PICTURE-PERFECT DEATH

It was Eben who found her that Monday morning at seven-thirty, on his way to get the lawn mower from the Talbot garage. He saw what looked like a black cloth lying among the syringa bushes which bordered the path, and stooped to pick it up. It would not lift, however, and then he saw that he had uncovered a woman's foot.

When I reached the place practically all the servants from the Crescent were already there, a huddled silent group. Daniels, curiously enough, had taken off his cap.

"Gone to her Maker, miss," he said to me. Then, seeing that I looked white, he added: " 'It is as natural to die as to be born.' "

She had been shot through the head, a quick and merciful death, at least. But like the others I dare say, my stunned mind could comprehend only the murder itself.

Or was it murder?

MARY ROBERTS RINEHART
THE ALBUM

ZEBRA BOOKS
KENSINGTON PUBLISHING CORP.

ZEBRA BOOKS

are published by

Kensington Publishing Corp.
475 Park Avenue South
New York, NY 10016

First printing: April, 1988

Printed in the United States of America

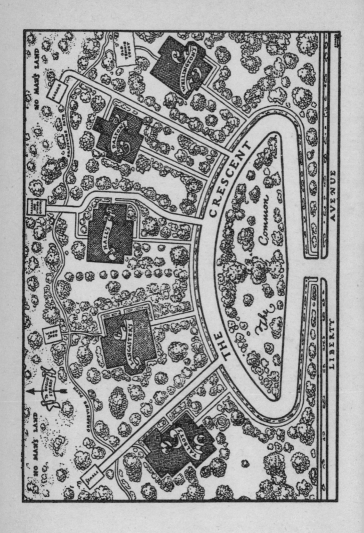

*The following
pages contain a gallery
of the principal characters in*
THE ALBUM

GEORGE TALBOT

Mrs. Talbot's son; he was often out late at night but was not allowed a latch key

LYDIA TALBOT

Mrs. Talbot's sister-in-law; a perfect specimen of the dependent spinster of the nineties

MRS. TALBOT

Her husband had vanished years ago; she had a mania for locking up everything and keeping the keys

JIM WELLINGTON

Young and in love with his wife, who led him a merry dance

HELEN WELLINGTON

Jim's wife; she gave lively parties, and the neighbors deplored her housekeeping

LOUISA HALL

Twenty-eight and attractive, but wilting under the thumb of her domineering mother

MARGARET LANCASTER

Emily's sister, not yet resigned to spinsterhood but devoted to her mother and stepfather

MR. LANCASTER

Husband of the bedridden first victim. Mild and elderly; stepfather to Emily and Margaret, who had taken his name

MR. DALTON

A big man, floridly handsome; jealousy may have caused the bitter quarrel with his wife

EMILY LANCASTER

A born old maid with an enormous pompadour, she waited hand and foot on her invalid mother — who was to be murdered

MRS. HALL

Her husband had been dead for twenty years, but she still wore deep mourning

HERBERT RANCHESTER DEAN

A criminologist who could work with the police

HOLMES

The Hall's butler-chauffeur; a strange little man who knew a little and guessed a lot

DANIELS

Nobody noticed him because he was a street-cleaner

MRS. DALTON

Middle-aged and sad; she had not spoken directly to her husband in twenty years

LIZZIE CROMWELL

Gaunt and faithful, she had been the Talbot's maid as long as anyone could remember

Chapter I

We had lived together so long, the five families in Crescent Place, that it never occurred to any of us that in our own way we were rather unique. Certainly the older people among us did not realize it; and I myself was rather shocked when Helen Wellington, after she married Jim and came there to live, observed that we all looked as though we had walked out of an album of the nineties.

"Including that iron clamp the photographers used to use to hold the hands steady," she said. "You're a stiff-necked lot, if ever I saw any."

I dare say she was right. Not long ago I was looking over the old red plush album which played such an important part in solving the crimes of which I am about to tell, and I found something or other of most of us there, especially of the women: Mrs. Talbot's faint mustache, Miss Lydia's spit curls, Emily Lancaster's enormous pompadour, Mother's pinned-on braids and Mrs. Dalton's square-cut Lillie Langtry bangs.

Even the hats were not unlike the ones which most of the Crescent still wears; those substantial hats, pinned high on their wearers' heads, by which at St. Mark's on a Sunday morning it was as easy to pick out our pews as to discover a palm oasis in a desert.

Just how unique we were, however, none of us, including Helen Wellington herself, probably realized until after our first murder. Then, what with police and newspaper men digging about our intermingled roots, it began to dawn on me that we were indeed a strange and perhaps not very healthy human garden.

Long ago Crescent Place was merely a collection of fine old semi-country houses, each set in its own grounds, and all roughly connected by a semicircular dirt road. Then the city grew in that direction, the dirt road was paved, and to protect themselves the owners built a gate at the entrance and marked it "private." The gate was never closed, of course; it was a gesture of dignified privacy and nothing more. The piece of empty ground which the road enclosed, and on which our houses faced, was common property, and in the course of time was planted like a small park at our mutual expense. Long ago it had been a part of a large empty area on which we had grazed our cows, and so now this glorified fragment was still called the Common.

The five houses face toward the Common, and were originally some considerable distance apart. Here and there additions have rather lessened this distance, but each house still retains that which it values above all price, its privacy and seclusion. When by the additions I have mentioned or for other reasons this in the past has been found threatened, a campaign of tree and shrubbery planting has at once been instituted; so that for more than half the year, save for certain weak spots in our defenses, we resemble nothing so much as five green-embattled fortresses.

We have these weak spots, however. One window of my own bedroom, for example, still commands an excellent view of certain parts of the house on our right, and from the end of our guest wing we have more than a glimpse of the one on the left. Both of which outlook posts, as well as the ones upstairs which command our own garage, were to play their own part in our tragedies. But in the main, until Thursday August the eighteenth of last year at four o'clock in the afternoon, each of the five houses had successfully for forty years or more preserved its seclusion and its slightly arrogant detachment from the others and from the world; had been neighborly without being intimate, had fought innovation to the last ditch — Helen Wellington maintaining that the last hatpin in the world with a butterfly top was the one Lydia Talbot still wore — and was still placidly unaware of much more of the living world than it could see through the gate onto Liberty Aveune.

My mother and I live in the center house, and thus almost directly face the little Common and the gate beyond it. Mother is still in deep mourning for my father, who has been dead for twenty years, and later on, when things began to happen, I was shocked to hear her described as the eternal widow draped in crêpe, and myself as a young-ish spinster — at twenty-eight! — who had been abnormally repressed and was therefore by intimation more or less psychopathic as a result.

This was the same tabloid which as our murders went on discovered that there were exactly thirteen people living on the Crescent, not counting the servants, and under the title The Unlucky Number ran an article a day for thirteen days on one or the other of us.

Yet the fact remains that of all the five houses along the Crescent ours was later proved to be the most normal, although we were to have our fair share of trouble and even horror. And that the next in normality and the first in peaceful and ordered living was the Lancaster house next door to us; until on that August afternoon last year old Mrs. Lancaster was murdered in such hideous fashion.

The Lancaster house lay to the right of us. The family consisted of old Mr. Lancaster, his wife, a bedridden invalid, and his two stepdaughters, Emily and Margaret. But so long ago had this second marriage taken place that no one seemed to remember the fact; not even the step-daughters themselves, now staid middle-aged women. They were devoted to their stepfather, whose name they had taken, and the entire life in the house centered on the small, rather dominant and not too agreeable elderly in-valid in her wide bed on the second floor.

Beyond the Lancaster house and nearest the gate on its side was the Talbots', and we had known them so long that

15

Mrs. Talbot's eccentricity was as much a part of her as her fall collection of dahlias or her ancient faded sables. Her mania, if one may call it that, was in locking everything up and keeping the keys. Miss Mamie, our local visiting dressmaker, said that she sat all day crocheting with these keys in her lap, and so she was constantly having new fronts put in her dresses! She was a big woman with a faint mustache and a booming voice, all of which made her peculiarity more marked. But as I say, habit had accustomed us to it, and the only time we ever remembered it was when she went asleep on her good ear and so could not admit her son George when she was out late at night.

Then it was necessary for her sister-in-law, Lydia, to rouse her and get a key. She would come down, her spit curls stiffly set and tied with a bandage, and admit him. Or if she too did not waken George would try the rest of us. There was hardly a house in the Crescent which had not given him a bed on one night or another when she was unable to awaken his mother, or when he had decided not to let him in at all.

The fact remains, however. The moment George Talbot left his bedroom its door was locked and the key taken to the old lady; and the same thing was done by Lydia Talbot, a perfect specimen of the dependent female of the nineties. Even the servants on their way downstairs left their keys in a basket outside her door, and a very good housemaid was dismissed once for forgetting to do so.

There was no Mr. Talbot. There had been, for one day when I was a little girl I found in the loft of the old stable on their lot a dreadful staring crayon portrait of a man with black hair mostly roached and a heavy black mustache; and George had said it was his father. Being utterly unable to associate it with a living man, after that I always felt that Mrs. Talbot had been married to a crayon enlargement, and when ultimately it disappeared entirely I had a strange feeling that George was suddenly fatherless!

On our left were the Daltons, a middle-aged couple who had not spoken directly to each other for twenty years.

Nobody knew what the trouble was, and we accepted them as calmly as the others. Twice a year they asked us all in for tea, and it was quite usual to have Mr. Dalton go to his wife's tea table and say politely to whoever stood by:

"Will you ask Mrs. Dalton for a second cup for me, please?"

Or to have Mrs. Dalton perhaps reply:

"I'm sorry. Will you tell him I have just sent out for some fresh tea?"

He was a big man, and still handsome in a florid fashion. The money was hers, and like many rich wives she was supposed to be niggardly with him, and it was said that that was at the root of their trouble. He had given up even the pretense of business since the depression, and spent a good bit of time tinkering with his car in their garage. But he was often lonely , I know. I used to see him talking to the butler now and then, out of sheer necessity for speech.

Mrs. Dalton was small, pretty, birdlike, and always slightly overdressed. Of the older women on the Crescent she was the only one who pretended to any sort of fashion, and I well remember the day she appeared at our house in her first short skirt! Mother gave one shocked look at her legs and from that moment on never glanced lower than her chin. But not one of us ever guessed, until our lives were thrown into chaos by the strange occurrences of last August, that Laura Dalton was still wildly and jealously in love with her husband.

The last house, nearest the gate on our left, was the Wellingtons', and they provided us with our only gaiety and with plenty of excitement. They were younger, for one thing; Jim Wellington had inherited the place on his mother's death. But they were always threatening divorce. One day Mary, our elderly cook, would report to us for the morning orders with the statement:

"She left last night. Called a taxicab and took her trunk."

And by "she" we always knew who was meant. Or again:

"Mr. Wellington, he lit out this morning. Gone to his club to live."

They would effect a reconciliation, of course, and celebrate it with a party. Pretty lively parties, they were, too. Sometimes after mother had gone to bed I would slip out and listen to the noise, or look in at a window. Sometimes I would see Helen Wellington on the dark porch with some man or other, in a dress which, as Miss Mamie would say, was cut clear down to nature. But Mother never let me go to these parties. She considered Helen a bad influence and a hussy, and she deplored both her morals and her housekeeping.

These were the five houses on the Crescent, and the people who occupied them on that appalling August afternoon of last year. People and houses, we were united by the old road in front of us which was now a street, by the grapevine path at the rear, and by a sort of mutual seclusion which more and more shut away the outside world.

To this world we made few concessions. Mrs. Talbot's basques and cameo jewelry were taken for granted as much as Mother's crêpe or Emily Lancaster's high pompadour built over a cushion of net and wire. The suspicious bulges on Lydia Talbot's thin figure we accepted as the curves of nature and not of art, and on Monday, which was of course the Crescent washing day, our clothes lines at the rear showed row on row of self-respecting but hardly exotic undergarments.

I remember meeting Helen Wellington on the back path shortly after her marriage, and seeing her stare at the Lancaster washing. She caught me by the arm.

"Listen!" she said, in her quick staccato voice. "Do they all wear things like that?"

"Most of them. You see, they always have."

"Do you?"

"Not always. But I wash them myself."

She gave me a sharp glance.

"Pretty well buried alive, aren't you?" she said. "Nothing ever has happened and so nothing ever will! Why don't you get out? Beat it? You're still young. You're not bad looking."

"Beat it? Where to? I couldn't even sell mothballs!"

"You *would* think of mothballs!" She cast a quick appraising glance about her. "Well, you never can tell. The older the house the better it burns! You may all go up like a tinder box some day. It isn't natural."

"What isn't natural?"

"This peace; this smug damnable peace. It's degenerating."

Whereupon she lit the first cigarette ever smoked by a woman in that vicinity, and moved along the path. The last I saw of her she was standing in fascinated awe, gazing unabashed at a row of long-sleeved nightdresses and Mr. Lancaster's long cotton underdrawers.

She was right in her prophecy, of course. But it was six years before it came true. Six years almost to a day until the match was applied to our tinder box and old Mrs. Lancaster, alone in her bed in the big front room of the white Colonial house, was brutally and savagely done to death with an axe.

Chapter II

As I have said, one of the windows in my bedroom on the second floor commands a view of a part of the Lancaster house. That is, I can see from it all of the roof, a part of the second story and a small side-entrance door which opens onto the wide strip of lawn with flower borders which separates the two houses. This area belongs, half to the Lancasters and half to us, and a row of young Lombardy poplars forms the dividing line.

At four o'clock that Thursday afternoon, then, I was sitting at this window sewing. Mother had just started for a drive, and old Eben, the gardener for all the five properties, was running his lawn mower over the lawn, the cut tips of the grass marking a small green cascade just ahead of it. When the sound ceased I glanced up, to find Eben mopping his face with a bandanna handkerchief, and in the sudden silence to hear a distant shriek.

Eben heard it too, and I can still see him standing there, the handkerchief held to his neck, staring over it at the Lancaster house and holding tight to the handle of his mower. How long he stood I do not know, for now the shriek was repeated, but nearer at hand; and the next moment Emily Lancaster, the elder of the old lady's two

20

daughters, stumbled out of the side door, screamed again, ran across the lawn toward Eben and then collapsed in a dead faint almost at his feet.

So rapidly had all this happened that Eben was still holding to the mower and to his handkerchief. When I got to them, however, he was stooping over her and trying to raise her.

"Let her alone, Eben," I said impatiently. "Leave her flat. And see what has happened."

"I reckon the old lady has passed on," he said, and moved rather deliberately toward the side door. But before he reached it a sort of pandemonium seemed to break loose in the house itself. There were squeals from the women servants, and hysterical crying, distinct because of the open windows; and above all this I could hear Margaret Lancaster's voice, high pitched and shrill.

Even then I believed as Eben did, that the old lady had died; and I remember thinking that there was an unusual amount of excitement for what had been expected for years anyhow. My immediate problem, however, was Miss Emily, lying in her spotless white on the path, her high pompadour slipped to one side and her face as white as her dress.

Eben had disappeared into the house by the side door, and there was nothing I could do until help came. I had expected him to send that help, but after perhaps two or three minutes I heard someone run across the front porch and out into the street, and I saw that it was Eben. He had apparently forgotten us, for he stood there for a second staring right and left and then set off, running again, toward the gate to the Crescent.

I knew then that there was something terribly wrong, and I tried to rouse Emily.

"Miss Emily!" I said. "Listen, Miss Emily, can't you sit up?"

But she did not move, and I stared around helplessly for someone to assist me. It was then that I saw Jim Wellington. It looked as though he had come out of the Lancasters' side door, although I had not heard the screen slam; and I have not lived all my life beside that door without knowing that it can slam.

At first I thought he had not noticed us. He was moving rapidly toward the back of the property, where a path connected the rears of all the houses. Our grapevine telegraph line, Bryan Dalton called it, because the servants used it to go from one house to another and to carry all the news. Then I felt that he must have seen us, for I in my pale dress and Miss Emily in white must have stood out like two sore thumbs.

"Jim!" I called. "Jim Wellington! Come here."

He turned then and came toward us. Like the screen door, I have known him all my life and been fond of him; too fond once, for that matter. But never have I seen him look as he looked then. His face was gray, and he seemed slightly dazed.

"I need help, Jim. She's fainted."

"Who is it? Emily?."

"Yes."

He hesitated, then came closer and leaned over her.

"You're sure she's not hurt?"

"I don't know. She didn't seem to fall very hard. She just slid down. What on earth has happened, Jim?"

But as Miss Emily moved then and groaned, he straightened up and shook his head for silence.

"She's coming to," he said. "Better tell them where she is. I have to get on home." He turned to go and then swung back. "See here, Lou," he said roughly, "you needn't say you've seen me. There's trouble in there, and I don't want to be mixed up in it."

"What sort of trouble?" I asked. But he went on as though he had not heard me, toward the back path and his house.

Still no help came. Apparently not even our own servants had heard the excitement, for our service wing is away from the Lancasters' and toward the Dalton house. Five

22

minutes had passed, or maybe more; long enough at least for Eben to have reached Liberty Avenue and to return, for now he reappeared on the run, followed by our local police officer. They had disappeared into the house when Miss Emily groaned again.

I bent over her.

"Can you get up, Miss Emily?" I inquired.

She shook her head, and then a memory of some sort sent her face down again on the grass, sobbing hysterically.

"What is it?" I asked helplessly. "Please tell me, Miss Emily. Then I'll know what to do."

At that she went off into straight hysterics, that dreadful crying which is half a scream, and I was never so glad to see anyone as I was to see Margaret, hastily clad in a kimono and standing in the side doorway. She too looked pale and distracted, but she came across to us in a hurry.

"Stop it, Emily!" she said. "Louisa, get some water somewhere and throw it over her. Emily, for God's sake!"

Whether it was the threat of the water or the furious anger in Miss Margaret's voice I do not know, but Miss Emily stopped anyhow, and sat up.

"You're a cold-blooded woman, Margaret. With Mother — !"

"Who do you think you are helping by fainting and screaming?" Margaret demanded sharply. "Do you want Father to hear you?"

"Does he know?"

"He knows. Miss Margaret's voice was grim. "I told them not to let him go upstairs."

Naturally I knew or was certain by that time that Mrs. Lancaster was dead, and as everyone had known how faithfully Emily had cared for her mother, I could understand her hysteria well enough. She was an emotional woman, given to the reading of light romances and considered sentimental by the Crescent. Margaret had been a devoted daughter also, but she was more matter-of-fact. In a way, Emily had been the nurse and Margaret had been

23

the housekeeper of the establishment.

The screen door was still unfastened, and together we got Emily into the house and across the main hall to the library. Margaret was leading the way, and I remember now that she stopped and picked up something from the floor near the foot of the stairs. I did not notice it particularly at the time, for the patrolman, Lynch, was at the telephone in the lower hall, and well as I knew him he stared at me and through me as he talked.

"That's it," he said. "Looks like it was done with an axe, yes. . . . Yeah, I got it. Okay."

He hung up and ran up the stairs again.

Suddenly I felt sick and cold all over. Somebody had been hurt, or killed with an axe! But that automatically removed Mrs. Lancaster from my mind as the victim. Who would kill that helpless old woman, and with an axe! Confused as I was, I was excited but still ignorant when we reached the library door; and it was not until I saw old Mr. Lancaster that I knew.

He was alone, lying back in a big leather chair, his face bloodless and his eyes closed. He did not even open them when we went in, or when Margaret helped me get Emily onto the leather couch there. It was after we had settled her there that Margaret went to him and put a hand on his shoulder.

"You know that it was murder, don't you, father?"

He nodded.

"Who told you?"

"Eben." His lips scarcely moved. "I met him on the street."

"But you haven't been up?"

"No."

"I'll get you a glass of wine." She patted his shoulder and disappeared, leaving the three of us to one of those appalling silences which are like thunder in the ears. It was the old man who broke it finally. He opened his eyes and looked at Emily, shuddering on the couch.

24

"You found her?" he asked, still without moving.

"Yes. Please, father, don't let's talk about it."

"You didn't hear anything?"

"No. I was dressing with my door closed."

"And Margaret?"

"I don't see how she could. She was taking a bath. The water was running when I called her."

Margaret brought in a glass of port wine, and he drank it. Always small, he seemed to have shrunk in the last few minutes. A dapper little man, looking younger than his years, he was as much a part of the Crescent as Mrs. Talbot's dahlias, or our own elm trees; a creature of small but regular habits, so that we could have set our clocks by his afternoon walk, or our calendars by his appearance in his fall overcoat.

But if he was stricken, I imagine that it was with horror rather than grief. After all, a man can hardly be heartbroken over the death of a wife who has been an exacting invalid for twenty years or so, and a bedridden one for ten.

The wine apparently revived him, for he sat up and looked at the two women, middle-aged and now pallid and shaken. It was a searching look, intent and rather strange. He surveyed Emily moaning on the couch, a huddled white picture of grief. Then he looked at Margaret, horrified but calm beside the center table, and clutching her flowered kimono about her. I do not think he even knew that I was in the room.

Apparently what he saw satisfied him, however, for he leaned back again in his chair and seemed to be thinking. I was about to slip out of the room when he spoke again, suddenly.

"Has anyone looked under the bed?" he said.

And as if she had been touched by an electric wire Emily sat up on the couch.

"Under the bed? Then you think—?"

"What else am I to think?"

But no one answered him, for at that moment a police

25

car drove up; a radio car with two officers in it, and a second or so later another car containing what I now know were an Inspector from Headquarters and three members of the Homicide Squad.

Chapter III

I was still shocked and incredulous when I went into the hall and watched that small regiment of policemen as they trooped silently up the stairs. The clock on the landing showed only twenty minutes after four. Only twenty minutes or so ago I had been peacefully sewing at my window, and the Lancaster house had gleamed white and quiet through the trees.

Now everything was changed, and yet nothing was changed. The hall was as usual, the old-fashioned brass rods on the stairs gleamed from recent polishing, and the men had disappeared overhead. The only sound I could hear was of women softly crying somewhere above, and toward that sound I found myself moving. It came from the upper front hall, and there I found Lynch, the patrolman. He had rounded the three women servants outside Mrs. Lancaster's door, and he was holding Eben there also.

Two of the maids were elderly women and had been there for years; Ellen the cook and Jennie the waitress. Only Peggy the young housemaid was a comparative newcomer, but none the less shocked and stricken. All three of them were crying with the ease and facility of people who know that tears are expected of them, but as I looked Peggy pointed to the doorsill and gave a smothered cry.

"Blood!" she cried.

Lynch told her gruffly to keep still, and so we stood until one of the detectives came out into the hall. He surveyed the drooping group grimly.

"And now," he said, "let's hear about it."

There was apparently nothing to hear. Ellen had been beating up a cake on the back porch, and Jennie had been cleaning silver, also on the porch for coolness. Peggy was off that afternoon, and had been about to leave by the kitchen door when they heard Miss Emily screaming. None of them had seen Mrs. Lancaster since Jennie had carried up her tray at half past one o'clock, and all of them swore that all the doors, front, rear and side, had been locked.

The detective took Eben last.

"Where were you?"

"Where was I when?"

"When this thing happened."

"I don't know when it happened."

"Let's see your feet."

"There's blood on them most likely. When Miss Emily ran out screaming I thought most likely the old lady had passed away, so when the noise began I came on up here. But Miss Margaret was here ahead of me. She had the door open and was looking in. She told me to see if her mother was still alive, but I didn't need to go far to know that."

"I can corroborate that," I said. "Eben was cutting the grass near my window. I saw Miss Emily come out, and I sent him in to see what was wrong."

I had to explain myself then, and what I had seen from my window. He listened carefully.

"That's all you saw?" he asked. "Didn't see anyone going in or coming out?"

"No," I told him; and suddenly for the first time since I had entered the house I remembered Jim Wellington. What I might have done or said then I hardly know now. I remember that my chest tightened and that I felt shaky all at once. But the need did not arise. There was a sound like

28

a mild explosion from the death room at that moment, and one of the maids yelped and turned to run.

In the resulting explanation, that a flashlight photograph had been made inside the closed room where the body lay, I was asked no more questions. The servants were dismissed and warned not to leave the house, and the detective, whose name I learned later was Sullivan, turned and went into the death chamber again.

I was left alone in the upper hall, but entirely incapable of thought. I remember hearing Miss Emily's canary singing loudly in her room and thinking that it was dreadful, that gaiety so close at hand. Then I went, slowly and rather dazedly, down the stairs and out the front door.

I have no clear recollection of the rest of that afternoon, save that on the way back I met Lydia Talbot on the pavement staring at the police car, with her arms filled with bundles and her face white and shocked.

"Whatever has happened?" she asked me. "Is it a fire?"

"Mrs. Lancaster is dead. I'm afraid she's been murdered, Miss Lydia."

She swayed so that I caught her by the arm, and some of her bundles dropped. She made no attempt to pick them up.

"But I was there," she said faintly. "I was there this afternoon. I took her some jellied chicken, just after lunch. She was all right then."

In the end I took her home, cutting across the Common to save time, and was glad to find that she had rallied somewhat.

"How was it — was it done?" she asked.

"I'm not sure. I believe with an axe. Don't think about it," I added, as I felt her trembling again. "We can't help it now."

And then she said a strange thing.

"Well, she was my own sister-in-law, but I never liked her. And I suppose they stood it as long as they could."

She tried to cover that up next moment, saying she was upset and not responsible, and that the girls had been

29

devoted daughters. But I remembered the strange look Mr. Lancaster had given them one after the other, only a short time before, and I wondered if he had not had the same thought as Lydia.

That is all I really saw or heard that afternoon. Now I know something of what went on in that shambles of a room upstairs in the Lancaster house: of the discovery of the axe, thrown on top of the big tester bed and discovered by the stain which had seeped through the heavy sateen; and the further discovery that it was the axe from the Lancaster woodshed, and that the only prints on it were old ones, later found to be Eben's, and badly smudged. I know that they took measurements of this and that, and opened the windows and looked out, and that the medical examiner arrived with a black bag some time later, and went upstairs as briskly as though we had a daily axe murder in the Crescent.

When I say that I know all this, I mean that all the Crescent knows. It knows the exact moment when Mrs. Lancaster's body was taken away, the exact moment when the police decided to hold Eben for further interrogation, and the exact moment when Miss Emily toiled feebly up the stairs and asked if there had been a key on a fine chain around her mother's neck.

"A key?" one of the detectives is said to have asked. "Anybody find a key on a chain?"

Nobody had, and our information was that Miss Emily immediately began to tear apart that dreadful bed, crying and moaning as she did so. But that no key or chain had been found, either there or elsewhere; elsewhere in this case being the morgue, a word which we avoided on general principles.

But the Crescent still knew practically nothing at all of what had happened when I went home that late summer afternoon to break the news to Mother. Save for Mrs. Talbot, who heard the news from Lydia and rushed over at once, only to be summarily if politely ejected by the police, the rest remained in ignorance for a good two hours, and the Daltons even longer. The usual crowd which follows police cars had either been daunted by our gates or was being held outside them by a guard. Helen Wellington was away, having made one of her periodical breaks. The Lancaster servants were being held incommunicado, and even the reporters who had converged on the spot had, due to our planting and our semi-isolation, failed to rouse any suspicion.

This is shown by the fact that I found Mother sitting on the porch when I returned. She was fanning herself, and complaining of the heat.

"I wondered where you were," she said rather fretfully. "Is Mr. Lancaster worse? I see a car there."

This was not surprising, since by that time there were at least six cars in a row before the Lancaster walk which led to the house. But I had to break the news to her, and I did it as tactfully as I could. That she was shocked and horrified I could see, but the Crescent carries its emotions, when it has any, to its bedroom and there locks the door. Never by any chance does it show them to the servants or to the casual passer-by. She got up suddenly.

"I must go over at once," she said. "They will need help."

"I'm afraid the police won't let you in, mother."

"Don't be absurd. They let you in."

"They wanted to ask me some questions."

"Precisely," she said drily. "My only daughter is interrogated by the police, and I am not even consulted! Besides, the Lancasters are my best and oldest friends, and when I think of that lonley old man and those two devoted daughters—"

Well, that is as may be. Mother had hardly spoken to Mr. Lancaster for years, due to a disputed boundary line, and I had frequently heard her refer to the daughters as two spineless women who allowed themselves to be dominated by an unscrupulous and hard old woman! But the tradition of the Crescent is more or less to canonize its dead, which is not so bad after all.

I got her into the house finally, and there she asked for

such details as I knew of the crime. It seemed to me that she listened with singular intentness, and that toward the end she relaxed somewhat.

"You say that all the doors were fastened?"

"The maids say so. You know how particular they are."

"And Emily, when she ran out? She was fully dressed?"

"In pure white, mother," I said, and smiled a little. "With not a stain on it!"

She looked up quickly, startled and annoyed.

"What on earth do you mean by that, Louisa?"

"Just what you meant, mother," I told her, and went across to my own room.

Chapter IV

I dare say every woman retains a sentiment for an old lover, even if he is inevitably lost; retains it at least until a new one effaces him. And at one time, ten years before, when I was eighteen and Jim was twenty-five, we had been engaged. Nothing came of it, for Mother had never wanted me to marry and leave her alone, and Jim made things rather painful by accusing her of selfishness and declining to share me with her. All in all it had been an unhappy business, and two years later he had married Helen and had now been married to her on and off for eight years.

The women of the Crescent had never much liked Helen. That was natural, for she flouted their prejudices and was openly scornful of their profoundest convictions. Besides she was young and attractive, a combination they found it hard to forgive.

"A silly flighty little fool," Mrs. Dalton said one day, shortly after the marriage. And Bryan Dalton had smiled into his teacup.

"You might say to my wife," he stated to the room at large, "that she is very easy to look at."

But Helen or no Helen, I carried into my room that late afternoon a terrible and gnawing fear. It could not be long before the police discovered that Jim Wellington had been in that house at or about the time the crime was discovered, that he had slipped away without letting his presence be known, and that I had concealed that fact from them.

I was bewildered, too. Why on earth run away from a thing like that, if he knew what it was? Why not raise an alarm, shout, call for the police, do any one of the normal things which normal people do under abnormal conditions? I dressed—the Crescent would dress for dinner in the middle of an earthquake—in a state of anxiety bordering on frenzy; and dinner itself proved to be trying beyond words, for Mother had found a grievance and was worrying it like a dog a bone.

"What I cannot understand, Louisa," she said, "is that you did not come back and tell me at once. I was back here by four-thirty. You seem to think you owe me no consideration whatever."

Perhaps my nerves were not what they should have been, for that upset me.

"I've shown you every possible consideration for twenty-eight years, mother," I said; and what with one thing and another I burst into tears and left the table to find the Daltons coming up our porch steps, and the three Talbots not far behind them.

It is not strange, to anyone who knows the Crescent, that the news had not spread its entire length until the late extra edition of the evening papers came out! For one thing, our servants, as I have already said, provide our grapevine telegraph, and the Lancaster servants were being held strictly incommunicado in the Lancaster house. For another, so well has our planting grown in the last forty years or so, that we ourselves are practically incommunicado unless we choose otherwise. Whatever its faults, the Crescent considers it a sin to cut down a tree or prune back its shrubbery.

The Crescent reads the evening paper after dinner, not before it. When the paper is finished, it is carefully refolded and sent back to the servants. And the Crescent never reads extra editions. When the reporters from the various papers, having exhausted the patience of the police, began to ring doorbells along the road, most of the occupants were concerned with the sacred rite of dressing for dinner, and later with the even more sacred rite of dining.

Not one of them gained access to any of the five houses. But undoubtedly they told the servants, for Lizzie at Mrs. Talbot's sent her down to dinner that night in a pair of odd shoes, and the Dalton butler, Joseph, forgot to place dinner napkins for the first time in twenty-five years. But as our servants speak only when spoken to, it was fully seven-thirty when this same Joseph walked into the library with a tray on which lay a neatly folded copy of an extra edition of an evening paper and then quietly retired. And it was seven-thirty-one when Mr. Dalton, leaping to his feet, pressed the library bell for him again and said:

"Will you tell Mrs. Dalton that Mrs. Lancaster has been murdered, brutally killed with an axe?"

Incredible all of it, of course, unless one knows us.

It was after half past seven then, by the time the Crescent was fully informed, front and back; and only slightly after that when, having made their polite inquiries and offers of help at the Lancasters', the Talbots and the Daltons gathered at our house. I showed them into the drawing room, Mrs. Dalton mincing along on her high heels, Bryan Dalton looking immaculate but shocked, Lydia carrying and dropping a knitting bag, and Mrs. Talbot laden as usual with the heavy old-fashioned reticule which carried her innumerable keys. George trailed behind them all, uncomfortable and apparently feeling that, being more or less in the presence of death, he should walk on his tiptoes.

Or perhaps for fear that because of his youth — he is only thirty — he might be sent away if noticed. George and I still constitute the children of the Crescent.

"Looks like a coroner's jury!" he whispered to me. "Be

careful. And anything you say may be held against you!"

Actually it turned out to be something of the sort, with his mother acting as a sort of star witness who regarded the entire catastrophe as a direct result of old Mrs. Lancaster's failure to lock herself in.

"Always told her that," she boomed in her heavy voice. "Told her to lock things up. Told her to have her bedroom door locked. Told her so this very day. Her lying helpless in that bed, and all this crime going on!"

For, as it turned out, Mrs. Talbot had been the last one outside of the family to see Mrs. Lancaster alive.

"Except the man with the axe," she boomed, and all of us shuddered.

She was a kindly woman, in spite of her eccentricity, and for many years almost her only outside contact with the world had been her occasional visits to Mrs. Lancaster, who was connected with her by marriage. Mrs. Lancaster's first husband having been a brother of the crayon portrait.

We listened to her story with avid interest. She had gone at two-thirty to sit with the invalid, as she sometimes did. Everything had been normal at that time; the old lady lying quietly in the big four-poster with the tester top, and Emily with her. It had been Margaret's afternoon off, for the sisters alternated that part of the day in the sickroom, and she was shut away in her room.

Old Mrs. Lancaster, however, had been rather fretful. She was feeling the heat, and as she did not like electric fans Mrs. Talbot had taken the palm leaf fan from Emily and sat beside her, fanning her.

"Then I noticed that key she wore on a chain around her neck, and I gave her a good talking to," she said, or rather shouted. "In the first place, I hate people who hoard gold these days, and I told her so. Then I said that I was certain that more people than she believed knew she was doing it, and that it wasn't safe. But she told me Margaret had been protesting too, and to mind my own business!"

36

That was the first time I had heard of any gold, and I sat up in my chair.

"Where did she keep the gold?" Mrs. Dalton asked curiously. "I've often wondered."

"In a chest under her bed, of all places. I told her anybody might climb the porch and get in a window, but she wouldn't believe me. She said: 'I've still got my voice. I keep telling the girls that. Emily's so nervous that she's always hearing burglars on the porch roof.' And now," Mrs. Talbot finished with a final boom, "I haven't a doubt that it's all gone. Or most of it. George says it would be too heavy to carry away in one trip."

"Has anyone an idea how much she had?" Mr. Dalton asked; and looked at George, who is in a bank in town.

"No," George said. "She got plenty from us. I don't know how many other banks she looted. But does anyone know it is gone?"

"The key's certainly gone," Mr. Dalton said decidedly. "I saw Margaret for a moment before we came here. They've hunted everywhere, there and—elsewhere. The police are opening the chest tomorrow."

I sat as well as I could through all the talk. It is characteristic of the Crescent's attitude toward what it calls the younger generation that this evening was the first time I had known that Mrs. Lancaster had been hoarding gold under her bed. But I felt a sense of relief. Here was a motive at last, and vague as I was as to the weight of gold coins in quantity, I knew that Jim Wellington had left the house empty-handed.

Lydia Talbot's story differed little from that of her sister-in-law. She too had seen Mrs. Lancaster that afternoon. At a quarter to two she had carried over a small basket containing a bowl of jellied chicken and some fresh rolls for the invalid. The front door as usual was closed and locked. Jennie had admitted her and she had carried her basket upstairs. She was sure Jennie had locked the door behind

37

her.

"I sat with her for a while," she said, as Emily wanted to clean her bird's cage. We talked a little, but nothing important, except that I thought she seemed upset about something. But she kept things pretty much to herself, always. When Hester came I left. Ellen let me out by the kitchen door."

"What do you mean, upset?" boomed Hester, who was Mrs. Talbot. "She wasn't upset when I got there. Only peevish, and that was nothing new."

Miss Lydia colored and looked rather frightened.

"I don't know. Emily looked queer too. I thought perhaps they had been quarreling."

Everybody felt uncomfortable at that, and Mrs. Dalton chose that moment of all moments to throw a bomb into our midst.

"The police think it was an inside job," she said maliciously, and smiled.

Her husband glared at her.

"Will someone have the goodness," he demanded furiously, "to ask my wife where she got an idea as outrageous as that?"

"From the servants," she said, triumphant over her sensation. "While Mr. Dalton was ringing the front doorbell tonight I went around to the back of the house. I found Ellen in tears, and the others in a fine state. The police have not only searched the entire house from roof to cellar, including the furnace and the soiled clothes hampers and the coal pile — there's a man still moving the coal — but they actually got a woman there and made the women take off their clothes! Or at least show what they had on. To see if there was blood on them."

The Crescent, as represented there, sat in a stupefied silence; not so much because an inside job was suspected, but at the power of a police force which could thus violate its privacy and offend its dignity.

It was only George Talbot who grinned.

"I'd better be getting home," he said. "I had a nose-bleed yesterday, and I have a little washing to do!"

But no one laughed. The picture Mrs. Dalton had drawn was too graphic. For the first time in its existence the Crescent was threatened with the awful majesty of the law, and it did not like it. It covered its fear with talk, much of it rather pointless. Nevertheless, out of that welter of talk and surmise, certain things finally emerged.

The afternoon at the Lancasters' up to or about four o'clock had apparently been quiet enough. The family had lunched at one, and at one-thirty Jennie had carried up the invalid's tray. Miss Emily had fed her, and the tray had gone down at two.

At a quarter before two Lydia had brought her basket, too late for lunch, and had been admitted by Jennie, who cautioned her with a gesture that Mr. Lancaster was asleep in the library. As she had gone out by the kitchen door shortly after her sister-in-law arrived, she had not seen the old gentleman again.

At two-thirty Mrs. Talbot had gone in, remaining until half past three, which was when Mrs. Lancaster took her afternoon nap. When she went downstairs she found Mr. Lancaster awake and in the hall, and about to take the brief half-hour saunter which was his daily exercise. Emily had gone downstairs with her; and she had not only seen them out, she had for Mrs. Talbot's benefit shown her that the spring lock was on the front door, and in order.

"I'm not afraid of the door," Emily had said. "But I don't like the porch roof off mother's room; especially just now."

"It's a fool idea anyhow," Mr. Lancaster had said. "If a good bank isn't safe, then nothing and nobody is."

He and Mrs. Talbot had then gone down the walk to the street together, separating at the pavement; he going left toward Liberty Avenue and Mrs. Talbot going back home. The last thing Emily had said was that she was going to put

39

on a fresh dress, since Margaret intended to go out. This fresh dress we all understood perfectly, since most of us dress before four in the afternoon to receive the callers who are more of a tradition of past social importance than present fact.

From that time, three-thirty or so, until Miss Emily came in that awful fashion through the side door, no one knew anything of what had happened. Emily had dressed, Miss Margaret had taken or prepared to take her shower, Eben had cut the grass, Ellen had beaten up her cake, Jennie had polished her silver, and up in the hot third floor Peggy had prepared to go out.

Not once in all this, however, had anyone mentioned Jim Wellington's name. It was George Talbot who came nearest to it.

"It looks like a premeditated thing, all right," he said. "Somebody who knew that Mrs. Lancaster always slept at three-thirty and that the girls dressed then." They are, of course, still the girls to us. "Also that the old boy always took his walk at that time." He looked around the room mischievously. "Might be any of us!" he said, and grinned. "Anyone along the Crescent, from Jim Wellington at one end to me at the other. Of course he'd have to know the axe was kept in the woodshed, too. That's another point."

"That isn't funny," said Bryan Dalton.

"Well, even you knew it was there, didn't you, sir?" said George, still grinning. "Matter of fact, I saw you near there early this morning."

"And what were you doing there yourself?" said Mr. Dalton, red with anger.

"Looking for a golf ball I lost yesterday," said George, smiling and unruffled. "And you, sir?"

"That's none of your damned business," Mr. Dalton shouted, and would have continued in the same vein had not his wife hastily risen.

"Will someone tell my husband," she said sweetly, "that it

is time to go home? *And* that I do not like his language?"

Almost he spoke to her! We all waited breathlessly, for it was common opinion among us that, the ice once broken, they would get along at least amicably. But he remembered in time, gave George an angry glare and stalked out. Mrs. Dalton followed him, tripping on her high heels, and at the foot of the front steps he waited for her. I watched them going side by side down the walk, in their usual silence; but it seemed to me that night that it was less companionable than usual, if a silence can be companionable, or if people can be further separated who are already entirely apart.

Chapter V

Mrs. Talbot remained that night after the others left. Lydia had pleaded fatigue, and so George took her home. Probably the line-up of cars on the street had changed since afternoon, but there were still several there, and the Lancaster house seemed to be lighted from attic to cellar.

I knew Mother and Mrs. Talbot were settled for at least an hour, so I slipped on a dark cape in the back hall, and letting myself out the kitchen door, took an inconspicuous route toward Jim Wellington's.

This was not the grapevine path the servants use, but one even more remote. Behind all our houses lies a considerable acreage of still unoccupied land, which since the war we have called No Man's Land. Children used to play in it, but the Crescent frowned on that after some one of us got a baseball through a pantry window. Now it is purely a waste, where George Talbot and sometimes Mr. Dalton practice short golf shots; a waste bordered on one curved side by our properties, on a rather narrow end by the bustle and noise of Liberty Avenue, and directly behind us, but some distance away, the rear yards of the modest houses on Euclid Street. The Talbot's old stable, now a garage for George's dilapidated car, bordered on it; as did the Lancasters' woodshed, our garage and the Daltons', and what was once the Wellington tennis court but was now the weed-grown spot where Helen — to our horror — took sunbaths in a steamer chair and a very scanty bathing suit. She and Jim had no garage. Their car was kept in a garage on Liberty Avenue.

This area did not belong to us, of course, but during the process of years we had adopted it as our own. Thus a path led across it and through some trees and an empty lot to Euclid Street, and was used by our servants and sometimes ourselves as a short cut. Also Eben burned there our dead leaves in the fall; and even the street cleaners, finding their little carts overfull, had been known to slip back and surreptitiously empty them there, sometimes setting a match to their contents.

It was through this waste land that I made my way that night. Not too comfortably, for there is something about a murder — any murder — that disturbs one's sense of security. However, I had a little light at first. Holmes, our chauffeur, was evidently in his room over the garage, for his windows were fully illuminated, and out in No Man's Land itself there was still the flicker of a small fire.

But beyond the Dalton place I found myself plunged into thick darkness and a silence closed about me which the distant noise on Liberty Avenue did nothing to dispel. Then something caught at my cape and held it, and I stopped dead in my tracks and went cold all over. It was only a briar, but that unexpected stop had done something startling and rather terrible. It had enabled me to hear that someone was close behind me, someone who had stopped just too late to save himself from discovery.

I never even turned to look. Pell-mell I ran on, blind with terror, until I fetched up with a crash against the wire netting of the tennis court and there collapsed onto the ground. When I dared to look back it seemed to me that between me and the fire someone was standing and watching; but he made no move and so at last I pulled myself to my feet.

It was a picture of demoralization I must have presented

to Jim Wellington when, a few minutes later, he himself answered my ring at the door.

"Good heavens, Lou!" he said. "Come in and sit down. You look all in."

I obeyed him in silence. To tell the truth, I was almost unable to speak. He led the way, himself silent, back to his den and pulled out a chair for me.

"It's not very tidy," he explained. "Helen's gone again, as you know. And as I find she hadn't paid the servants for two months—" he shrugged his shoulders—"they've gone too."

Well, not very tidy was a mild way of putting it. But that night I was not interested in Helen's slovenly housekeeping. I was looking at Jim, neat enough but tired and pale. I saw that he had changed his clothes.

"Aren't you going to sit down?"

I shook my head.

"Jim, I was followed here."

"By the police? Well, does that surprise you?"

"I hadn't thought of the police. I thought it might be whoever killed Mrs. Lancaster, Jim."

He eyed me steadily.

"That's very nice of you. Rather handsome, considering everything! But it was probably the police. I'm expecting them, I suppose that you, being the honest person you are, have told them you saw me there?"

"No."

"Why not?"

"Well, nobody asked me, Jim, and so—"

He dropped his light manner, and coming to me, put a hand on my shoulder.

"You're a good girl, Lou," he said, "and we were a pair of young fools once. Well—I suppose Emily will bring it out before long, if she hasn't done it already. She was coming out of her faint when you called me. Maybe not right away, but sooner or later she'll remember. You see," he smiled down at me, "you can't save a fool from his folly. Or a man from his stomach," he added cryptically.

44

When I merely stared at him in bewilderment he put me into a chair and sat down himself.

"Here's the story," he said. "You can believe it or not; if you do you'll be the only one who will. I had a key to the front door, so I let myself in. There was nobody about, and I went upstairs and found her—like that! I went up to her room and opened the door, and—God! I couldn't believe it. The house was quiet. Old Emily was talking to her canary across the hall, and the door into the old lady's room was partly open. Luckily I didn't touch the knob. At least I don't think I did." He laughed shortly. "But I didn't stop at the door. I went in and looked down at her to see if she was—She was dead, of course."

"Why on earth didn't you raise the alarm?"

"You're asking *me* that? Because I am God's worst fool. We'd had a quarrel; she'd been hoarding gold for months under that bed of hers, and I got sick and tired of facing the bank people every week and getting it for her. I was her messenger boy. The girls wouldn't do it, nor Uncle James. Too decent. So we'd had a row, and she—well, she threatened to cut me out of her will. And," he added with a return to the light tone I hated, "this is no time to be cut out of wills, my dear Lou."

"So you went back to make peace, and found her?"

"So I went back because I was sent for, like the good boy I am."

"Oh, stop it, Jim," I cried. "I can't bear it."

"Well, that's my story, and I'm sticking to it. If my cousin Margaret, who hates me like sin, will only acknowledge that she telephoned me this morning to come out at four o'clock to see her beloved stepfather, maybe I'll have a chance. Otherwise I'll get what the police so practically refer to as the 'hot squat.' Meaning the chair, my dear."

I got up, rather wearily.

"I'm sorry, Jim. I came here to help if I could. Even to get you some dinner—" He made a gesture at that. "But you don't want any help. I'd better go."

Then he became the old Jim again, kindly and consider-

45

ate.

"I'm just shouting to keep my courage up, Lou. And I haven't told you the whole story. Maybe you don't remember, but the sight of blood always makes me sick. It does something to me, always has. But it's too damned ridiculous to tell the police. I think I'd have raised the alarm. God knows it was the first instinct I had! But I was going to be sick. Can you imagine it?" he demanded savagely. "Can you imagine a full-grown man in an emergency like that rushing off to be sick somewhere? Well, that's what I did. And when Emily raised the alarm I was in the lavatory off the downstairs hall, throwing up my boots! That's a laugh for the police, isn't it?"

"They might believe it, Jim."

"They might. It's too irrational for a good killer to invent, I suppose. And it happens to be true. You see, I couldn't show myself after it was all over. I had blood on my clothes. Not much, but some."

"You could get rid of your clothes."

"How? Burn them, and let the police find whatever's left over. Nails, buttons or what have you? No, my child. I know exactly what a real killer is up against. I've been down twice to start that damned furnace; in August, mind you! But what's the use?"

"I could take them with me. They'll never search our house."

"And have them take them from you as you leave here? Use your head, Lou! Now run home and forget me and this mess."

"Maybe later on tonight you could bury them, Jim? Out in No Man's Land."

He refused that idea, too, and I remember standing there and trying to think of some place where the inevitable police search would not discover them. It is strange how little the average house offers against that sort of hunt, especially for bulky objects.

"You haven't a concealed closet for your liquor?" I asked at last.

"I have a closet; but if you think at least fifty people don't know about it, then you don't know Helen."

"Still it would give you time, Jim," I pleaded.

Without a word he turned, and going to the bookshelves beside the fire, took hold of the frame and swung it out. Books and shelves, it proved to be a small door, and behind it was a neat liquor closet.

"Of course, once I hide the things I am committed by my own act," he said. "Still—"

"Did anyone see you?"

"In this house? No, I have my own key to the front door. Of course the police know that now.

"Or outside, on the way back here?"

"How do I know? We'll have to take a chance on that. Luckily I left my car here and walked there. That may help some."

We made it without a minute to spare. I had drawn the front shades while he was upstairs, and he was on his way down when the doorbell rang. Luckily the hall was dark, and the front door solid. He slipped the things to me through the stair-rail, and fumbled long enough at the door to give me a minute or two. But I was trembling all over by the time I had hidden the trousers and the shoes, and had swung the shelves back in place.

He gave me a bit more leeway by stopping to turn on the hall lights after he had opened the door. Then I heard him bringing in some men, and although I dread to think of what the Crescent would have said had it known, I was lighting one of Jim's cigarettes when they entered.

There were two of them, an Inspector Briggs from Headquarters and the detective, Sullivan, whom I had seen in the hall upstairs at the Lancaster house.

They eyed me curiously when Jim presented them.

"Miss Hall, eh? Then you are the young lady who found Miss Emily Lancaster in the garden?" This was from the Inspector.

"I didn't exactly find her. I heard her screaming, and ran out. It was Eben who got to her first."

47

"I see."

I was bracing myself for the next question, but to my surprise it did not come. Instead he suggested that Mr. Sullivan see me home, and then come back. Evidently he had no idea of letting Jim overhear what I had to say. I had a horrified moment as I rose when I realized that in my anxiety to hide the clothing I had overlooked that with Jim. What would he tell them? Or deny?

But Jim settled that for me in surprising fashion.

"Don't worry, Lou," he said. "We'll tell the truth and shame the devil! And you can throw away that cigarette. I don't think it's fooled anybody."

Inspector Briggs smiled slightly, but his face altered as Jim walked deliberately to the shelves and swung them open. "There's the evidence," he said.

Sullivan took me out, and I came as near to fainting then as I ever have, right there on the Wellington front porch.

Chapter VI

Mother had notified Holmes that he was to sleep in the house that night, on the general principle I suppose that having had one murder we might expect any number of them; which was not so absurd after all as it seemed that night.

But Holmes as a protection did seem absurd; a scared little rabbit of a man, he trailed at our heels as we locked up that night, careful not to get too far away from one or the other of us. It was from Holmes that I first heard the theory of a homicidal maniac.

"I don't mind saying, miss," he confided to me, "that I'm just as glad to be in here tonight. Somebody around here's gone crazy, and that's the truth."

"It would have to be a lunatic who knows all about us, Holmes."

"Well, that's not so hard to do, miss, with everybody living by the clock, as you may say."

"Except you, Holmes!"

He grinned at that. Mother still insists that the servants be in at ten o'clock at night; but still Holmes has an easy and unobserved exit by the path across No Man's Land, and I knew perfectly well that there were times when he not only disobeyed the rule, but did not come back at all.

But I think now that Holmes tried to tell me something that night, that his following me was not without reason. Later on he must have changed his mind, but I often wonder what would have happened had he followed that impulse. We would not in all probability have had our second murder, for one thing. Also it might have brought into the open the fact that all our servants knew or guessed a great deal more than any of us.

As I have indicated, however, the Crescent keeps its domestics in their places, the result being a sort of tacit cabal among them; the backs of our houses, so to speak, against the fronts. And Holmes had no chance that night to speak. Mother returned before he had decided, and having had the best linen sheets ceremoniously removed from the guest room next to hers, installed Holmes there with instructions not to snore, and to rap on her door if he heard anything suspicious during the night.

Poor Holmes! Unscrupulous he might have been, and was, but I always had a sneaking fondness for the little man

Incredible as it seems, it was only half past ten when I finally got to my room, leaving Mother locked and bolted inside hers. It had been only six and a half hours since I had seen Miss Emily run shrieking out of that door and collapse on the grass, but it had been innumerable years emotionally for me.

Not only the murder. Not only fear for Jim Wellington, possibly even then under arrest. Alarmed as I was for him, even I knew that a man could not be sent to the electric chair because he had stumbled on an old woman dead in her bed. What also worried me was a sort of terror that I still cared for him. Perhaps it was only sheer pity for his danger, and because I had seen him alone in that empty disordered house, with his servants gone because Helen had spent their money on the exotic clothes, the perfumes and whatnot which seemed more important to her than he ever was.

I knew as well as if I had seen her that she was out that night at some club or roadhouse or hotel roof, dancing, and I felt that I hated her for it.

This is not a love story, however, and perhaps here I should attempt to tell what the police had discovered up to half past ten o'clock that night, and to outline the Lancaster house itself for better understanding. The first I learned a bit at a time over the next two weeks, but the house I knew as well as I knew our own.

Indeed, for all practical purposes the two houses were the same. The same builder had constructed them fifty-odd years ago, at the time when elaborate scroll and fret-saw work decorated most pretentious country houses; and later on the same architect had added what we called our guest wings, removed his predecessor's adornments and given the dignity of both white paint and plain pillared porches.

The Lancaster house, then, is broad and comparatively shallow, presenting its long dimension to the Crescent. On the lower floor a wide hallway runs from front to back of the main body of the house; from this hall the front door opens onto the porch, shaded with vines, while the rear door opens on what was the old carriage sweep in front of the long-gone stables, and is now a vegetable garden with the woodshed beyond and shielded from the house by heavy shrubbery. As the Lancasters kept no car, there was no garage.

The four main living rooms of the family open from this hall on the first floor, while a narrower hall runs the length of the floor, one end opening by a door onto the lawn toward our house, and the other connecting by a door with the service wing. The staircase rises, not from the main hall but from this transverse one. Under this staircase is the lavatory of which Jim had spoken.

Thus, entering by the porch and the front door, there is the wide hall from front to back, bisected by the narrower transverse one. The parlor — a word we still use — lies on the right, while Mr. Lancaster's library is on the left. Then comes the transverse hall, with the staircase going up on the left, and an extension, rather narrower, leading to the

51

side entrance to the right. Behind this is the morning room, done in chintz, where Margaret keeps her accounts and writes her letters, and across the main hall the dining room, the latter to the left and connecting through the pantry and underneath the back staircase with the kitchen beyond.

A servants' dining room and closets to the front of the house, the kitchen, pantry, kitchen porch and laundry comprise the service wing and connect through a door with the body of the house; while a rear staircase, rather awkwardly placed to open onto the kitchen porch, and thus separating the pantry from the kitchen, leads to what we call the guest wing on the second floor, and then continues to the servants' bedrooms on the third.

This rear staircase, playing a certain strategic part in our first crime, opens on the second floor not far beyond the first landing of the main staircase; for the second floor wing is on a lower level than the body of the house. One who ascends the front stairs may thus look through an archway along the guest wing passage, and then turn and go on up the short flight of six steps to the hall and four large bedrooms which are — or were — occupied by the family.

All these rooms and passages are large, with high corniced ceilings, and the effect is one of great dignity and space.

Practically the same arrangement holds upstairs; that is, the four main sleeping rooms open on the broad hall, while the guest wing, with its lower ceilings, contains two guest rooms to the front — almost never used — with a connecting bath between them, and to the rear a sewing room, a linen closet, a housemaid's closet, and reached by a narrow hallway, the entrance to the back staircase.

The servants sleep on the third floor.

Of the four main sleeping rooms, Mrs. Lancaster occupied the large corner one in the front of the house; this being somewhat noisier and more exposed to the sun than the others, but being by all tradition of the Crescent

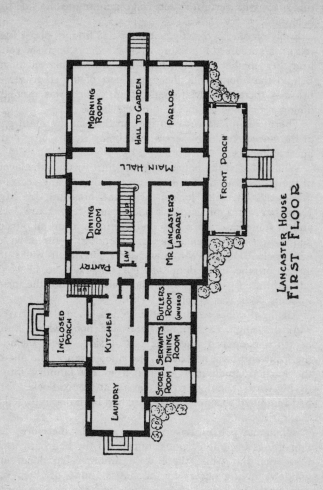

LANCASTER HOUSE
FIRST FLOOR

53

the room belonging to the mistress of the house. Through a bathroom it connected with her husband's room behind, this space with certain closets corresponding to the side hall below.

Emily's room lay directly across the hall from it; also a front room, she occupied it because with both doors open she could hear her mother if—or when—she needed her at night. Behind this room, with the upper part of the staircase-well between them, lay Margaret's room, which was over the dining room and at the rear of the house.

There was no staircase to the top floor in the main part of the house, the only access to it being by the one in the guest wing.

What puzzled the police from the start was not the layout of the house, but the seeming impossibility of any access to it. Always carefully locked, with the hoarding by Mrs. Lancaster extra precautions had been taken. Extra locks and in some cases bolts also had been placed on all outside doors, and the screen doors and windows were provided with locks. During Mr. Lancaster's afternoon walks the screen on the front door was left unlatched so he could admit himself with his key to the main door, but the inside wooden door was carefully locked.

All these doors were found fastened when they arrived, with the single exception of the side door which Emily herself had opened when she ran outside. These included the front and back hall doors, the side entrance, the one on the kitchen porch and another from the laundry into a drying yard. The door to the basement was padlocked, and had remained so since the furnace had been discontinued in the spring.

When the police arrived that afternoon, therefore, certain things became obvious, outside of the bedroom itself. One was that while there were innumerable doors and windows giving access to the house, none of them had apparently been used. Another was that the kitchen porch,

54

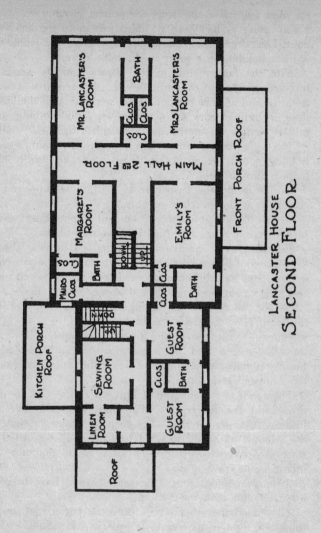

LANCASTER HOUSE
SECOND FLOOR

Mr. Lancaster's Room

Bath

Clos.

Clos.

Clos.

Mrs Lancaster's Room

MAIN HALL 2ND FLOOR

Margaret's Room

Emily's Room

Front Porch Roof

Bath

Maid's Clos.

Clos.

Clos.

Clos.

DOWN

UP

Bath

Kitchen Porch Roof

DOWN

Sewing Room

Guest Room

Bath

Clos.

Linen Room

Guest Room

Roof

55

the most vulnerable spot since the women servants were constantly using it, had been occupied ever since the luncheon hour: Ellen resting and later beating up a cake, and Jennie the waitress polishing her silver at the table there.

With the family shut in the library and the servants huddled in their own dining room, the detective named Sullivan had at once made an intensive survey of the lower floor, including doors and windows. He found nothing, and at last went back to the death chamber itself.

"House is like a fortress," he reported. "One thing's sure; nobody got in or out of it unless someone inside here helped him to do it."

But he found the Inspector at a front window, gazing curiously at the porch roof outside.

"Looks like he got in here," he said. "Something's overturned that flower pot. And look at this screen!"

Sullivan looked and grunted. Margaret Lancaster always kept a row of flower pots on her mother's window sill. Now one of them had slid off and overturned on the porch roof, and the screen itself was raised about four inches.

"Might ask one of the daughters if this screen was like this earlier in the day," the Inspector said.

Sullivan went down to the library, and came back to say that the screen had not been opened, and that Mrs. Lancaster had had a horror of house-flies; that she would have noticed it at once.

The medical examiner had finished at the bed by that time, and the fingerprint men were at work; and not finding anything, at that. The medical examiner went to the window and, still wearing his rubber gloves, tried to raise the screen from the top. But it would not move an inch and he gave it up.

"Nobody got out there," he said. "Might have tried it, however, and then gave it up."

They tried the other screen onto the porch roof, but it too stuck tight in its frame. It was not until Sullivan had crawled out the front hall window that they reached the roof at all, and that window he had found closed and locked. The three men were puzzled. Then Sullivan stooped suddenly and pointed to a small smear on the wooden base of the first screen.

"Looks like blood here," he said.

He straightened up and looked about him, then he creaked his way across the tin roof. There, lying wilted but fairly fresh in the hot sun he picked up two or three bits of newly cut grass. Just such grass indeed as I had watched cascading from the blades of Eben's lawn mower.

"What's that?" said the Inspector.

"Grass. How'd it get here? There's no wind."

"Birds, maybe."

None of them were satisfied, however. They went across into Emily's room, where her bird was still singing in the sunlight by a front window, and tried her screens. They too were locked, but they opened fairly easily.

"Anyhow that's out," said the Inspector. "She was in here herself, dressing, when it happened."

"So she says," said Sullivan drily, and the two men exchanged glances and went back across the hall.

Up to that time, oddly enough, they had not found the weapon. The medical examiner had suggested a hatchet, but there was none in sight. Then one of the fingerprint men happened to glance up, and he saw a stain on the tester top of the bed. Somebody got a chair, and being tall he was able to reach up with a clean towel and bring down the axe.

"It made me kind of sick," said the Inspector later. "I'm used to blood and all that, but an axe! And that little old woman not weighing a hundred pounds! It—well, it just about got me."

The discovery of the axe, while gratifying, was not particularly productive, however. It was a moderately heavy wood axe, with the usual long handle, but it bore only what looked like old and badly smeared fingerprints. At the extreme end there were no prints whatever.

"Either wore gloves or wiped it pretty carefully," was the comment of the fingerprint man, after a look at it.

None of them knew then, of course, that it belonged in the Lancaster woodshed, and practically all of them except Sullivan had veered to the idea of a homicidal maniac. The brutality of the crime, its apparent lack of motive, and as the Inspector said later, the utter recklessness of the entire business looked like that.

"You've got to get your lunatic into the house," was Sullivan's comment. "He hadn't wings, that's sure."

They began to study the room once more. The chest under the bed had at that time no significance for them, and the room was not particularly disturbed. Mrs. Lancaster's bed stood with its head against the wall toward her husband's room, and she had been found lying on the side toward the door into the hall. On one side of the bed was the entrance to the bathroom, which the police had found shut, and on the other a closet door, also closed. Beyond the closet door in the corner was a small chest of drawers, and one of these drawers was partly open, although its contents, mainly the dead woman's nightdress and bed jackets, were undisturbed.

There had apparently been no struggle, but that part of the room was a shambles. Not content with the first blow, probably fatal, five or six had been struck. In other words, as the Inspector said later, either some furious anger or pure mania lay behind the attack; or possibly fear, he added as an afterthought.

And, to quote him again:

"Well, there we were," he said. "We had some clues, as you might call them. We'd sliced that sliver with the blood off the window screen, and Sullivan was taking care of those bits of grass. But there was nothing on the axe or anywhere else. Also the house was shut, and shut tight. We didn't know about the hoarding then, but those lower floor windows and screens had new catches on them, and everybody in the house swore — and they were right at that — that every door had been locked and kept locked!

"Take the outside of the house, too. Here was the gardener. Nobody got past him, as we know, and I had my doubts about anybody except a professional strong man being able to climb one of those porch pillars with that axe, as you may say, in his teeth. Even the ground outside didn't help us any. Of course the earth was baked hard, but take a house like that with grass right up to the building itself, and there's mighty little chance of a print anyhow.

"Then there's another thing. I can understand that nobody heard anything. It's likely they couldn't, with that canary wound up tight and going hard. But it's not credible that whoever did that thing wasn't covered with blood from head to foot, and yet beyond a mark or two we spotted on that red hall carpet, probably from the gardener's shoes, there wasn't a sign of blood outside that room.

"For those wounds had bled! Especially the one in the neck. They bled and bled fast. Our medical examiner said that it would be practically impossible to strike those five blows and then cover the poor woman as she was covered, without the killer showing something. And maybe a good bit. You see she'd been arranged. In a way, that is; the body was straight in the bed and a sheet drawn up part way. And the mere matter of getting that key meant stains, and plenty of them."

The key had puzzled them, and Miss Emily's frantic search for it. No one explained it to them, and still of course they knew nothing of the gold.

"We were pretty much at sea about that time," he acknowledged. "Either it was an inside or an outside job, and there were arguments against either or both! It looked like one of those motiveless crazy crimes which drive the Department wild," he added. "The least to go on and the most showy from the press point of view! You could guess a crazy man with a pair of wings, and you could say that a bird went crazy with the heat and carried three blades of grass up onto that tin roof. But short of that where were we? And nobody, axe or no axe, had climbed those porch pillars. We caught a camera man shinning up a porch column that night to get a picture, and the marks he left were nobody's business!

"That's the outside end of it. Then take the inside. Take the matter of time as we figured it out that day," he said. "It was four o'clock when Miss Emily Lancaster ran out that side door and fainted on the grass. It was three-thirty when Mrs. Talbot left and the old lady turned over to take her nap. How much time had anybody in that house had to clean up a mess and get rid of a lot of bloody clothes? Whoever it was hadn't burned them and they couldn't hide them. We didn't merely examine that furnace; one of our operatives crawled inside it, and we had the devil of a time getting him out!"

And this, so far as the police were concerned, was the situation up to six o'clock that night when, Margaret being the calmest of the lot, they showed her the axe. She went white and sick, but she identified it at once as belonging to the household.

Normally it hung, from May until November, on two nails in the woodshed at the back of the lot; a woodshed which was purely a shed, having a door which usually stood wide open from one year's end to the other, but which Eben had noticed that day was closed. Investigation inside the shed, however, revealed nothing to show when it had been entered. The nails were there, the axe gone. Nothing else had been disturbed. The narrow shelf where Miss Margaret potted her plants for the porch roof and for the house in winter showed nothing save the usual crocks and a heap of loose leaf mold.

There was no sign of blood, nor of any stained clothing,

60

anywhere in the shed.

It was the discovery of the ownership of the axe that finally convinced the police that the crime had been an inside one. But nobody mentioned the gold, or intimated that it was in the house until approximately ten o'clock that night. Then Emily Lancaster suddenly broke down under their questions and admitted that Jim Wellington had been near her when she recovered from her fainting attack in the garden.

With that Peggy was recalled and broke down, and, as the Inspector would have said, the fat was in the fire.

Chapter VII

Out of that interrogation, of family and servants, certain statements were finally collected by the police and put into shape. Copies of these I now have, and as they illuminate the events of that day far better than I can repeat them here. I have stripped them, of course, of inessentials and repetitions, but they are correct in every other respect.

That of Emily Lancaster, as being the one who found the body, I give first.

"Mother had been restless all day. She felt the heat terribly, but an electric fan gave her neuritis, so I fanned her a good bit of the time. Except that I slipped over to the library in the morning to change that book I was reading aloud to her, I hardly left her at all. Indeed, I had not even a chance to clean my bird until Lydia Talbot arrived after lunch.

"Mrs. Talbot came in at half past two, and she relieved me of the fanning for a while. We sat and talked, but I thought that something Mrs. Talbot had said had annoyed Mother, and I was relieved when she went away. I went downstairs with her, and we met Father in the hall and they left the house together.

"I closed and locked the front door, and then went back to the kitchen porch for a glass of ice water. Jennie was

62

there, cleaning the silver, and Ellen was beating up a cake.

"As I went up the back stairs I thought I heard the housemaid in one of the guest rooms. It was a sound of some sort. I called 'Peggy, is that you?' No one answered, so I looked into the guest rooms, but they were empty.

"All that took about five minutes. I then went to Margaret's door. I knew she meant to go out and was afraid she had fallen asleep. I asked her if she would listen for Mother while I changed for the afternoon, but she said she was going to take a long shower to get cool before she dressed, and that she had just seen Mother, and she was asleep.

"I went on forward to my room and took off my dress, but just then I thought I heard Mother pounding on the floor with her stick, which is the way she often calls if she thinks I am downstairs. There is a bell over her bed, but it rings in the kitchen. I put on a dressing gown and went across, but she seemed to be asleep. I know that she—that nothing had happened then. I left the door partially open, and went back to my room.

"I know the exact time, for I looked at my clock. I like to be dressed for the afternoon by four, and it was not quite fifteen minutes before four.

"I dressed as fast as possible. My bird is a great singer, and he was making so much noise that once I opened my door and listened, for fear Mother was awake. She did not like birds much. I heard nothing, and so I finished dressing. It was almost four when I was ready.

"I went across to Mother's room, but I did not go all the way in. I saw her and I think I screamed. Then I ran back to Margaret's room, but I had to go all the way into the bathroom, for the water was running and she did not hear me. After that I ran down the stairs and out into the yard. I don't know why, except that I had to get away somewhere."

That was Emily's story, told in fragments between attacks of hysteria, and in some ways the most fully detailed of the lot. Neither in it nor in the others, until the situation was forced, did any of the family mention the dead woman's hoard. Partly I dare say it was pride, the fear that the newspapers would exploit the fact; partly it must have been because of their unwillingness to involve Jim Wellington. And it must be remembered that at that time the police still attached no significance whatever to the wooden chest under the bed.

Margaret's statement, which followed Emily's, is less exact as to time.

"This was my afternoon off. By that I mean that my sister and I take — took — alternate afternoons with Mother. Usually I go out on my free days, but today was very hot.

"I rested and read in my room until I heard Mrs. Talbot and Father leaving at half-past three. Then I remembered that Peggy, the housemaid, was having her afternoon off and that Mother had scolded her severely that morning. She was a good maid, and I did not want her leave.

"I went upstairs and spoke to her. She was crying, but at last she agreed to stay. I was there only a few minutes, but as I used the back staircase my sister may have heard me as she came up from the kitchen porch. I did not hear her call, however.

"I was running the water when she — Emily — came into my room with the news. She could hardly speak, and at first I did not hear her. Then I threw on something, took a glance into Mother's room and after calling to the servants I ran downstairs. In the lower hall I met Eben, and the two of us ran upstairs the front way while the servants hurried up the back.

"Eben then closed the door into Mother's room and started out to get a policeman. He was running. I have no real idea how long all this took, but at last I remembered Emily and went out to look for her. She was lying on the ground, and Lou Hall was stooping over her.

"Lou and I brought her in. Father had met Eben on the street and been told. We found him collapsed in the library, and soon after that the police came.

"The axe is one belonging to us. It was never brought into the house, and I have no idea how it got there. I know

64

of no reason why my mother was attacked, and I trust our servants absolutely. Two of the women and Eben have been with us for many years. Peggy has been with us only a short time, but she had neither reason nor opportunity to do this thing."

All of which sounds rather like Margaret, clear and unemotional and—even in the police notes—told without Emily's hesitation and indirection.

Mr. Lancaster's story to the police was much more vague. He was still profoundly shocked, but in his account he was quite clear as to the essential facts.

He had not been well for several days, and had not slept at night. He and Mrs. Lancaster had for several weeks disagreed on what he called a matter of policy, by which undoubtedly he referred to her hoarding of gold currency; but which he didn't explain that night. In her condition he did not like to argue with her, but he had been considerably upset.

That day he had read all morning in the library. Before going in to lunch he had made his usual noon visit to his wife. Emily was out, and he found Mrs. Lancaster silent and rather fretful, and had laid it to the heat. But here he added, after a certain hesitation, that he had been under the impression when he entered the bedroom that she had hidden something from him.

Asked what it might have been, he said that he had no idea, and might even have been mistaken. He was merely trying to remember all that he could. She had not said anything to suggest that it might be true, nor had he questioned her.

At noon he had eaten a light meal, largely fruit and tea, and had then slept for some time. He had not gone upstairs at all, but being roused by Mrs. Talbot's voice as she started down, had got his hat and left the house when she did. He had taken his usual walk, and had heard the news on the street as he returned from Eben, who was running for a policeman.

Asked as to his usual walk, he stated what we all knew,

that it was his habit to go out through the Crescent gates, and to go past the hospital and toward the shopping district a half mile away. For the city had grown and apartments had appeared on our horizon, so had sprung up six or eight blocks of small shops to supply their needs. Even the Crescent, which for a long time ignored them and did its buying downtown, had at last recognized and patronized them.

His walk that day, he said, had merely taken him to the tobacconist's shop on Liberty Avenue and back to the gates, where Eben met him. Unfortunately, and this is when the police determined to make a second and intensive search of the house, there were two things about Mr. Lancaster's statement which set Inspector Briggs to thinking, and thinking hard.

One was that he had stopped at a small and unimportant drug store, and had there had a glass of coca-cola.

"As we happened to know," the Inspector said later, "the drug store he mentioned had been padlocked that day for an infringement of the Volstead Act on the premises. Wherever he'd been, the old gentleman hadn't been there. And then came this girl Peggy with her story and — well, we began to wonder. That's all!"

For Peggy, seated uneasily on the edge of a chair in the dining room, her eyes swollen with crying, had finally admitted that she had been standing at her window overlooking the front street, had seen Mr. Lancaster go out with Mrs. Talbot; and return five minutes later.

"I don't want them to know I said so," she had whispered, "but that's the truth."

"You may be wrong about the time."

"No, sir. I didn't stand there more than five minutes at the most. Miss Margaret will tell you that she came up to speak to me, and that I was standing at my window then. Maybe she'll know the time."

"Did you tell Miss Margaret that Mr. Lancaster had come back?"

"I didn't think of it. You see the old — Mrs. Lancaster

had acted very mean to me that morning, and I was thinking about leaving. I couldn't make up my mind. Miss Margaret came up to ask me to stay on, and I said I would."

The Inspector had heard Emily's story by that time, and so he asked her if she couldn't be mistaken.

"Looking down from a third story window," he said, "people look different, you know, Peggy."

"I'd know that old panama of his anywhere," she said stubbornly.

"Lots of men wear old panamas. Was there nothing else?"

"He was getting out his keys. I saw him as plain as I see you. Besides," she added triumphantly, "anybody else but Mr. Wellington would have had to ring the doorbell, and it didn't ring. It rings on the third floor as well as in the kitchen."

But there is to Peggy's credit the fact that she then set her small and pretty chin, and that she said nothing more about Jim until she was recalled later that night. That was after Emily had remembered that Jim had spoken to me in the garden; and they brought the girl in, anxious and with reddened eyes, and inquired if the man she had seen on the walk could not have been Jim Wellington.

She shook her head obstinately, but they kept at her, and at last she admitted that she had seen Jim that afternoon.

"Where? On the walk?"

"No. In the house. On the second floor." And then seeing the Inspector's expression, she burst into a flood of tears.

But of course she had to go on, and at last they had a fairly coherent story from her.

Shortly before four, feeling comforted by Margaret's visit, she decided to go out after all. She did not know the precise time. She put on her hat and went down to the second floor, where in one of the guest rooms there was a better mirror. She fixed her hat there, and then went out into the hall. On her way to the back stairs, however, she heard someone coming up the front staircase and saw that it was Jim Wellington.

He was bareheaded, and he was coming up quietly, but without any particular stealth. Of one thing she was certain. He was empty-handed.

He did not see her, but passed the landing and went on up toward the main part of the house. Certainly his presence there did not surprise her.

"He always had the run of the house," she said, rather naively.

She had not seen or heard him go out. She herself had gone on down the back stairs, and she was there with Ellen and Jennie when the alarm was raised. Not in a thousand years would she believe Mr. Wellington committed the crime. He wouldn't hurt a fly, and she didn't care what anybody thought.

"So there we are!" said the Inspector, summarizing the case later on. "Wellington had been in the house and slipped away, and old Mr. Lancaster had pulled a fake alibi on us! But if this girl was right, the old gentleman came back at twenty-five minutes to four, and at a quarter to four or about that Miss Emily finds her mother all right and goes to dress. At four she discovers what has happened, and not more than ten minutes after four Eben meets the old gentleman on his way in at the gates, immaculate and not in a hurry, apparently on his way home, and not more than five or ten minutes past his usual schedule!

"I don't mind telling you that when I got home at three o'clock that morning I took a triple bromide."

Chapter VIII

I suppose some of the Crescent people went to bed that night. That some of the women stood before their old-fashioned bureaus, stuck their brooches into their fat pin-cushions, unhooked dresses and hung them up, slid off petticoats, unpinned false curls and braids and put them neatly into their boxes, unhooked their tight laced stays and unbuttoned their tight shoes; and having got so far, mod-estly slipped their nightgowns over their heads and then removed the remainder of their clothing.

Or that some of the men also retired, after taking a final nightcap or two, the material for which rumor reported that our chauffeur, Holmes, surreptitiously supplied at a profit.

They had had the first real thrill of many years, and now behind them, visible in the mirrors before which they brushed their hair or took off their collars, were their wide beds with their bolsters, opened and waiting for them, the starched linen pillow-shams of the day laid aside, the day spreads neatly folded and the night spreads as neatly in place. The single bed had no place on the Crescent.

Looking back, I can see them all with an understanding I lacked at the time. I can see Mrs. Talbot, attended by her faithful Lizzie, removing one of the black transformations which she wore rather as other women wear a hat, and of which she claimed to have a half dozen or so. I can see Lydia taking off her pads and hanging them up in a window to dry after the hot day. I have seen them there myself, early in the morning. I can see Emily Lancaster, filled with who knows what horrors, asleep at last after the Crescent physician, Doctor Armstrong, had given her an opiate; and Margaret walking the floor of the morning room downstairs while police overran the house, listening for any approach to the library and the old couch there, where far down under the upholstery she had hidden something which she must somehow get out of the house.

And downtown, in an office in the City Hall, I can see Jim Wellington sitting in a hard chair and being questioned, his key to the Lancaster house on the desk, the Commissioner behind the desk, and the District Attorney walking the floor and smoking one cigarette after another.

"What time was it when Miss Margaret Lancaster telephoned you?"

"Between eleven and twelve. Perhaps a little later."

"And what did she say?"

"She said her father wanted me to go over the chest and see what was in it."

"A chest? What chest?"

Jim was astonished.

"Then they haven't told you? The chest under my aunt's bed. She had developed a nervous terror of banks, and she'd been turning her fortune into gold and currency for some months. Mostly gold."

After that he had to explain the entire procedure, and they listened spellbound. Here at last, they felt was the motive for the crime. But they were not satisfied with his explanation of why he had gone to the house that afternoon.

"You carried no money today?"

"No. None whatever."

"Then why did they send for you?"

"I've told you that Mr. Lancaster wanted the chest opened and investigated. A sort of audit, I suppose."

"Why an audit? Did Margaret Lancaster explain?"

"No, I haven't an idea. None of them had liked the hoarding. I hoped it meant the stuff was to go back to the bank. It was a fool idea from the start."

"This key the family was searching for, was that the key to this chest?"

"I don't know what they were searching for," he said rather sulkily. "My aunt wore the key to the chest on a chain around her neck."

"You know how much gold was in this chest. Is it your idea that robbery was the motive for the crime?"

"I have no ideas about it at all. More than half the stuff was in gold, the rest in currency. I'd say nobody could carry the gold away in a hurry. It's pretty heavy. As to the currency —" He looked at them. "Why in God's name don't you look and see?"

But this, as it happened, was not possible that night. On the first information from Jim that the chest had held a fortune in gold and currency Inspector Briggs had been notified and the chest examined. Not only did it show no signs of having been tampered with, but it was still so heavy that the mere act of getting it out from under the bed was a difficult one.

No key had been found, and the officers stood about the chest, eyeing it. It was almost midnight by that time, but Sullivan went downstairs and after getting an ice pick from the back porch, the only tool he could find, was on his way back when he met Mr. Lancaster in the lower hall.

"I'm glad you're here, Mr. Lancaster," he said. "We want to take a look into that chest under your — under the bed upstairs. I suppose you have no other key to it?"

The old man eyed him stonily.

"The chest is not to be opened," he said.

"But if there has been a robbery —"

71

"There has been no robbery. The chest contains a large part of my wife's estate, and will not be opened unless her attorney is present; perhaps not until her will has been probated. I know very little about such matters."

Sullivan, I believe, went up the stairs, swearing softly. There was apparently nothing to be done, since the chest itself showed no signs of having been disturbed. He and the Inspector agreed to let it ride until morning, and it was only the discovery of fingerprints on it that changed their minds. These checked with none belonging to the household, all of whom had been printed that evening, and were quite distinct; that is, two hands had been laid on the lid, on either side of the lock, as if to raise it.

They made no further attempt to open the box that night, but they put a policeman in the room on guard over it; and at last after a rather acid exchange with that office in the City Hall they went home, the Inspector to take his bromide and Sullivan to ponder over those prints on the box. For they were the prints of a small hand, and Jim Wellington was built on large and fairly substantial lines.

That, as nearly as I can describe it, was the situation that night of Thursday August the eighteenth, following the murder. The police had gone over every inch of the house and were still examining the grounds outside, but what they had as a result of seven hours or more intensive labor was the body of an aged and bedridden woman, almost decapitated by the blows of an axe; the picture of a family, stunned but still bearing with dignity its terrible catastrophe; and for clues a blood-stained axe, two or three blades of grass, a smear outside a window screen, a locked chest with some unidentified prints on it, and the knowledge for what it was worth that both Mr. Lancaster and Jim Wellington had been in the house at or about the time the murder was committed.

I myself was faint and confused when I got back from Jim's that night. Mother was asleep, locked in and probably with a vase set on each of her window sills so it would fall if anyone tried to enter by the porch roof. Holmes was snoring lustily in the guest room, and the night air was heavy and close, as though rain were in prospect.

I remember standing in the center of my room and looking about me. My sense of security was badly shaken that night, and suddenly I realized that I had given up everything else for it, had sacrificed to it my chance to live and even my chance to love. And for what? That my bed should be neatly turned down at night and the house run smoothly, with fresh flowers in the proper season and the table napkins ironed first on the wrong side and then polished on the right?

Perhaps I was hysterical that night, for I found myself looking at the fat pincushion on my bureau and laughing. I had done that only once before. That was when I came home from boarding school for the last time, and tried to throw it out. I had done it, too; but the next day it was firmly in its place again. I had laughed then, and then burst into a storm of tears.

After that the pincushion was always symbolic to me. It stood for everything: for no children to play with when I was small; for long hair when I had wanted to cut mine; for fried chicken and ice cream at hot Sunday midday dinners; for the loss of romance and the general emptiness of life. And that night it squatted there as if to remind me that life was short, but that it was still there; that it would always be there.

I did not undress at once. Instead I stood by a window, in the room which corresponded with Margaret Lancaster's, and thought over all that I had learned. Out of the chaos in my mind certain things were emerging. For one thing, everyone at the house that night had, either tacitly or openly, suspected that the crime was essentially a crime of the Crescent itself. Apparently George Talbot suspected Bryan Dalton, and Mr. Dalton suspected George! Both Lydia Talbot and Mrs. Dalton, not to mention Mother, seemed convinced that the answer lay in the Lancaster house itself; and only Mrs. Talbot openly believed that it was a plain case of robbery.

But that last theory seemed to me to be absurd. Even I knew that gold was heavy. One did not pick it up and simply run away with it. Again, none of us actually knew that the gold and currency were missing. And if they were, I wondered vaguely if there had been time between Mrs. Talbot's departure and Jim's entrance for the old lady to be killed, the chest dragged out and opened, bags of gold or bundles of notes placed on the porch roof, and the chest replaced under the bed.

For that at least we did know that night, although I do not remember how we knew it, unless it was from Lydia Talbot, who had an uncanny way of securing information. The chest was under the bed when the police got there.

I wondered about Eben, only to dismiss him. It had been half past three when I sat down at my window, and the sound of the mower had not ceased once until that time at four o'clock when he stopped to mop his hot face, and Emily had screamed in the house across.

No, not Eben. Not even any of our servants, so far as we could tell. All of them save Peggy at the Lancasters' had been with us for years on end. All save Helen Wellington's, that is, and they had packed and gone long before the crime. I thought of Peggy and dismissed her; a slim soft little creature, whom I had once seen walking with Holmes on the path through No Man's Land, but whose face showed only a sort of weak amiability.

Then who else? Not a delivery driver for one of our shops. The Crescent rigidly insists on delivery at the rear, and the Lancaster rear porch had been occupied all the afternoon. Not Holmes, more recent than most of the others, but driving Mother that afternoon until half past four; nor the Daltons' butler, Joseph, identified in the general canvass that night by Laura Dalton as having brought her iced tea at a quarter to four.

Who else but Jim, then? I began again that sort of

desperate roll call of the Crescent: Helen Wellington in town, and with no possible motive: Mrs. Dalton drinking iced tea and Bryan Dalton in a pair of dirty overalls working over his car in their garage, Mother out, Eben mowing, Lydia gone shopping at two-thirty and sitting the rest of the afternoon in an air-cooled moving picture theater, George downtown at his bank, and Mrs. Talbot carefully locked in her bedroom and taking a nap.

It was Lydia Talbot that afternoon who had come nearest to making plain statement. "I suppose they stood it as long as they could," she had said, and then became uneasy and spoke of what devoted daughters they had always been.

One thing was clear even to me, however. That was that the secret of the Lancasters' gold was not a secret at all. Probably from the moment Jim Wellington had brought out his first canvas sack, with its neck neatly wired and sealed with lead, our grapevine telegraph had sent the news from one end of the Crescent to the other. There would be even no secret as to where it was kept, with Peggy wiping the chest daily with an oiled cloth — as we wipe all our furniture — and brushing the floor under that tragic bed.

A dozen people knew, a hundred might have learned. And as I did not then know of those screens which would not move, it seemed to me that some one of those hundred could have scaled the porch roof, slid into the room, opened the chest with the key after his deadly work was done, and escaped with his treasure.

But how? In a car? No car had passed our house from three-thirty to four. That I knew. Then who else? The street cleaner? I had hardly ever noticed him. No one seems to notice the street cleaner, for some reason. But now I recalled him, a tall thin gangling man in dirty white clothes and helmet, who was a constant source of irritation to the Crescent, which regarded him as especially employed by the city to brush its leaves into heaps and then let the wind blow them about again.

Perhaps I was not entirely rational that night, but the

picture of this individual pushing his waste can on wheels persisted in my mind. After all, if the Crescent knew of the gold and the key to the chest around the old lady's neck, then its servants knew it. And what the servants knew he might know.

In a way, too, he had access to all our properties; for whenever his cart was filled he had a way of trundling it back to No Man's Land and there, against a city ordinance, dumping and burning it.

He could have known not only about the gold. He could easily have known about the axe in the woodshed. Moreover, so regular are our habits, it might have been possible for him to know that Emily dressed while Mrs. Lancaster slept between three-thirty and four, that the old gentleman walked at that time, leaving the screen door open, that it was Margaret's afternoon off, as well as Peggy's; and he could have seen that the other two maids were in the rear of the house.

Moreover, the times coincided. While I had not noticed him that day, he generally reached us by mid-afternoon. And again, it seemed to me that his cart answered the question as to how the gold had been taken, if it had.

I have told all this circumstantially, not because it made any real contribution to the solving of our crimes, but because it explains how I myself in a small way became involved in them. For shortly before midnight, and while the Inspector and Sullivan were still gazing at that chest as it was being dragged from under the bed, I was on my way to the Lancaster house with my theory!

I got out of the front door without rousing anyone, but no sooner had I set foot on the street pavement than a shadowy figure in a rubber coat looked up and flashed a light in my face.

"Not allowed to go this way, miss," a voice said.

"Don't be absurd. I want to see Inspector Briggs."

"I don't think he'll see you. He's busy."

"Nevertheless I intend to try," I said firmly; and with that he fell back, although he followed me all the way. At the Lancaster walk he stopped.

"I'll be here when you come out," he told me. "It isn't a healthy neighborhood just now for young ladies alone."

With which cheerful remark he lighted a cigarette and lounged away.

The Lancaster house was more fully lighted than I had realized until I stood before it. Saving of lights is one of the Crescent's pet economies, although most of us are safely beyond want, and it is an actual fact that the house in front of me, blazing from attic to cellar, was more indicative to me of the sharp break in our lives than anything else I had so far seen.

For a time, however, it looked as though I might not be admitted.

There was an officer on the porch, and he asked me sharply what I wanted.

"To see Inspector Briggs," I told him. "Or Mr. Sullivan. He's a detective, I believe."

"The Inspector's upstairs, miss," he said doubtfully. "But I don't think he'll see you."

"Tell him I have something to say that may be important. I am Miss Hall. I live next door."

He went in then, and I stood on the porch waiting. The expected storm was closer now, and I remember distant thunder and a thin spatter of rain on the roof overhead. Then the front door opened again, but it was not the policeman. It was Margaret Lancaster.

"Louisa?" she said, in a whisper.

"I'm here, Miss Margaret."

"Quick, take this," she said. "Have you a pocket? If you haven't, slip it into your stocking. And for God's sake don't tell anybody I gave it to you."

She had thrust a small package into my hand; an envelope rather. I took it, but I must have seemed uncertain, for she urged me in a desperate voice to hide it.

"He'll be down any minute!" she implored me. "Hurry!"

77

I slid it into my stocking, and then slowly straightened.

"I don't like it, Miss Margaret," I told her. "If it has anything to do with —"

"Listen to me, Lou! All I'm trying to do is to save somebody who is innocent. I swear that, Lou."

The next second I was alone on the porch, and soon after that the officer returned.

Chapter IX

I was in a poor state of nerves when I was finally shown into the library. Only Mr. Lancaster was still there, and he looked as though he had not moved since the afternoon. He was lying back in the same chair, with his delicate immaculately kept hands on the arms, and his face a waxy yellow. He did not rise as usual on my entrance. At first he seemed not to know that I was there; then he opened his eyes and looked at me, a strange and unfriendly look.

"What brings you here?" he asked, still without moving.

"I want to talk to the Inspector."

"About what?" He still lay back, but I got an impression of sudden tension.

I took my courage in my hands.

"About the money, Mr. Lancaster," I said. "I may be wrong, but I have thought of a way by which it could have been taken out of the house."

"Taken out of the house! How do you know it has been taken out of the house?"

Luckily for me Inspector Briggs came in just then, looking rather annoyed, and took me to the morning room behind the parlor. He put me into a chair, and then drawing one close in front of me, sat down himself. At that moment I thanked heaven for long skirts. Whatever it was Margaret had given me, it felt bulky and uncomfortable in my stocking.

"Now, Miss Hall," he said, "let's have it. I presume it's about this murder."

"The murder and the gold," I told him.

"Gold? What do you know about any gold?"

That was the first time I realized that the family had not told the police about it, and I was pretty well confused. But I managed to say that there was a story that Mrs. Lancaster had been hoarding it and that, trying to think how it could be taken away—if it was—I had thought of the street cleaner.

"After all," I said, "somebody did this killing, Inspector. And it wasn't Jim Wellington, no matter what you think."

He smiled rather grimly.

"Somebody did it, that's sure," he agreed. "Well, we'll look up your friend with the cart; but I wouldn't be too hopeful. You live next door, eh? Then I suppose you know this family fairly well."

"I've lived next door to them all my life. But as to knowing them well, if you knew the Crescent you wouldn't say that."

"Why?" He eyed me, absently pinching his upper lip; a habit I was to learn well as time went on.

"I don't know. We are rather a repressed lot, I imagine. We see a good bit of each other, but no one is particularly intimate with anyone else. We still leave cards when we call after four o'clock," I added; and he seemed to find that amusing, for he smiled.

"But you have certain powers of observation," he pointed out. "Take this family here, in this house. Did they get along together? Just shut your eyes and tell me what you can think, or remember, about them; their relationships, their prejudices, their differences if they had any." And seeing me hesitate, he added: "Nobody is under suspicion,

80

of course. As a matter of fact, it is practically impossible for any of them to have done it; for reasons I won't go into now. This is routine, but it has to be done."

"I don't really know much," I told him. "They seemed to get along very well. The two girls were devoted to Mrs. Lancaster, although she was a fretful invalid. In a way Miss Emily bore most of that burden; but Emily was her favorite."

"And Mr. Lancaster? Was he fond of his wife?"

"He was most loyal and careful of her. But she was not easy to get along with. You see," I explained, "our servants talk back and forth, and so we learn things we wouldn't otherwise."

"And—since you seem to know about this money—how did Mr. Lancaster regard the hoarding?"

"He disliked it. All of them did."

He leaned back and pinched his lip again. "Now that's interesting," he commented. "Very interesting. It doesn't look—well, let's get on. What about Miss Margaret? Rather more worldly, isn't she? Doesn't like being a spinster and doesn't like getting old. Isn't that it?"

I colored uncomfortably.

"No woman likes either, Inspector."

But he grinned at me cheerfully.

"Tut, tut!" he said. "You're still a young woman, and a good-looking one at that. Well, what about her?"

"I don't know very much. She's a good housekeeper, and she helps with her mother. She goes out more than Miss Emily, almost every other afternoon; and she dresses more carefully. That is, Miss Emily is frightfully neat, of course, but Miss Margaret is more—well, I dare say more fashionable."

"Hasn't give up hope yet, in other words!" he said, and laughed a little. "All right, that will do for the family. Now tell me about this afternoon. Close your eyes again. But first; have you any idea just how this gold was put into the chest? The old lady was helpless, wasn't she? Then who did it, or was there when it was done?"

"I haven't any idea. I never heard of it until tonight."

"And then Wellington told you?"

"I heard before that. All the Crescent seems to have known about it, except myself."

He pinched his lips again, thoughtfully.

"They did, eh? Just how did they know? I gather the family here hasn't been very communicative about it."

"I really don't know. George Talbot is in a bank, and I suppose even bankers have their human moments—in clubs or wherever bankers go when they are not banking."

"The Talbots knew then, I take it?"

"They must have. Mrs. Talbot says she remonstrated with Mrs. Lancaster only this afternoon about having it there. And Mrs. Lancaster was peevish, and said Margaret had been scolding her too."

"Humph!" he said. "Quite a lot of interest in that money all at once, wasn't there? Well, let's get back to you, and what you saw before Emily Lancaster came out of her faint, and found young Wellington with you."

I had begun to have a queer unwilling sort of confidence in the man, but I hesitated then.

"Don't be afraid," he said. "It takes a lot of trouble to send an innocent man to the chair these days, and something as much to send a guilty one!"

So I told him all I knew, which was not a great deal. I began at three-thirty that afternoon, and ended when I left the house perhaps an hour and a half later. He listened with his eyes closed, and still pinching that upper lip of his, until I had finished. Then he thanked me and got up.

"It's the sort of case that sets a police department by the ears," he said. "A crime probably by a non-habitual criminal, and so ordinary methods are no use in it. Well, we'll have to hope for some luck. Maybe it's in the chest! Certainly from the weight of it the gold still is!"

And I imagine that it was after that talk with me that Mr. Sullivan went down for the ice pick and met Mr. Lancaster in the hall, only to be forbidden to open the chest at all.

My friend of the pavement was waiting for me when I left the house. It was after midnight by that time, and raining hard, and I still remember the street lamp shining on his glistening rubber coat, and his injunction to me that I "had better make a run for it."

It was not until I had got back to my own room that I missed Margaret's parcel! My heart almost stopped beating, for whatever it was I knew that it probably lay, white and gleaming, somewhere on the pavement between the two houses.

I turned out my light and surveyed what little of the street I could see from my window. My friend of the rubber coat was not in sight, but toward the rear and No Man's Land men seemed to be still moving. Their flashlights at that distance looked like fireflies moving close to the earth. I did not know just what they were searching for, unless it was footprints. But they gave me what the Inspector had not, a terror of the relentless process of the law that turned me cold.

For I knew I would have to go out again, retrace my steps and find that envelope which was to save someone who was innocent. And who could that be but Jim?

The rubber coat was not in sight when I reached the pavement again, and I found my parcel easily enough. No sooner had I picked it up, however, than the now familiar voice spoke close behind me.

"I thought I'd put you safely to bed!"

"I lost my handkerchief while I was running," I said, and dropped the wet object down the neck of my frock.

He saw the gesture and seemed undecided. After all, he could hardly have up-ended me there on the street and shaken it out of me. But he did not believe the handkerchief story, and he lost some of his amiability.

"I'd like to see what you picked up just now, miss."

"My handkerchief. I've told you. If you don't believe me take me over to Inspector Briggs and watch him laugh at you!"

"And you won't show it?"

"Why should I? Unless I'm under arrest?"

That decided him, for with a sharp warning to go back home and stay there he let me go. When I reached our porch, he was still standing there in the pouring rain, looking uneasily after me. And so frightened was I was that I was locked in my room with the shades drawn before I so much as looked at what Margaret had given me.

Then I examined it. It was a fair-sized white envelope on which the rain had already done its work, for as I examined it it fairly went to pieces in my hands.

There was no concealing its contents. What it contained was a man's glove, a glove belonging to a large man, and of heavy leather. Nor was there any concealing the fact that the glove was stained with blood. It was wet and faded on the back, but the palm and fingers were stiff with it.

I stood there, literally frozen with horror. It was a glove that would have fitted Jim Wellington, but could on no account belong to Mr. Lancaster, with his small delicate hands. Like a woman's, his hands. And instantly I was seeing Margaret running down the stairs after poor Emily, and coming across that glove, maybe in the lower hall. Finding it and hiding it. She liked Jim. She had said: "All I'm trying to do is to save somebody who is innocent."

But how, if that glove was Jim's could she believe him innocent?

I took it to the light and examined it carefully. It was an old right-hand glove. The marks on the inside showed that it had made several trips to the cleaner's, and ignorant as I was of such matters I knew that the police could easily identify it from those marks. Also it bore, in addition to the stains, some curious black streaks that looked as though it might have been used while the owner worked about the engine of a car, but which had a pungent odor, familiar but hard to identify, except that it was apparently not engine grease. Still, it might have been.

I sat back and thought. Beginning at the house nearest the gate, Jim Wellington and Helen had a car, but it was kept at a garage on Liberty Avenue, not far away. The Daltons had a car, and Joseph drove it on state occasions. Mr. Dalton often worked over it in the garage. Holmes I eliminated; he had true mechanic's hands; usually dirty, to Mother's disgust. The Lancasters had no car at all, using a hired one when necessary, and George Talbot had an ancient Ford, notorious in the Crescent for its noise and for George's boast that he had never looked under the hood since he bought it.

Also, I was more and more certain that the black smears were not engine grease; that they were something else which I should be able to identify, but could not; and which was pungent enough to rise above the odor of wet leather and the dreadful flat smell of dried blood.

One thing I did know. That glove held the key to the crime next door. It had been worn by the killer, and now I was to hide it where even the police could not find it. For I knew well enough that the man in the rubber coat had not believed me.

I could not even burn it. Not at once, anyhow. It was wet, and besides, Margaret had told me to hide it. I might get her permission later to destroy it, but for that night at least I had to secret it. But where? And as though to add to my troubles that night, Mother had to choose that moment to waken and to come through the connecting bath into my room. I had only time to slip the dreadful thing under a chair cushion before she entered.

There was nothing to do but to face it out, so I stood there while she gazed in amazement at my sopping head and dress.

"Louisa! Where in the world have you been?"

"I couldn't sleep, mother. I walked to the corner, and the storm caught me."

"You went out? Like that?"

"No, I came back like this, mother."

But she refused to smile. I can still see her, as I see so many things belonging to that dreadful time; her hair in its usual kid rollers, her dead black dressing gown about her, and her face grave and somber.

"Louisa, she said, "if I ask you to stay in the house especially at night, until this crime is solved, will you believe me when I tell you that there is a real reason for it?"

"I should think you would have to tell me more than that, mother."

She shook her head.

"It is not my secret. And it is particularly necessary that the police should not know."

"But if it has any bearing on this terrible thing they ought to know."

"The thing is done. Nobody can bring her back."

"It all sounds stupid and silly to me," I broke out. "And if the rest of us are in danger it's criminally wrong. That's all."

But Mother's face took on the obstinate look I know so well.

"I am sure all possible steps will be taken," she said. "The only reason I have told you is that you will realize that you must not leave the house at night. Or even in the daytime, alone."

"So, to avoid publicity, we are all to be prisoners! Mother, if you don't tell the police I shall."

I was frightened after I had said it, for I do not remember ever before coming into open conflict with her. I had the little girl feeling that probably the lightning outside would strike me dead the next minute, but Mother took it better than I expected.

"If you do," she said, coldly but without indignation, "I can only tell you that you will spoil two lives, and may completely destroy one of them."

With that she went out, leaving me to make of it what I could.

Chapter X

I remember that I spent the time until Mother slept again in undressing and in trying to think of a safe spot in which to hide that sickening glove.

Perhaps that seems a simple matter in a house as large as ours, but it does not take into account the Crescent type of housekeeping. For thirty-odd years, in four of our five houses, the week has been divided into certain household "days." Thus, although we have imported certain labor-saving devices, we still wash on Monday and iron on Tuesday. We bake — we still bake our own bread — on Wednesday and Saturday, we clean our silver on Thursday, we do our marketing three times a week and do it ourselves, and on Friday we have a general cleaning, upstairs and down. Saturday is a sort of preparation day, being devoted to the preparing of elaborate food for Sunday, and to the changing of beds, the listing of Monday's wash and a complete tidying up of house, porches and grounds.

Nothing is sacred from this system, and I myself have rather less privacy than the elephant in our city zoo. It is nothing unusual for me to find Mother seated before my bureau and putting into order the contents of its drawers, and it was in the course of such an investigation that she once found hidden there a letter from Jim Wellington, and thus ended my first and only romance.

So it was that, there waiting for Mother to go to sleep, I was wildly canvassing the house for some safe hiding place for the glove. I considered the library and dropping it behind the books there; but although we use the room the books are my father's and so are held virtually sacred. No hand but Mother's ever dusts them, and only that week I had heard her say that she meant to get at them again. On the third floor the storeroom was always locked, and Mother carried the key. And it was now Friday by the clock, a day which meant the lifting of all liftables and the moving of all movables in the entire house.

Never before had I realized what must be the mental condition of a criminal faced with the problem of hiding the clue to his guilt; and never before had I considered that it might be practically impossible in a house of eighteen rooms, baths, pantries and innumerable closets, to conceal an object as small as a glove. Certainly I did not believe that, having at last found a spot which seemingly answered all requirements, it would be discovered in less than twenty-four hours by anything so ironic as a mere turn in the weather!

But that is precisely what happened, for the place I finally located was over the radiator at the end of the guest wing hall.

Some years ago the Crescent had decided that our hotwater heat was hard on its furniture, and almost all of us had installed new patented radiator covers in our upper and lower halls. These covers were of metal and resembled all other covers of the sort, with one exception. The top of each one was hinged, and underneath lay a flat zinc water pan. One might examine them for days, and unless one knew the secret he would not discover that shallow pan, which was filled only when cold weather stared our furnaces.

In our house there were two in the upper hall, one

underneath the front window and outside of Mother's door; the other near the end of the guest wing, where a window faced the Daltons'. It was this one I decided to use, and it was there, at something after one o'clock in the morning, that I placed the glove.

My spirits rose at once, I remember. The storm had passed, and a cooler air was coming through the open window near at hand. To add to my relief I heard a car drive in at the gate, stop at the Wellington house and then go round the Crescent and out the gate again. That could only mean that they had brought Jim back, and I drew my first full breath of the evening when far away I heard his front door slam.

It was then that I went to the window, to discover that the Dalton house, like the Lancasters', was lighted from top floor to basement.

It startled me, that blaze of light. The Dalton house is rather closer to ours than the Lancasters', and as Mother has her cutting garden there, it is not obscured by trees. Ordinarily it is a dark house. The strange silent life which goes on there is not conducive to the gaiety of many lights, and never before had I seen it fully lighted.

Mrs. Dalton's room at the front was brilliant, and also her dressing room behind it. Downstairs both drawing room and dining room were alight, and even the windows in the cellar. Nor was that all. Beyond the shrubbery at the rear there was a faint gleam as though the garage itself was lighted, although I could not see it.

At first all I saw was this blaze of light. Then I realized that someone was moving about in it, and at last that this moving figure was that of Mrs. Dalton. She appeared to be still fully dressed, and she was doing a peculiar thing. So far as I could make out, she was systematically searching her house!

She would enter a room, appear and reappear as though moving about it, end by examining the windows and the sills

90

beyond them, and then turn out the light and go through the same process in the next room. Even from that distance that silent search of hers had something remorseless and determined about it.

She was in the dining room when I first saw her, and in Bryan Dalton's den next. Then came a few minutes when I lost her, only to have her reappear in the basement. She was there for so long that I wondered if she had gone up again, when I saw her again at one of the windows, carefully peering out into the areaway beyond it.

To say that I was puzzled is rather to understate the situation. On a night when, shattered as to nerves and profoundly shaken as to its sense of security, the Crescent was presumably locked and bolted into its bedchambers, the most timid woman among us all was carefully and systematically making a search of her house. For what?

Odd memories wandered through my mind: Miss Lydia Talbot's statement a year or so before that Laura Dalton was still madly in love with Bryan. Helen Wellington's conviction that he, Bryan, had a wandering foot as well as a wandering eye, and that he was too good-looking to be let alone and too dangerous to trifle with.

"But he's so old," I had said to that.

"Old? At fifty-something? Don't be the eternal ingénue, Lou. That's not what I meant anyhow. When I say he's dangerous I mean that she is. She's insanely jealous of him."

Up to that time when at last she put out the basement lights, then, I had not connected any of all this with our murder. If I had any coherent thoughts at all, they were that she was searching for something which might show that he was involved with another woman. For it was no casual search; even I could see that. She was carrying it on with too desperate an energy for that.

It was not until the light went up on the rear porch that I began to wonder, for Bryan suddenly appeared in the picture, towering over her — she barely reached to his shoulder—and to my utter amazement seemed to be protesting not by gestures but by words. Not only that, but she seemed to be making brief staccato replies. This complete reversal of all that I could remember was more than human nature could bear, and I started running back to my room for my dressing gown and slippers. I must have made some noise, for the next minute I had run full tilt into Holmes and scared him nearly to death.

"Oh, my God!" he gasped, and darting back into his room, closed and bolted the door.

Luckily Mother had not wakened, and I dragged on some things and went downstairs without further interruption.

Perhaps one should have been born and have lived along the Crescent to realize what any break in our routine means to us, or the avid curiosity which hides behind our calm assumption that each house is its family castle. Perhaps, too, I should invent here some excuse for what I meant to do, which was nothing less than to get as near to the Daltons' as possible, and to see if the old deadlock actually had been broken; and if it had, why?

But there was more to it than that. I was remembering that neighborhood meeting downstairs only a few hours before, with Laura Dalton's loquacity and her husband's comparative silence. More than that, for I had happened to be looking at Mrs. Dalton when George Talbot said he had seen Bryan near the woodshed that morning, and I remembered that her eyes had narrowed and her lips tightened.

A dozen ideas were surging in my mind as I went down: reports that Mr. Dalton had been caught in the market and badly squeezed, stories that he had found consolation for the separation from his wife, pictures of him working over his car, his hands protected by old kid gloves and swearing sometimes at the top of his voice. A quick-tempered man he was, but I had thought him rather kindly. The feminine part of the Crescent had always blamed him rather less than his wife for their troubles.

92

And now something, something crucial, had driven him to speak to her, and to her to reply. What was it? Was she merely jealous, or was it in some way connected with the crime?

But I had no time for surmises. I had barely reached the kitchen door and let myself out onto the porch when I realized that the two of them, she in the lead and he following, had left the house and were coming quickly but quietly toward where I stood. They came through the darkness by the grapevine path, moving swiftly because of long familiarity, and so far as I know neither one spoke until they were immediately beneath me. Then he said, cautiously:

"It's sheer madness, Laura. With all these policemen about!"

"What do I care about the police? The more the better!"

"I suppose you know what you are doing?"

"Didn't you know what you were doing, all these months? And today?"

"For God's sake, Laura! What do you mean?"

But she did not reply to that, and the next moment they had passed by our porch, going as nearly as I could determine toward the Lancaster house itself, and leaving me there on the porch with the solid foundations of the Crescent fairly rocking under my feet. What had driven them into speech together I had no idea, but from the cold fury in her voice and the fear in his I knew that it was something terrific, something beyond any knowledge of mine.

I had never doubted that they were on the way to the Lancaster house, now only dimly lighted. To my amazement, however, the next thing I saw was that the flash was being used in the woodshed. Mrs. Dalton was apparently examining it from roof to floor, and by going down to the end of our garden I saw that this was so.

It gave me a strange and eerie feeling, for now again they were not talking. He was standing in the open doorway, and she seemed to be moving about rapidly. Luckily for them, for she seemed beyond caution, the doorway opened in our direction and there were no windows. Also the rain had apparently driven the outside searchers within doors somewhere.

It had stopped raining by that time, but the grass and shrubbery were dripping, and I began to feel cold and uneasy. In the Lancaster house Margaret's windows at the back, which had been dark, were suddenly lighted. Evidently she, too, could not sleep. And in the shed I heard Mr. Dalton's voice, now cold and angry.

"Well, what have you found?"

"I know what I'm after. That's something."

"I think you've gone crazy."

"Then what about you? Ask yourself that. And I'll find them, don't worry. You're clever, Bryan, but I'm clever too. Wherever you put them I'll find them."

That broke his icy calm, for he went in suddenly and caught her by the shoulder.

"No, you won't," he said. "I'll tell you that right now." Then he released her and his voice softened somewhat.

"You're a little thing to have so much hate in you," he said. "If you'd been any sort of wife to me, Laura—"

"And whose fault was that?"

Sheer recklessness had carried them safely through all this. I know now that there was a policeman on the Lancaster back porch at the time, but as I have said the woodshed is at some distance, and is screened by shrubbery as well. Not that Mrs. Dalton cared, at that. She was in one of those cold rages where she cared nothing for consequences. This was evident when she started back with the flash still going.

I had beat a hasty retreat, but I could hear him protesting.

"For God's sake, Laura! Do you want us both arrested?"

· "They couldn't hold me. Not for a minute."

But she put out the light, and as they passed our porch again they were only two shadowy figures once more, silent and unhappy. I had a feeling of tragedy about them that night, for their frustrated lives and their wasted years.

It was not until I was back in my room and in my bed that the full significance of that visit and that conversation began to dawn on me. Surely Laura Dalton could not suspect her husband of that ghastly murder. What possible motive could he have had? The money? But according to the Inspector, the money was still in the chest.

Chapter XI

Mother had one of her headaches the next morning, and I was awakened late with the word that George Talbot wanted to see me downstairs.

I dressed as quickly as possible, and George came into the dining room while I ate my breakfast; the Crescent frowns on meals in bed except in case of illness. I sent Annie out as soon as possible, although I had an uneasy feeling that she was not far from the pantry door.

George looked tired and anxious.

"See here, Lou," he said. "I suppose you know that Jim is in pretty bad with the police, although they've released him. And if you've seen the morning papers you know that they'll have to arrest somebody, sooner or later. The town's gone crazy. The middle of a bright afternoon, a house full of people, and a helpless old woman killed with an axe. It doesn't make sense, but there it is!"

"So they pick on Jim, of all people!" I said bitterly.

"Jim's all right so far. People don't go to the chair simply because they are remembered in wills. It's that infernal chest; they're opening it this morning. That's what the servants say. Lizzie was over there at the crack of dawn!"

Lizzie, as I may have said, is a sort of major domo at the

Talbots'. She had been there for thirty years, first as George's nurse and later on as an underpaid and overworked pensioner; a tall gaunt woman who, like Lydia, missed nothing of what happened to us. In fact, they were not unlike, and between them they formed a sort of machine, Lizzie collecting small items of interests and Miss Lydia disseminating them.

"You think it may be gone?" I asked weakly.

"I'm trying not to think that, Lou."

"But listen, George, I saw Jim when he left that house. He hadn't a thing in his hands."

He shook himself impatiently.

"That's not the point. If it's gone the police may wonder — well, if he ever put it in the chest at all. Don't look like that, Lou; we've got to face it. Why should Mr. Lancaster have sent for Jim yesterday, if he didn't think something was wrong? It wouldn't be so hard, under the circumstances. Just the two of them in that room and a little act of substitution. He carried it out in a bag, and if he had another bag ready, filled with silver dollars for instance —"

I was too horrified to speak, and George leaned over and touched my hand. I had known him all my life, and he had grown into a not unattractive man of the heavy-chested middle-height type, the sort that has to shave twice a day and still has a blue-black look about the jaw. But his eyes were still the eyes of the boy I used to play with, and now they were filled with pity.

"I'm sorry, Lou. I thought maybe we could work this out together, but I've only scared you to death. I know damned well he never killed her. But something queer has been going on around here for the last few weeks. And if you don't beleive it, look here."

He reached into his pockets and pulled out a shining new twenty-dollar gold piece.

"I picked this up back in No Man's Land, about ten days ago. I'd lost a ball, hooked it into the trees toward Euclid Street; and I turned over some grass and found this. Of course it may not mean anything, but there it is! Thank God I found it and not Dalton. It might as easily have been him."

And then and there I told him about what I had seen the night before. It seemed to stun him as much as it had stunned me, and he sat thinking for some time. Then he said abruptly:

"I wouldn't tell the police that Lou."

"Why not? I don't want to, but if they arrest Jim Wellington—"

"They won't arrest him. Not yet anyhow. No, it looks to me as though— You saw Dalton last night when I said I'd seen him at the woodshed that morning, didn't you? If you saw his face you know he was scared."

"He'd never have taken the axe, at that hour."

But he was not listening.

"Look here," he said, "do you know why the Daltons broke off diplomatic relations?"

"I don't know. I believe she was jealous, or something of the sort."

"Exactly. Well, Bryan Dalton has been a pretty gay lad in his time, and he's not so darned old now. What I'm wondering now is— What about this Peggy at the Lancasters'? She's pretty and she's nobody's fool. She'd know about the chest, of course. She could have kown also that Mr. Lancaster meant to make an inventory yesterday; the telephone's in the hall. And she'd have several chances every week to get an impression of that lock. You know, wiping the floor, or dusting under the bed. You see what I mean. She could have let him in the house yesterday, too. Opened one of the lower windows, for instance, and fastened it later. Of course it's horrible, but it's all horrible anyhow."

"And you think Mrs. Dalton suspects that, George?"

"How do I know? What was she looking for last night? What might be in the woodshed? The duplicate key maybe. Or perhaps we're just crazy, and the money's still there."

"And we fall back on a lunatic!" I said, trying to smile. "What is there to do, George? I'll go crazy sitting here."

"Well, the police are opening the chest this morning, according to Lizzie. Apparently they tried it last night with an ice pick and failed." Which shows I think not only the high efficiency of our grapevine telegraph, but the fact that all along we underrated the intelligence of our servants. "If the money's gone, I wish you'd take a look around No Man's Land. I have to work, or I'd do it." He picked up a pencil and began to draw a crude sketch on the table cloth. We still use table cloths; the Crescent regards doilies as an attempt to evade laundering the heavy damask cloths we affect.

"Here's the Crescent," he said. "And here's where I found the gold piece. If I were you I'd go in by way of Euclid Street, and examine that woodland. You see, the chances are that if the money is gone it's been buried; and if it's been buried it may be buried there."

He looked at his watch and got up.

"Better rub that out," he said as he rose. "God knows the servants have enough to talk about already. If you can get into the Lancasters' and learn what the police discover I wish you'd call me up."

I agreed, and I went with him to the door.

"I wonder if anyone has told Helen Wellington about Jim," I said. "If she knows he is in trouble —"

"She'll like it!"

"Still, there should be someone there. Even the servants have gone, George. He's all alone."

"If you're asking me, he's better alone than with Helen any time." He patted me on the arm. "He's able to take care of himself, Lou. He won't mind a little dust in the house and he can get food, of course. We'll begin to worry about him if that money's missing, not before."

"And if it is?"

"Then, as sure as God made little fishes, they'll arrest him."

When I went back to the dining room Annie was gazing with interest and disapproval at his drawing.

"It's a pity he couldn't use a piece of paper, Miss Louisa."

"I'll rub it out in the lavatory," I said hastily, "and you will

99

only have to press it."

She took away the dishes and I was gathering up the cloth when she came back and said: "Old Mr. Lancaster has taken to his bed, miss. He had only a cup of black coffee this morning. And Ellen is threatening to leave. She doesn't like the way the police went through her clothes yesterday."

I remember standing there, the table cloth in my arms, and feeling that she wanted me to ask her something, that her return had been solely for that purpose. But her face was carefully blank.

"Listen, Annie," I said at last, "if you know anything, anything whatever that the police ought to know, you should tell it."

I realized at once that I had made a mistake. At the word "police" she stiffened.

"I don't know anything, miss."

"Not the police, then. Is there anything you can tell me? Anything out of the ordinary? Someone has committed a terrible crime, Annie. Do you want them to get away with it?"

"Maybe there's plenty out of the ordinary been happening," she said darkly. "But it hasn't anything to do with that murder."

"How do you know that?"

"I know it all right."

"Annie," I said desperately. "You can tell me this at least. Has it anything to do with Peggy at the Lancasters'?"

But her astonishment was so evident that I hastened to add: "Or with any of the maids there?"

All of which was most unfortunate, for she froze immediately and departed for the pantry with her head in the air.

It was after nine when I went to the Lancasters' to ask Margaret what I was to do with the glove. Mother was asleep, and I slipped out without saying anything. I had not told George about the glove, but it was one of those cool mornings in August which with us sometimes turn into downright cold, and I could not run the risk of our furnace being lighted. That meant water in the radiator pans and discovery.

Cool as the wind was, however, the sun had come out and everything looked fresh and green after the night's rain. Even the Lancaster house, white and immaculate, looked cheerful, and the only strange note was the officer on guard in front of it, and a camera man on the Common, trying to find some spot where the trees did not hide it completely, for a picture.

I met Mrs. Talbot at the walk, and I was shocked to see that she looked almost ravaged. For all her eccentricity she was in the main a cheerful woman, but even her voice had lost its vigor.

"I'm taking over some beef tea," she said, "Mr. Lancaster is ill."

We went in together; or rather I went in. She merely gave the jar of beef tea to Jennie and went away. Jennie admitted me without speech, and I saw a group of men in the library, to the left of the front door, as I entered the hall.

"I want to see Miss Margaret."

"She's in the morning room, miss."

Margaret was there, fully and as usual carefully dressed, except that now she wore deep black. She did not hear me at first. She was sitting in front of her desk and staring at the wall above it, without moving. For the first time it occurred to me that morning that Margaret Lancaster was a handsome woman. I had known her so long that I dare say I had never considered her before. She had been like any familiar thing which, after years of familiarity, one does not see at all until some shock or change forces it on one's attention.

Looking back as now I can, I realize that to a woman like Margaret Lancaster, good-looking, intelligent and restless, those years in that house must have been nothing less than a long martyrdom. She had never given up, as had Emily. She still dressed beautifully, and had her hair marcelled. I can remember that there was an almost fresh wave in it that morning and that her hands, spread out before her on the desk, were well kept and carefully manicured.

But she was also thoroughly poised. When at last she realized that it was I who had entered the room she turned quietly and looked at me.

"Close the door, Louisa. I want to talk to you."

When I came back she indicated a chair close by her, and she lowered her voice.

"What did you do with it?"

I told her and she nodded.

"That ought to do, for a day or two. Later it will have to be burned, of course. I want you to burn it without opening the envelope, Louisa."

"It opened itself."

"Then you know what is in it?" She sat erect and stared at me, and two deep spots of color came into her cheeks.

I explained and she listened. But the explanation was plainly less important to her than the fact that I knew and had seen the glove. There was a long silence when I had finished. Then she made up her mind and turning to me put a hand on my knee.

"First of all," she said. "I wanted that glove out of the house because it was Jim Wellington's. I give you my word that that is true. And I give you my word that I found it here in the house, after he had gone. But I don't believe for a minute that he — that he killed Mother. But he left the pair here two or three months ago, in the spring, and I dropped them into a table drawer in the hall. I always meant to tell him they were here, but I forgot. And I'm pretty sure he had no idea himself where he lost them. I had to get rid of that one last night; that's all."

It was my turn to sit silent for a time.

"Then anybody in the house might have known it was there?" I said finally.

She made a gesture.

"Anybody. And I can't find the mate to it. I'm sure there were two."

I got up, with an uneasy feeling that she had not told me all she knew.

"Very well," I said. "I'll burn it. I'll have to do it at night in the furnace."

She nodded, and then leaned forward and put a hand on my arm. "I can only say this, Louisa," she said in a low voice. "I believe that glove was deliberately planted where I found it, and that it was the most cruel and diabolical thing I have ever known."

Chapter XII

Before I left I inquired about Emily, and she gave me a quick hard glance.

"She's all right," she said. "Doctor Armstrong gave her a hypodermic last night, but I don't think she slept much. It only dazed her."

Emily was not asleep. As I went out I heard her voice in the upper hall querulously demanding some paste, and Peggy replying that there was none in the house.

"I'll get you some, Miss Emily," I called. She did not hear me, however, and so I started up the stairs. The men were still in the library at that time, and I recognized the voice of Mr. Lewis, who has been the attorney for most of the Crescent ever since I can remember. As I mounted I could hear Emily's canary, singing gaily, and in the upper hall Peggy was using a carpet sweeper. It might have been any house in the Crescent on a sunny August morning, had it not been for a policeman in uniform, eyeing Peggy with admiration from his position outside Mrs. Lancaster's bedroom door.

"Where is Miss Emily, Peggy?" I asked.

She glanced at the other.

"She's in *there*, miss. There was a leak in the night, and

they let her go in."

I saw then that the door into the death chamber was open, and I went to it and glanced in.

The big bed had been stripped of its sheets and mattress, but apparently nothing else had been touched, except that the chest had been drawn out from under the bed and now rested on two chairs in the center of the room.

The leak was at once evident. The rain had seemingly come in from the third floor by the way of the roof, for the heavy paper was soaked and loose from ceiling to floor just beside the big bed. There was a pan on the floor to catch the water, and stretching over this Emily Lancaster was carefully patting the paper back into place. She had not heard me, for she did not turn until I spoke to the policeman.

"May I go in?"

"No, miss. Sorry, but it's orders."

Then Emily turned, and I was horrified by the change in her. Her face was simply raddled. Not only that; usually the perfection of neatness, she looked as though she had slept in her clothes. She still wore yesterday afternoon's white dress, but it was incredibly wrinkled. When she came toward me she moved with the tottering gait of a very old woman.

"I'm afraid the paper is spoiled," she said, as though that was the most vital matter in the world. "I've spoken to Father ever since Ellen reported the leak upstairs, and now it has come all the way through."

She held out her hand to me, seemed to forget why, and turned back to look again at the paper.

"Even when it dries it will leave a stain," she said. "It did it once before, but not so much. I fastened it back with thumb tacks, but now I'd like to glue it."

It was rather dreadful, that escape of hers from reality to anything so unimportant. And she would not stop. She sent me down to Margaret to see if she had any paste, and Margaret gave it to me grimly.

"Still at it, is she? She's been carrying on about it since seven this morning."

"I suppose it gives her something to do."

"There's plenty to do, if she'd pull herself together. Tell her not to use that paste while the paper's wet, and get her to bed if you can, Louisa."

I did not manage all that, but I did coax her to bathe and lie down. She kept up an incessant rattle of empty talk all the time I was with her, and what with that and the singing of the bird I felt as though I were on the edge of hysteria myself. It was fortunate for my nerves that Doctor Armstrong came in just then, and seemed to grasp the situation without words from me.

"Now see here, Emily," he said sternly. "You stop talking and take this medicine. I told you to take it last night. After that Louisa here will draw your shades and settle you. And get rid of that damned bird, Lou."

"I'm used to him," Emily protested.

"I could get used to a riveting machine," the doctor retorted, "but I don't intend to. Out he goes."

He handed the cage to me and I carried it into the back wing of the house and left it in one of the guest rooms. It seemed the obvious thing to do at the time, but I still have moments when I waken and think of the cheerful little creature, and that by not looking at its seed and water cup I signed its death warrant that day. Perhaps another death warrant too, but that does not bear thinking about.

When I came back the doctor met me in the hall and asked me to stay for a while.

"Margaret is arranging for the funeral," he said, "and all of them have got the inquest to go through tomorrow morning. If you'll be about in case the old gentleman needs anything it will help."

I was astonished, when I went back into Emily's room, to find that she was already asleep. Evidently Margaret had been right, and she had not slept much during the night.

That left the upper hall to the policeman and myself. Peggy having disappeared, he had taken a morning paper from his pocket, and sitting on the front window sill, was doing a crossword puzzle. I was about to get a chair from Margaret's room to place outside Mr. Lancaster's door when

I heard the men below leave the library and start up the stairs. The Inspector came first, followed by Sullivan, the detective; then Mr. Lewis, who nodded to me, and a strange dark man carrying a shabby valise.

They were very quiet. They filed along and into Mrs. Lancaster's room, and it was Inspector Briggs who spoke: "That's the box, Johnny."

When I tiptoed forward they were gathered about it, and no one noticed me at all. The dark man, Johnny, produced a bunch of keys, tried them in turn, selected one and filed at it, and then in a businesslike manner stepped back and said:

"That does it. All right, chief."

I could not see into the box, but I could see the Inspector's face, and I am certain he was disappointed.

"All here, apparently," he said. "Is there anybody about to show this to?"

"I represent the family," Mr. Lewis said rather pompously.

"Ever see this before? Know how much is in it?"

"No, but—"

"Get somebody, Sullivan."

I moved away from the door just in time, and a few minutes later the detective returned with Margaret. She gave a look into the chest, and her expression changed from one of apprehension to relief.

"It's there, then," she said. "Well, all I can say is, thank God."

The Inspector eyed her quickly.

"Why?"

"Because now we know," she said. "There was no motive. Someone got into the house, that's all."

But Sullivan had bent slightly and was prodding something with a finger.

"Any objection to opening one of these bags, chief?" he asked.

Margaret answered, instead.

"Not unless my father is present," she said, "and I don't want to disturb him just now."

I saw Sullivan and the Inspector exchange a glance, but

nothing more was said about opening anything. Instead the Inspector asked her about the method used when the money was put into the chest.

"It was very simple," she said. "We all disapproved, of course, but sometimes one or the other of us would be in the room. Jim Wellington got the gold for Mother, and currency when gold was scarce. She had accounts in different banks, and most of them would give only a little gold at a time. He brought it out in these bags, and Mother would count it out on the bed.

"After that she would put the gold back into the sack, and twist the wire around the neck of the sack. Or — when it was bank notes — into one of those brown envelopes. After that, whichever it was, Jim would put it into chest."

"How did he do that?"

"Well, at first he would put the box on two chairs, as it is now. But it got pretty hard. After that he simply dragged it out from under the bed. Mother would give him the key, and he would raise the lid and place the money inside."

"You don't know how much there is, I suppose?"

"Not exactly. Jim said once that five thousand dollars weighed over eighteen pounds, and that he didn't like carrying so much at once anyhow. Something might happen to it. Then the banks objected, too. He hated the whole business. He brought less at a time after that. He's the only one who would know exactly, if he kept a record; as I'm sure he did. I imagine she had between fifty and a hundred thousand dollars, but that is only a guess."

Sullivan had been doing some figuring on an old envelope. Now he picked up one of the handles of the chest and lifted it. Inspector Briggs watched him, but said nothing.

"Sure is heavy," was Sullivan's only comment.

"Just one thing more," Margaret said. "I'm sure Mr. Lewis will agree with me, and I know the family will. I'd be glad if that money went back to the banks, and now; today. Under police protection. It can all go to the First National and be counted there."

Then she went out, followed very shortly by Johnny with

108

his bag. The others remained for some time, having closed the door on me, and so again it was not until the afternoon papers came out that the Crescent as a whole learned that there was no gold to go back to any bank; that practically all the currency was gone, that most of the brown envelopes with their tapes contained merely scraps of the local newspapers, and that the canvas bags had been looted of their gold and carefully filled with lead weights.

Just such lead weights, indeed, as Miss Mamie uses to hold down the none too modern dresses she makes for most of us, and which all of us buy to weight the bottoms of flower vases, and plant crocks, so that they will not upset in a wind.

But I knew nothing of that that morning. I went back home convinced that everything was all right, and that there was no need of the search George Talbot had suggested in No Man's Land. Which was as well, for Mother with a sick headache is rather difficult and I spent the remainder of the morning putting iced cloths on her head—we do not approve of rubber ice caps—and in raising and lowering the window shades.

At two o'clock Doctor Armstrong, who is the Crescent doctor as Mr. Lewis is its attorney, came in and I sent him up to see her. Before he went he followed me into the library, and I saw that he looked anxious and as though he too had not slept much.

"It's a bad business, Lou," he said. "Any way you look at it. Matter of fact, this whole Crescent is bad business."

"I don't understand, I'm afraid."

"It's not hard to understand," he said testily. "It's neurotic; it's almost psychopathic. That's what the matter is. Outside of yourself and the Wellingtons—and even then Helen Wellington is not all she might be—there is hardly a normal individual in the lot of you. By circumstance or birth or exclusion of the world or God knows what, this Crescent has become a fine neuro-psychiatric institute!"

"We are a little cut off," I agreed.

"Cut off! Look at the Talbot woman, with her mania, no less, for locking doors! Look at Lydia, suppressed within an inch of her life! Look at Laura Dalton! Look at your own mother. Is it normal for a woman to wear deep mourning and shut out the world because of the death twenty years ago of a man — of her husband? Unless there's remorse in it? About fifty per cent of these crêpe-draped women are filled either with remorse or self-dramatization!"

Then he realized what he had said and apologized rather lamely.

"Your mother is different," he added. "With her it is escape. People and the world generally rather bore her, so she escapes. But take the Lancasters. Margaret has apparently managed, with the aid of an outside life, to keep fairly normal. Emily has been on the verge of a nervous breakdown for a year or two. Even Mr. Lancaster has felt the strain of the last two years. Now on top of all that this comes, and — well, I'm uneasy, Lou. Something or somebody over there is going to blow up. I've been in and out of this Crescent for ten years, and it's — well, I've said what it is!"

He was a youngish man, with a thin tired face and a habit of drumming nervously on his professional satchel while he talked.

"What do you mean by blow up, doctor?" I asked.

"How do I know? Yell, scream, go crazy, escape! Take your choice, Lou, but keep normal yourself."

He got up then, and prepared to see Mother. But he turned back at the door.

"You found Mr. Lancaster in the library, didn't you? Well, what was your idea of the old gentleman's reception of the news? How did he take it?"

"He was shocked, of course. He said very little, but he looked faint. He asked Emily if it was she who had found the body, and later on he asked if anyone had looked under the bed."

"Who was there when he asked that?"

"Both the sisters."

"Not too shocked, then, to think of the money! Well, what about the two women? How did they react?"

110

"Emily was hysterical. Margaret was calm. I think she was angry with Emily for acting as she did. That's really all I noticed."

"In other words, they each conformed to the pattern you'd have expected."

"I suppose so. I was pretty well excited myself."

When some time later I let him out he said rather whimsically that he had given Mother a sedative, and that so far he had doped practically the entire Crescent, beginning with Lydia Talbot; and that the only reason he had omitted Helen Wellington was because she was not there.

"Although I've got an idea that she ought to be," he said. "This is no time for the police to know that Jim's wife has deserted him. They may not understand that little habit of hers!"

Which explains in part what I did later that afternoon, with Mother safely asleep in her bed and the usual Friday turning out and cleaning being done in a sort of domestic whisper.

What I did was nothing less than to call on Helen Wellington, and to beg her to come home.

I had meant to go in, calm and collected, and merely tell her the situation, but circumstances changed all that. On my way downtown in a taxi I heard the newsboys calling an extra and bought one. That was how I learned that the money was gone, and I remember leaning back in that dirty cab, strewn with cigarette butts and ashes, and feeling suddenly faint again and as though I needed air.

I had pulled myself together somewhat when I reached Helen's hotel, but I must have looked rather queer when I went in. And I knew there was no use appealing to either her pity or her pride the moment I had entered that untidy little suite strewn with her belongings, and where she met me in a gaudy pair of backless and sleeveless pajamas, a cigarette in her hand and a cool smile on her face.

"Come in, Lou," she said. "Wasn't it just my luck to leave the Crescent when it was about to provide some real excitement? I wouldn't have missed it on a bet."

"Well," I said, "it isn't too late. Helen, Jim's there alone, and he certainly needs you."

"Did he send you?" she asked sharply.

"No. But the servants have gone, and the way things are —"

She laughed a little, not too pleasantly.

"Gone, have they? Well, they were a poor lot anyhow," she said. "Always wanting money, the wretches! So Jim's there alone, and you think I ought to go back to make his bed and cook for him!"

"I think he needs moral support, Helen."

"Ask Jim if he would expect moral support from me! I'd like to see his face."

"There's another reason, too," I said soberly. "It doesn't look well just now."

"Yes, the Crescent *would* think of that!"

"Not to the Crescent. To the police."

But she waved that off with a gesture.

"They've been here already. They know I don't believe Jim did it. He had too much common sense. It was his common sense that separated us, by the way; always asking me to be sensible and taking the fun out of life. But that's neither here nor there. I'm not going back just to save Jim's face, and that's flat."

"You mean never?"

"Well, never's a long time. Don't be too hopeful! But I'm very comfortable here."

"Listen, Helen," I said. "Probably Jim would want to kill me if he knew I'd been here, but I must tell you how things are. Then maybe you'll reconsider."

I did tell her, from the stains on his clothes to the money in the chest. It was not until I reached the money, however, that she really sat up and became intent.

"And to think he never told me! How much was there?"

"I don't know. Between fifty and a hundred thousand dollars, they say."

Her reaction to that was typical. She simply lay back on her hotel sofa and groaned.

112

"What I could do with all that money," she wailed. "I owe everybody, and I'm completely out of clothes. Now some fool has got it and buried it, and will turn it into government bonds and live on the interest! I simply can't bear it."

After that I went away. Thinking it over since, I believe she staged a good bit of that for my benefit, and that she deliberately overplayed her attitude of indifference. That had always been her reaction to the Crescent, and it still remains so; a carefully thought-out defiance.

I still remember her last words as she stood in that untidy room, with the scent she affected almost overwhelming and her eyes shrewd and keen.

"Sorry Lou," she said. "I'm not a very satisfactory person, am I? But your Crescent scares me to death. Too much steam in the boiler and no whistle to use it up."

Chapter XIII

I found Annie carrying a tea tray in to Mother, and a copy of the extra on Mother's bed. That newspaper alone, if nothing else, would have marked the change in our habits since the murder. But I was astonished to find Mother looking relieved and almost cheerful.

She looked up as I went in.

"Get that tray fixed and get out, Annie," she said, "and close that door behind you."

Annie went in a hurry, and Mother turned to me.

"I suppose you've seen this?"

"No. But I dare say I should have suspected it. I was there when they opened the chest."

"Oh, you were, were you? Really, Louisa, sometimes I wonder how I ever bore a child so—so undutiful. To think—!"

"You've been sick all day, mother. Anyhow, I wasn't certain. I was there when they opened the chest, but not the bags in it. I simply remember now that one of the detectives looked skeptical when he touched the bags. That's all."

She eyed me.

"I suppose you realize that this will probably be very damaging to Jim Wellington, to say the least."

"I don't see it," I said stubbornly. "Anyone who knows

114

him—"

"Stuff and nonsense. Do use your head, Louisa. Who else could have done it? It would have been easy for him. All he had to do was to show her one bag, and have another ready to put into the chest."

"You can't believe that, mother! You can't."

"Never mind what I believe," she said sharply. "What I want you to do is to get Hester Talbot here. I've got an apology to make to her."

That must have been at five, or perhaps later. At six o'clock Mrs. Talbot came, carrying her bag of keys as usual, and from then until almost seven she and Mother were shut away in Mother's room. When she came out I thought she had been crying, a fact so astonishing that I should have been less startled if I had seen a hippopotamus weep. But her voice was as loud and resonant as ever when she met me in the upper hall.

"Well, I understand they've taken Jim Wellington in again for interrogation. It's about time they took him and kept him!"

"If all the Crescent is determined to think him guilty it *is* time, Mrs. Talbot."

I let her out myself. It was dark and windy and growing much colder. But I was too utterly miserable to notice it then. I was thinking as hard and as fast as I have ever done in my life. If the police found that money buried in No Man's Land, I knew what it would mean, especially if it was buried among the trees where George had found the gold piece. That bit of wood was not far from the Wellington house, and began perhaps two hundred feet from the end of the tennis court.

I went back to the kitchen and told Mary I should want no dinner. Then I put on a heavy coat and started out. On the back path I met Holmes coming in, and it seemed to me that he stopped and looked after me; but I was beyond caring. Nevertheless, I did not strike for the wood land at once. Instead I took the grapevine path which connects the rear of each house with the other; and I remember wondering to see the Dalton place as quiet and orderly as ever, with Joseph in the dining room and a faint aroma of something spicy coming from an open kitchen window. It was hard to believe that I had actually seen what had occurred the night before.

It was beyond the Dalton garage that the Wellington house, as it came into view, surprised me by showing a light in the kitchen. My first feeling was one of relief, that Jim had been released once more and was at home again. That changed to surprise, however, as I kept on until I was close under the kitchen porch.

There was a man inside, a tall man in an apron, who was smoking a cigarette and eyeing rather dubiously a can of something or other which he held in his hand. He might easily have seen me, but he did not, and as I watched him I felt certain that I had seen him before. I had no time to think about that, however, for the next moment he commenced a curious performance which kept me rooted to the spot in amazement.

That is, he first did something or other to the gas range and then backing off from it, began to toss lighted matches at it from a distance. On what I think was the third try the effect was simply astounding. There was a roar of exploding gas, and the door to the stove oven came hurtling through the screen and landed on the rear porch, followed almost instantly by the strange man himself, who proceeded to fall over it.

There was a second or two of silence. Then the man sat up and commenced a soft and monotonous swearing which I interrupted.

"Are you hurt?" I asked.

"Hurt! I've damned near broken my leg."

He was getting up by that time, and now he looked out and saw me.

"Sorry, miss. I must have turned on the oven and forgotten about it. I'm not used to a gas range."

"So I imagine," I said drily. "Has Mr. Wellington come back?"

"No, miss."

"Then you'd better let me come in and show you about that stove."

He did not want me; I saw that. But he put as good a face on it as he could, and I went in and lighted the stove properly. He watched me carefully.

"It's really quite tame, isn't it, when you get the hang of it?" he said, and then added "miss" as an afterthought. I noticed then that he had lost his eyebrows and some of his front hair, but he was distinctly amiable in spite of it. "You see, miss, I'm not a cook; but I told Mr. Wellington I'd try to carry on until — well, until things got settled."

"If you carry on the way you've started, they'll never be settled. And you can tell him, when he comes back, that Miss Hall called. Louisa Hall."

He gave me a quick look, seemed to hesitate and then opened the screen door, or what was left of it, for me.

"Very well, miss," he said. "I'll tell him."

I started out from there for the wood land toward Euclid Street, but once I turned to look back, and he was at the window watching me. Take it all in all, I was puzzled and not too easy. Had the police taken over Jim's house in his absence, and was this man an officer of some sort, trying to get himself a bit of a meal? Or was he a friend of Jim's, there for some purpose I could not know? He was no servant. That was certain.

But I could not take a chance on him. I looked regretfully toward the wood land and then turned back home, to see when I turned the corner of the Dalton house something which set me running as fast as I ever ran in my life. That something was a thick column of smoke from one of the chimneys of our house, and I knew that Mother had ordered the furnace to be lighted.

That, with all the Crescent, meant that immediately the water pans on all the radiators would be filled.

I ran like a crazy woman. Luckily it was now dusk and the dinner hour, so that the kitchen windows which are like so many eyes peering out were untenanted. I shot into our own kitchen, collided with Annie in a passage carrying down

117

Mother's tea tray, and took the stairs two at a time. But I was too late. Mother in her dressing gown was standing by the radiator in the wing, and gazing down at that awful glove.

"Is that you, Louisa?" she called. "Come here a moment. What do you think this is?"

"It looks like an old glove," I said as calmly as I could.

"Then what is it doing there?"

"It doesn't matter, does it?" I picked it up and looked at it. "It has stove polish on it or something. I'll throw it away."

But Mother reached out and taking it from me, delicately held it to her nose and sniffed at it.

"It's boot polish," she said.

I knew at once that she was right. It was boot polish. That was the scent that had escaped me; a scent which took me back to my childhood days, with my father standing with one foot on an old-fashioned boot-box and fastidiously rubbing at his shoes.

"But who in the world polishes boots in this house?" Mother said. "Not Holmes. He never polishes anything unless he's forced to do so. I must ask Annie."

But the one thing I did not want was that Mother should ask Annie, or show her that glove. Luckily the collision and the resulting damage had delayed her somewhat, but I could now hear her slowly plodding up the stairs, ready to see the significance of that glove, or of the stains on it that Mother's older eyes had overlooked. Ready to run downstairs with it, examine it, talk it over.

I thought desperately of some way to divert Mother's attention. She was still holding the glove, and Annie was on her way down the hall with a pitcher with which to fill the pans.

"There's a new butler at Jim Wellington's, mother," I said breathlessly. "And he blew up the kitchen range."

"He *what?*" said Mother.

"Blew up the range. I was walking by, and the explosion blew him and the oven door out onto the back porch."

"And serves him right," said Mother, outraged at this crime against domestic order. "I never heard of such a thing. It was

118

a new range, too. They only bought it last year."

But this expedient had had the proper effect. Glove in hand and still indignant, Mother watched Annie fill the radiator pan and then sailed back to her room. Inside it she looked absently at the glove, seemed surprised to find she still held it, and finally dropped it into her wastebasket.

This did not mean necessarily that the glove was safe. Rather the contrary indeed, the Crescent expecting that its wastebaskets be emptied at night when the beds are turned down, just as it demands fresh towels in its bathrooms. And this waste goes into cans provided for the purpose at the extreme rear end of each property. Rain or shine, bright morning or late evening, our servants make these excursions. And I knew enough about police methods by that time to realize that examination of waste cans might well be a part of their routine.

Even if the glove escaped Annie's sharp eyes, there was the question whether I could safely make a night trip for its recovery. Lightning did not strike twice, and I could hardly hope to repeat the Dalton's foolhardy and reckless excursion. I managed to drop the advertising portion of the paper into Mother's basket so that it covered the glove, and when Annie came up to turn down the beds I waylaid her in the hall.

"Annie," I said, "I don't think I'd go out by the rear door at night for a while. We don't know what all this is about, but it might not be safe."

"I haven't any intention of doing that, Miss Louisa. Not with a murdering lunatic about."

"You might suggest to Holmes that he bring the waste cans onto the kitchen porch."

"They're there now, miss," she said primly. "Although what your mother will say I don't know."

"I'll take the responsibility for that, Annie."

She gave me a small and cynical smile. Both of us would get it, it implied, when the time came. But there was appreciation in it too. Annie and I understood each other.

"Very well, Miss Louisa," she said. "And it's Mary's evening out, and she says she's going out by the front door. I

119

suppose you haven't a key for it?"

"You know very well that I have no key for it, Annie."

She was standing beside me with the coffee tray in her hands, and I was surprised a look of sympathy on her face. She knew that I had no key, had never had a key of my own.

"I've told her I'd wait up, so she needn't ring the bell, miss. She'll be back at eleven."

I agreed, of course. It meant that I, too, must wait until eleven or later before I could retrieve the glove, but there was nothing else to do. And I have reported this conversation in detail because it led to what was to be the most exciting night of my life up to that time.

Chapter XIV

I got Mother to bed by ten o'clock, putting her book and her glasses on the table beside her, along with her folded clean handkerchief and her glass of water. Her prayer book, of course, always lay there. And as I did it I wondered about Miss Emily next door. What was she feeling that night, after all her years of service? Was she utterly lost? Or was there some sense of relief from the demands of that petulant and querulous old woman, with the stick by her bed with which to summon Emily remorselessly, day or night?

She had built herself no life at all, had Emily, save for her incessant reading, her trips to the library for books. Margaret was different. She had a life of her own, slightly mysterious but very real. She dressed carefully, went out — to concerts, to the theater now and then. It was even rumored that she had a small group where she played bridge for infinitesimal sums of money; something of which the Crescent disapproved on principle, although it bought lottery tickets at hospital fairs without compunction.

When at last I went back to my room I was still wondering. Not only about Emily and Margaret; about all our women. Save Helen Wellington, none of us lived interesting or even active lives. It was as though our very gates closed us away. The men went out, to business, to clubs, to golf. They came back to well-ordered houses and excellent dinners. Even old Mr. Lancaster had a club, although he rarely went there. But the women! I remembered a call I had made on Helen Wellington shortly after she married Jim.

"What do you do, all of you?" she asked. "You'll got twenty-four hours a day to fill in."

"We have our homes, of course. You'll find that we consider them very important."

"And that's living? To know how many napkins go into the wash every week?"

"We manage. It isn't very exciting, of course. It was harder when I first came back from boarding school, but I'm used to it now."

"Used to it! At twenty! That's ridiculous."

And because she too was young I had told her about having to let down my skirts before I came back for each vacation—that was when skirts were very short—and turning them up laboriously as soon as I reached the school again. She had thought it so funny that she had screamed with laughter. But I wondered that night if it was really funny at all.

"Twenty," she had said, "and they've got you. Well, they've never get me."

And perhaps it was as a result of those reflections that I took a book that night and went down to the library.

By years of custom, on nights when Mother has gone to bed early I have sat in my room with the door open, in case she might need something. Now I went down and turned on all the lamps. Not the few we ordinarily use, but all of them. And it was into this blaze of light that, at ten-thirty, Annie showed Inspector Briggs.

He came in, pinching his lip thoughtfully, and with a faintly deprecatory smile.

"Sorry to bother you again, Miss Hall."

"That's all right. I'm interested, naturally, if that word is strong enough. That's a good chair, Inspector."

He sat down, remarking that the night was cold and the room warm; and then said rather abruptly that he had dropped Jim Wellington at his house on his way in.

"I thought you'd like to know," he said, rather too casually.

"I can't see why you took him in the first place," I said.

"Well," he replied, smiling again, "the police aren't miracle workers. They are only a hard-working plodding lot at the best, and the fact that we've released Wellington doesn't mean so much at that. The plain fact is that we've got a fair case against him now, but nothing to take before a jury. There's a difference, Miss Hall!"

"And you've come here for help?"

He shook his head cheerfully.

"No," he said. "I hadn't meant to come here at all, but I saw the lights, and you're an intelligent young woman and as near to a witness as we've got. I'd like to know, of course, what you dropped on the pavement last night and went back for, but I suppose you won't tell me, eh?"

"My handkerchief."

"You would swear to that, on the witness stand. Under oath?"

I was silent, and he nodded.

"You see what we're up against," he said. "I'll not try to bully you. Whatever it was, you've probably destroyed it anyhow. But it's just possible that that sort of silence can send the wrong person to the chair. You might think it over. Our man thinks it was an envelope of some sort."

And when I still said nothing, he went on:

"We've followed up Daniels, the street cleaner you spoke of. Nothing doing there, no blood, no indications whatever, no police record. He's a quiet man, rather eccentric, living alone on a street behind the hospital. Has lived where he is for the last ten years with no interruptions. Got a bit of shrapnel in his leg in the war. Seems to have volunteered early in spite of his age, and not to have asked for any compensation since. Rather likeable chap, but reticent.

123

Better than his job, I imagine, although he doesn't say so. In these times a man takes what he can get."

"So, because you like him, you would rather suspect Jim Wellington! Is that it?"

He grinned.

"Well," he said, "you see this shrapnel lamed him. He might have climbed a pillar of that porch, but he'd need two arms and two legs. And I don't see him carrying the axe in his teeth."

I had to confess that I had not noticed that the man was lame.

"I suppose nobody ever really sees a street cleaner," I said. "You just take them for granted."

He nodded absently; he had already eliminated Daniels from his mind.

"These two women over there, the daughters. They are Mr. Lancaster's stepdaughters, I understand."

"Yes. I suppose they really should be called Talbot; but they were quite small when their mother married again. They have always used Mr. Lancaster's name. The Talbots didn't like it much at first, I've heard."

After that he asked me once more to go over what I had seen the afternoon before, both inside and outside the Lancaster house. He was particularly interested in my entrance when Margaret and I helped Emily inside.

"Mr. Lancaster was in the library?"

"Yes. Lying back in a leather chair with his eyes closed."

"Can you remember what he said?"

"Margaret asked him who had told him, and he said Eben. Then she asked him if he had been upstairs, and he said no. She went out to get him a glass of wine, and then he asked Emily if it was she who had found Mrs. Lancaster, and if she had heard anything."

"What did she say to that?"

"She said that she was dressing with her door closed, and that when she ran to tell Margaret, she was running a

124

shower. That about all, Inspector. It was not until after he got the wine that he asked about the money."

"Oh, he asked about the money?"

"Not in so many words. He asked if anybody had looked under the bed. Them Miss Emily remembered the gold, and she sat up and asked him if that was what he thought. He said: 'What else am I to think?'"

The Inspector considered this for some little time.

"Then, in your opinion, all these people acted as people would normally act, under the circumstances?"

"I don't know what is normal in such circumstances, but I should think so."

"Shocked, rather than grieved, eh?"

"Perhaps. I really don't know."

"You didn't think Miss Margaret rather cool?"

"She is always like that, Inspector."

"And you yourself, you have no suspicions whatever? Now listen, Miss Hall. A particularly brutal murder has been committed. This is no time for scruples. People are not sent to the chair on suspicion anyhow. It takes a water-tight case before any jury imposes a death sentence, and they don't do it easily even then. It's a pretty serious matter for any group of men to send another one to the chair."

I shivered, there in that warm room.

"I've thought of nothing else since it happened, Inspector. I am being as honest as I know how when I tell you that I simply cannot conceive of anyone I know killing that poor old woman."

"Not even for money?"

"Not even for money. And as to that, you know as well as I do that money went before the murder. Unless you are willing to believe that somebody had time to break into that house, kill Mrs. Lancaster, open the chest, put the bags on the roof, drop them to the ground and carry them to a car which nobody saw — even Eben or myself — all in about fifteen minutes."

125

He smiled again, and resumed his thoughtful pinching of his lip.

"And also carried into the house those bags of lead weights. Don't forget them! And, now we're on them, what about those weights, Miss Hall? They're used for other purposes, of course, but in the main I believe they're used in women's clothes. Now, you're a woman. Suppose you wanted a lot of them. How would you go about it?"

"I haven't an idea. Try a wholesale house, maybe."

He nodded.

"Or several wholesale houses," he added. He looked at his watch and got up. "Well, it's a queer case. Generally speaking, an axe is a man's weapon. Women run to pistols if they have them and are in a hurry; and to poison when they have time and opportunity. If anyone in that house had wanted to do away with the old lady, why not poison? Nobody would have been surprised at her death, I gather; or suspicious, either."

I remember all that, although I was listening with only half my mind. What he had said about scruples had aroused something in me. All the Crescent, I knew, regarded the police with distaste and resentment. It would tell as little as it could, and yet expect them to solve the crime. It was not fair. And people were not sent to the chair on suspicion.

I had to make my decision quickly, for the Inspector was ready to go. The gold piece, found not far from the rear of Jim's house, I decided to keep to myself. The glove also, although I was soon to realize that in that I had committed an error so grievous that even now I wake up at night to think about it. But the Daltons were different.

Then and there I told him about the night before.

He listened with fascinated interest, and I saw that he lifted his head suddenly when I repeated Mr. Dalton's speech on the path: "It's sheer madness, Laura. With all these policemen about." And her reply, that she did not care, and the more the better. He seemed irritated too that they had

126

reached the woodshed without the officer on guard at the back discovering them; although I pointed out that the Lancaster planting had been expressly devised to conceal the shed. But it was over the last words that he pondered for some time.

"Well, what have you found?"

"I know what I'm after. That's something."

And over Mr. Dalton's odd and angry explanation: "If you'd been any sort of wife to me." And her statement that the police couldn't hold *her*, not for a minute.

"Intimating of course that we could hold him," he said pinching his lip again. "Well, that's interesting to say the least. You're sure she said *them?*" 'I'll find them'?"

"Absolutely certain."

"And young Talbot suspects Peggy of knowing something! Well, she could have got an impression of the lock to the chest, that's sure. When was it that Talbot saw Mr. Dalton around the shed?"

"Early yesterday morning. The morning of the crime."

"And what was Talbot doing there himself?"

"He was looking for a lost golf ball. Both he and Mr. Dalton often practice short shots back there."

The Inspector got up and held out a large capable hand.

"Thank you," he said. "I know this hasn't been easy. But if Dalton is mixed up in this it's time we knew it. I'll keep you out of it, of course. They needn't know who overheard them. We've got to remember too that it may be only a jealous woman, hot on a trail of nothing more than a letter or two! I suppose you don't know why they live the way they do? Not speaking and all that?"

"There may have been somebody else. But that's years ago, of course."

"It takes a jealous woman to hold a grudge, Miss Hall. They seem to get some sort of a kick out of it. But one thing's sure: she wasn't jealous of old Mrs. Lancaster!"

He said only one more thing that night that I recall, and

127

that was partly to himself.

"What I don't understand," he said, "is about the key to that chest. The only object in doing away with it would seem to be to gain time; for an escape, maybe, or to get rid of the gold. But nobody connected with the case so far has apparently made a move to do either!"

From which I gathered that perhaps we were all being more closely watched than we suspected.

Chapter XV

The Inspector had given me plenty to think about after he had gone. Once more I went over in my mind the Lancaster household and what I knew of it: over Mr. Lancaster taking his daily walk, and Emily living her vicarious life out of a loan library, and Margaret holding desperately to her youth. Over Peggy too, cheerful and pretty, and maybe carried away by Mr. Dalton and the attentions of a gentleman. But it was only the same vicious circle. Who among them all would have done so terrible a thing, or could have done it? And how was it possible for any criminal literally smeared with blood to have escaped out of a locked and bolted house into a brilliant summer day, without being discovered at once?

Mary came in at half past eleven, an hour which would have shocked Mother, and I waited until both she and Annie had gone safely up to bed. Then I went out to the kitchen porch on my rather grisly errand.

I found myself oddly nervous and apprehensive. The excitement of the day before had vanished, and with it much of my courage. The fact that the night was bright, with a clear cold moon, only seemed to make matters worse. It exaggerated the shadows, and the wind turned every tree and bush into a moving thing, alive and menacing. There was not even the comfort of Holmes in his room over the garage, for he was once again sleeping in the house at Mother's order. Rather sulkily, I had thought.

I intended to burn the glove in the furnace, and even while I was fishing in the can for it the thought of the dark basement rather daunted me. And then, with the glove in my hand, I looked up and saw a man standing on the path just below! That settled it. Police or not, that glove had to go into the furnace before it was found; and in a perfect hysteria of terror and anxiety I shot into the house and down the cellar stairs.

I remember pausing only long enough to press the switch at the top of the basement steps which lights the cellar, and then of running on down. At the foot of the stairs, however, I stopped abruptly. I had not even closed the kitchen door, an act so foolhardy that my first impulse was to rush back again and do it. But there was the glove, damaging and maybe damning, and ahead of me the long passage forward to the furnace cellar, with the darkened doors which opened off it.

I had my choice and I took it. I went forward toward the furnace, and it was when I had almost reached the small room where we store our fire wood that I heard somebody coming down the cellar stairs.

I managed to turn and look behind me, but I could not have moved if the house had been on fire. And still those awful steps came on, heavy steps that were trying to be light. With their approach I made a final superhuman effort, rushed into the wood cellar, fell over a piece of wood that had slipped from the pile and simply lay there, half-conscious.

I was aroused by the light of an electric flash on my face, and a strange male voice that was not entirely strange, saying:

"Oh, I say! I *am* sorry!"

"Who is it?" I managed at last. I could see nothing; and the voice laughed a little.

"Well, I'm a friend," it said, "although I don't blame you for doubting it. Are you hurt?"

I sat up, and between me and the door I could make out the figure of a tall man, now bent forward.

"I'm mostly shocked and scared," I said. "If you'll get out into the light so I can see who you are—"

He did so at once, and I saw that it was the man who had blown up the Wellington range. But I saw something else; he had a flashlight in his left hand, but his right held a blue automatic. He realized that too at that moment, for he slipped it into his pocket.

"Sorry again!" he said lightly. "You see, I thought you were a burglar when I heard you on the porch. And these being unhealthy days around this neighborhood, I simply followed you in. Why in the world did you leave the door unlocked? You ought to know better."

"I forgot it," I said lamely.

"Now that's interesting." He looked at me cheerfully. "That's very interesting. With everyone around here locked in against a possible lunatic or against poor Jim, you forget to fasten the kitchen door!"

And then suddenly I remembered him.

"I know you now. You are a friend of his, aren't you? I saw you there one night, when Helen was giving a party."

"Great party giver, Helen," he commented briefly. "Well, every man to his taste; every woman too," he added. "And now, shall I go up and see what you put into that can? Or will you tell me?"

"You are not a policeman?"

"Are you insulting me, young woman?"

But his eyes were sober enough.

"Look here," he said, "can't we go into the laundry and sit on the tubs or something? You and I have some matters to discuss, and I've got a stiff leg from that fall." And when I hesitated: "Jim is counting on you, Miss Lou; on you and

131

me. He's in a pretty tight place."

Then and there I made up my mind, and I went back into the wood cellar and got the glove. I simply handed it to him.

"I didn't put anything into the trash can. I got this out of it," I said shakily, "and it can send Jim Wellington to the chair."

He took it and examined it. Then without another word he led the way back into the laundry, and while I sat on a box and he used the ironing table (all the Crescent irons its table linens on a table) I told him the whole story. When I had finished he did as Mother had done. He put the glove to his nose and sniffed.

"Boot polish, of course," he said. "And something else too," he added with delicacy. "Well, it's hard to believe, isn't it? Yet there it is."

"There what is?"

"Our case. I wonder —" he checked himself, and smiled at me. "You've given Jim a break tonight," he said. "The first he's had, and he certainly needed it. Now go over it again, and let me listen."

So I did, and he sat awkwardly on the laundry table and took it all in without a word. When I had finished he nodded, put the glove into his pocket and then slid to his feet.

"Good work, Miss Lou. It would be interesting to know just how Margaret Lancaster found it, and whether she's getting rid of it out of pure altruism or not. But that can wait. The main thing is that we've got it. We have a long way to go, little lady; it's going to be darned hard to prove Jim's innocence. But that's what I'm here for, and you too, I gather."

"I'd do anything I can," I said shakily, and suddenly burst into tears. He came over then and patted me on the shoulder, and I was conscious that there still hung about him a faint odor of scorched hair. In spite of myself that made me smile, and he touched his eyebrows ruefully.

"I admit I've lost something in looks," he said. "You may not believe it possible, but it's true. Just now I'm glad it's a cool night, for lacking my eyebrows I'm like a house that has lost its eaves!"

His nonsense gave me back my control, which is no doubt what he intended.

But he was noncommittal about himself and his presence there. It seemed that his home was somewhere else.

"I'm here because Jim is in trouble," he said lightly. "Frat brother, you know; the good old grip and the magic word. Which, by the way, in this case is silence."

That was my second encounter with Mr. Herbert Ranchester Dean, usually referred to by Helen as Bertie Dean; the criminologist who, working with our own police, finally solved our crimes. Not for some days was I to know his profession, nor for weeks of that laboratory of his which, when I finally saw it, looked not unlike the one where Mother goes annually for her various tests.

But of the man himself and his work he gave me the best description when, after almost two weeks of death and absolute horror, the answer was spread across the newspapers of every city in the country, and our reign of terror was over.

"I am not a lone wolf," he said. "I hunt with the pack. The actual fact is that I'd be helpless without the police, while they need me only now and then. They have the machinery, for one thing. What I have is a line of specialized knowledge, odds and ends. Actually, I look after the little things, while they do the big ones.

"They've got their machinery, men, radio, teletype, files—the whole business of law and order. I've got mine. Mostly it's a microscope! But in this case I played in luck. Ordinarily the gloves, for instance, would be their job; they'd find them and I'd tell them there was boot polish on them, if their noses didn't!

"To get back to the gloves. There had to be gloves. Two gloves. The police knew that well enough; it takes two

133

hands to use an axe. But you turned up both of them for me, one after the other, and the story of the crime was right there. All," he added, with his quizzical smile, "but the identity of the criminal."

But as I say, I knew nothing of all this that Friday night, the second after Mrs. Lancaster had been killed; nor of Herbert Dean's reputation among the police of various cities. I did not know of Jim's wire which had brought him in a plane some five hundred miles in less than as many minutes, although the police did! As a matter of fact, Mr. Dean's first visit on his arrival had been to the Commissioner. That had been on Friday afternoon, after he had heard Jim's story.

"What I would like to do," he said, "is to look over the lay of the land for a day or two, before even your own fellows know I'm on the case. If that's all right with you—"

"Anything's all right with me, Dean. We're in a hole over this case and it's falling in on us. It's sink or swim." And having thus neatly mixed his metaphors, he inquired as to how Herbert Dean proposed to go about it.

"I'm taking a job in the Wellington house. The story's somewhere along that Crescent, Blake. It has to be. And maybe the servants will talk."

Which last reveals an optimism not justified by the facts. Our servants may have talked among themselves, almost certainly they did. But never did they more than pass the time of day with Mr. Herbert Ranchester Dean, expert criminologist and for a few days what he called gentleman's gentleman and cook-butler to Jim Wellington.

But I knew nothing of this when, the glove carefully wrapped in a bit of old newspaper, Mr. Dean slipped out the kitchen door like a shadow, and I closed and locked it behind him. It was not until I got upstairs that I became uneasy. After all, I had only this man's word that he was working for Jim, and that vague recollection of having seen him there once on the porch at a party. It was well after twelve then, and from that time until almost two in the

134

morning I simply walked the floor, uncertain and wretched.

It was two by my clock when I finally undressed, put out my light and went to a window to raise the shade.

I was in that state of exhaustion which makes sleep a remote thing, and so I stood by the window for a moment or two. Beneath me lay the two gardens, the Lancasters' and our own; and that strip of lawn where Eben had been mowing the grass when Miss Emily had run shrieking out of the house. Between the two properties is a thin line of Lombardy poplars, slim and graceful, and suddenly a movement among them caught my attention.

There was a man standing there, close to the trunk of one of the trees and rather behind it. As I stared down he left his hiding place and sliding from tree to tree began to make his way silently and more rapidly than it sounds toward the rear and No Man's Land. When he had left the poplars he abandoned all caution and commenced to move rapidly toward the rear. Who he was, whether tall or short, heavy or lean, I could not tell.

I stood by the window, stunned with astonishment. Before me was the Lancaster house, shrouded in trees save for that side entrance and for the roof which rose above them. It was dark, except for the faint light in Mr. Lancaster's bathroom which he always kept on. Only when my eyes traveled to the roof did I see anything unusual, and then my previous astonishment turned to real alarm.

There was another man up there. A figure, anyhow. It was not erect. It was crawling on hands and knees, slowly and cautiously; and now and then it seemed to stop and to peer over the edge to where the mansard of the third floor ended in a gutter. There was something so deliberate and dreadful about the whole thing, outlined as it was against the moon, that at first I could scarcely move. Then at last I got myself under control and rushing down to the telephone, called the Lancaster house.

It was Emily who answered, her voice heavy and thick with sleep.

"What is it?" she said.

"It's Louisa Hall, Miss Emily."

"Good heavens, Louisa! Is anything wrong? I've had a sleeping powder, and I'd just got to sleep."

"Listen, Miss Emily. Please don't be frightened, and don't make a noise or anything. I think there's someone on your roof."

"On the roof?" she said dully. "Are you sure?"

"Yes. He must have used a ladder to get there. If you'll waken someone and take away the ladder you'll have him trapped, and I'll get the police."

She made no immediate reply. She seemed to be standing there, undecided and heavy with whatever narcotic had been given her. But at last she spoke again.

"I can't believe it; but I'll tell Margaret."

She did not even hang up the receiver, and I wondered what had happened. Then I heard the sound of her rather heavy footsteps in the hall, and knew that she was on her way to call Margaret.

When I went back to look at the roof the figure was gone. Perhaps through the open windows it had heard the shrill sound of the telephone bell. Indeed now I think there is no doubt of it. Anyhow that part of the roof which I could see was empty; and when I had reached the street and located the officer who was still on duty around the Lancaster house, we could find no sign of any ladder whatever.

The officer was skeptical.

"Maybe you dreamed it, miss."

"Dreamed it? I haven't even been to bed!"

He eyed me in the moonlight.

"Keep pretty late hours around here, don't you? For a quiet place."

"Perhaps you consider it quiet. Personally I don't."

Margaret joined us on the front porch then, and was as much at a loss as we were.

"It doesn't seem possible, Louisa," she said, with a wor-

136

ried frown. "I got Father's revolver, and Emily and I went up to the cedar room. The ladder is where it ought to be, and nothing has been disturbed."

I explained to the officer. Both the Lancaster house and ours have on the third floor a small cedar room, with a trap door in the ceiling; and each house keeps in the cedar room a portable ladder for the use of the men who periodically go over the roofs and paint the gutters. It was to this ladder that Margaret referred, and to this room that she took the policeman while I went back home. Only a few minutes later I saw the officer himself on the flat roof and staring about him, but apparently he discovered nothing suspicious, and soon he too disappeared.

That was, as I have said, on Friday night, or rather early Saturday morning. It was two-thirty when at last I crawled into bed, and fell into the sleep of utter exhaustion.

Chapter XVI

We do not oversleep in the Crescent, no matter what our nights have been, and as I think I have said, we breakfast downstairs. Mother was better that next morning, Saturday, and we were still at the table when Miss Margaret came over and through the French door into the dining room.

She was shrouded in black, even to her hat with its crêpe-edged veil, and although it was not yet nine we knew she was ready for the ordeal of the inquest. She had come to ask if Holmes could or would stay in the house while they were all gone.

"It will be safe enough," she said, "and I have never left the house empty. You see we all have to go, even the maids."

"Of course, Margaret," Mother agreed. "Although I'd as soon put a rabbit on guard. Still, if you want him — Certainly. Louisa can go with the Daltons although why she should want to go at all I cannot understand."

Emily, Margaret said, was still asleep and not well. She had been in a sort of daze for the last two days, and she would not rouse her until the last minute. Upon which Mother insisted on ordering some creamed chicken prepared and sent over later, and by going back to speak to Mary left us alone for a minute or two.

I can still see Margaret suddenly throwing back her veil

and bending toward me.

"Tell me something, Louisa," she said in a low voice. "Just what did you see on our roof last night?"

"I don't know," I said honestly. "It looked like a man, on his hands and knees."

"On his hands and knees!" she repeated, astonished. "Just crawling about, you mean?"

"He seemed to be that way so he could get to the edge; for safety. Or so I thought."

"And when he got to the edge?"

"I thought he looked over, into the gutter."

"You didn't dream all this?"

"I hadn't even been to bed, Miss Margaret," I said.

"At two in the morning?" Her keen eyes searched my face, and I felt myself coloring.

"I've been worried. Naturally."

That seemed to satisfy her, for she drew down her veil again and nodded.

"Jim, of course. Well, Louisa, I wish you'd keep it to yourself. The servants are ready to bolt at any minute anyhow. And you may be wrong. By the time I'd got Father's revolver, and Emily and I got to the cedar room, the trap was fastened and the ladder where it belongs. I've convinced Emily that you had a nightmare, so it would better rest at that. I wouldn't even talk to her about it. Or to anybody."

And of course I agreed.

Perhaps in writing all of this I have left out too much of the excitement our murder had caused; have said too little of the curious crowds which were held back at the gate by a uniformed policeman, but which had discovered Euclid Street and No Man's Land, and had periodically to be driven out of the latter; have ignored the press, bored and in the summer doldrums and so now in a state of hysterical excitement. And it is possible too that I have underestimated the local importance of the Crescent families.

Every city I dare say has its group of old families which in

139

their day have written the local history. In time they pass out of the social columns and into the obituary; indeed sometimes they have to die to be remembered. Nevertheless, the names still are important, and even their ordinary deaths are news.

Now in one of these families had occurred a savage and shocking murder, and since the crime both press and people had shown not only curiosity but a very real pride in us. We discovered to our own surprise that we were the last stand of fashionable exclusiveness, that we were among the few survivors of an earlier and more formal age, that even royalty was more accessible, and that our rare invitations were eagerly sought by all the *nouveaux riches* of the town!

And that propaganda had had its result by the time our various cars started out that Saturday morning. There was a large crowd outside our gates as I drove out with the Daltons, and downtown in the city proper police reserves had had to be called out to control the masses who had gathered to see the grieving family arrive for the inquest.

I had not been prepared for all this, and to add to my discomfort the ride was constrained and painful. Bryan Dalton had barely spoken, devoting all his attention to the car and now and then running a finger around his immaculate collar as though it choked him. And Mrs. Dalton, beside me in the rear seat and looking pale and drawn, had chattered all the way; not so much to me as at him.

"Of course, Louisa," she said. "You know and I know that no lunatic did this thing. It's my opinion it was thought out and worked out to the last second of time. And who could do that?"

"I haven't an idea," I replied dutifully.

"Well, think about it! It had to be someone who knew all about that house, didn't it?"

"You can't mean a member of the family!"

"I didn't say that," she said sharply. "There are other ways of finding out. And even with all this money gone she must

140

have left something. Those two women ought to be well fixed."

That was the only time Mr. Dalton spoke, and he spoke without turning his head.

"You might say to my wife that I regard this talk about money just now as execrably bad taste."

She laughed her small frozen laugh.

"I would be interested to know when Mr. Dalton ever before regarded any talk about money as in bad taste," she said.

All in all, I was glad when we had reached the building, passed through a barrage of camera men and the aisle made for us by the police, and into the building itself.

It was my first experience of an inquest, and I had never even seen a coroner before. This one turned out to be rather a hortatory person, who explained to us and to the six men of the jury that a coroner's inquest is a preliminary inquiry, that it corresponds in many ways to an examination before a magistrate, and that testimony is taken under oath.

"What we shall want here today," he said to the jury, "is a truthful statement from all witnesses so that you may render a verdict in accordance with the facts."

I suppose the jury had already seen the body, for one or two of them looked rather white. And the formality of identification took only a moment, Doctor Armstrong doing this for the family.

After that the medical examiner was called, to testify as to the nature of the injuries. These he said had consisted of five blows with an axe, any one of which must have rendered the victim unconscious immediately. Most of them had been delivered on the right side of the head, but there was one which had struck the neck, and severed both the carotid artery and the jugular vein.

He considered it unlikely that the dead woman had survived the first blow, or had suffered any pain whatever; this I suppose for the benefit of the family.

141

The jury was then shown a map of the Crescent, and a detailed plan of the Lancaster house. And following that came the first witness, Emily Lancaster, who had discovered the body.

I do not think Doctor Armstrong had wanted Miss Emily to go on the stand at all. She had insisted, however, and after giving her some aromatic ammonia in water he helped her to her place. There was a murmur of sympathy as she took the stand, and a breathless silence while in a low voice she gave her testimony.

As to the time, she was absolutely certain.

"I have lived by the clock for so many years," she explained. Otherwise her story was as before, save that she added something to what the police already knew. This was that while she was partially dressed she had again heard a sound from the direction of her mother's room, and that she had then opened the door into the hall, but heard nothing and went back to her dressing.

"What was the nature of the sound?"

"It was—I can hardly say. Maybe a door closing, or a chair being overturned."

"It did not occur to you to investigate further?"

"No. I listened and everything was quiet."

They let her go at that. She looked so ill that even the coroner seemed moved to pity. And after that the rest of us followed along with our stories, Margaret, Eben, myself—highly nervous, Mrs. Talbot, the house servants, and the police. Testimony was offered that the house was carefully locked that day, and was still found locked after the crime. Details of the search throughout the house for bloodstains of any sort brought the crowd to the edges of their chairs, only to sit back when it was learned that none whatever had been found. The events of that afternoon were carefully detailed for the jury, Lydia Talbot's brief call, her sister-in-law's longer one, her departure with Mr. Lancaster at three-thirty, and the careful locking of the front door behind them.

142

I looked around the room. In the rear and standing I could see Mr. Dean and in a corner, looking more interested than anxious, was Helen Wellington. Mrs. Dalton had hardly moved since the inquest began, while on the other side of me her husband was restless and clearly uneasy.

The crowd, avid for sensation, was growing restless when at last Peggy, the Lancasters' housemaid, was called, and the first stir came when she told her story of seeing Mr. Lancaster return some five minutes after he had left with Mrs. Talbot.

It stunned us all, including the old man himself. I saw him draw himself up, and then subside into a chair again. Yet when he was finally called he made rather a better explanation than we had expected.

"I had hoped to say nothing about this," he said, straightforwardly enough. "But since it is known—My wife and I had had an argument that morning. When I left the house I was still irritated, but on thinking it over I decided to go back and apologize. After all, she was a sick woman, and after so many years of marriage—"

His voice broke.

"Did you see her when you returned?" asked the coroner, smoothly.

"No. Everything was quiet, and I decided she was asleep. So I went out again. I was not in the house two minutes."

"Did you go up the stairs?"

"I did not."

"Can you tell us just what you did do?"

"Easily. I walked into the hall, decided my wife was asleep, decided as it was hot to leave my gloves on the hall table, and having done so went out again."

"That is all?"

"Absolutely all."

"Now, Mr. Lancaster, will you tell us what this controversy with your wife was about? I'm sorry, but it may have some bearing on this inquiry."

"It was a family matter."

"Can't you be more explicit than that?"

He hesitated.

"I can be entirely explicit," he said at last. "It concerned the amount of gold and currency she kept in the house. I considered it, among other things, highly dangerous. In these days of crime—"

"It was not until you had left the house that you thought of that?"

"I had thought of it all along. But as I left the house with Mrs. Talbot she spoke of it. She is here. You can ask her if you like."

"Had there been any other reason for this anxiety of yours? As I understand it, this hoarding had been going on for some months."

It seemed to me that he hesitated again.

"No particular reason, no. My daughter Emily had claimed once or twice to have heard someone on the roof at night."

"So, as I understand it, you decided to go back and urge that the money be placed in a safe place, and then changed your mind?"

"Precisely that, sir."

"Are you certain that the front door was locked behind you when you left?"

"Absolutely certain. In view of what was worrying me, I tried it after I had closed it. It was locked."

The remainder of his testimony referred largely to the events of the earlier part of the day, which I have already given. To my surprise and the disappointment of the crowd the matter of the chest and its contents was dropped for the time.

I know now that the police, working with the coroner, had determined to limit the inquiry as much as possible to the actual events of the day and particularly of the afternoon of the murder. Then too there may be rules as to evidence given before a coroner which eliminated the chest, save as it actually bore on the movements of certain people on that day. At the best I can only give my recollection of the questions and answers, but I think I have been fairly accurate.

And then at last Jim Wellington was called and sworn.

Chapter XVII

Jim seemed calm enough as a witness and he made — at least at first — a good impression. But there was no getting away from the fact that he had been in the house and in the room, and that he had tried to get away without this being known. Questioned on this, however, he was firm and unshaken in his statement.

Earlier in the day, he thought between eleven and twelve o'clock, he had received word from Margaret Lancaster that her father wanted to see him at four that afternoon. She gave as a reason his anxiety about the amount of gold and currency in the house, and he had agreed to go.

He had left his car at his own house and walked to the Lancasters'. As he had a key he opened the door and went in, but Mr. Lancaster was not in his library and so, having waited a few minutes, he finally decided to go up the stairs to his aunt's room.

That must have been, he said, at four o'clock or perhaps a couple of minutes earlier.

Mrs. Lancaster's door was slightly ajar, and everything was quiet save for Emily Lancaster talking to her bird across the hall. He pushed open the door to his aunt's room. The shades were drawn and at first he did not notice anything

146

wrong. Then he reached the bed and saw her.

He saw no axe or other weapon, nor did he look for one. His first thought was that the family must not see the body as it was, and he tried to draw the sheet over it. Unfortunately it lay partly on the sheet and he did not succeed. And then he added, he had grown suddenly wildly nauseated; the sight of blood had always done that to him, and of course he was horrified as well.

He had made for the downstairs lavatory in the side hall and been violently sick.

He was still there and still sick when Emily began to scream. Then his own position began to dawn on him. There was blood on him. He decided foolishly to try to slip out the side door and to get home. When he saw through the screen door that Emily was on the grass and that I was bending over her he knew it was no good; but by that time bedlam had broken out upstairs in the house, and he did not try to go back.

"I was a fool to do what I did," he added, "but I was still incapable of consecutive thought."

Some of all this had been question and answer, of course, but in the main he told his story directly and frankly. It was only over a question which followed that he seemed to hesitate.

"Did you hear any suspicious sounds before you went up the stairs?"

"Not sounds exactly. I thought someone was running upstairs."

"You heard someone running?"

"Not exactly. There's an old crystal chandelier in the hall, and it jingled as though someone were moving very fast. The prisms swing and strike each other. They did it then."

"That was before you went up?"

"It was while I was walking back to the stairs."

The coroner did not pursue the subject. He asked: "Were you familiar with the key to the chest?"

"Very."

"Where did the deceased keep it?"

"On a thin chain around her neck."

"Did you see this key when you went to the bed?"

And then Jim's nerves broke.

"Good God, no!" he said. "Do you suppose I was thinking about a key just then?"

Peggy was recalled after that, and her statement as to when she had seen Jim on the stair landing patiently gone into.

She had come out of a guest room in the wing and was on her way to the back stairs when she saw him. She had not seen anyone else, or heard anyone running.

"In other words," as the coroner said later on, "if Mr. Wellington is correct and someone was actually running just before he started up the stairs, then that person's escape was cut off from three directions; from the front stairs, from the rear hall and from the back stairs leading down to the kitchen porch where two women were at work."

It was then that one of the jurors spoke up, much, I fancy, to the annoyance of the police.

"The jury would like to inquire about the windows, Mr. Coroner. The newspapers have stated that one of the screens in the—in Mrs. Lancaster's bedroom was found partially raised, and a flower pot was overturned. If that is the case we would like to know it. If someone entered by the porch roof, or could have done so, we should know it."

And much to his irritation the Inspector was recalled and obliged to tell the facts. Even then there was no mention of the bloodstain on the screen or the grass on the roof, but he admitted that the screen had been found raised some four inches and the flower pot overturned. Immediately following this, however, Mrs. Talbot insisted on being recalled, and announced in her booming voice that the flower pot had been overturned when she left her sister-in-law at three-thirty that afternoon.

"Are you positive about that?"

"Certainly I'm positive," she boomed in her big voice. "I tried to raise the screen to set it up again. But I couldn't move it an inch. It was stuck tight."

It was bad luck for Jim, and I felt my hands and feet growing cold. Beside me Mr. Dalton muttered: "Damn the

148

woman! Why couldn't she keep her mouth shut?" And Mrs. Dalton heard him and gave him one of her sharp glances.

Nevertheless, the verdict when it came in was of murder by someone unknown. Whatever the police believed, clearly they had no case against Jim at that time, and I imagine the verdict gave them what they wanted, which was time. I know now of course that they had been tracing back his life for several months and had found nothing suspicious about it.

He was in debt, but not more so than any man with an extravagant wife and a limited income. He was well known to all the banks, and had so far as they could find no safe deposit boxes save his own. His dislike of Mrs. Lancaster's gold hoarding was a matter of record. He had not speculated or been caught in the market, and his presence in the Lancaster house that day at that hour was acknowledged by the family to be the result of a summons by telephone.

But the press was disappointed by the whole procedure. It commented rather sharply of the fact that little or no mention of the chest and its contents had been made, although there seemed no doubt that the gold — it preferred to ignore the fact that part of it was not gold at all but currency — had provided the motive for the murder.

"The police admit that this gold is missing," one paper said. "Then where is it? How much of it was there? Gold is bulky and heavy. Could the murderer have escaped with it, and if so, how?"

One enterprising journalist had figured that seventy-five thousand dollars in gold, an amount which he seemed to have guessed with uncanny accuracy, would weigh a total of two hundred and seventy-six pounds. But on that morning when the Crescent left the inquest and started home, all we knew was that Jim Wellington had won the first round in what might be a fight for his life, and that the Crescent itself had for a time at least been vindicated.

All of us saw Helen on the pavement outside. She was with another young woman, both very smartly dressed, and before they got into a car Helen had already lighted a cigarette. There was a man in the car, and he was grinning cheerfully. But I was fortunately the only one who heard what followed.

"Well," he said, "which of them did it?"

Helen smiled back at him.

"Can you see them and still believe that Queen Victoria is dead? No verdict. If you ask me, they're all capable of it. Given a reason, of course."

"Such as?"

"Protection, pride, dignity — how can I tell?"

"What gets me is how you yourself overlooked that money, Helen!"

"I didn't know it was there."

Then they drove away.

Chapter XVIII

Mrs. Lancaster was buried that same afternoon from a downtown mortuary chapel. Owing to the enormous curiosity aroused by the case, admission to the services was by card only, and for these Margaret had herself made out the list.

It was the brief but beautiful service of the Episcopal church, and we were back home again by four o'clock. The funeral had tired Mother, so she went to her room, and thus at last I found time to follow George Talbot's suggestion of a visit to the woodland where he had found the gold piece. For now at last I realized the vital importance of that money, gold or whatever it had been, from the chest.

I was too late, however. To my astonishment the woodland was already occupied by four strange men, and their procedure was so curious that I stood fascinated, watching them. They had eight wooden stakes, a spade, a hammer, several long pieces of twine and a can of water which I recognized as Miss Emily's watering can with the sprinkler removed; and what they were doing was to drive the four stakes to form a large square, outline it with cord and then divide it in the same manner into four smaller squares.

Each man then took one square and on his hands and knees examined it carefully. Every now and then one of them got up, took the can and poured water onto the ground, while the others watched intently. How long they had been doing this I did not know, nor did I know the purpose of the water until that night, when Herbert Dean enlightened me.

"Looking to see if the ground had been disturbed," he explained. "If it soaks in quickly and there are air-bubbles, then they can know that the earth has been dug up recently. And the woodland is obvious; it's sheltered, while the rest is open. But of course they'll not find the gold there."

"Why not?" I asked.

"Because, my dear young lady, the person who committed that murder and got away with that money is too smart to have buried it there."

That conversation took place in Jim Wellington's house late that night. Mother, as if to make up for her inaction the day before, had stayed down until eleven, insisting on game after game of cribbage until I had gone nearly wild. Whatever she had feared after the murder, whatever had made her bring Holmes into the house and speak so mysteriously to me, she had been much more calm since she discovered that the gold was gone. But my attempt to sound her out that night met with failure.

"Mother," I said, summoning all my courage when at last she prepared to go upstairs, "don't you think that now you can explain what you said to me on the night of the murder?"

"What in the world are you talking about, Louisa?"

I was chilled, but I had to go on.

"You know perfectly well, mother. I was not to go out of the house, day or night. You said there was a reason."

"Why should I explain that? It's self-evident. And you did go out. I happen to know that! You deliberately disobeyed me. If anyone had told me that a daughter of mine—"

"Listen, mother," I said earnestly. "It's frightfully important. It may be vital. What was it about spoiling two lives? That's certainly not self-evident."

She was putting away the cribbage set, and I thought she

stood for a minute with her back to me as though she were undecided, if one can imagine Mother being undecided about anything. Then very deliberately she put away the set and closed the drawer. When she turned to me her face was quite blank.

"I dare say I was merely sharing in the general hysteria," she said blandly. "I am not certain precisely what I said, but I was certainly anxious about those two poor women next door."

With that she admonished me as usual about locking the windows, and in her long heavy black swept out of the room and up the stairs. Mother must be well over sixty, for I was the child of her middle age, but she still sits erect in a chair and moves with the dignity which is a part of her tradition. I felt rather helpless as I watched her go, for I was as certain then as I am now that she could have helped if she had wanted to. I still marvel at her silence, at the pride or whatever it might have been that kept her suspicions to herself, or to herself and Mrs. Talbot. But here again I am up against the Crescent itself, its loathing of publicity, its distrust of the police, and its firm belief that every man's house is his castle.

That was of course on Saturday night, and I had no intention of doing anything but follow Mother up to bed.

But I did not get to bed until hours later.

Due to that false sense of security of Mother's, that the thing was over and done with, Holmes was no longer sleeping in the house; and as I went upstairs myself I stopped at the rear window which overlooks the garage and saw him in his room. Probably he had forgotten to draw the shade, or was indifferent, for he was still fully dressed. Mother had gone into her room. I stood by the window and gazed in surprise at what he was doing.

What he was doing, so far as I could see, was cutting the pages out of a book. He would take a knife, bend over a table, cut carefully and then take out the page and drop it, either onto the floor or into a basket. I could not see which. And he was working carefully and deliberately, so far as I could tell, doing only one page at a time. It seemed to be slow work, or perhaps he was clumsy; for he managed to take out only two or three while I watched, and the whole performance was so mysterious that when at last Mother called me I could scarcely tear myself away.

When finally I was free I was still curious. Holmes's window was dark by that time, but it occurred to me that in all this dreadful business perhaps I had considered Holmes far too little. Certainly he knew a great deal about us. If the Lancaster servants had known about the money, for instance, he could easily have known also. I remembered that time I had seen him with Peggy on the path.

Then too he could easily have known of the axe in the woodshed, and the habits of the Lancaster house. True, he had had an alibi for the hour of the murder; Mary had said he was having a cup of tea in the kitchen at the time. But our kitchen clock is notoriously unreliable; that is Mary has a habit of turning it ahead, so that the other servants will get down in good time to breakfast.

Therefore Holmes, having his tea before taking Mother out, might actually have had it some fifteen minutes or so before four. And Holmes, like Bryan Dalton, had an eye for a pretty girl. If the Lancasters' Peggy was involved, it seemed to me that she was far more likely to have been his tool in securing the gold than anyone else. The only stumbling block seemed to be that, having already secured the money, the murder in that case was utterly unreasonable. Unless of course he had needed more time in which to dispose of it, or unless Mrs. Lancaster herself had been suspicious.

But apparently she had not been suspicious at all. It was Mr. Lancaster who, for some reason still unknown, had insisted on the audit on that previous Thursday.

It was all too much for me, and so I determined to carry my new theory to Jim and the Dean person. I had to wait for Mother to settle down, of course, and she took a maddening time about it that night, making her usual Saturday preparation by putting her hair in kid rollers and laying out her church clothes for the morning. At last she slept, however, and once again for the third successive night I crept out of the house.

I had expected to have to rouse the Wellington house when I got there, and even to defy any officer detailed to watch the place. But neither was necessary; there was a light in the library windows, and my tap on one brought Jim himself to it.

"It's Lou, Jim," I said. "Can you let me in?"

"Go to the kitchen porch. I'll open the door there."

There was something conspiratorial in our movements; in the silence with which the door opened and I slid in. But there was nothing conspiratorial in the library, now miraculously restored to order, where Mr. Herbert Ranchester Dean was hastily putting on a coat and lamps were cheerfully burning.

"Well!" he said, "it's the young lady of the cellar! Are you like your fellow creatures who live in the basement, and only emerge at night?"

"I was at the inquest today."

"Were you indeed? And what did you think of our little performance?"

"I'm more interesting in one I saw an hour ago," I told him, and took the chair he offered me.

Suddenly his light manner left him and I saw him as he was, shrewd, keen and observant. But he finished lightning his pipe before he asked me about it.

"What was that?"

"It's about our chauffeur, Holmes, Mr. Dean," I said. "Why do you suppose he would be cutting the leaves out of a book tonight and then throwing them away? What is he trying to get rid of?"

He sat up suddenly and put down his pipe.

"He was doing that?"

"I watched him in his room, about an hour ago."

"What sort of book? Could you tell? Was it large or small? And what did he do with the pages?"

"He threw them down, either onto the floor or into his

155

wastebasket. I know there is one there. And it seemed an ordinary sized book. It might be a detective story. He reads a lot of them."

"Has he an open fire in his room?"

"No. It is heated by a radiator, from the house."

I thought even Jim was puzzled by his intensity and the speed of his questions. He got up, as though he were about to start out after Holmes at once. Then he reconsidered and sat down again.

"That will keep," he said. "Either he's burned them already, or he'll dispose of them early tomorrow morning. If they're gone they're gone. If not—"

He did not finish this, but sat drawing at his pipe and thinking.

"Just what do you know about this man?" he asked at last.

"Well, very little really. What does one know of people like that. I believe he bootlegs for George Talbot and Bryan Dalton now and then, although Mother doesn't suspect it. And he speaks sometimes of a place in the country; just a small place, but I imagine he either stores liquor there or makes it."

"You don't know where it is?"

"No."

He seemed to consider that too, but the next moment he startled me.

"By the way," he said suddenly. "Did you by any chance ring up the Lancasters last night, about two hours after I left you?"

"Yes, I did. Good heavens, don't tell me you were the man on the roof!"

He smiled and shook his head.

"No, but I was the man on the ground if you happened to see me. You scared him away, you know. That telephone bell did it. What did Margaret Lancaster say when she came down to the front porch?"

I told him; that the cedar room trap was closed and the ladder in its place, and he nodded thoughtfully.

"I see," he said. "Of course it took some time to get there.

Emily isn't a fast mover. Well, it's all rather curious."

He lapsed into silence, and Jim spoke for the first time. He had remained standing since I entered, leaning against the mantelpiece with his hands thrust deep in his pockets, and I thought he looked tired and harassed.

"Thanks a lot about the glove, Lou," he said rather awkwardly. "It's mine, of course, or was, although I don't know how it got into that house, or when I saw it last. I don't wear gloves in the summer, scarcely ever carry them. I'd put the date at somewhere last spring; early in June, maybe."

"You didn't leave it at the Lancasters'?"

"I might at that. I simply don't know."

Mr. Dean looked up.

"You know this Crescent pretty well, Miss Lou. Who would you say uses boot polish around here? I suppose the butler, Joseph, at the Daltons'? And old Mr. Lancaster does his own, I imagine. Who else?"

"I don't know. Possibly Holmes, although Mother says he hates to polish anything."

He thought that over before he spoke again. "Well," he said, "of course we need the other glove, but I'd say the chances are two to one against our finding it. You see, Miss Lou, a man may and usually does polish his boots with one hand; but he uses two hands on an axe. He's got to. And that's why we want the second glove."

It was after that that he asked me about the Crescent itself.

"Funny place, this Crescent," he said. "What about the Talbot woman, for instance? And why does she lock herself away? What was Mrs. Dalton hunting for, the night of the murder? And why does he look like a whipped dog? Then whose prints are those on the chest? I've got an idea I know, but it's probably too late to prove it. Certainly they don't check with those of the Lancaster family or the servants.

"Then again, does anyone in the Crescent suspect anyone else? You might know that. They're a secretive lot, but they know each other well and some of them are interrelated.

157

Take Jim here, and I believe the Talbots are connected, aren't they?"

"Mrs. Lancaster's first husband was a brother of Miss Lydia's, and of Mrs. Talbot's husband. I think—" I added hesitantly—"I think Miss Lydia suspects that either Miss Emily or Miss Margaret did it."

"Did she say so?"

"Not exactly. She said she supposed they'd stood it as long as they could."

"Now that's interesting! Stood what? The old lady was hard to get along with, I gather."

"Probably, but I don't think Lydia meant it really. She was dreadfully upset."

"Well, nerves with women are often like wine with men; they bring out indiscreet facts. However—! I suppose there's a Mr. Talbot?"

And Jim gave me a real surprise when he said that there was.

"Although he may be dead now. He ran off when George was a baby, and has never been heard from since. It was pretty well hushed up at the time, and of course I don't remember it; but there was a miserable story connected with it. That was years ago."

It was so utterly incredible to me that I laughed. To learn all at once that that crayon portrait had had more than a head and shoulders; had had legs to run away with and emotions to feel and resentments to drive it off! But nobody noticed me.

"Is that why she locks up everything and everybody?"

"By George, it never occurred to me!" Jim said slowly. "It may be. Still, it's absurd on the face of it. It must be twenty-five years ago. Maybe thirty."

But Mr. Dean was apparently tired of ancient history. He asked me if Holmes was a hard sleeper and an early riser, to which I replied yes and no; and a little later on he explained to me, as I have said, the intensive method of search I had witnessed that afternoon.

"But they'll not find it there," he said. And added: "Whoever got away with that money was too intelligent for that."

I left him standing by the fire, and Jim took me back to the kitchen door again. He was silent until we reached it, then with his hand on the doorknob he said:

"What on earth made you go to see Helen, Lou?"

"I suppose — I didn't know about Mr. Dean, and I thought you needed looking after," I told him.

"Well, she's coming back. Not because it's her duty, she says, but because she doesn't want to miss anything!"

And with the memory of the utter bitterness of his voice in my ears I got myself home somehow and into bed. As I went back I could see that across toward Euclid Street the men were still at work with lanterns and electric lamps. They had moved considerably since the afternoon, and there was something sinister and ominous about that painstaking inch-by-inch search, and about the shadowy figures as they crept along close to the ground.

Chapter XIX

The second glove turned up the next day, but by the time it did we were too busy wondering about Miss Emily's adventure of the night before even to think about it.

For it was that night, a Saturday, or rather at two o'clock on Sunday morning, that Miss Emily Lancaster ran out of her home and sought sanctuary in the Talbot house. Ran just as she was, in a dressing gown over her long-sleeved nightdress and in a pair of bedroom slippers, and stood hammering on their front door until George Talbot opened it for her.

Just what had happened I do not know. Even now the Crescent can only largely surmise. I know that when I went back to our house at one o'clock I noticed that the Lancaster house, or such part of it as I could see, was still lighted; and that this surprised me. I know too that by the time I was ready for bed it was dark again. But I heard no noise, and I dare say I should never have known about that flight of Miss Emily's at all, had not George Talbot come the next morning to tell me.

It was a Sunday morning, and breakfast is later that day. But I was down early, anxious to see if anything had happened about Holmes and his book. Nothing had apparently, for he was sitting, small and semi-grimy and entirely cheerful, over a substantial breakfast in the servants' dining room.

He rose when I went to the door and grinned sheepishly; and I saw then that he had been reading Mother's newspaper, which is supposed to be untouched until it is placed beside the coffee tray for her.

"Just taking a look at the inquest, miss," he said. "Looks as though the press had it in for the police, as well as for Mr. Wellington."

"They have to have somebody, Holmes."

He gave me one of his furtive looks.

"Maybe. Maybe not, miss. I was wondering if I could have the afternoon off. I'd like to go out to my little place, if it's convenient."

"I think it will be all right. Just where is this little place of yours, Holmes?"

But he was noncommittal. "Out the North Road a ways," he said, and thanked me.

I did not pursue the matter, a fact which I have since regretted; but just then I saw George Talbot, aimlessly knocking a golf ball about and keeping an eye on the rear of our house, and I wandered out to the back garden, where he joined me.

"I want to talk to you," he said in a low voice. "How about the garage? Where's Holmes?"

"Eating his breakfast."

We sauntered as casually as possible toward the garage, George swishing his club about as though looking for a lost ball. Probably all this was unnecessary, for I knew the servants would have joined Holmes at the table, and except for the Daltons no one else could see us. Once inside, however, George's manner changed.

"Listen here, Lou," he said. "There was hell to pay last night. See what you make of this."

Then he told me. He had been out to dinner and bridge, and got home at one. His mother had been hard to rouse, but at last his Aunt Lydia had heard him, and securing the

161

front door key from Mrs. Talbot, had let him in. He was in a bad humor, apparently.

"It's such senseless absurdity," he said. "And she's getting worse, Lou. She's had bolts added to some of the window locks since the murder, and getting into her room is like getting into the Bastille. That with a woman who is normal in every other way! I've tried to get her to a good psychiatrist, but you'd think I'd suggested giving her poison."

The story, however, had little or nothing to do with Mrs. Talbot's aberration or whatever it was, except that Miss Emily was apparently escaping from something, and had chosen the safest place she could think of.

George had been too irritated to go at once to sleep. He had tried reading instead, and at two o'clock he heard someone ringing the bell and then pounding on the front door. He heard Lydia moving in her room, and he met her in the upper hall. She still had the front door key, and he snatched it from her and ran down the stairs.

Emily Lancaster almost fell into the hall when he opened the door. She was as white as paper and looked wild and terrified.

"Hide me, George," she gasped. "Hide me somewhere. They're after me."

He fastened the door behind her, and she seemed to come to herself again, enough at least to draw her dressing gown around her. Lydia had come down by that time, and Emily had collapsed into a hall chair and was staring ahead of her with a strange look in her eyes. As George said, there was no sentiment about his Aunt Lydia, so she went to her and shook her by the shoulder.

"Don't be an idiot, Emily," she snapped. "You've had a nightmare; that's all. Who on earth could be after you?"

George had brought her some brandy by that time, and she gulped it down. She looked better, but it had the effect of making her sorry for herself, and for the next few minutes she cried and told of her long years of service and no life of her own. But they could not get her to say what

162

she was afraid of, or to tell who she thought was after her.

In a half hour or so she was better, however, and her story was an odd one.

Her room is on the front of the house, as I have shown, and across the hall from her mother's. She had gone to bed early, after taking another sleeping powder. Her stepfather and Margaret were shut in the library talking, she thought, about her mother's estate. And she went to sleep almost as soon as she went to bed. She had locked her door, of course. They all did, since what she referred to as their trouble.

She did now know how long she had been asleep when something roused her. It was a movement or a sound on the porch roof, and she sat up in bed and saw a figure outside. It was quite clear in the moonlight, but not clear enough for identification, and it seemed to be crouching and trying to raise her window screen.

She herself was too frightened even to scream. She slid out of her bed and caught up her dressing gown and slippers. Then she unlocked her door quietly and escaped into the upper hall. She tried her sister's and father's doors, but they were both locked; and then she thought she heard the screen being raised, and she simply ran down and out of the house; much as she had run the day of her mother's death. Only this time she had used the kitchen door.

That was her story, and although by the time he got it more than a half hour passed, George got his automatic and went at once to the Lancaster house. He examined it carefully from the outside, finding no one, and had finally rung the doorbell. After some time Margaret admitted him, opening the door on the chain first, and only taking off the chain when she had turned on the porch light and identified him.

She had been fairly stunned by his story.

"Emily!" she said. "Do you mean she is at your house now?"

"She is. Aunt Lydia is putting her to bed."

"But I don't understand. Why didn't she rouse us? Father sleeps heavily, but I am easy to waken. Of all the ridiculous things to do!" She was puzzled and indignant, but George was not interested in how she felt.

"I'd better take a look at that screen," he said. "She may have dreamed it, but again she may not. I imagine," he added drily, "that it would be a pretty real dream to send her out of doors in her dressing gown and slippers at this hour of the night."

They went up the stairs quietly, so as not to arouse the household, and into Emily's room. The coverings on the bed had been thrown back, and on a chair neatly folded were her undergarments. Everything was neat and in order; her tidy bureau was undisturbed, her bookcase, her desk.

Only the hook where her bird cage usually hung beside a window was empty, and it was at this screen that Emily had seen the figure.

From the inside the screen had apparently not been disturbed, and Margaret was willing to let it go at that. George, however, was wide awake by that time and pretty thoroughly interested. He raised the screen and got out onto the porch roof, and there lighted a match or two to examine it.

"And if someone hadn't tried to lift it from the outside, I'll eat it," he said. "He'd put a chisel or something of the sort underneath to raise it; enough to get a fingerhold, I suppose. Then, he heard her either in the room or running out of the house, for her lowered it again and got away. Slid down a porch pillar and beat it. It was no dream of Miss Emily's, Lou. Somebody was there, and that with one policeman at the gate and another patrolling the Crescent. It doesn't make sense!"

"But why?" I asked. "Who would want to get at poor old Emily Lancaster? Who wants to wipe out the family, George? For that's what it looks like."

He sat on the step of the car, making idle circles with his mashie on the cement floor, and I noticed that his face had darkened.

"I had no idea once that maybe I knew," he said, "but this kills it."

164

"What sort of idea?"

"Oh, nothing much. If it had been our house I'd say that the thing one's afraid of is the thing that happens — whatever that may be. Meaning Mother!" He spoke lightly. "But this washes that out, of course."

He got up.

"I just thought I'd tell you. Otherwise we're to keep quiet about it, and I've advised Emily to have some bars up on the windows tomorrow. Now, if we had an alibi for old Jim for last night we'd be all right. As it is —"

"George! You don't think it was Jim?"

"No, but who cares what I think? There was somebody there, that's sure. You can see the marks he made climbing one of the porch pillars. He broke a part of the lattice too. Well, I've got to go. I've promised Margaret to bury Emily's bird."

"The bird?" I said. "It's not — dead?"

"Pretty thoroughly dead. No water. Everybody forgot it, and water evaporates pretty fast this kind of weather. Margaret asked me to take it, cage and all, for fear Emily finds it. If anyone wants it later and I'm not around, it will be behind the old barrel in the corner of our stable. No need to leave it where the poor old girl might see it and have a fit."

He went along then cheerfully enough, but leaving me filled with dismay and remorse. Long after he had disappeared I remained in the garage, grieving over a little yellow bird which had had to die of hunger and thirst. Indeed I was still there when Holmes came out, after his breakfast.

He did not see me at first. He came into the garage whistling and moved directly to a corner, where with his foot he stirred up and scattered a small heap of fine black ashes on the cement floor. It was only when that was done that he managed a grin.

"Burned some letters last night," he said. "Never keep anything around that will get you into trouble. That's my motto, miss. And your mother is down for breakfast."

165

I went out, my mind confused in many ways but entirely clear on one point. Mr. Dean would never find the pages Holmes had cut out of his book.

I was depressed when I left the garage. It seemed to me that we would never solve our problem, that clues came and went and still led nowhere. And yet it was that very morning that I found the second glove; found it indeed in a spot which had been examined over and over the afternoon and evening after the crime.

This was under the dining room window at the back of the Lancaster houser, and almost directly beneath Margaret Lancaster's bedroom.

Chapter XX

Outwardly that Sunday morning on the Crescent differed little from any of the innumerable ones which I can remember. Our servants divided as usual, one out and one in; where there were three one took the day off, one went presumably to eleven o'clock service and one remained at home to prepare the heavy midday dinner which after the week's light luncheons sent most of us into a coma during the afternoon.

And the Crescent allows no decent interval for grief. One submits to what Mother calls the Eternal Will, puts on one's heaviest black, and shows to the world an unbroken front of submission to God.

At a quarter to eleven then the road was lined with cars, the Daltons' sedan, our own limousine, the Lancasters' hired car and George Talbot's aged roadster with Lydia in the rumble seat, where she got all the dust and wind. But Emily Lancaster did not appear. She had been brought home and put to bed, and our Mary reported that she had looked like a ghost.

I was an interested onlooker at all this, have begged off with a cold which was real enough at that. I stood on the porch and waved Mother off, and I remember watching the other cars go by, each laden with black-draped figures; and wondering if there was not someone in that funereal group who would kneel that morning under the stained glass windows of St. Mark's and beg an unseen God for forgiveness and mercy.

It was a bright morning. The cold spell had gone, but there was a hint of autumn in the garden. Back in No Man's Land a small child, as if aware that the overlords had departed, was trundling a red wagon, and across the intervening strip I could see that Mrs. Lancaster's windows had been raised, as though by airing the room they could somehow remove the last trace of the little old woman who had died in it.

Except for those opened windows and what they suggested, the Crescent had resumed its normal appearance. The curious crowd had gone from the gate; hereafter it would follow our story in the newspapers and not on its feet. Reporters no longer lay in wait to trap us as we entered or left our houses. Even the guards were gone, and either the police were taking a Sunday holiday or the search in No Man's Land had been abandoned.

But if the front of the Crescent was quiet, the rear was not. The moment the cars had all departed it bloomed into life and activity. The maids sang or laughed, and after a time there was a gradual emergence from the houses, and a conversation apparently on the kitchen porch of the Dalton house, where I gathered that tea, and probably cake, was being served. Ellen from the Lancasters' was the first to go, followed by our Mary, Annie being out that day. And before long the austere black-robed figure of Lizzie from the Talbots' came into view along the path, and she too joined the party.

The thing interested me. It was the first time I had seen our grapevine telegraph in full operation, and I watched it from the rear window of the upper hall. What did they talk about together, these servants of ours, so many of whom

168

had lived with us for many years? What did they think? What did they know? For I was certain that they knew something, perhaps many things.

What, for instance, did Mrs. Talbot's Lizzie know about that strange locking up? Or the Daltons' Joseph of that search a few nights before? Or about the quarrel which long ago had separated master and mistress?

All this was running through my mind when I saw Mr. Dean emerge from across No Man's Land, casually following the path and looking in his dark clothes very much indeed like a gentleman's gentleman returning from a Sunday ramble. I saw him glance toward the Dalton porch and then look away; and I saw him finally reach our garage, well shielded from that porch, try the door to the staircase which leads to Holmes's living quarters, find it locked, and then—sheltered from any but my observation by the shrubbery—take a key book from his pocket and carefully experiment with the lock. It was less than a minute until the door opened and he disappeared inside.

St. Mark's is well downtown, and I was confident that he had an hour at the least before Holmes would return. Nevertheless, I was relieved when in some ten minutes Mr. Dean reappeared, cautiously closed the door, which has a snap lock, and then entered the garage below. But all this was more than any anxiety could bear, so I snatched up my garden scissors and a basket and was in time to come almost face to face with him as he emerged. He touched his cap and greeted me cheerfully.

"What! Not at church?"

"I had a headache. Or a cold. I forget which."

He laughed at that, and glanced quickly toward the Dalton house.

"Better cut some flowers," he said, "and I'll stand at a respectful distance. I don't think they can see us, but they might. Your man Holmes is a pretty clever rascal, Miss Lou."

"Then it was a crime book?"

"It was; it had to be. He has no other sort! By the way, you haven't missed any glue from the house lately, have you?"

I almost dropped the scissors.

"We have indeed," I told him. "Mary keeps some in the pantry, and she said yesterday it was gone."

He nodded, without surprise.

"You have no idea when, I suppose?"

"Some time in the last week."

But apparently he had no intention of explaining what he meant, and his next question surprised me.

"This Daniels, the street cleaner," he said. "He seems to have had a place back here where he burned his leaves, when he had too many of them. What about him? Pretty observant sort of chap?"

"I don't know. The servants say he is queer. I've thought of him already, Mr. Dean. But the police have looked him up; his uniform too, for stains. They couldn't find anything. Anyhow, Holmes burned the pages of that book in the garage, on the cement floor. I saw the ashes this morning."

He showed no signs of disappointment, but he was clearly surprised when I told him about Miss Emily's experience of the night before. He listened in his usual intent manner.

" 'They're after me,' " he repeated. "What did she mean by that, do you know?"

"Not unless she thinks all this is the work of a gang of some sort."

"Nonsense! What sort of a gang?" he demanded. "No gang did this job." Then he glanced toward the noise at the Daltons'.

"How long is that likely to last?"

"I don't know. Probably until twelve. They'll start then to cook the dinners."

He looked at his watch and nodded.

"See here," he said. "I'd like to get into the Lancaster

170

house. I have Jim's key and I've forty-five minutes. Who do you suppose is still there? Emily, of course. What servants?"

"No servants. Peggy is out for the day and Jennie is off for church. Only Emily, and she's probably asleep."

He looked at me with admiration.

"Just like that!" he said. "The more I see of you all, the more I am filled with wonder at our criminal. Everything known to the smallest private detail, and yet — ! Well, are you ready to chance it? I shall need a lookout, you know."

"I'll come, of course. But if you are working with the police, why not do it openly, Mr. Dean? Suppose Emily is awake?"

"I'll take care of Emily. And I'm not working openly with the police, I can do more under cover, and they know it."

I was uneasy, but the thing turned out to be simplicity itself. On any indication that the meeting at the Daltons' was over I was to ring the front doorbell as a warning. Then before Ellen had had time to return Mr. Dean would be out of the house. In the meantime I was to wander about the rear of the Lancaster property, ready to give the alarm.

It worked perfectly. No sounds of excitement came from within the house. I wandered about, first in the garden, then gradually reaching the kitchen porch. There I finally settled myself on the doorstep, curled up like a cat in the warm sun. I heard a window raised above my head, and as cautiously lowered, but Emily evidently still slept and no one emerged along the grapevine path to indicate that the gathering at the Daltons' was breaking up.

Then, idly following an insect of some sort as it crawled along the edge of the house wall, my eyes fell on a smallish round object underneath the dining room window, and I found myself staring at it. It lay in a wash of sand and gravel from Thursday night's heavy rain, and it looked not unlike a bit of rock itself, half buried as it was.

I got up and was stooping over it when Mr. Dean spoke, just beside me.

"So you've found it," he said calmly. "Well, don't touch it. Can you get me a trowel of some sort and a box? And we have only ten minutes, maybe less."

I took the hint and hurried back home. I dare say I was back in five minutes or so, but I was just in time. Louder voices from the Daltons' told me that that unofficial investigation over tea and cake was over, and indeed Mr. Dean had just time to shovel up the glove and drop it earth and all into the box when I heard Ellen and Lizzie on the path. When they came into view, however, he had disappeared around the far corner of the house, and I was knocking vigorously at the kitchen door.

Ellen came on a run.

"I just slipped out for a minute, miss," she panted. "Is there anything you want?"

"Only to ask for Miss Emily. If she's asleep I'll not bother her."

That was at twelve o'clock, and I went back home to find a rather irritated Inspector Briggs ringing our doorbell.

"Just began to think the whole Crescent had gone to church for absolution!" he said when he saw me. "I'd like to have a talk with you, Miss Hall. Something has come up, and I think maybe you'll know."

I took him into Mother's downstairs sitting room, which corresponds to the Lancasters' morning room, and put him in a large chair. But he did not sit back in it. He sat on the edge, fumbled in his breast pocket and brought out a letter.

"Of course," he said, "in a case of this kind we get anonymous letters. Everybody's got an opinion and wants us to have it without getting mixed up in it. This is different. It comes from around here. It was mailed from the Liberty Avenue branch post office, for one thing; and—well, read it first."

I took it. It was printed in pencil on a ruled slip of paper such as comes in tablet form; not unlike the sort we keep about the house for menus and dinner lists, and it read as follows:

"If you want to know who killed Mrs. Lancaster, ask her daughter Margaret. Ask her too who she has been meeting for the last few weeks at night near the woodshed. She has played a dirty game and ought to get caught. He has got the money, but she took it."

I put it down and stared at the Inspector, who was pinching his lip.

"Well?" he said.

"I don't believe it."

"Maybe. Maybe not. I'll bank that she didn't kill her mother; unless she's even smarter than I think she is. We found no blood and no bloody clothes in that house. But Dalton's different."

"Dalton!"

"Sure. Dalton and she have been pretty thick for some little time. The back of the Crescent knew it if you didn't. That letter probably came from one of the servants. Maybe one of yours! Remember, I'm not saying there was anything wrong about these meetings, but there you are. Now, if we suppose this Margaret was getting out the gold as fast as it went in, and notified Dalton that last day Wellington was coming for a sort of general audit, you get the idea."

"But her own mother!" I gasped.

"Worse things in this business than that," he observed. "Or as bad, anyhow. Every now and then some loving daughter blows up and there's trouble. I'm not saying it's true, and I have a pretty shrewd idea that you're close-mouthed or I wouldn't have told you. But you live here. You may know something. You may even have written that letter! Did you?"

"No," I said, feeling slightly dizzy. "Then that night after the murder Mrs. Dalton—"

"Sure," he agreed. "She'd got wind of something, and was on the hunt. For letters, very likely, and maybe for something else."

He got up.

"That's only theory, of course," he said. "But don't underestimate the passions of older people, young lady. They go to queer lengths sometimes, although you may not believe it. Funny thing," he added, "how two intelligent people like that think they can carry on an affair and not have at least a dozen people know all about it. We got our first hint from this gardener, Eben; but I expect most of the servants about here know what's been going on."

He went soon after that. I had said nothing about the finding of the glove, leaving that for Mr. Dean, and I gathered that the police were still at a loose end, especially as to the gold.

"For most of that money was in gold," he said. "A hundred and fifty pounds of it anyhow. Maybe two hundred. That took some carrying and some hiding, believe me."

And he assured me, as he went out the door, that the murder of Mrs. Lancaster had been, in spite of all appearances, no crime either of insanity or of sudden passion; but one long planned and skillfully carried out.

"Only thing I can say is that if she was killed because of that money, it's as sly and cunning a piece of work as I ever saw. If she wasn't, then we've got a lunatic loose somewhere and we've got to get him."

When Mother came home from church that day she found me locked in my room, and as close to hysteria as the Crescent traditions permit to any young woman. For I no longer doubted that Margaret Lancaster had killed her mother, either directly or with Bryan Dalton's help, and with the connivance of Holmes. And I nearly burst into shrieks at the dinner table when, Lydia Talbot coming in to talk over Emily Lancaster's strange experience of the night before, Mother at once decreed that Holmes was to sleep in the house again that night.

"Not Holmes, mother!" I said, while Miss Lydia stared at me curiously.

"Why not Holmes?" Mother said irritably. "He can at least make a noise."

Which is one reason why Holmes was never accused of our second crime, which was committed that night. For so strenuously did he object that Mother was finally obliged to order him to obey, and later on after he was asleep to send me to take the key out of his door and to lock him in! A confession which later brought a smile even to the faces of the police.

Chapter XXI

It was that night, Sunday, August the twenty-first, that Miss Emily Lancaster was shot to death on the grapevine walk.

Looking back over that day, I cannot help marveling at how peaceful it was, in view of all that was to come. Except for the background tragedy of Thursday, it differed in no particular from any other Sunday afternoon that I could remember.

As usual, Mother retired after our midday dinner for her rest, a device used by all the Crescent families to take care of the fried chicken and ice cream which is our summer Sunday meal, and which becomes roast beef and a fruit pie at the end of September. And also as usual Lydia Talbot stayed on after her self-effacing but tenacious fashion. She frequently came in on Sundays, and always remained until something or other finally forced her away.

But that afternoon she nearly drove me wild. We sat on the porch, and she insisted on discussing the crime and her various grievances connected with it.

"One would think," she said in her flat monotonous voice, "that we would have been called in to help. After all, we are the only close relatives the girls have. But can you believe that neither Hester nor I has been in the house since it happened? And they can't lay it to the police now; the police have gone."

She was actually moist with indignation. One gray spit curl had straightened out and hung rakishly over an eye. High priestess of all our funerals as long as I could remember, I understood her resentment and did my best to soothe her.

"Of course they're very upset, Miss Lydia."

"You'd think that would be when they need their own family. I'm their full aunt, Louisa; but that makes no difference. When Emily gets into trouble she runs to us, as she did last night, but that's all it amounts to."

On that night alarm of Emily's, however, she was rather reticent.

"How do I know what it was?" she said, in response to a question from me. "Or who 'they' are? Maybe she dreamed it, although George thinks not. But I can tell you this, Louisa; the minute I got her quiet she stopped talking. She always was a close-mouthed woman anyhow, but she shut up like a clam."

She changed the subject then as though she had said too much.

"I hear Helen Wellington has come back."

"Yes."

"I suppose she thinks Jim has all that money."

That was almost too much for me. I suppose I was constrained and rather silent after it, for soon she got up, straightened the hat which Crescent-fashion sat high on her head, and picked up her old beaded bag.

"Well, I'll move on," she said in her flat voice. "I intend to try just once more to see Emily and Margaret. Then if they don't let me in — well, I suppose I can take a hint as well as anybody!"

I watched from the porch as well as I could, seeing her absurd hat as it passed up the Lancaster walk and then losing it again. But apparently she did not have to take the hint, and I was really relieved when the hat did not reappear.

That was at half past three.

Usually Mother drives out at that time, but Holmes had

secured the afternoon off and Mother was settled upstairs with a book and some essence of pepsin, and the remainder of the afternoon passed with intolerable slowness. Around five o'clock I walked idly toward the Crescent, to see Helen Wellington on the front porch, carefully dressed in white and yawning over a book. I dare say it was a case of any port in a storm, for she saw me and asked me to join her. I did not go up, but I did sit on the steps, to find her eyeing me curiously.

"Look here, Lou," she said. "All this isn't *your* funeral. You look terrible."

"I've had a shock, of course," I told her lamely. "I'm glad you've come back, Helen. Jim needed you."

She laughed.

"Jim! He needs me about as much as he needs a cinder in his eye. Besides, I'm rather under the impression that he has had you to console him! Never mind that, Lou, I'm in a bad temper, that's all. If you could see this house! And not an agency open until morning!"

I looked at her.

"I suppose it hasn't occurred to you to do anything about it yourself," I said drily.

"You would think of that! That's what Bertie Dean says. I've just had a row with him. If he wants to masquerade here as a servant let him do the dishes! It's idiotic anyhow. I dare say the Crescent hasn't been fooled for a minute."

"The Crescent," I told her quietly, "has had other things to think about, Helen."

I did not stay long. It developed that Herbert Dean, after she firmly refused to wash the lunch dishes, had mysteriously disappeared around noon, and that Jim was pretending to read the newspapers inside somewhere.

"He's scared of course," she said easily. "But also of course he didn't do it. He hasn't the brains, Lou; no matter what you think of his intellect. And he is no prestidigitator, no matter what the police may think."

By which she referred to what has been called the substitution theory as to the money in the chest.

Since then I have seen a record of Mr. Lancaster's early statement after the discovery that the chest had been looted.

178

It runs much as follows:

Q. (by Inspector Briggs). "You are certain that nobody could have moved that gold in any quantity in a short space of time?"

A. "Practically certain, considering its weight."

Q. "But you were not afraid that the attempt might be made?"

A. "I haven't said that. I was not afraid in the daytime. The nights worried me, however. My wife often took an opiate at night to enable her to sleep."

Q. "Then it is your considered opinion that the gold was not taken yesterday afternoon after her death?"

A. "I do not see how it could have been."

Q. "Now, Mr. Lancaster, are you ready to state that this gold and so on actually went into the chest?"

A. "I'm afraid I don't understand."

Q. "I mean, are you certain that there was no substitution?"

A. "Substitution. Oh yes, I see what you mean. I think not. Once or twice I myself tied up the bags and placed them there. There was no substitution while I was present."

Q. "In that case, have you any explanation of the fact that this money has disappeared? Of any possible method?"

A. "None whatever."

Q. "Will you tell us the exact procedure which was followed when the gold arrived?"

A. "I was not always present, or even often, but I suppose it did not vary. Mr. Wellington brought the money in a small black bag. Usually it was gold, tied up in small canvas sacks with the necks wired and a lead seal on each one. He would cut the wire, and my wife would then count the money as it lay on her bed. Mr. Wellington would then enter the amount in the book and my wife would sign it."

Q. "And after that?"

A. "It was simply a matter of putting the sacks — or the folder with the currency — into the chest. He would draw out the chest, my wife would give him her key, and he would then deposit the money and lock the chest again."

Q. "Your wife could see all this?"

179

A. "I am not certain. She could at first. The box was taken out and placed on two chairs beside the bed. Later on it was too heavy, and was merely drawn out and opened."

Q. "Then it would have been possible for a substitution to be effected later? That is, a second bag containing these lead weights might have been placed in the chest, and the bag with the gold have gone back into the valise? And so on?"

A. "I suppose it might be possible; yes. But I think it highly unlikely. I have known Mr. Wellington all his life," etc., etc.

This was the theory to which Helen referred that afternoon, and her comment on it was characteristic.

"Now can anybody see poor Jim figuring all that out?" she said. "Jim, who remembers that a party needs gin after all the bootleggers have put on their dress clothes and gone to the opera! He's a good sort, and he's mine and so I like him — no matter what you may think, Lou; and not all the time either. But that's neither here nor there." And she added in her casual fashion: "I suppose Emily really did it. I know I would, in her case. She was a horrible old woman."

With which I finally went back home, to a light supper and a heavy but disturbed sleep through which Helen Wellington moved gaily and irresponsibly; and our own Annie was writing an anonymous letter to the police — which is the only time in my life when a dream turned out to be true, as we learned after the case was over.

It was from this dream that I wakened early the next morning to the discovery of our second murder; that of Emily Lancaster herself.

Chapter XXII

The circumstances were peculiar as well as tragic. Miss Emily, having slept most of the day, had apparently been wakeful that night and at one o'clock in the morning she had gone out to the kitchen porch. There she had evidently sat for a time, eating an apple, a portion of which with the knife for paring it was found on the table there later on. As the porch is an enclosed and locked one, this is understandable enough, although rather strange after the events of the night before.

What followed was less so.

For some reason then unknown she had left the porch, gone out onto the rear path and followed it toward the Talbots'. She was clad much as she had been the night before, for under her wrapper she still wore her nightdress, although she had put on her shoes and stockings and a petticoat.

The path, familiar to her for many years, she had apparently followed without difficulty; although the night was dark and overcast. There were no prints on her flat-heeled shoes to show that she had left it at any time. But only thirty yards from the rear of the Talbot house that tragic walk of hers had ceased. Someone, perhaps hidden in the shrubbery, had shot at her and killed her.

That is the brief story of our second murder as it was reconstructed at the time, and it is not the least dramatic part of it that George Talbot had not only heard the shot but had gone outside to investigate it; and that because she had fallen into the shrubbery he must have passed close by her body without seeing it.

"I heard a shot," he told the police, "and I got my gun at once. I knew it was not a car back-firing, for it came from the rear of the property and there is no road there.

"Well, it's pretty hard to get out of our house at night in a hurry, so I used an old kid trick of mine. I got out onto the roof of the summer kitchen, which is low, and dropped from there. I had no flashlight, but I took a pretty good look around and I saw nothing and nobody, although I thought once I heard some movement near our stable.

"I gave it up then, and I had a hard time getting back into the house. But at last Mother came down to admit me. She had heard no shot, nor had my Aunt Lydia; but Lizzie, who has been with us for years, had heard it. She was awake with a toothache. That's all I know about it. I went back and went to sleep. It was a quarter to two then. The shot was at half past one."

And that for some time was all anybody seemed to know about it.

It was Eben who found her that Monday morning at seven-thirty, on his way to get the lawn mower from the Talbot garage. He saw what looked like a black cloth lying among the syringa bushes which bordered the path, and stooped to pick it up. It would not lift, however, and then he saw that he had uncovered a woman's foot. It was after that that he yelled and the street cleaner, Daniels, who was in No Man's Land with some débris from Euclid Street, heard him and came running. He seemed stricken when he saw the body, and neither he nor Eben had touched it when the Talbot's Lizzie came on a run.

When I reached the place practically all the servants from the Crescent were already there. As in the case of Mrs.

182

Lancaster, they stood more or less together, a huddled silent group with the women silently and conventionally weeping. George Talbot had arrived and taken charge, sending Lizzie to telephone for the police; and Daniels, curiously enough, had taken off his cap.

"Gone to her Maker, miss," he said to me. Then, seeing that I looked white, he added: "It is as natural to die as to be born."

How was I to know that he was quoting from Bacon's "Essay on Death"? He went away quietly soon afterwards, leaving word that he would be on Euclid Street when he was wanted. But he was not there. His brush and his rubbish cart was there, all the simple paraphernalia of his business, but it was late afternoon before he used them again. Then I saw him, and he said he had felt sick.

"She'd been very kind to me," he explained, as though that was the answer.

Looking back I see him moving through all our troubles, an untidy white figure who came and went, hardly noticed; a mild-faced man with no particular characteristics save a slight limp and the thick glasses of a man who had been operated for cataract. At some time he had suffered a paralysis of one side of his face, which drooped. But he was cheerful and a steady worker. Who could have guessed that he was the key to so much that we could learn only slowly and painfully?

He had drifted away before the siren of the police car sounded at the gates to the Crescent. By that time, some of them only casually attired, the Crescent families were appearing. George Talbot tried to wave his mother back, but she came on, and so did Miss Lydia. Mr. Dalton appeared in his dressing gown. Mother had arrived, and insisted that the body be removed at once into the Talbot house, regardless of police regulations. And almost before the police car had had time to stop I saw Helen Wellington, in pajamas and carrying a cigarette, walking toward the group and looking interested and nonchalant.

183

All of this, of course, is only a picture, photographed on my mind; the background for Emily Lancaster, lying on her side on the warm summer earth and looking clumsy and heavy even in death.

She had been shot through the head, a quick and merciful death, at least. But like the others I dare say, my stunned mind could comprehend only the murder itself. Or was it murder?

The two policemen, having driven us all back, were searching for a weapon near the body in case of suicide, and being careful not to step on the ground beyond the path. There was no weapon in sight, however, and unless it lay under her they knew that a second crime had been committed within less than two hundred yards of the first.

That was the situation when Margaret Lancaster came running down the steps of their kitchen porch; a wild-eyed and half-crazed woman. Ellen was the first to reach her and to try to get her back into the house, but she shook her off and came on toward us, dreadfully and determinedly.

"I want to see her," she said. "I must see her. Let go of me, Ellen. Let go, I say."

She went through us without seeing any of us, and she paid no attention whatever to the two policemen.

"Please don't touch her," one of them said. "Sorry, miss, but that's a regulation."

I doubt if she heard him. Moaning softly she got down on her knees and looked at her sister. Then something of the inevitability of the situation must have come to her, for when she rose again she seemed calmer.

"I'll go back now," she said, to no one in particular. "I must tell my father."

Mother and Ellen went back with her along the path, but I heard later that she shut them both out and went in alone.

"She was certainly not herself," Mother told me later. "Anyone could smell Ellen's oatmeal burning on the stove, but she simply slammed the door, and of course it has a spring lock. She was in no condition to break the news to

184

anybody. No wonder he collapsed."

For that was the next news we had. It came while the Homicide Squad was still at work in the morning sun, and shortly after the body had been taken away, carefully covered, on a stretcher. Mr. Lancaster had had a stroke, and Doctor Armstrong's car drove up just as the police ambulance was carrying Miss Emily away.

It was the doctor, coming in later to give Mother her hypodermic of iron, who told us.

"It's not surprising," he said. "He's almost seventy, and he has been in very poor shape ever since his wife's death. As a matter of fact, I believe he had his stroke in the night."

"In the night!" Mother said. "Then he doesn't know about Emily?"

"I doubt it. Margaret went in to tell him as best she could, poor woman. The room was still dark, and she sat down on the edge of the bed and took his hand. Apparently he opened his eyes, or at least she thinks so. She told him to be brave, and that she had some bad news for him, but he did not move. That did not alarm her. He was always pretty well-controlled. When she finally said what had happened and he was still quiet she was alarmed, and raised a window shade. Then she saw there was something wrong. I've sent for a nurse. She's about ready to collapse herself."

He himself doubted if the old gentleman would be able to rally. Not only because of his age, but because he had neither eaten nor slept properly since the first murder.

"Kept an iron hand on himself, but was boiling inside all the time," was the way he put it.

As to Emily's death he had no theory whatever, except that it was an accident.

"Where's there a motive?" he asked. "A quiet peaceable middle-aged woman, a devoted daughter and a good neighbor. Who would want to do away with her? Trouble with all of us is that we're trying to connect it with Mrs. Lancaster's murder. Well, I'd say offhand that there's no connection. There is no relation between the impulse that wielded that axe next door and this shooting. There was fury behind the axe."

"What sort of accident?" Mother demanded, refusing since nothing could bring Miss Emily back to be done out of a second crime. "If you're talking about George Talbot's idea that someone was shooting at a cat—!"

"I didn't say that, although it's possible. But with the amount of crime there is today, and especially after what had happened here, almost anyone would feel justified in shooting at a figure moving along that path at something after one o'clock in the morning."

"But why was she moving along that path? Have you any idea? Was she running for shelter again, as she did before?"

"Hardly. So far as we can make out she'd been sitting on the porch eating an apple, just before." And then he turned abruptly to me and faced me into the sun.

"See here," he said, "don't you let this get too far under your skin, Lou. You have your own life to live, you know."

And out of sheer tension and strain I spoke out as I had never spoken before.

"Have I?" I said. "I wonder, doctor. I haven't lived any of my own life yet. I'm like Miss Emily in that."

"Louisa!" said Mother sharply. "Control yourself."

"I'm sick and tired of controlling myself. What does it lead to? A bullet in the dark, and nothing to carry away with one. No life, no anything. I wanted to marry and I couldn't and now—"

Then of course I broke down, and Mother went out of the room and I did not see her again for hours. But I did not tell even Doctor Armstrong that the sight of Helen Wellington walking down nonchalantly in her gaudy pajamas to where poor Emily lay dead by the path had been the first strain. Not, I think, that I really cared for Jim, but because of sheer contrast.

I do remember muttering that the path of duty led but to the grave, and that the doctor immediately sent for Annie and had me put to bed. But he understood rather more than

I thought he did, for before he left he sat down beside me and took my hand.

"There is only one safe way to carry on in this world, Lou," he said gently. "That is to let the past take care of itself and to look ahead. No use looking back. What's over is over, so bury it decently. But always look ahead. That's the game."

"To what?"

"Well, we may evolve some ideas about that later," he said, and soon after he went away.

That collapse of mine is the reason I can relate the events of that day, Monday the twenty-second, only at second hand.

Chapter XXIII

Miss Emily had, it developed, been shot from the right side, which if she had been on her way toward the Talbot house made it appear as though the bullet had come from No Man's Land. But as she might have stopped and turned, particularly if she had heard a sound of some sort, this was only important in view of the lack of clues elsewhere. Thus the area between the Talbot and Lancaster houses, largely garden with soft flower beds, showed no footprints whatever.

The idea had someone had fired from an upper window at a possible prowler was also not tenable. The post-mortem showed that the bullet had entered and left the head in an almost horizontal line. The time of her death was set at between one and two in the morning, due partly to George Talbot's story of the shot, and partly to her sister Margaret's statement that she had heard someone moving about in the upper hall at one o'clock.

The story of that night, as it gradually drifted to the rest of the Crescent, was that on hearing Emily Margaret had called out, and that Emily had replied that she was going downstairs to get an apple.

As Emily when unable to sleep often went downstairs at night for something to eat, this had not surprised her. Save for one thing, and that was the alarm which had driven her out the night before. She had thought it odd for Emily to be prowling about after that experience, and her first inclination had been to offer to go with her. She was very tired, however, and Emily knew her way about. She was not surprised that she wanted food; she had eaten almost nothing since the Thursday before. But she was sorry now, tragically sorry; she had simply gone to sleep again and let her go alone.

The evening, she said, had been quiet. Emily had slept most of the day, although late in the afternoon she had wakened and had agreed to see Lydia Talbot, who had been downstairs. Lydia had suggested nailing shut the two windows opening from Emily's room onto the porch roof, and she and Ellen had done it together.

The two women, Emily and Lydia, had talked for some time. Although aunt and niece, there was no great disparity in their ages, and Emily had never had Margaret's dislike of the older woman. But after Miss Lydia's departure Emily had been restless. She had got up and prowled around the house, especially on the second floor. When Margaret found her she said she was looking for her bird, which Lydia had missed, and Margaret had had to tell her that the bird was dead.

Emily had taken the news very hard, but had become more quiet as the day wore on.

She — Margaret — and Mr. Lancaster had spent the evening downstairs. Mr. Lewis had brought out a copy of her mother's will, and had gone at nine o'clock. After that the two of them had sat in the library discussing it. Like every other value, Mrs. Lancaster's estate had shrunk greatly during the depression. She had, however, left some three hundred thousand dollars, including the money in the chest, and fifty thousand of this was left without restriction to Jim Wellington.

It was an old will made when the estate had been valued at more than a million dollars. Now that legacy to Jim loomed large and formidable, and Mr. Lancaster had seemed undisturbed.

He had gone up to bed at eleven, although she herself had remained below until almost midnight. Since her mother's death her stepfather had refused to enter her mother's room, and had in fact locked it off from his own by the connecting bathroom. When he was ready for bed, therefore, he called down to her that it looked as though it might rain that night, and for her to close her mother's windows. She had unlocked the door, gone in and closed them.

Emily was still awake and still worrying about her bird, for she opened her door when she heard Margaret and asked where the cage was. Margaret told her that George Talbot had taken it to the stable, and Emily had seemed satisfied.

That was all she knew, and examination of Emily's room supported this part of her story. The book Emily had been reading was face down on the table beside her chair, and her bed jacket lay across the foot of the bed. What the police could not understand, nor those of us who learned it by the grapevine, was why Miss Emily should have at least partially redressed herself later; have put on her shoes and stockings and her petticoat, in order to do what she had done so many nights before; to go downstairs for something to eat.

Miss Margaret, distracted as she was by her father's grave illness, could give no explanation.

"She never bothered to dress," was what she said. "She often went in her nightdress and slippers, or sometimes in a wrapper. No, I can't understand it. The bird cage? But why in the world would she want it? She knew the bird was dead."

That was the way the case stood until three o'clock that afternoon. Then the police, still searching for the empty shell, found two things which only added to our mystery.

One of these was a garden spade, identified by Eben as belonging to the Daltons and left by him on Saturday leaning against the wall of the Dalton garage. This spade was discovered in the shrubbery near the body, but at first seemed to have no significance. It was Eben's identification which set them to thinking.

The other was the discovery late that afternoon of the bullet itself, deeply implanted in a small tree in No Man's

Land. There was no empty shell to be found, however, and no spot could be found where, if Miss Emily had indeed carried the spade to where it lay, she had used it for any purpose whatever.

Inspector Briggs sumed it up later.

"Well, there we were again, with the newspapers howling like nobody's business and the Commissioner and the District Attorney carrying on like two lunatics. What had we? She didn't shoot herself; that's certain. And we couldn't get a search warrant and tear all five houses wide open to look for a gun. Not the Crescent! There would have been hell to pay.

"All that bullet did until we'd examined it the next day was to show us approximately where she'd been shot from; the direction. That pointed to the walk itself, or to the space between those two houses. But we couldn't find the shell to prove it.

"What we figured was that she'd been shot from close range. It was a dark night, remember; no moon. Not exactly pointblank, but close enough. And that she was out on some business of her own, maybe the gold. She'd carried that spade. Her prints were all over it."

"That was another thing that threw us off, for it wasn't far from the body that we found that key to the chest and its chain. We didn't announce that, but it was there all right; looked as though it had been buried and the rain had uncovered it. But there it was."

"As for the prints of those heels, well—they looked pretty fresh, but by the time we'd got there women had been swarming all over the place. They might be important and they might not. Just one of those things!"

For, although we didn't know it at the time, the search had finally revealed between where the body lay and the Talbot's old stable, two or three prints of a high French heel. Just such heels as Helen Wellington and Mrs. Dalton wore as a matter of habit, and as I myself used now and again in spite of Mother's protests and as a small assertion of independence.

The police made molds of them; spraying them with some sort of liquid shellac first, I believe, and then pouring in

191

some melted paraffine. The earth was fairly firm and the molds successful, but they offered no characteristics of any sort to identify them. As the Inspector said with disgust:

"There were at least four women along the Crescent including the housemaid Peggy, who could have made those prints. But there were about a hundred thousand in the city who could have made them too."

We knew nothing of this on that Monday, however. All we knew was that Emily Lancaster had been killed, and that our morale had for the second time been pretty completely shattered.

We carried on as best we could. Monday is the Crescent's wash day, and murder or no murder, at or before nine o'clock its various laundresses converged on it as usual. By eleven that day the drying yards revealed as usual to all and sundry the most intimate garments of its owners, and inside our houses we were calling up the butcher and ordering soap from the grocer, much as we always had.

Not quite as usual, however, for about the middle of the morning the Talbots' laundress, setting the pole for her clothesline into its cement foundation in the drying yard was unable to seat it properly and made an examination of the hole. The empty shell was lying in it, and with the aid of a clothespin she got it out.

But here is one of the things which I dare say has hanged an innocent man before this, or sent him to the chair. All our laundresses are negresses, and of a grade which has an almost superstitious fear of the police. Amanda therefore put the shell in her pocket and said nothing about it.

"Ah didn' want to get mixed up with that kind of trouble," was her later explanation.

This, when we learned it, seemed definitely to fix the position of the killer on that Sunday night as in the Talbot drying yard, a small piece of ground which borders the path toward the Lancasters', and which is protected from the street by an open lattice covered with vines. On the side toward the garage and the path, however, there is only shrubbery, and rather low shrubbery, at that.

We knew nothing of Amanda's discovery that day, however. Mother spent most of it at the Lancasters', with Mrs. Talbot there also, and reported on her return that Mr. Lancaster was still unconscious and Margaret going about in a daze. She had, it seemed, decided to clear her mother's bedroom of its personal belongings, and so the three women had unlocked the room and gone to work. Mother was hot and tired when she came back, and I noticed that she carried a square package of some sort which looked like a large book.

She said nothing about it, however, and as it was wrapped in white paper and tied, I did not ask her about it. In fact I quite forget about it until that evening when by ones and twos the neighbors drifted in.

The package was on top of one of the bookshelves, and it was Mrs. Talbot who noticed it.

"I see she gave it to you."

"Yes," Mother said. "She didn't know what to do with it. I don't know that I do, either. I suppose it will go to the third floor."

"To the third floor" is Crescent usage for any sort of storage.

I cannot remember now that anyone except Mrs. Talbot showed any interest in the album. There was a time coming when I was to think back and try to recall that scene, but without result. George wanted to see it, "to cheer him up," and was sharply rebuked by his mother. Bryan Dalton eyed it and then looked away, while his wife watched him. But that was all.

I myself knew it well, its imposing size and the clasps which fastened it. I could remember it lying on the Lancasters' parlor table when I was a small girl, and the awe with which I examined the strange clothes and stranger attitudes of the people pictured inside. But now as I say it aroused no interest. We sat in an informal circle, much as we had once before, but the excitement of Thursday had given place to a strained anxiety which showed itself in Mrs. Talbot's lowered voice and strained mouth, in Lydia's pallor and the hands which shook over her knitting, in Mrs. Dalton's shrill high laughter, and in Bryan Dalton's increased taciturnity.

So far as I can recall he spoke only once all evening.

"What it comes to is this," he said. "We have a murdering killing brute somewhere around us, and I've already asked for extra police protection."

"Police!" said Mrs. Talbot. "We've been overrun with them, and what good are they? What we need is more bars and more locks."

"And more fires out back!" said Mrs. Dalton surprisingly. Everyone looked at her, but she only laughed rather maliciously and on that the bell rang and Helen Wellington came in.

She stood in the doorway surveying us with her faintly ironic smile.

"Well," she said, "I suppose you think that Jim has been busy again!"

That shocked us into action. Bad taste always does. Perhaps she had meant to do just that, for Mother got up and faced her squarely.

"Really, Helen!" she said. "If you think we have been discussing Jim in this — in this tragic connection, you are mistaken. We have done nothing of the sort."

"Discussing or thinking or just plain wondering, I came in to tell you what I have told the police. Jim Wellington slept in my room last night, and he didn't leave it." And she added more lightly, seeing how indelicate most of us considered that statement: "I'll swear that on a stack of Bibles if necessary. I'm sure the Crescent could produce a stack of Bibles!"

"Come in and don't be silly, Helen," George Talbot said. "We've been talking about self-defense here; nothing else."

Her eyes, made up as usual but shrewd behind her mascara, swept the circle.

"Self-defense?" she said. "With everybody here but poor Jim? That's funny!"

Then she turned and went out, and we heard the front door slam behind her.

She had effectively broken up the gathering. They all left soon after she had gone, but I noticed that where the Daltons had once walked side by side, even if it was in silence, he now stalked ahead and let her follow as best she might. At the end of the path, where it reaches the street, I saw him turn and look back toward the Lancaster house, where a light showed from the sick man's room. After that he squared his shoulders and marched on, with his wife mincing along on her absurd heels behind him.

George stopped long enough behind his mother and his aunt to tell me that Margaret had asked him to stay the night in the house, and that he had agreed.

"She's frightened," he said. "And I don't blame her. It looks like a plot to wipe out the whole lot of them."

"You think it's the same person, then?"

"It's stretching things rather fine to premise two killers after one family, isn't it?"

Then he left, and I locked up the house while Mother carried the album upstairs with her, still in its paper wrapping.

Chapter XXIV

Holmes slept in the house again that Monday night, and locked in once more, although he did not know it. Miss Emily's death had destroyed any theory I might have had about him, and I was confused and rather hopeless. Even granting that he could have escaped by the window, there was no possible way by which he could have reëntered the house. Unless — and that came to me suddenly as I commenced to undress — he had dropped out the window, reentered by one of the long ladders we all have for tree pruning, and in the morning taken it away again.

Somewhere I had read that such a method had been used, and discovered by the marks left in the earth by the ladder. So, because I was not sleepy and because I could not hear Holmes snoring loudly in his comfortable guest room bed, I decided to go downstairs and investigate for myself. There seemed nothing else to do. Since the morning of the day before I had lost all contact with Herbert Dean.

Mother was tired, and after locking all her windows for her and placing a vase on each sill, "in case someone tries to enter," as she said, I went downstairs and out the front door.

It was another cloudy night, with another storm in the air but with no wind; which was fortunate, Mother having demanded our only flashlight and I being armed merely with a box of matches. I had lighted one and found no marks, and was stooping with my second one when a low voice suddenly said:

"Don't be frightened, Miss Lou. It's Dean. And put out that match. There's nothing there. I've looked."

The shock made me tremble violently, and I imagine he knew it, for he caught me by the arm and drew me away.

"Steady!" he said. "And where can we talk? The cellar?"

"The garage is all right," I managed to say.

"Oh! Then Holmes is in the house again tonight?"

"Yes. How did you know he was, last night?"

"Knowing about Holmes is my business. Not for what you think, however. Your Holmes is a smart young man, as I believe I've said before. Some of these days he and I are going to have a good old-fashioned gam."

"A gam?"

"A talk, a gossip. Whatever you like to call it. In the meantime, can't we have one ourselves? I need to know a lot of things."

This I agreed to and so I went back into the house, closed and bolted the front door, and on reaching the kitchen porch found him waiting for me on the back path. His matter-of-factness was solid and dependable. In silence he led the way to the garage, put me on a bench, sat down on the running board of the car and got out his pipe.

"Well!" he said at last, "things are getting interesting! Day by day, in every way, they're getting hotter and hotter."

That surprised me. "You're hardly human, are you?" I said. "I believe you actually *like* this situation!"

"Human enough, but it's my business," he said calmly, and smoked thoughtfully and in silence for some time.

"I understand Helen broke up the meeting tonight," he went on after the pause. "Very typical of Helen, if slightly indiscreet. Still she had a good enough reason, although I'd have kept her back if I'd known, but you see I'm not there any more. She's filled up the place with servants, and I had to get out."

"What was her reason? She was rather dreadful."

"She was scared," he said quietly. "You see, Jim owns a forty-five automatic. However, the police have the bullet now, and by tonight or tomorrow the experts will know that his pistol never fired that shot."

He had little to say as to his own movements during the day, and he flatly refused to discuss the second glove.

"I'll tell you all about that some day."

But he was more concerned about Miss Emily's murder than he had seemed at first.

"You see," he said, "there can be only two or three reasons for killing her. First, that she was mistaken for someone else — possible, but unlikely to my mind. Again, she may have had to be put out of the way for some reason we don't know; because she knew something or obstructed some plan. I have an increasing feeling that there is a plan. And still again, she may have had something in her possession which somebody else wanted or had to have. I say all this because we have to count out the usual motives of revenge or jealousy or love. She was hardly a person to inspire any of them. And of course there's the possibility of a lunatic. We can't eliminate that entirely."

"But you don't believe that, do you?"

"No. You see, Lou, — you don't mind my calling you Lou, do you? it's easier — you see there are two types of killers, roughly speaking. One is a low type, a subnormal mentally, who generally belongs to the underworld and who kills impulsively, out of fear or rage or liquor. The other type is the intelligent one. Its crimes are carefully planned and subtly carried out. But that of course is its great danger. Everything in such a plot depends on something else; it's all fitted together like a machine. Then a cog slips and the whole business goes to pieces."

"Does that mean that poor Emily Lancaster was such a cog?" I asked.

"It's possible. Why else kill her? She was inoffensive, to say the least. If she knew anything she hadn't told it, at least to the police. You see, Lou — I rather like calling you Lou. I hope you do too! — it's my belief that somewhere buried in this Crescent is a story. I'm leaving the rest to the police and going

198

after that story. But I don't mind telling you that if and when I get it, it won't be from the Crescent itself. Of all the tight-lipped mind-your-own-business people I've ever seen! But let's forget them. Are you tired? Do you want to go in?"

"Not unless you do?"

"What, me? With a pretty girl and a summer night and a handsome running board to sit on? Never. Besides, it helps me to talk out loud. You're a good listener, you know; any man prefers no voice even to a soft low voice in a woman at times."

Then he dropped his bantering air.

"What gets me," he said, "is why she left the house last night at all. It doesn't fit, Lou. Why did Miss Emily get up, put on part of her clothing, eat an apple on the porch and then go out? She wasn't scared off that porch. She'd have rushed into the house and locked the door. Unless," he added, "she was afraid of someone in the house. And in that case, why the apple?"

He was annoyed, I could see. He had had a theory of some sort which had satisfied him, and then along came something, which, as he said, didn't fit.

"One night she runs out of the house and hunts sanctuary at the Talbots'," he went on, "and the next she sits on the back porch at one in the morning with that damned apple and then goes and takes a walk! Lou, we've got to find out why she took that walk."

I thought for a moment.

"Of course," I said, "she might have gone for the bird cage."

"The what?"

"Well, Margaret had told her that the bird was dead, and about giving the cage to George Talbot to put in their stable. And she would know that he doesn't lock the stable at night. He's been hoping for years that someone would steal his car."

He put his hands to his ears with a wild gesture.

"I look at you, Lou," he said, "and you are uttering words in a very nice voice. But they don't mean anything. What is this about a bird cage? Do you mean that Miss Emily Lancaster would go after it at one o'clock in the morning? Why would she do such a thing?"

"She was terribly fond of the bird. But of course she knew by that time that it was dead — You see, I really killed it. I put it in a back room and nobody gave it any water. I — I really can't bear it, Mr. Dean. If she was after that cage when she was killed I'll carry a scar all my life."

Upon which, to my intense surprise, I found myself crying. I had been calm enough comparatively until then, and I think I scared Herbert Dean as much as I astonished him.

"Stop it, Lou," he said sharply. "You've been a grand girl up to now, and this is no time to heat up and boil over. Stop it, do you hear? Of course you didn't kill the fool bird, or Emily Lancaster either. Here's a handkerchief. And this is a nice sentimental time, when you are softened with grief, to tell you that I'm often called Bert — or even Bertie! Silly name, but these things are like warts. You don't know what brings them on. You only know you've got them."

Which I dare say served its purpose of making me laugh, for it did.

He harked back to the bird cage almost at once, however, and so I told him the story. He listened until I had finished.

"Curious," he said at last. "If Margaret told her about it she knew the bird was dead. Of course that might account for the spade too; that she meant to bury it. Still, to start out for a thing like that after her scare of the night before simply doesn't make sense, unless the whole business was an excuse, a sort of camouflage. But that would mean —"

He rose rather suddenly and held out both hands to me.

"Up with you, my lady Lou. Poetry, did you notice! You are going into the house and to bed. I have an idea, although I can't see you, that you look ghastly. And young ladies shouldn't look ghastly, Lou. It isn't becoming."

"I'm afraid I haven't cared much how I look. Not for years and years."

He stood silent in the darkness, still holding my hands.

"No," he said. "I suppose not. Why should you? The whole effect of this Crescent has been to defeat youth. That's a rather terrible thing, Lou. And you submit. The difference between you and Helen lies right there, you know. You submit. She revolts. She has more courage."

"Perhaps I want peace more than Helen does," I said.

"Peace! It is only age that craves peace, Lou my dear. It has lived and so it is willing to rest. But why should you want peace? Conflict is the very essence of life. And speaking of conflict — " He released my hands.

"You're going to bed," he told me, "and I am going to the Talbot stable or garage or whatever it is, to look at that bird cage; although if anyone had told me a week ago that I would start with an axe murder and end with a bird cage I don't know that I'd have believed them."

He gave me a little shove and started toward the house.

"I'll wait until you're safely inside," he said. "And listen to this, Lou. We may be through or we may not; but I want you to promise that you'll not do any more night investigating. There are only two theories of these crimes: one is that they are inside crimes, done by someone on the Crescent; the other is an outsider and possibly a lunatic, and he's not eliminated even yet. And I don't know which is the worst. Let me do the dirty work. Is it a promise?"

"I thought you said I had no courage."

"Moral courage, child. I haven't a doubt you would fight your weight in wildcats, but there's a difference."

With that he let me go, and stood watching me until I was safely inside the house. Then he swung rapidly but silently toward the Talbot garage, and I turned to the front of the house and an experience which I still cannot remember without a shiver.

One of the strangest things during all those hectic days was the comparative immunity with which our killer apparently moved about among us. Police might be scattered here and there, and usually were; we ourselves might be on guard, our houses locked and our windows bolted. But with uncanny skill both were circumvented.

Thus, although I cannot say that our kitchen door was in full view from the garage that night, it was at least dangerously close to where Herbert Dean and I sat talking. Yet in that interval of a half hour or less what followed seemed to prove later that someone had crept up the steps of the back porch and slipped inside.

I had no idea of this, of course. I remember feeling happier than I had felt for a long time, in spite of our tragedies; feeling younger too, and determined to go upstairs and get the beauty sleep Herbert Dean had suggested that I needed. I think I was even humming a little under my breath as I went forward through the dark hall, although I stopped that at the foot of the stairs for fear of Mother.

I went up the stairs quietly for the same reason. There was a low light in the upper hall, but it only served to throw the shadows into relief, and it was while I stood at the top of the stairs that I thought I saw Holmes moving back in the guest room passage.

That puzzled me. He was locked in, or should have been, and after a moment's hesitation I went down to the landing again and back along the hall. There I tried his door, but it was securely locked; and either he was asleep or he was giving an excellent imitation of it, from the sounds beyond.

I decided then that I had been mistaken, so I wandered to the end window of the guest room and glanced out at the Dalton house. Our hall was dark, but there was a light in Mrs. Dalton's bedroom, and the shades were up so that I could see into the room.

She was there, and so far as I could make out she was walking the floor and crying. She was in her nightdress, and without her high heels she looked small and pathetic. Old, too; I had never thought of her before as an old woman. It came to me then that there was real tragedy in the picture framed by those windows, the tragedy of loneliness and some mysterious grief which was the more terrible because it was so silent and repressed.

But it seemed almost indecent to spy on her, and I was about to turn and leave when I heard something behind me. It was not a step; it was a stealthy movement, almost inaudible. And with that something or somebody caught me by the shoulder; I screamed, and that is all I remember.

When I came to Holmes was beating on his locked door and shouting murder, and I was absolutely alone in the dark and flat on the floor. Deadly sick at my stomach, too, and with a queer numb feeling in my head. Then I heard sibilant whispering, and I knew that Mary and Annie were on their staircase and afraid to come down.

"Mary!" I called. "Please come. It's all right."

My voice was feeble, but they heard it and slowly emerged. I must have looked a strange object lying there in the dark, and the noise Holmes was making did not lessen the excitement. With the lights on they gained some courage, however, and Annie roused Mother and told her I was half killed—which seemed to me to be the truth at that time.

The three of them got me to bed finally, and at last someone released an outraged and indignant Holmes and called the doctor.

I had a huge lump on the top of my head, and a nausea from concussion which bothered me more than the bump. But all the time I was being petted and patted, as the doctor put his examination of my skull, the police were carefully searching the house. And they found exactly nothing, except that the kitchen door was unlocked.

The weapon was neither an axe nor a pistol, but a poker from the kitchen stove, and it bore no prints whatever.

I believe they suspected Holmes that night. Certainly they examined his room and himself for the key to his door. But as Annie observed, he would have had to jump like a grasshopper to get down and unlock the kitchen door and then get back again and lock himself in, between my scream and the time she and Mary had reached the bottom of the stairs.

So far as they worked it out, I had trapped someone in the back hall. There is a space there where the hall widens, and whoever it was hid in the angle of the wall there. Almost certainly I had passed close by the intruder in the dark, and there must have been a momentary hesitation; an indecision whether to chance an escape while my back was turned, or to put me beyond raising an alarm.

"But you raised the alarm all right," the Inspector said that night with a chuckle. "Understand down on the Avenue they thought it was a fire engine!"

I can still see him, standing beside my bed and pinching his lips as he surveyed me. He was holding a bit of the green stem of some plant or other, in his free hand.

"Well, I'm glad it's no worse," he told me. "It's a good thing you've got all that hair. A poker's kind of a mean thing away from a fireplace. And so you're pretty sure you didn't drag this in?"

"Not if you found it in that corner of the back hall."

"That's where it was, and close to the wall. Well, I suppose I've got to go back to the Commissioner and tell him I'm running an agricultural show. Three blades of grass and a piece of stem! That's a hell of a layout to put before anything but a jackass."

Chapter XXV

I believe that Mother and Annie took turns that night in sitting up with me, but I was in the pleasant lethargy of a small dose of morphia, where the mind suddenly develops enormous dynamic activity, and everything extraneous is so remote as to be non-existent.

Pictures succeeded one another with dazzling sharpness and activity. I was helping Margaret Lancaster take Emily into the house, and Margaret was stooping and picking up something from the floor, almost under Lynch's eyes. I was in the upper hall, with a thin line seeping out under the door, and Peggy pointing to it and yelling "blood!" I was meeting Lydia Talbot on the street, and she was saying in a dazed fashion that she supposed "they had stood it as long as they could." I saw Mrs. Dalton going through her house again, and the two of them in the woodshed. I saw the lid of the chest raised and the detective, Sullivan, prodding a sack with his fingertips. I watched Holmes carefully cutting pages out of a book, and after burning them stirring the ashes with his foot. And once again Miss Emily was lying in the bushes, and the street cleaner was saying: "It is as natural to die as to be born."

That phase passed rather quickly, but it was followed by

one less dramatic but no less sublimated. Hidden motives seemed entirely clear to me while it lasted, the very secret springs of the Crescent's hidden life, love, hate, jealousy and fear. Fear? They were all afraid. I thought of that gathering downstairs earlier in the night. They were terrified. But they were more than afraid. Some common bond of secret knowledge held them together, as it had brought them together. They had sat with their carefully tended hands idle and with their eyes wary and their mouths tight; and although they had gathered voluntarily, there was no real friendliness among them.

That was my last thought when I finally fell asleep.

I wakened late to a stiff neck and an aching head, to find that Mother was taking a needed sleep and that Annie was beside the bed.

"That butler who was working at the Wellington's — he's downstairs, miss, and he's got a message for you from Mr. Jim."

"I can't see him like this, Annie."

"He says it's important, miss."

I caught her eye, and I was fairly confident that whatever Herbert Dean might do in the way of helping with our troubles, he had never fooled our servants for a minute.

"All right, Annie," I said. "Give me something to put around me and another pillow. And — please don't waken Mother."

"Not me, miss," she said, and I caught her eye again. Incurable romantic that she was, she was almost palpitating with excitement.

That is how I learned of Herbert Dean's experience of the night before with the bird cage; and while less sinister than my own adventure, it had certain points of interest, to say the least.

After he had left me he had moved quietly along the grapevine path toward the Talbot stable. In the dark pullover sweater and dark trousers that he wore he was almost invisible, and his rubber-soled shoes made no sound whatever. He had gone perhaps half the way to the

Lancasters' when he thought he heard a door cautiously closing behind him, and he stopped and listened.

He heard nothing more, however, and so he went on. It was after twelve by that time, and the houses were dark save for the lights in Mr. Lancaster's room, and a low one in Margaret's across the hall.

He was almost stunned then when, about fifty teet from the woodshed he fairly collided with a man standing there.

"He leaped me," he said. "I was off guard, of course, and the two of us went down in a heap. I knew in a minute that he had a gun, but he couldn't use it; and I don't know exactly what would have happened if a policeman hadn't heard us and come on the run. Each of us had a death hold on the other, and then the officer pulled a flash and it was George Talbot."

"George Talbot!" I said faintly.

"George himself and no other. He'd been taking a regular round of the house and grounds, as he'd promised Margaret Lancaster. Luckily I'd had occasion to see him yesterday downtown, and he identified me to the guard so he wouldn't arrest me. Then we got up and I went on about my business. Or tried to."

All that had taken time, of course. The officer had never heard of Herbert Dean and was still suspicious, and George had lost a cuff-link in the scuffle which had to be found. In the end, however, they went their several ways, after perhaps ten minutes of delay, George back to the Lancasters', the officer apparently to the street, and he himself toward the Talbots' again.

The house itself was quiet and dark. He had an impression, however, of a light coming out of the stable; not a flashlight, but apparently matches. The light came, went out, then flared again.

"Either matches," he said, "or somebody shading a flash every minute or two."

The last two hundred feet he took on a run. Then he slowed down and slid around a corner to a window. There was no light inside the stable by that time, but there was

207

someone there, moving or trying to move something heavy.

"At least that's the way it sounded," he said.

He waited a moment, hoping that whoever it was would light a match or use a flash; but nothing of the sort happened, and so he began to work his way toward the door again.

He had not gone half the way before a hand caught him by the shoulder, and the same officer who had found him fighting with George had a death grip on his collar and was shoving a revolver into his back.

"Now," he said, "come along and no trouble."

"Get the hell out of here," Dean yelled, and made a break for the front of the garage. But he as too late. The officer caught him again at the corner of the building and neatly tripped and threw him, and there was a rush out of the garage door and then a complete silence.

"Get up, you murdering devil!" yelled the policeman, standing over him. And then he blew his whistle and all at once policemen of all sorts began to converge on the stable and the two of them there.

"There were six of them there in three minutes," he said rather wryly, "and when I gave them my name they didn't believe me. Well—!"

They took him into the Lancaster house finally, but they would not let him telephone. That was before Inspector Briggs had been called to our house, and he was still on duty when the call reached him.

"You have, eh? Where did you find him?"

"Outside the Talbot stable, sir."

"What was he doing there? What does he say?"

"He says he was after a bird cage, Inspector."

"A what?"

"A bird cage."

"Listen," roared the Inspector, "if you have a bird out there who thinks he's a canary, I want to see him. That's all."

So they held him for the Inspector to see; putting him into a chair in that library of Mr. Lancaster's while four of them stood around the room. They had locked out George Talbot and the nurse from upstairs, who had come running down; and although they had taken his automatic they jumped at him when he reached for his pipe.

And that was the situation when a police car screeched to a stop, and two men ran for our house while the Inspector panted into the Lancasters' and banged at the library door. When they opened it he stood staring.

"Where is he?"

"This is the man, sir."

And then Inspector blew up.

"Why, you blankety-blank sons of jackasses," he shouted. "That's Dean. I told you he was on this case. Is this a joke, or what the hell do you think you're doing?"

When, leaving an Inspector exhausted from sheer flow of vocabulary, the four of them accompanied Herbert Dean back to the stable they found the stable closed and the bird cage gone. Some time later we were to learn that it had been found lying in their back yard by a family on Euclid Street, and by them carefully washed and refurnished with a new canary. But when that discovery was made known it no longer mattered.

He told me a considerable amount that morning, while Mother slept and I ate the light breakfast I was permitted; although I know now that he told me only what he wanted me to know.

Thus, in spite of the Crescent's critical attitude toward them, the police were busy with the infinitely patient detail which only they could cover. They were handicapped, of course. By the very prominence and isolation of the Crescent, there was no chance to introduce the usual operatives to watch us. No window cleaners could be brought in; the Crescent washes its own windows and polishes them until they shine. No detectives driving taxi-cabs could sit at our curbstones, eyeing all who came and went. No house painters or roofers could work on adjacent buildings while watching us, and no agents or canvassers could pass our rightly locked front doors.

209

True, at noon on Monday an individual in the outfit of a city park employee had, for the first time in history, appeared with the proper tools in No Man's Land, and for the next three days raked, cut and burned while keeping a sharp watch on our comings and goings. And after Monday Daniels, our street cleaner, was superseded by a gimlet-eyed gentleman with a walrus mustache which Helen Wellington later claimed to have seen him drop and pick up hastily one day. But otherwise our policemen were frankly policemen. They came and went, or stood guard at night, uncamouflaged and known to most of us.

Their inquiries, however, had brought only negative results. Sunday had been a lost day, but in three days since Mrs. Lancaster's murder they had located neither the source of the lead weights in the chest nor the hiding place of the gold. It looked as though the weights had been bought a box at a time, the usual box containing only two pounds and thus the process necessarily continued over a long time.

Inquiry among the reputable locksmiths all over the city had discovered no one of them who had made a duplicate of the key to the chest, and although some of the banks were able to give the names of people who were hoarding gold in safe deposit boxes, in every case apparently their identity was known, and in most cases they were regular customers of the bank.

But Herbert did not tell me of the intensive examination of Mrs. Lancaster's bedroom, made the night before by the Inspector and himself after the bird cage incident. Or of the hour just at dawn when he himself had sat down by one of Daniel's old fires in No Man's Land and had patiently, inch by inch, gone over the ashes.

It was two weeks before he told me all this, and then only as a part of the summary of the case.

"The Inspector needed help by that time," he said, grinning reminiscently. "He knew me, of course; but this was a big case and he wanted it himself. Not only that. He was so sure of Jim at first that he couldn't see anything else, and I was Jim's man. That galled him, and he held out on me.

"Then things began to thicken up, and after Emily Lancaster was shot he sent for me to talk it over. I'd moved away from the Crescent, and he seemed to think I was going off the case. We didn't lay all our cards on the table. He held out about the Daltons, and I kept still about the two gloves, but outside of that we were like brothers!

"Then you get hit on the head, and that happens while he's got two men in sneakers watching the Dalton house and ready to swear that Bryan Dalton went to bed at eleven o'clock, and that not even the cat left the house after that. In the meantime he comes on a run to find the lunatic he's had in the back of his mind all along, and—well, I'm it! It was after that he offered me a free hand, and I took it."

The first result of this armistice, which took place that same night in the Talbot stable as a sort of neutral ground, was that Herbert Dean requested a chance to examine Mrs. Lancaster's bedroom; and that that be given him without the knowledge of the family.

"What's the use?" said the Inspector, "You don't know these people. That place has been scrubbed and polished until it's as pure as—as pure as—"

"The water which falls from some Alpine height?" Herbert suggested.

The Inspector glanced at him suspiciously.

"It's clean, I'm telling you. Floors scrubbed, pictures wiped, fresh curtians. I'm telling you;. You'll not find anything there."

"I know all that. I've seen it once, but I hadn't much time."

"Oh! You've seen it? When?"

"On Sunday morning," said Herbert pleasantly. "It looked extremely clean then, but you never can tell."

The Inspector was rather silent after that. They got to the Lancaster house and saw George Talbot asleep on the library couch, with his automatic on the floor beside him. They wakened him finally by rapping on the window, for

Herbert Dean was firm about not ringing the bell. Once inside the house, however, the problem was not solved.

"What about the nurse?" George said. "She's settled in the hall up there. She's probably asleep, but she may not stay asleep. What's the idea anyhow?"

"Why not ask her down? Tell her you're lonely?" Herbert asked.

"I've tried that. She's not having any," said George gloomily.

"Well, make some coffee. She probably has *one* vice."

In the end that is what they did; and at something after two o'clock that morning Herbert and the Inspector got into Mrs. Lancaster's room; while George, who had relieved the nurse in the hall, stood guard at the head of the stairs.

Chapter XXVI

It must have been an odd performance, all in all. For I believe Herbert took at first only a casual glance at the room, and then immediately got down on his stomach and wriggled under the bed. The chest had not been replaced, and with his searchlight he examined every inch of the under-side of the bed, including the box mattress.

All this was in silence, with the Inspector watching him and half-amused.

As I have said before, Mrs. Lancaster's bed stood with its head toward her husband's room behind it, and she had been found lying on the side toward the door into the hall. This was her customary place in it. Beyond the closet door stood a small chest of drawers, and it was to this corner, between the bed and the door to the hall, that Herbert Dean practically confined his activities that night.

From the bed he moved to the bed table beside it and followed much the same procedure there. The chest of drawers he examined, not only from beneath, but by pulling out each drawer and minutely inspecting its edges. And at last he took down a picture or two from the wall.

"Has it ever struck you," he asked the Inspector, "that she may not have been in the bed when she was killed?"

"How the devil could she get out of it?"

"I'm leaving that to you. I'd say at a guess that she was

213

standing in front of this chest when the first blow was struck, and that the others followed after she fell to the floor. It's hard to explain blood on the under-side of the box springs in any other way, Inspector, and it's there. It's under the bottom of this chest too, and under the edge of the top drawer."

"The woman couldn't walk. Hadn't walked for years."

"I wouldn't be too sure of that."

"Listen, Dean," said the Inspector. "I'm not saying you don't know your stuff. You do. But I'll put this to you. She was back in bed all right when she was found. Remember, I'm taking your word now for this idea of yours. I'll go as far as to say that she didn't weigh a whole lot, and she could have been lifted back easily enough. But I'm saying this too; that wasn't done without leaving any marks. I'll go so far as to say that whoever did it would have been smeared with blood from head to foot. It isn't pleasant but it's a fact."

Herbert agreed grimly.

"I've never doubted that, myself. Of course blood washes off."

The Inspector eyed him.

"What do you mean by that? We examined every inch of this house, and if anyone left it in that condition he wouldn't have got a hundred yards. Unless — look here, Dean." He lowered his voice. "I suppose somebody in this house could have stripped mother-naked and done it? This Margaret — by the Lord Harry, Dean! She was taking a shower when the other one called her!"

"Getting ready to take a shower. That's not quite the same thing."

"We've only her word for that, and I haven't been any too sure of her right along."

And then and there, and with some considerable excitement, he told Herbert Dean of the Daltons' strange excursion to the woodshed that Thursday night, and of the anonymous letter.

"There's your motive," he finished triumphantly. "She and Dalton were about to hop it, and of course they needed money. Probably Emily knew or suspected, and so she had to be put out of the way. It even explains the axe. She could get it in any night and nobody would be the wiser."

"Precisely," said Herbert. "That's one of the reasons why I

know she didn't do it. You see, the axe wasn't brought in that way, Inspector. It was tied to a cord and brought in through an upper window. I'll not explain that now, but you can take it as a fact."

"The hell you say!"

"And before anyone does any more cleaning around here," Herbert added smoothly, "I'd see if there's print on that bell over the bed, and compare it with the ones on top of the chest. I think you'll find them the same."

"And I suppose you know that, too!"

"I can only guess. I think you'll find that both are Mrs. Lancaster's."

It was then that George Talbot tapped warningly at the door, and the two men slipped down the back staircase as the nurse came up by the main one.

The Inspector was upset and uncomfortable. The two men had some coffee in the kitchen, but he was taciturn and annoyed. He asked only one question, and he brought that out of a brooding silence.

"Then where is the bird cage in all this?" he inquired. "And what's the big idea as to Louisa Hall next door? Why try to bump her off? What's more, how? I've got two operatives on the Dalton house next door; good men too, and they don't see or hear a thing until she screams. It isn't natural, Dean."

"It's not so hard, Inspector. Take someone who knows every foot of these grounds and every house, as all these people do, and it's not as difficult as it sounds."

"But the Hall house was locked too. The mother states that positively. She went over it herself."

"Not all night. The kitchen door was open for an hour or so, earlier in the night."

The Inspector actually dropped his cup.

"How do *you* know a thing like that?"

"I watched Lou Hall open it." And although he explained, the Inspector continued to eye him grimly.

"Damn it all, Dean," he said at last, "I believe in my soul that you're the criminal yourself!"

It was four in the morning when he finally departed in the police car which, with its uniformed driver, had been waiting patiently all the time. And at a quarter to five any interested observer could have seen a tall man in dark trousers, sneakers and a pull-over sweater, sitting in the August dawn beside a pile of ashes out in No Man's Land, and carefully combing them over with his fingers.

By six o'clock he had finished. No one was about except the operative at the rear of the Dalton house, who was watching him with fascinated interest. The tall man got up, stuck an old envelope into his trousers pocket, and carrying something warily in his hand, padded on noiseless feet to the Wellington house.

There I believe he roused a sleepy butler and was admitted. His coat and hat were there in the hall, but he did not take them. Instead he went to the lavatory off the lower hall.

"Got plenty of hot water?" he asked.

"I think so, sir. There's an automatic heater."

"Good. Then I'll need a sieve, if you have one, and — What's your name?"

"John, sir."

"I'll need two flat pieces of glass, John. Window glass. Know of any about?"

And it speaks well either for John's training or for certain private instructions that he never turned a hair.

"I'm new to the house, sir. But I dare say one could break a basement window."

"One could, and one might as well hurry and do it."

He went away, with only the faintest flicker of a glance at what lay in Herbert Dean's palm, and in five minutes he was back with a wire sieve and two flat pieces of glass.

"Afraid they're rather irregular," he apologized.

"Well, breaking a window is irregular too, John. And I'm not doing this for looks."

The thing he was doing, it appeared, was to place very carefully in the sieve a small charred piece of heavy paper, badly curled and black. After that he turned on the hot water and held the sieve in the steam; held it until the butler offered to relieve him. But he shook his head.

"Hold one of those pieces of glass," he said. "I'll be ready to dump it soon."

And John held it, much as he would hold a card tray at the front door. It is, I think, like the bird cage incident, one of the few light notes in all that grisly business of ours, that picture of the two men in that lavatory, the one dirty and unkempt, the other in an old dressing gown, and both enveloped in a cloud of steam while one of them held a sieve and the other the glass from a broken window.

"What do you think it is, John?"

"Perhaps they'll be able to say at the laboratory, sir."

Herbert Dean glanced up quickly, but the man's face was as impassive as ever.

"Headquarters?" he asked quietly.

"Yes. The Inspector got me the job, Mr. Dean. I'd be glad if you kept it to yourself. I do a good bit of inside work of this sort."

"All right. Now I'm ready."

And that was how Herbert Dean after a bath, shave and breakfast, turned up rather early in the morning at a downtown laboratory with a piece of heavy charred paper, still bearing along one edge a bit of dingy gilt and securely fastened between two plates of ragged window glass; and also with an envelope containing eight discolored buttons, each with a miniature automobile stamped on it, and a bit of flower or plant stem, an inch or so long.

He was indeed probably leaning over a microscope in that same laboratory when, at a quarter to nine that Tuesday morning, George Talbot was taken to police headquarters for interrogation as to the murder of Emily Lancaster.

Chapter XXVII

So quietly had this been done that even Herbert Dean had not known it when he had made that visit to me between ten and eleven o'clock of that day.

It was Jim Wellington who came bursting in to tell me at noon, fortunately finding Mother at the Lancasters' again and myself up and in a chair. But he wasted no time on polite inquiries.

"Look here," he said. "Where's Dean? We've got to locate him."

"Why? Is there anything new?"

"New? They've arrested George Talbot for killing Emily Lancaster. That's new, isn't it? And the devil is that they've got it on him. The bullet that killed Emily fits his gun. And when I say fits it, I mean fits it; scratches and all."

He was almost inarticulate with fear for George and anger as to the whole situation, but at last I got the story pretty much as I know it now.

Early that morning there had appeared at Headquarters a rather frightened negro woman, the Talbots' Amanda, accompanied by a pompous black man who was her husband; and prompted by him Amanda had told when and where she had found the empty shell in the Talbots' drying yard.

The Inspector after his long night was still at home and in

bed, but Mr. Sullivan was there and heard the story. He let the negroes go but kept the shell, and he apparently sat back and thought about it for some time. Before him on his desk was the report of that scuffle on the grapevine path between Herbert Dean and George the night before, and also of the incident of the stable later on. It seemed to him, and he has repeated this since, that things in general, including Emily Lancaster's murder, had rather shifted toward the Talbot end of the Crescent, so at last he got a car and drove out there.

George had a forty-five; he knew that. Not only that. George had acknowledged being outside the night of the shooting, and having had to be admitted to the house later on. The more he thought it over the less Sullivan liked it, or the better; I suppose it depends on the point of view. But he had no intention of arresting George Talbot at that time.

He had taken a uniformed man with him and they found George, grumpy after an almost sleepless night, in the stable and ready to get out of his ancient car. Rather apologetically they asked if they might see his gun.

"What for?" he demanded. "Am I under suspicion now? You seem to have tried everyone else."

"Not at all, but you understand that there is a routine to all this. We're checking all the guns in the vicinity."

That seemed to satisfy him, for he produced it at once from the pocket of the car. He was not particularly gracious about it, however.

"It's such damned nonsense," he complained. "I sit up all night and lose my sleep to protect the Lancaster house with that gun, and now I'm a suspect myself. I've got a permit, by the way. Do you want that?"

He seemed astounded when they did, but he produced it and they checked the number on it, which was correct. Certainly it was his own gun.

"I've cleaned it recently," he said. "Yesterday evening, as a matter of fact. I knew I was taking it with me last night."

"And when did you fire it last?" Sullivan asked him. But he could not remember. In the spring, he thought, or early summer, at a picnic. They had been shooting at empty bottles.

He was rather affronted than alarmed apparently when they took it away with them. After all, he had been up most of the night and was generally disgruntled anyhow. But in less than an hour he was at Police Headquarters. Examination had showed that bullets fired from his gun corresponded exactly under the microscope with the one which had killed Miss Emily.

Confronted with this fact, even shown the pictures, greatly enlarged, he either maintained a stubborn silence or reiterated his earlier story. He had slept with the gun under his pillow ever since Mrs. Lancaster was killed. He had put on the safety catch and crawled out the window with it in his hand. He had not fired it at all; had had no reason to fire it.

What was more, no one else had fired it. It had never left his possession. Since the Thursday before he had slept on it at night and carried it with him by day.

On the night before, knowing he was to spend the night as he had, he had taken it entirely apart, had taken out the barrel and the spring, had oiled and rubbed it and then reloaded it.

"Why would I keep it, if I'd killed poor old Emily?" he demanded. "Don't you suppose I know that every gun puts its mark on a bullet? I'm not a fool."

"Then you ought to know that these marks are identical."

They showed him the enlargements of photographs, but he only shook his head.

"That's your business," he said. "Mine's to get out of here with a whole skin. But don't fool yourselves that anybody else has had that gun of mine. If you think that you don't know our house. We're not only locked up against the world. We're locked up against each other!"

That was the best they could do. They held him all day and well into the night, and then they had to let him go home. They let him go because there were some things they could not understand about the automatic; especially about that empty shell of Amanda's. I am no expert in ballistics, but I believe it had to do with a firing pin. There was some microscopic deviation there, but small as it was it released George.

He was not free, of course. Thereafter, and until our third

mystery was solved, I was more than once to meet George walking briskly along with a detective following at a discreet distance; and to have George say:

"Just taking him around the block before I turn in. I've offered to put him on a leash, but he doesn't fancy the idea."

It must have been about the time in our reign of terror that the Commissioner of Police sent for Inspector Briggs and asked him ironically if he would like to take over the public library on Liberty Avenue as headquarters for the men on the case.

It was after luncheon on that same Tuesday that Mrs. Talbot and Lydia heard the news of George's arrest, and they reacted in characteristic fashion. Mrs. Talbot at once called a taxi and fairly took Police Headquarters by assault.

"Where is my son?" she boomed. "Get out of my way, young man. My son is being illegally detained, and I'll get him out of here if I have to engage every lawyer in this town."

Lydia, indignant and frightened as well as agonized at being left behind, came in to see me.

"Of course he didn't do it," she said sitting as usual bolt upright on the edge of her chair. "Why should he? Anyhow I heard him getting out onto that shed roof, and there was no shot fired after that."

"You should tell them that, Miss Lydia," I said.

"I'll tell them when they ask me."

If she was alarmed for George, she was also highly curious about my own adventure. I had to sit and wait while she went back to look over the scene of it, and I can still see her after she came back, prim and late-Victorian on the edge of her chair, opening that bead bag of hers and taking out the clippings from the morning papers and giving them to me to read.

"I have kept them all," she said. "I'm pasting them into a book, but I haven't told Hester. It's surprising, Louisa, how many there are."

Strange, that casual little speech of hers, when I am writing this story largely from that very book, so neat and yet so lurid.

She did not stay long. She wandered into Mother's room to see if a camera man who had been hidden in the bushes all morning was still there, and on discovering that he had gone she went away.

"I sent Lizzie out to drive him off," she said, preparing to go. "But he only offered her ten dollars if she could get you to the front porch with a bandage on your head. Or he said a towel would do!"

I rather affronted her by laughing at this, and finally she went away. I remember watching her go out the door, and smiling at the butterfly hatpin in her hat. It was set on a bit of coiled wire so that the insect took on a curious activity as she walked, jerking and glittering uncannily. There was certainly nothing that morning to tell me that the time was near at hand when I was to see that same butterfly trampled into the ground; or that Lydia Talbot herself was soon to be added to our list of tragic mysteries.

I was much stronger that afternoon, and after she left Annie helped me into a dressing gown and put me into a chair. Mother, who had escaped the moment she saw Lydia, was still at the Lancaster house; for Margaret had had to go to the inquest over poor Emily, and somebody had to stay in the house.

It was still, incredible as it seems to me now, only Tuesday. The smell of hot irons on wet linen penetrated to my room, and now and then far off I could hear the thud of one as our own black Lily thumped it on the stove. All along the Crescent, though death and trouble seemed everywhere, the same process was going on. Dark hands were taking dampened rolls of this or that from our baskets, spreading them on tables and boards and ironing them. On clothes horses the finished products were hung to dry, and then folded down into their various hampers. Ruffles were fluted with fluting irons, and old damask carefully polished until it shone.

Yet the situation that Tuesday afternoon was strange enough, what with suspicion suddenly shifting from Jim to George Talbot; with reporters ringing our doorbell; with Mr. Lancaster slowly sinking in the white house across from my windows; with poor Emily still lying on a slab in the morgue, and nothing so far discovered as to the hiding place of the stolen gold.

Of actual physical clues, in the sense of something material, there were still only a half dozen. The police, so far as I can recall now, had only the series of photographs taken after each of the crimes; a number of fingerprints on cards, each card carefully marked; an automatic pistol, an empty shell and a bullet; the chest under the bed, and George Talbot! Somewhere put away they probably had those stained clothes of Jim Wellington's, but I do not know. Also I dare say they still had those ridiculous and now withered blades of grass from the porch roof, but the sliver of wood from the screen I know had been mounted on a card and carefully kept.

I know that because after the whole thing was over the Inspector presented it to me!

They did not have the bit of stem which had been found in our hall, however. That the Commissioner of Police had gravely handed to Herbert Dean.

"Briggs here seems to think I need a salad!" he said. "He'll be bringing me a rose geranium leaf next and asking me to smell it! Maybe you can find out what that stuff is, Dean. Not that I think it matters, but — well, take it along if you like."

However, the police added another clue that Tuesday, and then sat around a desk at Headquarters and wondered just where it left them. That was the magnified photograph of a fingerprint from the bell which hung over Mrs. Lancaster's bed, presumably hers, and beside it another one, of the thumbprint from the chest which had contained the money. There was no question but that they were the prints of the same thumb, and I believe the District Attorney sent for the Inspector on the strength of his discovery and told him he was the only man on the job worth a hill of beans.

"Good work, Briggs," he said. "Now I suppose we have to guess whether the money was taken out of the chest by the old lady and hidden somewhere; or whether she found out it had been taken and was killed before she could make a fuss. No chance it's still in the house, I suppose?"

"Not a chance, unless someone there is smarter than I think."

Nevertheless, I believe they made another intensive search of the house that day, rapping walls and even examining the chimneys and the roof. But they found nothing whatever.

"And of course, Miss Lou," the Inspector told me later, "it was still only a presumption that those prints were the old lady's anyhow. The whole thing was guesswork, and how could we prove it? We didn't like to ask for an exhumation order; the family would never have given it. And under the circumstances we hadn't printed her before she was buried."

Herbert Dean had one or two bits of evidence which he had not given to the police, however. Among these were the gloves, a short piece of hemp cord, and the buttons and charred paper from the fire in No Man's Land. Also he now had the stem of the unidentified plant, over which that same day the botanical department of our local university was working. But he also had, carefully stowed away, the end of a rather expensive cigar, flattened as though it had been trampled into the ground.

These — "and an idea" — he says, were his total equipment up to four o'clock that day when, Mother still at the Lancaster house, Laura Dalton rang our doorbell, pushed Annie aside, walked deliberately up the stairs and into my bedroom, and locked the door behind her.

Chapter XXVIII

I have thought a great deal about Laura Dalton since that day. In the Crescent her position was somewhat isolated; not because she did not belong, for she had been born there. But as Herbert says, she was suspended like Mahomet's coffin, between heaven and earth. She was too young for that close triumvirate which had consisted of Mother, Mrs. Lancaster and Hester Talbot, and her marriage had placed an unbridgeable gulf between the local spinsters and herself.

Doctor Armstrong, calling that morning to look me over, had expressed some anxiety about her.

"It's the wrong time of life for her to go through all this," he said. "Head looks all right to me, Lou; you can go down to dinner if you feel up to it. But I'd be glad if you could talk to her a little. She's got something on her mind. She's still pretty much in love with Bryan, you know, and I imagine she's got some sort of bee in her bonnet about him." He went into the bathroom, washed his hands carefully and came back still holding the towel.

"I suppose people make their own hell in this world," he went on. "They're fond of each other, you know; probably a good bit more than that. But they're both stubborn. It's twenty years since she locked her door against him for some peccadillo or other, and I haven't a doubt myself that there have been a good many times since when she's unlocked it; and others when he had brought himself to try it, and had to go away. Pitiful, isn't it, with life so short!"

All that was in my mind that afternoon when Laura Dalton walked into my room and locked the door behind her. I can see her now, in her pale lavender summer silk, her too-youthful hat sitting high on her head, and under it a pair of devastated eyes and a mouth that twitched with nerves.

She did not even explain that locking of the door. She moved directly across the room and stood over me, and for a moment I was startled. She did not look quite sane. She wasted no time in preliminaries.

"Is it true," she demanded, "that they have arrested George Talbot?"

"I don't know about an arrest. They have taken him to Headquarters."

"The fools. The fools!" she broke out. "Listen, Louisa, George never killed Emily Lancaster, or her mother either. I know that. But I can't tell the police. I can't. I *can't.*"

It was some time before I could quiet her, and at first I did not realize what she was trying to tell me. It was only after a full half hour, while I listened to the bottled-up miseries of a jealous and suspicious woman, still passionately in love with her husband and now terrified beyond all control, that I knew that Mrs. Dalton believed that her husband, with the assistance of Margaret Lancaster, had killed both Margaret's mother, and her sister!"

Stripped of inessentials, her narrative ran something like this:

Years ago, Margaret Lancaster had been engaged to Bryan Dalton. He did not live on the Crescent then; but he used to come in his high trap and take Margaret for drives. Mrs. Lancaster had opposed the match, however.

"She didn't like Bryan," was what she said. "And when Margaret insisted on marrying him anyhow she simply went to bed for six months. I was very young then," she added quickly, "but my father had built here where we are now, and I can remember my own mother saying that Mrs. Lancaster

226

had gone to bed because it was the one way she could keep Margaret at home."

Then one day Bryan asked *her* to drive with him, and after that they became engaged and were married. "And I had the house by that time," she said, "so he came to live on the Crescent, although it wasn't the Crescent then. It was just country, and he never really liked it."

It was to that, his boredom and his revolt against the Crescent, that she laid his unfaithfulness. There had been somebody else, as she put it, every now and then since. And for the past few months it had been Margaret Lancaster again.

She was, I thought, trying to explain something to herself rather than to me, for all this came out only by degrees. She would stop, stretch the fingers of the gloves on her lap and start again, as though by going over the whole business and trying to coordinate it for me, she was trying to follow the steps by which she had come to her tragic conviction.

"I thought it was all over," she said. "I still can't see — I think she led him on, Louisa; for her own purposes. He hadn't been faithful. We separated years ago over a maid in my own house. But after all a man of fifty — well, I thought all that was over. I suppose," she added doubtfully, "that I shouldn't be telling you all this, Louisa. You're still a young woman."

"I'm twenty-eight," I said briefly. "I don't think you're telling me much I don't know. I can't believe what you are telling me about Margaret Lancaster. That's all."

I was, however, uneasily remembering that anonymous letter sent to the police, and I felt that my voice lacked conviction. If it did she did not notice.

"It's true," she asserted. "I don't know how far it's gone, but she's smart and not bad-looking; and after all the time comes when any man has to learn that young women aren't interested in him."

There was apparently no mistake about the situation. He had even taken Margaret out driving, meeting her some place downtown; that was early in August, and once she had found Margaret's bag in the car. It had slipped down beside a seat cushion, and she had given it to her husband without speak-

227

ing. He had simply shrugged his shoulders and taken it. But she had no other proof. She had set herself to watch, but so far as she could tell no letters passed between them. She believed now that they had; that they had used the woodshed on the Lancaster place as a sort of post office.

The affair, so far as she knew, had commenced late in June or early in July.

Then abruptly she went on to the day of Mrs. Lancaster's murder.

"Bryan was in the garage," she said. "He had put on a pair of old overalls, and I was at a window at the back of the house upstairs. I wasn't watching him," she added. "I was measuring a window for new curtains. And at half past three I saw him, in his overalls, go toward the Lancaster woodshed. I could not see him all the way, of course. The path curves, and you know how the shrubbery has grown. But I was curious and I waited. And he didn't come back *until a quarter after four.*"

She began to cry again, and I saw that she was trembling violently.

"Look here," I said, "haven't you just worked yourself into a state of nerves over all this? Suppose he was near the Lancaster house at that time? How could he get in? And why in heaven's name would he want to get in? It all sounds rather silly to me."

"It won't sound so silly when I've finished, Louisa," she said with a return of her dignity. "I'm not an utter fool. Perhaps I would be a happier woman if I were!"

I was inclined to agree with her as she went on; for she did go on. What she believed was that for a long time Margaret had been taking gold from the chest under the bed, either with a duplicate key or by securing at night the one from her mother's neck. That she had carried it out of the house, a little at a time, and hidden it; and that all of this was known to Bryan Dalton. That it was in effect a part of their plan to run away and live together somewhere, probably in Europe or South America.

"You see," she said, as though the entire Crescent did not know it, "I have the money. Bryan has very little of his own."

Then, on the day Margaret had telephoned Jim Wellington

228

that her father wanted an audit and to examine the chest, they had both known the game was up.

"He might have found a note in the woodshed, telling him," she said. "And of course there was the axe, right there in plain sight. I know it sounds crazy, but wait, Louisa. How do we know he didn't slip around the house, and Margaret admit him by the front door?"

I am afraid I shivered, for she said then that she should not have come to me after my own dreadful adventure; but that she was simply desperate.

"I can't let them hold George Talbot," she wailed.

"Listen, Mrs. Dalton. Do you think Bryan Dalton shot Emily Lancaster, or did this to me last night? Because I don't."

"God forgive me, Lou! I don't know."

"Well, I do know," I told her. "He never left the house last night. They had two men watching it."

I remember that she got up then, her face colorless and still twitching.

"Then they suspect him! What am I to do, Lou? What am I to do? For he's guilty, Lou. He must be, or why did she give him that note last night to burn his overalls? He did burn them, last Thursday night. There was a fire still going out there and they disappeared. What else could he have done with them?"

I was too stunned to speak.

"And why, when he heard Emily run out screaming, didn't he go to her? He must have been near enough to hear her. Who could help it? And why did he come into the house from the garage after he took off his overalls and tell Joseph to get him some whisky? In thirty years I've never known him to take a drink before dinner. I tell you, Louisa, Bryan Dalton knew that afternoon that Mrs. Lancaster had been murdered; for all his asking Joseph to tell me that night, as though he had just read it in the newspaper."

When he came back into the house that afternoon she had been quietly drinking her iced tea, and he never knew she had seen him. But of course she still knew nothing of the murder. She was still without suspicion that evening, in the library after dinner. He had looked very strange when he called

Joseph, however. She remembered that later on when they had reached the Lancaster house. They did not enter it together. Bryan rang the front doorbell. She herself had gone around and in by the kitchen, fully aware that the servants would be more talkative than the family. It was still only a crime to her, bad as it was.

But on emerging from the service wing into the side hall, she had seen her husband and Margaret together for a second near the foot of the front stairs. The Talbots were there also, but she had seen Margaret slip a note into Bryan's hand, and he had slid it into his pocket. She was fishing in her hand-bag while she was telling me this, and I do not even now know how or when she had got it from him later on. She passed it to me, and I must say my flesh crept when I read it. It was in Margaret's clear strong hand.

"Please burn all letters at once, and destroy what I gave you this afternoon. M."

Just how she got possession of that note I do not know, nor did she say. He had no idea that she knew he had it, and certainly she got it. But after that, I imagine, all hell must have broken loose in the house when she read it. To her, then, and since, it had meant only one thing: that Margaret and Bryan Dalton had killed Mrs. Lancaster as a preliminary to a flight together, and that the crime was the result of a plot long concocted and carefully carried out.

For she had never found the overalls.

That night, Thursday, she had searched for them, and for any letters from Margaret. He had discovered what she was doing and had tried to stop her, but she was like a crazy woman. There was no sign that he had burned anything in any of the fireplaces, or in the furnace either. But of course that idiot Daniels had had his usual fire in No Man's Land, and during that three or four hours in the afternoon after the murder he could easily have walked out and dropped something there. Nobody would have been likely to notice. Or maybe he did it at night. She did not know.

That was the story Laura Dalton told me the Tuesday afternoon after our two murders; stripping away for once the hypocrisies and traditional reticences of the Crescent and revealing a naked and suffering soul. She had done it with a certain amount of dignity at that, save for one or two outbursts; stretching and pulling at her gloves, keeping her voice down, and even — heaven help us! — once settling her skirt so that it hung at the correct length about her ankles.

All I could do was to make her promise that she would not go to the police for a day or so at least; and at last she drew on her gloves, straightened her hat, and went away with that odd self-possession which seems to characterize all the older women of the Crescent. Time takes its toll of them, death and tragedy come inevitably, but they face the world with quiet faces and unbroken dignity.

I even heard her thanking Annie as she let her out the front door.

Chapter XXIX

I had another visitor that afternoon; Helen Wellington looking, I thought, rather edgy, but determinedly cheerful. She came in, demanding Herbert Dean, and seemed to think I might have him somewhere in a closet.

"I thought he'd be here," she said. "He seems to spend a lot of time hanging about this place! Either he's fallen for you or he suspects you; you never can tell with him. Love or business, he's equally secretive about both."

She inspected me carefully, including my rising color.

"I hope it's love, of course," she went on. "I'd just as soon see you out of my way, Lou! Every time Jim and I have a fuss he spends hours secretly convinced that I'm the Big Mistake and lamenting that he missed out with you."

"Don't be so foolish, Helen."

"Oh, I'm not foolish. After he has been noble and taken me back I spend hours too, telling him how interesting I make life and how you would have bored him. But it's a fixed idea. However, don't bother about that. I want to wash my hands, and after that I want to choke Bertie Dean with them. Do you know that I've spent the afternoon in the public library? Believe it or not!"

She did not explain at once. From the bathroom she kept up a running fire of talk; my own injury, the bombshell she had

232

thrown the night before "if anyone is going to abuse Jim I'll do it myself" — and George Talbot's detention.

"They've been all around the mulberry bush," was her comment, "and I dare say they'll be back to us now. I haven't a doubt myself but that your mother did it. They've suspected everybody else."

It was characteristic of her to return from the bathroom carrying both a bottle of hand lotion and a towel; and that she immediately spilled the one on the carpet and mopped it up with the other. But it is also characteristic that just then Annie came up with an enormous bunch of expensive roses which Helen had brought in with her.

"Don't thank me," she said. "They're simply an expression of relief. Failing with my little poker last night, I now hope that Bertie Dean may carry you off out of sheer anxiety for your safety! Lou, why do you suppose he sent me to the library today? I'll give you three guesses, and don't guess a book. He knows me better than that."

When she finally dropped her bantering air, it was to reveal that her errand had been to look over old files of the local newspapers; not so old, really, but from the first of March to the first of August, and to look in the proper section for someone either advertising for a room in our vicinity, the reply to be sent in care of general delivery; or for a room advertised to let, furnished.

"Although just why anybody would come voluntarily into this vicinity is a mystery to me," she finished. "There you are. That's what he wanted, and I never suspected that anywhere in the world there were so many bright, attractive rooms, 'nicely furnished, run. water, use parlor, rent reasonable.' "

She had eight in all, copied out in her square modern script, and she laid them on my lap. Only one of them concerned a room in our immediate vicinity, and I could not see how it could possibly have any bearing on our situation. I read it over twice:

"Wanted: By trained nurse, furnished room near General Hospital. Must have telephone in house."

"I can't see how that could mean anything," I said.

"No? Then you don't know our Bertie. If you did you would realize that our murderer, masquerading as a lady, has probably been living in that room and stroking fevered brows between crimes, so to speak. The telephone, of course, is pure camouflage! Well, I've done my job. I have to save my man; he's a poor thing but mine own. And now I'm going home to take a bath."

Writing this record and piecing together from this and that the whole story of our crimes, I have often thought of that visit of Helen's and wondered exactly what would have happened had those angular notes of hers reached Herbert Dean and the police in time. But they did not. She was cheerful enough when she left me, apparently even gay. I heard her whistling as she went down the street, a gesture of bravado with which she often shocked the Crescent. She was fighting Jim's fight for him with a certain gallantry, as witness the night before.

Yet she and Jim quarreled again that afternoon, and I think there is no question but that the two deaths which followed were due entirely to that. Possibly she knows it; it is a different Helen who now lives in the house nearest to the Crescent gate. She still swaggers, but the old casual careless ways are gone.

Even John, that suave and impassive police agent who was in the Wellington house as a butler, did not know what it was about. Although he was certainly suspicious; and I have never held Jim guiltless. He was in a bad state of nerves, irascible and impatient, and Helen was not a person to stand for either.

However that may be, at seven o'clock when Annie brought up my supper tray she was pop-eyed with information.

"Mrs. Wellington's gone again, miss."

"Gone? Gone where?"

"That I can't say, miss. I believe they had a few words, and she just called a taxicab and went away in it. I must say it's a poor time to leave Mr. Jim, with him needing all the comfort he can get."

All of which, as I have said, is not important. What was vitally important was that she carried away with her in her hand-bag those notes made at the library, and that she did not

234

go to her usual hotel. When she was finally located — she really located herself — she still had the notes in her bag, having forgotten them completely; but they were useless then.

I have wondered since what would have happened, or not happened, had Helen gone to the police that day with what she knew. The notes in her bag and her story of that Sunday night. But she did not. She was frightened, like all the rest of us.

Would we have seen it all? Perhaps it was not possible even then, although Herbert Dean came closer than any of us to guessing the truth. But as Doctor Armstrong said afterwards:

"Upon my word, Lou, if everyone on the Crescent had had a dose of some drug like hyoscine, and been so released from all his normal repressions that he'd had to tell the truth, we'd have saved some of these people. Not hyoscine perhaps; it causes fantasy; but something to put the brain censors to sleep. All we needed was a little openness, but everybody was afraid."

Which was true enough, for it was not until that evening, Tuesday, that I learned that Peggy from the Lancasters' had had her purse snatched from her in No Man's Land on Sunday night; and had been so terrified to report it for fear of some reprisal that even our servants did not know it for a day or two. Here too Annie was my source of information. She came up to turn down my bed that night, and her mouth was set hard and tight. She had just heard the news, from Peggy herself.

"She's a little fool, and I've told her so," she said. "Because, Miss Lou, whatever these police may think — and so far as I can see their thinking isn't getting them anywhere anyhow — the whole thing ain't what you'd call natural. Why did he bring the purse back? If that isn't the act of a lunatic, what is?"

And Peggy's story as related by Annie had indeed an unusual element.

She had been at home that evening; she lived somewhere in the neighborhood. And as she had been late, which is a grave offense with us, she had taken the short cut across No Man's Land. In the woodland behind the Wellingtons', where the

235

path is shady for two hundred feet or so, she had suddenly seen a man emerge from the shadows and come toward her.

She was startled and stopped dead, but the man said: "Don't be afraid, please. I have no idea of hurting you. But I want that bag."

She gave it to him. He wore a soft hat pulled down on his head and she thought a pull-on sweater, one of those with a high rolling collar which covered the lower part of his face. But he made no effort to attack her, and perhaps the most unusual thing about it was that he thanked her when she gave him the bag.

He took it and moved quickly back among the trees, and Peggy ran as fast as she could to the Lancasters'. She had been in a bad state when Ellen let her in, but she had only said that she had hurried and that she had lost her bag while running.

"And the next morning," said Annie with unction, "when Ellen opened the porch door to get the milk, there was that bag hanging on the doorknob. All her money in it, too! If that's not the act of a lunatic, then I'm crazy myself."

I did not tell Mother. She was sufficiently uneasy as things were, and I gathered that she had demanded a police guard for our house that night. Which was perhaps the time when the Commissioner sent for Inspector Briggs and asked him if he would like the library on Liberty Avenue as headquarters for his operatives on the case! Or—I believe he added—should he wire the governor to send the National Guard!

Mother was very silent that night. Conditions in the house next door were simply lamentable. Mr. Lancaster had not spoken since Sunday night and was slowly sinking, and Margaret was a ghost. She did not eat or sleep, and she scarcely spoke.

"Really," Mother said, "I don't understand her, Louisa. She will hardly go into her stepfather's room! I relieved the nurse for sleep this afternoon, and Jennie did it yesterday. Yet she has always been devoted to him. She is not like herself at all."

The verdict of the inquest over Emily had been much the same as that over her mother. It had not taken long, and the funeral was to be the next day. Margaret had returned from

236

the inquest only to shut herself in her room, and Mother had not seen her again.

I watched Mother as she talked. She was excited and unusually loquacious, but in spite of all that had happened I came definitely to the conclusion that night that Mother had shown a certain relief ever since Emily Lancaster's death. It was much the same as she had shown that day when she had sent for Mrs. Talbot. She was bitterly sorry for Emily, but it was as though some doubt in her mind, some suspicion, had been definitely allayed by it.

It was that night that George Talbot was released on bail as a material witness. The ballistics expert of the Department was, I believe, still firing test bullets out of George's automatic and examining the results under a microscope, for late that night he telephoned in to Headquarters a rather surprising report. George was on his way home by that time, angry and bewildered as well as more than a little frightened; and it was several days before he knew anything at all about that report.

"I'm not committing myself yet," said the expert cautiously, "but what it looks like to me is that somebody has switched the barrels of two pistols. Mind you, that's only a theory so far. The bullet that killed Emily Lancaster came out of this barrel. That's certain. But I'm not sure it was fired out of this gun."

Chapter XXX

That was on Tuesday night.

Perhaps I have said too little so far about the effect on our community of our two murders. That belongs here, for it directly affected our situation and what was to develop out of it. Because of it the local hardware dealers were busy selling extra bolts and locks, and also chains for entrance doors; and because one woman in our vicinity had bought such a chain for her front door, that Wednesday found us at the beginning of a new mystery and another tragedy.

The reign of terror, as the press called it, was never limited to the Crescent. The public was convinced from the start that a homicidal maniac was loose in that part of the city, although statements from the nearby State Hospital for the Criminal Insane had shown not only that no such patient had recently escaped, but also that an hour-by-hour check was made of all patients and all attendants.

The rumor persisted, however, and the killing of Emily Lancaster, apparently as motiveless as that of her mother, served to magnify it. Our delivery boys ran in with their parcels of meat or groceries and got away as fast as they could. No children slipped into No Man's Land to play, and many of them were escorted to school and back again. Servants in the early morning peered out of windows before opening kitchen doors to take in the milk. There were no curious crowds watching from beyond our gates; and at night those people who were compelled to pass the Crescent on Liberty Avenue chose, not the long area bounded by the Wellington and Talbot hedges, but the other side of the street.

To all this had now been added the attack on me. One tabloid came out with the statement that there had been thirteen people on the Crescent at the beginning of our troubles, and went on at length to discuss the number thirteen and the almost universal superstition concerning it; the fact that no house in Paris bears that number, that it is left out of Italian lotteries, and that the superstition itself runs back into Norse mythology, although in Christian countries it is supposed to have originated from the Last Supper.

What is important in all this is that the Crescent locally at least had become taboo, a fact which left us without possible witnesses for the remainder of that dreadful week, and without even our rare visitors from other parts of town for a far longer period.

For on that Wednesday we were involved in another mystery and another death.

There is so far as I know only one coincidence in this record, and that was that the day of Emily Lancaster's funeral was also the anniversary of my father's death. Yet it was to have its consequences.

For twenty years Mother had observed this anniversary in almost ritualistic manner. Thus in the morning, accompanied by my Aunt Caroline, my father's remaining sister, she visited the cemetery, and generally had a discussion and a quarrel with the Superintendent over the condition of our lot. From there she went into the city to lunch sadly but substantially with Aunt Caroline, after which they took a drive to Aunt Caroline's husband's grave, and the morning's procedure was repeated there.

On this particular morning therefore the only variation was that the two first witnessed the final rites over Emily Lancaster, and on the departure of the funeral procession of cars, carried out the usual program. With a difference, however.

It was after one o'clock, and I had managed to dress and get downstairs, when Mother called me on the telephone in an exasperated voice and demanded to know if I had heard from Holmes and the car.

"From Holmes?" I said, astounded. "I thought you had him. Where are you?"

"I'm at the cemetery with your Aunt Caroline," she said shortly. "That wretch drove us here and then simply drove away again. And the Superintendent has gone to lunch and the office is locked. I never heard of such a thing! We've walked for miles."

Well, I must admit that the picture of Mother and Aunt Caroline in their best black left stranded at the Greenwood Cemetery was almost too much for me. It is miles from anywhere, and I doubt if either of them has walked four blocks in as many years. But I agreed that it was dreadful, and to send a taxi for them at once. Which I did immediately.

When I turned it was to find Annie at my elbow.

"I suppose that Holmes has gone, miss?"

"How in the world did you know?"

"Because he carried his clothes away last night," she said promptly.

"Why on earth didn't you tell us that?"

"And get my throat cut?" she said darkly. "No, miss, I know my business and I value my life."

I went back to his room over the garage at once; and discovered that Annie was right. He had slept there; with a guard around the house he had been no longer needed inside it. His bed was untidy and his bathroom had been used. But his closet was stripped bare of clothing and his battered suitcase gone from under the window where it always stood.

There was no question but that Holmes had gone, and it looked just then as though a three-thousand dollar car had gone with him.

Mother got out of a taxicab shortly after that, and limped into the house. What with the heat, her heavy black and a very considerable indignation, she was in a state of almost complete demoralization.

240

She sat down in a hall chair and closed her eyes, and she said nothing whatever until Annie had unlaced and taken off her shoes. Then:

"That wretch!" she said. "I never did trust him, and I never will."

"And right you are, ma'am," said Annie. "You'll be lucky if you ever see him or the car again. That's what I think, besides making you walk on that bunion in this heat. Look at it!"

"That's arthritis, Annie," Mother said sharply.

We got her upstairs and into bed, and I turned on the electric fan. Then Mary sent up some luncheon on a tray, and what with rest and some food she grew more calm. It was not until she was comfortable and quiet that I told her that Holmes's clothes were gone and that whatever his reason might have been for leaving her and Aunt Caroline in the cemetery, it had evidently been planned at least a day ahead.

After that I notified the police, but it was half past two by that time, and too late, as we knew later on.

So far as we were concerned, the remainder of the day was uneventful. At three in the afternoon I saw Bryan Dalton, perhaps less florid than usual but impeccably dressed, get out his car and drive off in it. But I did not know then that he was on his way to a downtown office, where the District Attorney and two or three other men were grouped around a desk on which were lying, carefully tagged, a handful of scorched buttons and two irregular pieces of window glass, held together more or less neatly by two rubber bands.

"Then, as I understand it, you do not identify these buttons?"

"How can I? I suppose automobile overalls are much alike. I wear them to save my clothes."

"But you admit burning your overalls the night following the murder. That's the fact, isn't it?"

"Admit? What do you mean admit? I burned them, certainly. It isn't the first time I've done so, either. You can ask my man, Joseph. I wear them until they're soiled and then have them destroyed."

"Precisely. But isn't this the first time you've done it your-

241

self, Mr. Dalton? I mean, hasn't this Joseph always done it before?"

"Perhaps. I don't remember. And before I go on, I want to know my status here. Am I under suspicion, or am I merely to help you with your investigation? If I'm under suspicion I shall want my lawyer."

"In a way, everyone is under suspicion just now," said the District Attorney smoothly. "I can only remind you that an open statement of fact has never hurt an innocent person, and that I don't think you have been particularly open so far. Now, as to this — er — exhibit under glass. You know nothing about it?"

"Nothing whatever."

"You could not, by examining it, even venture a guess as to what it is? Or has been?"

"I have examined it. I don't know what it is."

And it was then that the District Attorney received a note in Herbert Dean's writing, read it and laid it on the desk before him. When he looked up his examination took a new and different angle.

"Mr. Dalton," he said, "do you know of any poison ivy around the Crescent? In that vicinity, I mean."

"Poison ivy! Are you trying to be funny?"

"I'm afraid not. It's entirely pertinent to our inquiry."

Bryan Dalton shook his head.

"I don't know of any," he said. "I suppose you fellows know what you're talking about, but — poison ivy!" Then he smiled rather grimly. "You don't know us or you wouldn't ask that! Of course I can't speak for the waste land behind us; although I've never noticed it there."

There was, I believe, a pause here. The District Attorney picked up the note from the desk and handed it to the Commissioner, who looked surprised but nodded. And it was the Commissioner who, note in hand, asked the next question.

"Just how long," he inquired gruffly, "on the afternoon of Thursday of last week, did you stand beside the Lancaster woodshed, Mr. Dalton?"

242

He must have looked around him then at that ring of intent faces, all turned toward him. There was no pity in any of them. They were hard; set and grim, like those of men peering into a microscope at some imprisoned insect. Probably after his habit he ran a finger inside his collar, as though it was too tight for him. Then he smiled again.

"I suppose if I refuse to answer that it will be held against me!"

"I can only repeat what I said before, Mr. Dalton."

"I was there perhaps ten minutes."

"You are certain that is all?"

"Absolutely certain."

"Will you explain just why you were there? There must have been a reason. If you'll tell us that reason frankly, I assure you we will hold it as confidential — unless, of course, it turns out to have an important bearing on the case."

But there he surprised them.

"Why I was there had nothing to do with this inquiry," he said shortly. "If you want a reason for your record put it down that I was hunting for a golf ball. That's as good as another. It's as far as I care to go anyhow, and you can take it or leave it."

That practically ended the interrogation. There was not a man there who did not know he was concealing something, although they could not be certain that what he concealed had any bearing on the case. But there was also not a man there who did not believe that he had lied about his ten minutes, and that he had stood beside the woodshed of the Lancasters' long enough to smoke almost in its entirety one expensive Belinda cigar, made for him in Havana.

"Although," as the Inspector said to me a long time afterwards, "that in itself didn't mean a lot. It was pretty hard to believe that in the half hour to forty minutes he was there that afternoon he could have smoked a cigar of that size and still killed the old lady. And he wasn't smoking either when his butler saw him go or when he came back."

A little statement which once more bears out my conviction that from the very start our servants knew more of our crimes than we did.

We knew nothing of all this that afternoon, of course. Mother was too fagged to relieve the nurse that afternoon, and Lydia Talbot did it instead. Margaret was still shut in her room, refusing to allow Lydia to call the doctor. Mrs. Talbot was still with ire about George's interrogation, and her Lizzie reported that she was sitting locked in her room, shouting infuriated house orders through her door. In the house nearest the gate Jim Wellington was trying to locate Helen; partly for himself and partly for Herbert Dean, who was annoyed at her absence. And next door to us Laura Dalton was nursing for jealousy and her suspicion, while I dare say Joseph watched her out of eyes that saw a great deal more than they pretended.

Holmes was still missing.

Chapter XXXI

There had been a little by-play enacted that Wednesday morning, however, of which I knew nothing at the time. With the household at Miss Emily's funeral and only the nurse in charge of the Lancaster house, Herbert Dean and Inspector Briggs had gone there. The nurse opened the door, and after a short talk with her she went upstairs and returned shortly carrying a small object under her apron.

This object the Inspector pocketed, and after that the two men went quietly up the stairs. They remained for more than an hour, the Inspector an interested bystander most of the time, and before they left Dean, as the slimmer of the two, had crawled through a small window onto the roof of the kitchen porch and had there carefully examined the guttering and the opening of the water spout. Whatever he had found inside the house, he found nothing there and at last the two had departed, Herbert to a microscope in a laboratory downtown, where I believe he examined an ordinary house-sponge, and the Inspector to that interrogation of Bryan Dalton which had so exasperated everyone working on the case.

Mother rallied long enough that evening to eat a squab and some blanc-mange, but she was in a bad humor. Doctor Armstrong had come in at six o'clock to give her her hypodermic of iron, but he was too much interested in Holmes's disappearance and too little in her own annoyance to please her.

"That's another instance of what I'm talking about," he said. "The servants here know Holmes is taking out his clothes, but do they tell? They do not. The whole damned Crescent is a conspiracy of silence!"

Mother eyed him coldly.

"The people who could talk will never talk again, doctor. Besides, why go further than we have gone? This deliberate disappearance of my chauffeur can mean only one thing."

"You honestly believe that Holmes is guilty?"

"Why not? He's probably had that gold hidden somewhere all the time, and now he's got away with it. And who but Holmes could have attacked Louisa?"

"He was locked in, wasn't he?"

"How do we know he hadn't a second key?"

"But why attack Lou, of all people?"

"That's for the police to find out," said Mother loftily. "Although I must say what they have found so far doesn't justify any hope in that direction. But people do very strange things sometimes, doctor. I well remember when our dear Bishop got up one night, walked into his wife's room and simply jerked the footboard off her bed. He said afterwards that he had been asleep, but I have always wondered."

When I left the room to see the doctor out he voiced what I was feeling.

"Let her think it, if she can," he said. "Maybe she's right at that, but I don't believe it. Still, it probably comforts her to blame him. She's got in him a criminal she can accept. He belongs to the class, which, according to her ideas, normally produces criminals. And she's been afraid it was somebody else, Lou. Don't forget that. She's been afraid of that from the start."

That was at six o'clock, and both the car and Holmes remained among the missing until nine o'clock that night. Then it was Inspector Briggs who brought me the word that the one had been found, if not the other.

246

"We have your car, Miss Hall," he said. "It was abandoned quite a way out of town, and a sheriff's car picked it up. They'll bring it back in the morning."

Annie had shown him into the library, and now he sat pinching his lip as usual and with his eyes fixed on me intently.

"You know, Miss Hall, the deeper I get into this thing—and God knows I'm over my head already—the more I believe that it's the story we're after. A story. Get the story and you understand the rest. And maybe when we understand—well, maybe this piece has a villain and maybe it hasn't, if you see what I mean."

"It was a pretty wicked thing to kill those two women, wasn't it?"

"It's a pretty wicked thing to kill anybody. And it's a pretty wicked thing, too, to send somebody to the chair unless he deserves it. I could lie awake nights worrying about things I've never been so sure of as the public has been. Well—!"

He leaned forward in his chair.

"Let's get this Crescent of yours clear," he said. "Relationships, old quarrels, all the freakish ideas, like that one of Mrs. Talbot's about locking herself in. What's wrong between young Wellington and his wife, if anything? And even here, in this house. What about yourselves? And where does this Holmes come in? As I recall it, he had your mother out for a drive on the day Mrs. Lancaster was murdered."

"He did. But he has been rather queer, Inspector, ever since."

He listened while I told him about that night when I had seen him tearing pages out of a book, although he seemed to set rather less store by it than Herbert Dean had done.

"Funny performance," was his comment. "I don't suppose you know what sort of book it was?"

"It was a detective story."

"Was, eh? Well, that doesn't mean he's a criminal. I believe our best people read them nowadays! And don't jump too fast to the idea that Holmes is a killer. He didn't kill Mrs. Lancaster. That's sure. It's just possible that he has had all along a pretty shrewd idea of where that money is; and that as it's heavy stuff he had a motive in taking the car today. Although even that's curious. He takes a conspicuous limousine and wears a uniform. Now if a fellow wants to get away with something like that he generally does it at night, and as inconspicuously as he can. Still—now let's start with this Crescent, beginning at the gate. This Jim Wellington; he was a nephew of Mrs. Lancaster's, isn't that it?"

"Of her first husband. He and George Talbot are cousins. Of course his uncle has been dead so long that we always think of Mrs. Lancaster as his real aunt. Jim's mother was a Talbot."

"Humph! Pretty well related, all of you, aren't you?"

"We are not. Or the Daltons."

"All right. Let's get back to the Wellingtons. He's an orphan, I suppose?"

"Yes. His mother died ten years ago. She was rather queer; but Jim isn't, of course."

"How was she queer?"

"I don't exactly know," I said vaguely. "She was very religious, if that's queer! And I remember that she walked a good bit, and talked to herself. She frightened me when I was a little girl. But she was all right otherwise. She was a very intelligent woman really. I—it seems rather awful, Inspector, to talk about people like this. She was really very kind. She gave a great deal to charity."

He nodded.

"Well, queer or not she's dead and out of it. I suppose you know Wellington has refused to profit by his aunt's will? Must have money of his own, eh?"

"He has a good income, but of course—"

"He has an extravagant wife! But, all sentiment aside, you don't think Jim Wellington would steal and kill. That's it, isn't it?"

"I'm sure of it. He—well, he simply hasn't that sort of courage, if you call it courage, Inspector."

"I gather you didn't always feel that way about him."

I could feel my color rising.

"That has nothing to do with it."

He sat forward in his chair.

"Why didn't you marry him, Miss Hall? That isn't an impertinent question. There must have been a reason."

"I couldn't leave my mother all alone."

"And she objected? Why? Because his mother was what you call queer?"

"No. But you see she had felt my father's death very deeply, and of course—"

"Of course, as a good daughter, you made your sacrifice. Well, it takes all sorts to make a world. Now let's move on. The Daltons related to anyone here?"

"No. Mrs. Dalton inherited the place, and he came there to live when they were married."

"Why don't they speak to each other? And how long has that gone on?"

"Twenty years."

"My God! What a life. Do you know what started it?"

"He used to be rather gay," I said carefully. "It may have been something like that."

"Were they on good terms with the Lancasters?"

"Very good. Rather formal, of course. We are rather formal here, you see, Inspector. We don't do much running back and forth."

"And she has the money?"

"I think he has a little of his own. I really don't know."

"Now what about him and Margaret Lancaster? You needn't worry about telling, for we know anyhow. We know he was in his garage that afternoon working in a pair of old overalls over the engine of his car, and we know that those overalls have disappeared and he's got a new pair. That may not mean anything, of course. I'm telling you so you won't feel—well, too scrupulous. And we know he's been meeting the other woman. Why? Have you any idea?"

"I never heard anything about him and Margaret Lancaster until you showed me that letter, Inspector."

He was not satisfied, I knew. He sat with his eyes drilling into me, but at last he moved and spoke.

"All right," he said. "Let's get on. Now what about the Lancasters? What about the way they got along together?

249

How did the old gentleman like his stepdaughters? What about Mrs. Lancaster? Did she put up the money, like Mrs. Dalton, or did he?"

I tried my best, but they had been so long a part of my exterior life that I found it hard to detach myself.

"I really don't know," I said at last. "Both of them were well off, I believe. They lived quietly always, even before she got sick. As a matter of fact, she had had bad health long before I was born. I suppose that's one reason why the girls never married. She didn't have a stroke or anything like that, you know. She just grew more and more feeble, and at last she took to her bed. She hadn't left it for a good many years; she couldn't take a step. I think it was something wrong with her spine, but I don't really know."

"But they got along all right?"

"They did indeed. Of course Mr. Lancaster disliked her hoarding the gold — you know that — and Margaret was impatient sometimes. Her mother was rather fretful, especially in the summer; she fussed about her food, and Margaret was the housekeeper. But I think that's all."

"In other words," he said, "the usual rather disagreeable old invalid! Well, she's gone, so we'll let her alone. Now — how did the others like Miss Emily? What about her, anyhow? What sort of a life did she live? Try to think about her and make a real picture. Look back a bit."

I found it very hard.

"She used to be rather pretty. When I was a little girl she was still pretty. Later on she had to sit with her mother so much that she got heavy. I really don't know anything more, Inspector."

"She had no one outside the family? No close friends?"

"I never heard of any. She adored a canary I gave her one Christmas. It was almost sad, the way she fussed over it, as though — well, you know what I mean. If she had had children —"

He nodded again, as though even a male could understand that vicarious maternity of Emily Lancaster's.

"I get you. No reason then to suppose that the old gentleman disliked her, or was afraid of her, or anything like that?"

"None whatever," I said rather stiffly. "Why on earth should he do either?"

He ignored that, pinching his lip thoughtfully.

"Humph! Well, what about Miss Margaret? Not so even-tempered as her sister, I understand. Gets angry easily, isn't that it?"

"She's over it in a minute, Inspector."

"Do you think the family knew about this affair with Dalton?"

"No. I don't think it was an affair."

"Maybe. Maybe not. Then according to you there's no story in that house. Just a lot of elderly and middle-aged people living their own lives, until someone comes along and without reason wipes out two of them. Is that it?"

"I can't see it any other way."

"All peaceable and calm, until the old lady begins to hoard that gold under her bed, and somebody who knows about it takes it out and loads the bags with dress weights!"

"But that's not so strange as it sounds," I told him. "We all have them. We all use them. I remember seeing a lot of them in a keg in the Lancasters' woodshed last spring. Miss Margaret was potting some plants, and putting them in the bottoms of the pots. But I imagine she used them all."

He was thoughtful for a moment. Then he reached into his pocket and drew out his notebook. After examining it, he glanced at me.

"What about this seamstress, anyhow? She must know a lot about this Crescent, and the people in it. Is she a tall thin woman, angular, with gray hair?"

"Miss Mamie! No. She's very short and very fat."

"Can you place such a woman, anywhere in the Crescent?"

"Only Miss Lydia Talbot, and a maid of theirs, Lizzie Cromwell. Our own cook, Mary, is rather like that, too."

"All right," he said as he put the book away. "Now we're up to the Talbots, and a queer kettle of fish they are. What do you know about them? What goes on behind those barred windows and locked doors? Or do you know?"

I tried to tell him. How Mrs. Talbot rarely left her room at the back of the house, but sat there with her doors locked doing enormous quantities of crocheting — not a house in the Crescent but duly received its gift at Christmas of some terrible thing which it was supposed to use and display — and reading voraciously book after book. How she dominated her household, which was all in deadly fear of her except Lizzie Cromwell, who had been there for years, and in less degree George Talbot himself. How she measured out each morning the day's supplies from the store closet off the kitchen, and then locked the door; and how woe betide any cook who demanded an extra egg or spoonful of tea thereafter. Also how her sister-in-law, Miss Lydia, had to live there because it was all the home she had; and although she did the buying, was carefully audited to the last cent.

And yet, with all of this, how Mrs. Talbot was the first on hand in case of trouble; as witness her visits to Mrs. Lancaster, who was her sister-in-law by her first husband and who, in view of the fact that Mrs. Talbot had been deserted by that husband's brother, might well enough have been let alone, or ignored.

He listened carefully, his eyes intent and penetrating.

"Good friends, were they?" he asked. "She didn't resent Mrs. Lancaster's second marriage, or anything like that?"

"I think they had been better friends in the past few years," I said cautiously. "Before that there was some sort of trouble. I've never known what. Just a family quarrel, I believe. But that was years ago."

"You don't know what it was about?"

"I haven't an idea. I've always thought it was because when Mr. Talbot died — Mrs. Lancaster's first husband — his will didn't provide for Miss Lydia, who was his sister, and Mrs. Lancaster left her to Mrs. John Talbot to look after. But it may not have been that at all."

"Probably was," he agreed. "The more money people have the more care they take of it. That's why they have it. Well, we've got to the son there, George. How does he manage with all this locking up? It isn't a normal life for a young man.

You'll grant that."

"He's never known anything else. Of course he realizes it's unusual, but he is really fond of his mother. He dodges some of it by living his own life outside. That's only natural."

"What do you mean by his own life?"

"Tennis, golf, clubs."

"And women?"

"I don't believe so. I've never heard anything of that sort. But then, of course, I wouldn't."

It was nearly ten o'clock when he left, leaving me rather exhausted. I went to bed shortly afterwards, and I was sleeping soundly when between twelve and one o'clock that same night a motorist on the North Road found the body of Holmes lying on the cement a dozen or so miles out of town.

Chapter XXXII

Although when he abandoned Mother and Aunt Caroline he had worn a smart uniform, when found he was dressed in shabby clothes, and a cap which was badly worn lay a foot or two away. Apparently he had been struck by a hit-and-run driver, and with the feeling that he might be still alive the motorist brought him in, with his horn blowing like a police siren, to the General Hospital not far from us on Liberty Avenue.

The hospital, finding nothing on him to identify him and having discovered without any peculiar emotion that he was dead, then sent him downtown to the morgue. And it was at the morgue the next morning that Detective Sullivan of the Homicide Squad, taking what he called a general look-see after what looked like a double suicide but might be murder, saw him and found his face familiar.

"I've seen him somewhere," he said. "Seen him lately, too."

He walked away, intent on his other problem; but Holmes bothered him. He has, I believe, a reputation in the Force for a tenacious memory, and at last it came to him. He had queried this man on the Lancaster case, along with the other servants.

He shot back to the table and looked the body over carefully. There was no real indication that the man had been murdered, although there was a rather bad contusion on the back of his head. It looked like another hit-and-run case; but he knew that our car had been missing the afternoon before and found abandoned later, although not on the North Road. In almost the opposite direction, in fact.

It did not fit.

"Let's see this fellow's uniform," he said at last. "There's something not just right about this. Get his clothes, somebody."

Somebody did, laying them out on a white table, and Sullivan surveyed them with some surprise.

"Sure these are his? Last time he was seen he was in full uniform with breeches and puttees, and driving a limousine."

"Seems to have lost the lot, then," said the attendant; "including the car! Those are his, all right."

Mr. Sullivan looked over the layout. There were no papers. There was a five-dollar bill and some small change, and a very soiled handkerchief. For the rest, a suit of summer underwear, a new shirt, old and worn overall pants and a coat, a nondescript belt, the battered cap and worn shoes and socks. There was not a mark on anything that could identify him, but there was one thing that was peculiar. His left-hand pocket was filled with keys, small keys of almost every sort and description. There were about two dozen of them.

"Looks like a housebreaker," said the attendant. But I believe Mr. Sullivan made no comment. He was examining the shirt carefully, a new white shirt of an inexpensive type.

"Had his coat on when he was brought in, did he?"

"Yes, Mr. Sullivan. I took it off myself."

Sullivan was no talker. He gathered up the shirt, being careful not to smear certain marks on it, and carried it away under his arm. Then, having pocketed that vast array of keys and with a parting glance at the quiet figure on the slab, he simply walked out again.

It was eleven o'clock on that Thursday morning when he rang our doorbell. I was in the lower hall arranging the flowers; it being one of our traditions that a gentlewoman attends to the house flowers in the morning, and that the daughters of the house are particularly fitted for this task. Mother was fussing with Mary in the pantry, but she came forward when the bell rang, and I must say she received the news of Holmes's death heroically.

"Dear me," she said. "And almost a month's wages due him! Had he a family, Louisa, do you know?"

"I think not. He had a little place in the country. He never mentioned a family."

Which represents very clearly our attitude toward our men servants, when we have any. Our women are different. We watch over their health, their relatives and their morals, and in effect ring a curfew for them every night at ten. Our men, however, strictly preserve their anonymity. Even today I doubt if the Daltons know whether Joseph when he goes out leaves them for a family, for some less regular relationship, or to go to the movies! And it is also a fact that when Mr. Sullivan asked us what was Holmes's given name, we were obliged to consult Mary and eventually Annie before we remembered it.

"William Holmes," said Mr. Sullivan. "Well, that's something anyhow. And now, he'd better be identified. If either one of you ladies—"

To my astonishment Mother at once volunteered to do so.

"I do not want Louisa in such a place," she said, referring to the morgue and ignoring the fact that violent death and I were no longer strangers. "I shall go myself, Louisa. Order the car."

Then she remembered, and she showed for her what was almost emotion.

"Poor Holmes!" she said. "He was always so careful, especially at the corners. Order a taxi, Louisa."

It turned out, however, that Mr. Sullivan had his own car; a low open sports roadster. It took some effort to get Mother into it at all, and I still remember the almost shocked look of surprise with which she found herself, as they drove away, with her feet almost straight out in front of her, while of necessity she was more or less sitting on the small of her back.

Our household received the news without any great emotion. Neither of the two maids had cared for Holmes, and while they were shocked, they made no pretense at grief.

"Always snooping, he was," Mary said. "Not that I want to speak ill of the dead, miss; but it's a fact. He spent more time up in his room watching out the windows than he ever did over his work."

While Mother had prepared for her visit to the morgue, Mr. Sullivan had visited and closely inspected Holmes's quarters over the garage. Also he had questioned the servants. The sum total of their knowledge was unimportant. He was apparently unmarried, or at least had never mentioned having a family. He had the little place in the country I have mentioned, but he had never told where it was. And they believed that he had done a little polite bootlegging for George Talbot, the Daltons and the Wellingtons; and perhaps more than a little less polite liquor dealing elsewhere.

I went back again to his quarters after Mr. Sullivan had driven Mother off, going at the pace for which she would have instantly dismissed Holmes, or any chauffeur. The door to the staircase was locked as usual, but I had taken the house keys with me and I had no difficulty in opening it. The stairs were dirty, for, whatever Holmes's virtues, neatness was not among them. At the top they opened at the right into his bedroom, which with a most untidy bathroom comprised his living quarters.

There was no question as I looked about but that when Holmes left Mother and Aunt Caroline at the cemetery the afternoon before, he had not intended to return. As I have said before, his clothes were gone. On a shelf were a few books, all of them detective stories; a torn magazine lay on the floor, and on the table by the window was the missing tube of glue, and an empty tin spool which had once held adhesive plaster. The bed had not been made, and for all my suspicions it looked pathetic. Whatever he had done, he had arisen from it alive and well only the morning before, and now he was dead. For somehow I had no doubt that it was Holmes who lay on that slab in the morgue.

The bathroom showed only a soiled towel or two, and a worn-down shaving brush.

I realized, however, as I wandered around that these quarters of Holmes's offered a peculiar advantage to anyone who for any reason whatever, was interested in what went on in the Crescent. Our garage was set well back of the house, and from the windows on both sides he commanded portions of the Lancaster and Dalton houses, and even a small part of the Talbots' and the Wellingtons'. From the rear he could look out over No Man's Land, and his front windows almost impudently stared at our house.

To Holmes, then, the Daltons' garage and the Lancaster woodshed were in plain view, and even the rear end of the Talbots' stable where George now kept his car. The trees which obscured us from each other did little to shield us from him, and he was high enough to see easily over our shrubberies.

He must have known a great deal about us, I thought; through Peggy he could have known about the money under the bed, and it might be that he had killed Emily Lancaster. But now he was dead himself. Who had killed him? Was it some bootleggers' quarrel? Or had he finally got away with the gold and had there been, on that remote road, some quarrel over it? Or had it been, after all, one of those accidents which no shrewdness seems able to prevent?

I was still thinking as I went slowly back to the house. I reflected uncomfortably that suspicion, having moved from house to house along the Crescent, had finally and at last involved ours; and Doctor Armstrong, coming in again around noon and reporting that he could make no more money out of me as a patient, put that into words for me.

"That finishes the roll call, doesn't it?" he said. "Everybody's involved now, and I doubt if even that smart young man of yours, Lou, ever had anything like it."

"He is smart, but he is not my young man, doctor."

"Well, I hope to God he will be," he said, tapping his fingers on his bag as usual. "Too many virgins here now, and not only the unmarried ones at that. Virginity is a state of

258

mind, when all's said and done. But to get back to your young man; if Holmes was murdered it begins to look like a syndicate, and I think myself he *was*."

"Why a syndicate?"

"Well, take the average killer; the fellow who takes life the way he'd take a dose of salts. He's got his method and he sticks to it. The hammer killer sticks to his hammer, the rod man to his gun, and the bag murderer puts all his victims in sacks and leaves them around somewhere. But what have we got here? An axe, a pistol, a poker and probably an automobile. Let your criminologist make something out of that if he can!"

Not that he decried criminology, he said. It was a new profession and a hard one.

"Fellow's got to be an expert in a lot of things," he said. "Got to know everything from ballistics and chemistry to bloodstains and fingerprints; also photo-micrography, which is a big word you needn't bother about! But he's got to know psychology too, and that's where most of them fall down. They forget that most of us are naturally aggressive, and that enough repression of all the aggressive instincts drives us to extreme violence the moment we get upset. Even to murder. Your criminologist forgets that. He's dedicated to pure fact."

A conclusion which would have been borne out, had he known it, by what I now know to have been Herbert Dean's occupation that morning. He was, as a matter of fact, bending over that white shirt of Holmes's, examining the tire marks under a microscope and then photographing and enlarging them.

The result was a teletype from Headquarters ordering a search for a small light truck, showing signs of having been driven through tar, and of which the right front tire was of a certain designated make and carried embedded in it a short nail with a broken head.

That was at noon on Thursday. Mother had not returned at lunch time, nor by two o'clock, when she was due at the Lancasters'; so I telephoned to Lydia Talbot that she had been called downtown, and Lydia agreed to substitute for her. Somewhat later however she appeared at the house and said that her sister-in-law had gone instead.

"Hester seems to think I've been butting in where I'm not wanted," she said. "And she's so queer. Really, Louisa, I feel as though I've got to get away from here. I've got to. My nerves are going. I told Hester this morning and she's furious. She says she's given me a home for more than twenty years, and that's true. But a home isn't a life. I'm not as young as I used to be, and it's like living in a jail. I don't care where I go. I have a little money, and I can still work. I work where I am for that matter, only I don't get paid for it."

Her voice was more bitter than her words. All my life I had seen her about, had known her as well as any woman of my age could know a woman of fifty or so. Her thin figure plodding on its innumerable errands was almost as familiar to me as my mother's. But now she looked actually desperate.

"I'm sure it hadn't been easy," I agreed.

"Easy! It's been plain hell. As though John Talbot would ever come back and bother her again, or want even to see her! The house locked and barred as though—" She caught herself then, and I saw that her face was twitching. "I'll have to get away, Louisa," she said. "Look at me. And she won't let me go."

"Do you mean," I said, "that she has locked herself away all these years from—from your brother?"

"I didn't say that," she said more calmly. "No. She knows he wouldn't do her any harm. He was the gentlest soul alive. I—" She lowered her voice and looked about her. "Sometimes I worry about Hester, Louisa. She's not herself. She's very queer sometimes; and lately I've thought even Lizzie is not herself. Maybe I'm only nervous, but—"

She checked herself then and got up, dropping her gloves as she did so.

"I do hope you won't say I've said all this, Louisa. I just had to talk to somebody. I feel better now. And of course it's all nonsense about my going away. Where would I go?"

She hurried off through the August heat, and I went into the house. It seemed strange to me that day to remember how, only a week ago, we were living our complacent orderly lives; that on the surface at least we were a contented group of householders, and that our only skeleton was the occasional violent separations between Jim Wellington and Helen. The Daltons too, but we were so accustomed to that situation, and it so little affected our normal living that we hardly noticed it.

Now every house on the Crescent had been shown to have its story, for the death of Holmes had involved even ours. Under those carefully tended roofs, behind the polished windows with their clean draped curtains, through all the fastidious ordering of our days there had been unhappiness and revolt. We had gone our polite and rather ceremonious way while almost certainly somewhere among us there had been both hatred and murderous fury.

I remember standing in the darkened hall and once again calling the roll. It could not be; but when Annie came to say that our car had been brought back and the driver wanted to see me in the garage I was gazing fixedly through the door into the library, where my father's portrait in oil hangs above the mantel. I was not seeing it, however. I was seeing instead the old crayon enlargement of George's father which used to be in the stable loft, and hearing Lydia's flat voice:

"She knows he wouldn't do her any harm. He was the gentlest soul alive."

I went back to the garage, to find a man in rough clothes and a cap who had raised the engine hood and seemed to be entirely engrossed in what poor Holmes had always called the car's innards.

"Seems all right, miss," he said, and then looked up. It was Herbert Dean, in a mechanic's overalls and a dirty cap.

"Sorry to be so long, miss," he went on. "I suppose, like most women, you never notice your mileage?"

"Considering that we never go anywhere, why should I?"

"True. Too true!" he observed. "Of course that's all over now," he added cryptically. "Still, if you had it might help. Or it might not. I have an idea that if this baby could talk it would tell us a good bit about poor Holmes, and his

261

movements yesterday. But I can make a fair guess at that."

"Am I supposed to ask what you are guessing?"

He looked gratified, or pretended to.

"Certainly you are." But he dropped his light manner then. "I'm guessing," he said slowly, "that at some time yesterday, probably toward noon, this car drew up at a house not far from here, but outside the Crescent; that a chauffeur in livery, Holmes, impressively delivered either a note or a message — probably a note — to a lady who rents rooms; and that in all probability this landlady was a tall thinnish woman who was duly impressed by the whole outfit, and who received that message in good faith. And — I am still guessing but I believe — that that same Holmes went back last night with a light truck of some sort and took away from that house one new trunk, which would be unduly heavy for its size, and which may have required help; say, the landlady's son, if she had one. Most landladies have no husbands. That's the reason they are landladies."

"Are you saying that the gold was in that trunk?"

"I am guessing, dear Lou of the nice quiet eyes. But I think it's true. And so that poor little shrimp lost his life."

"Then he *was* murdered for that money!"

"I haven't said that, I'm not sure. But either by accident or design he was killed, my darling. He was knocked on the head, and after that the truck — it was almost certainly a truck — went over him."

"It's horrible."

"Well, it's queer. And some of the other things are queer. I can understand putting his coat on to hide the tar marks on his shirt; the truck had been through tar. It was smart, you see. In nine cases out of ten he'd be picked up as a hit-and-run case, and that would be the end of it. But why lay him out neatly on the road, and then anchor his handkerchief on his chest with a stone, so that he would be sure to be found?"

"Herbert," I asked feverishly, "was Holmes killed by the same person who killed Mrs. Lancaster and Emily?"

He shook his head.

"God knows," he said. "It is all connected somehow, but I

can tell you this. So far as it is possible to be sure of anything, nobody left the Crescent last night. But all I'm certain of this morning is that somewhere, perhaps still on the road but more probably hidden somewhere in a house, is the new trunk in which—brace yourself for this—the new trunk in which Emily Lancaster hid the gold which she systematically took at night from under her mother's bed."

He was getting ready to leave by that time, going by way of the path across No Man's Land to Euclid Street, and under Mary's prying eyes I could only stand and stare at him.

"I think you'll find the car all right, miss," he said, touching his cap. Then he lowered his voice. "Oh, yes, I meant to tell you. That bit of stem from your upper hall was poison ivy. Better be careful, if you're susceptible. The Commissioner is. I wish you could see him today!" And he added, with his attractive smile: "Are you susceptible, Lou?" You are such a suppressed little person that I can't be sure. But I hope you are, for I'm coming to see you tonight."

Chapter XXXIII

He went away at once and I went into the house and up the stairs, dazed and dizzy with this new knowledge, and wondering where it led us. It should have explained so much, and yet it really explained so little.

How could I believe that Emily Lancaster was a thief? To accept that was to revalue all the Crescent, to doubt everyone of us, and to wonder whether under our cloaks of dignified and careful living we were not all frauds and hypocrites. To suspect Emily was to suspect everybody.

I stood in the upstairs hall and gazed about me. The door was open into the guest room and where Holmes had slept, and which still seemed to retain his particular aroma of oil and grease. The sun poured in on the radiator at the end of the hall where I had hidden that glove of Jim Wellington's, through the window from which I had watched Mrs. Dalton making her frantic search of the house that same night. And from the back window in the main hall I could see that room of Holmes's, and his patient experimentation with the book.

Holmes had known about the money, and that knowledge had killed him. But how long had he known that Miss Emily was carrying it away? How had he discovered where she was taking it? As I have said before, not only did he occupy a strong strategic position over the garage, but he undoubtedly used No Man's Land for purposes of his own. Had he, like George Talbot, found some of that dropped money? Or had he followed Miss Emily for some unknown reason, discovered where she went, and then formulated his plan?

I stood by that rear window and tried to think it out. There seemed, with the plot he had apparently conceived, no actual reason for killing Miss Emily. Whatever its details were, so far as I knew it could have been carried out as well with Emily alive as if she were dead. And that conclusion of mine was borne out only a few minutes later, while I stood at the window.

A woman was slowly crossing No Man's Land from the direction of Euclid Street; a tall thin woman, not unlike the Talbot's Lizzie, and moving toward the Lancaster house. She had a rolled newspaper in her hand, and even from that distance I could see that she was both uncertain and uneasy. I lost her when she reached the woodshed, but picked her up again as, still moving with a certain unwillingness, she went up the path toward the Lancasters' rear porch.

There evidently Ellen turned her away. Mr. Lancaster was very low that morning, and I dare say Ellen, who had been fond of him, was extremely short with her. At all events the woman stood uncertain for a moment and then reached a decision and moved toward our house.

All of this had interested me, and I went downstairs so as to meet her before Mary sent her off. She seemed startled when I confronted her.

"Are you looking for somebody?" I asked.

"I was looking for Miss Lancaster, but the old gentleman is pretty bad. She couldn't see me."

"Maybe I would do. I'm a great friend of Miss Margaret's."

She looked me up and down, with caution rather than suspicion. Then, right there in the path, she opened up her newspaper.

What I had expected was the morning paper, with its report on the finding of an unidentified man killed by a hit-and-run driver, and followed by an excellent description of

Holmes. But I was mistaken. What she produced was an illustrated section of one of our newspapers; and this she held out to me.

"I just saw this picture this morning," she said. "I was lining a drawer with the paper, and I saw it. Would you say this is Miss Emily Lancaster, miss?"

I looked at the paper. It was a Sunday morning edition, and the picture she referred to was taken as the family had gone in to the inquest on Saturday. It was a very clear picture. In it Margaret's black veil was down but Emily, emotionally unstrung, had raised her veil and was apparently about to wipe her eyes. In so doing she had seen the cameraman and with her handkerchief in her hand, had hesitated for a fraction of a second. That had been enough however; and the result was an excellent picture of her.

I rolled up the paper and glanced toward our kitchen. Mary was watching with interest from a window.

"Come into the house," I said quickly. "It's hot out here, and anyhow I think you have something to tell me."

"I have that," was her reply, and she followed me docilely enough around the building and into the library. Once inside I closed the doors.

"First of all I'll answer your question. Yes, that is Miss Emily Lancaster. I suppose you know she is not—living now?"

She nodded.

"But she didn't call herself Lancaster when she rented a room from me," she said. "I'm sorry to speak ill of the dead, but if that's Miss Lancaster she told me her name was Merriam, and she said she was a trained nurse. But that's neither here nor there. What worries me is about that trunk of hers. I don't know that I'm responsible, but I've got my living to make, and I don't want any trouble."

I reassured her as well as I could, and she told me the story.

On or around the first of April she had read an advertisement for a room wanted by a trained nurse, and as she lived near the corner of Euclid Street and Liberty Avenue, across from the library and only two blocks from the General Hospital, she had answered it at once.

She was a newcomer in the vicinity and did not recognize the middle-aged woman who called in reply. This woman had stated that she was a nurse with what amounted to a permanent position with an elderly invalid, and that she had only a little time now and then to herself.

"But she said," went on Mrs. MacMullen, for that turned out to be her name, "that she liked a place she could call home anyhow, even if she only spent an hour or two a day in it, when she went to the library for books or took a walk. She said it was the nearest she could have to a home. And she gave Miss Emily Lancaster as a reference; said she had nursed her mother at one time. Well, everyone around here knows about the Lancasters, although nobody saw them much. It sounded all right, but I did call up the house, and this Miss Emily answered herself. She gave her quite a good reference. How was I to know it was herself all the time, miss? And why did she want to play such a trick anyhow? It wasn't as though she was a young woman. You know what I mean."

"No," I said thoughtfully. "It was curious, of course. I think they did have a nurse named Merriam once for a short time, but that's long ago."

The end of it was that Miss Merriam took the room, and according to Mrs. MacMullen the arrangement went very well. Miss Emily, or Miss Merriam, came in almost every other day. Usually she went first to the library, and then to this room of hers. Once in a while she would stay two or three hours, but mostly it was less. She had sent in a new wardrobe trunk soon after she took the room, and she kept it not only locked, but padlocked. Apparently this padlock arrangement did not belong to the trunk, but had been added.

"I didn't like that much," the landlady admitted, "but women that age are peculiar sometimes. I never looked in a roomer's trunk in my life; I've got other things to do. But she was peculiar in other ways too. I had to do the room

267

while she was in it. Not that she mussed it much — she was very neat — but I could only send the vacuum when she was there. She kept the key herself."

Not once in that almost five months had she suspected that Miss Emily was other than what she seemed, and it shows very clearly the almost complete isolation of Miss Emily's life that she could move about our own neighborhood as she had and remained unrecognized. It was Margaret who did the marketing and buying. Liberty Avenue knew her well. But Emily Lancaster remained, in all that busy life which moved along Liberty Avenue, a lonely and unknown figure, a stout middle-aged woman carrying an armful of books to and from the public library.

Mrs. MacMullen had not finished, however.

"I did my best to please her," she said, "and she seemed to like me well enough. Then early this month she began to look tired and nervous, and I'd hear her walking up and down the room when she came. She'd lock the door and — well, she'd just keep moving like a woman who was too upset to sit still. You know what I mean, miss.

"So I wasn't so surprised as I might have been when one day about two weeks ago she came to me and said she'd liked the room very much, but that she might not keep it long. The old lady, her patient, was talking about going on a cruise around the world and taking her along. I remember she'd brought in a lot of steamer folders, and she read them while I did the room. They're there now, as a matter of fact. And that's why I let the trunk go."

She came then to the events of the last few days. On the Thursday morning of Mrs. Lancaster's death, at somewhere around eleven o'clock, "Miss Merriam" had come in in a worse state of nerves than usual. She had been there the morning before, but only for a few minutes. This time she stayed an hour, and Mrs. MacMullen said she could hear her walking the floor again.

"Back and forth she went, and me wondering what it was all about. Then she came out, and I asked her if there was anything wrong, or if her old lady was worse. She just acted as though she didn't hear me, and went past me and on out like a crazy woman. Then she came right in again, and said she'd have to give up the room in a day or two; that they were going somewhere, she didn't know where. But that she'd send for the trunk later. And she paid me up to the end of the month. That's the last I ever saw of her, until I recognized this picture this morning."

It was that afternoon that Mrs. Lancaster was murdered, and the whole neighborhood thrown in a state of frenzy. Mrs. MacMullen was interested, not only because of the crime, but because Miss Merriam had given Miss Emily as a reference. The general belief was that a homicidal maniac was loose, and along with a good many others the landlady inspected her window locks, and in addition she had put a chain across her front door the next morning.

"Some of my people didn't like it," she explained. "I put it on at nine every night and after that they had to ring the bell. Their keys were no good to them. But I did it to protect them as well as myself, and when that killer got Miss Emily herself on Sunday night, they stopped fussing."

She still, she said, had no idea that Miss Emily and Miss Merriam were the same woman. She was shocked nevertheless: "because only last spring I'd talked to her over the telephone. It was as if I knew her, if you see what I mean."

But on Sunday night she had had real reason to be thankful for the chain. It was about three o'clock in the morning and she was in the lower hall.

"Miss Anderson on the second floor had a toothache, and I'd offered to go down and heat some water for a hot-water bottle. I know my house pretty well so I didn't turn on a light—and I was in my slippers, and they don't make any noise.

"Well, I was down at the foot of the stairs when I heard somebody at the front door fumbling with the lock. All my people were in, and they knew about the chair anyhow. I was scared, but I stood still and watched, and that door opened! It opened as far as the chain would let it. Then—I couldn't help it, I guess—I yelled, and it slammed shut again."

"You didn't see anybody?"

"No, miss, and I'd be glad if you kept it to yourself. I don't want my roomers leaving."

I nodded absently, I'm afraid, for I was busy thinking. On Sunday night Holmes was locked in our guest room, and he was still there when I unlocked his door the next morning. Then it could hardly have been Holmes at that door and thwarted by that chain. Then who? Mrs. MacMullen was in no doubt, apparently.

"I guess I'd have yelled louder if I'd known Miss Merriam was Emily Lancaster and that he'd killed her that very night," she said trying to smile. "It's easy to see what happened, Miss Hall, isn't it? Whoever it was, he killed her to get that key, and I can only thank God that my chain held."

But of course she still did not know Miss Merriam's real identity, and she only wondered why she had not come to her room since the Thursday before.

"I thought maybe she'd gone away as she said," she explained. "But that seemed queer with her trunk still locked in that room of hers."

And then, after this long preamble, she reached the trunk itself. It had been taken away the night before, and the word had been brought at noon by a liveried chauffeur with a limousine at the curb. Naturally she had suspected nothing out of the way.

"Up the steps he came, as bold as brass, and he said to me that Miss Merriam's old lady was going out of town in a hurry, and that she'd send for her trunk that night.

" 'And what about getting into the room for it?' I said 'She'll have to send her key.'

"He said he would get the key, and that was all." She had not been surprised when he himself came for the trunk with a light truck. He had a negro helper, and the two went up the stairs. He had the key right enough, as she said; but the trunk was heavy and he himself was a small man. It had stuck too at the turn of the stairs, and finally she herself had gone out on the street, found a white man loitering on the pavement, and brought him in.

"The three of them got the trunk out and into the truck," she said, "and that's all I know, except that he paid the helpers off and drove away by himself."

She took a handkerchief out of her bag and wiped her face with it. I could see that she was trembling.

"Well, that's all, Miss Hall," she said, getting slowly to her feet. "I let him take the trunk. How was I to know that this Merriam woman was Miss Lancaster, or that she was dead? I gave it to him, and the police can believe it or not. I don't know what was in it and I don't care. Let them get him and they'll get it."

"They'll never get him, Mrs. MacMullen," I said gravely. "I'm afraid he is dead."

And I was astounded to see her crumple up in a dead faint, on the floor at my feet.

She came around before very long, after Mary over my protests had dashed a tea cup of ice water in her face. She was dazed at first, gazing at us all with blank eyes, but soon she oriented herself and tried to sit up.

"I'm sorry, miss," she began. "I don't know when I've done such a thing." Then memory came back and she closed her eyes and leaned back heavily against my arm as I held her.

"Dead!" she said. "O my God! What will we do!"

Chapter XXXIV

The remainder of that day, Thursday August the twenty-fifth, is a sort of nightmare to remember.

I had notified the police of Mrs. MacMullen's visit, and then followed the usual long hours when nothing seemed to happen. Indeed when everything was over and we knew that our killer would kill no more, I was to hear Herbert Dean say that a big crime case was like a war: a few dramatic moments and then hours and days of surface quiet and patient underground digging.

So far the Crescent as a whole knew nothing of Holmes's death. No boy selling extras ever intruded on our sacred privacy, and both Mother and I had been asked to let the police make the announcement when they were ready. The result was an extremely peaceful if hot August afternoon, with Eben once again systematically cutting the grass, and our housemaids or parlormaids or butlers, as the case might be, quite cheerfully doing the usual Thursday silver cleaning.

To them I dare say the crimes were over and the excitement ended. Whatever they knew or suspected, the curtain was down and they were ready to go about their business again. It had been exciting, but it was not their play. They had been interested and terrified spectators, but no more than that. The result was that for all our bars and locks, for all our guards at night and the incessant clamor of the press for action on the part of the police as to the Crescent Place murderer, there was a definite relaxation of tension.

Mary and Annie might, and actually did, barricade themselves on the third floor each night by putting a row of chairs on the staircase. But I know now that in most of the Crescent houses the attack on me was laid, either to a burglar after my grandmother's silver in the cedar room or to my having run head-on into an open door!

That was due to Mrs. Talbot who, coming in early on the morning after it happened, had gone ponderously back to the guest wing and carefully inspected it.

"That's what happened," she boomed. "This door was open and she ran into it in the dark. My George did that once and had to have three stitches. Who on earth would want to hurt Louisa?"

"Louisa didn't carry the kitchen poker up with her," Mother said.

"How d'you know? Whose fingerprints were on it? I don't know anything to hold a mark like a brass-handled poker."

But the poker had borne no prints, it seemed; not even mine. Nor could she account for the fact that even if I had run into a door, the bump was on the top and toward the back of my head!

It was then to a Crescent still ignorant of this third tragedy and quietly going about its business, that Mother returned rather late that afternoon. Her mourning veil looked rather the worse for wear, but she herself looked better than I had seen her look for a long time. She had, it appeared, not only gone to the morgue. She had lunched alone downtown for the first time in twenty years; a break in her routine so incredible that I almost gasped.

"It was quite pleasant," she said. "The chicken salad was much better than Mary's; I must speak to her about it."

"It was Holmes, wasn't it, mother?"

She nodded, taking off her hat.

"Yes, it was Holmes. Of course his uniform is missing. I shall have to buy a new one. But he looked very natural, considering everything. Quite natural. A hit-and-run driver, they say. But I cannot help thinking, Louisa that he was taken by a definite act of Providence; and Mr. Sullivan quite agrees with me. You see—I suppose I can say this now—I had suspected something quite different. If Holmes killed Emily Lancaster—"

"We don't know that it was Holmes, mother," I said. "You may have been right, you know. At least you ought to tell somebody what you suspected, or whom. It can't do any harm."

But she refused with a gesture, and I could not induce her to tell me. In her mind the case was settled, the mystery solved. She was certain that he had killed Mrs. Lancaster before he took her on Thursday for her drive, and that all the family had been wrong about the time; and she was even more certain that on Sunday night he had escaped from a locked room and shot Miss Emily.

This belief of hers was strengthened rather than weakened by the fact that the Department had no record of Holmes's fingerprints.

"You know, Louisa," she said, "the police have said all along that the murderer was a non-habitual criminal, and I dare say they'll find that he has that money out in that country place of his he used to talk about. It is all perfectly obvious."

Outside of that one matter, of the suspicion which was now definitely and comfortably allayed, Mother was more garrulous that afternoon than I had ever seen her. Mr. Sullivan had taken her to see the Police Commissioner after they left the morgue, and she had been surprised to find that he was what she called a gentleman.

"Quite good-looking," she said. "That is, he would have been, but he was suffering quite dreadfully from poison ivy. It seems he had got some on his hands and then rubbed his face. He was severely swollen. And he has very handsome offices. I suppose that is where our tax money goes. Then

274

the District Attorney dropped in and we had a very nice talk."

From which I gathered that Mother, rather pleased and certainly without suspecting it, had been that morning tactfully interrogated by the police!

Considering Mother since, in the light of that secret she so carefully preserved, I believe that she was as much a victim to the Crescent as its defender. It had done to her what it had done to most of us: it had definitely contracted our lives until it was a vital matter that in hot weather our candles be placed on ice before using so they would burn evenly on our dinner tables; or that our doilies be rolled over cones of old papers, and not folded.

Congresses might come and go, but it was still essential that our table napkins be ironed on the wrong side and then polished on the right side; that on certain dates our furs be brushed, sunned and put into domestic storage, and that on certain other days the process be repeated in reverse order.

Out in the world women were taking their places and living their own lives, but our small rules of living and conduct ignored all that. Our women servants still had to be in at ten and up at seven. Dependent women relatives were still cared for, if somewhat grudgingly; as witness Lydia Talbot. Mrs. Dalton, cutting flowers in her garden with her hands and complexion protected against the sun, was simply following the tradition; as was Mother when she served a glass of wine and a biscuit to one of our rare callers. And Mrs. Talbot might lock herself in to her heart's content; it was her house and her affair.

Was it from this slavery of the unimportant that Emily Lancaster had tried to escape? That was the problem I carried into my room that afternoon, for if Emily had taken that money, it opened up something so dreadful that I was afraid to face it.

Suppose that Mrs. Lancaster had roused some night or other to find Emily drawing out that chest, or fumbling with its locks as it lay underneath the bed? And suppose then that the invalid had asked for Jim, the next day perhaps, to come and examine her hoard, to count it for her bag by bag and coin for coin as it lay on the bed? Then what? Was it so hard to suppose the rest? Hadn't Lizzie Borden been accused of having killed her stepmother with an axe? And hadn't our own grocer's daughter turned on him a year ago and stabbed him in the neck with a knife, so that only the proximity of the hospital and assistance had saved his life?

I do not know when I have put in as utterly wretched an hour. All that I knew of Emily came back: the sacrifice of her life and of any real chance for marriage, and the possibility of some furious inner rebellion that had suddenly flared into desperate action. That was what Doctor Armstrong had said: "— to extreme violence. Even to murder."

For she could have done it. I saw that clearly. She had had that half hour between three-thirty and four, for we had only her word that at three-forty-five she had opened her mother's door and found her still asleep.

All of it, the plotting about the room on Liberty Avenue, the direct and indirect purchasing of the weights, the conning of various steamship folders, pointed to long and careful planning and the expectation of escape. Then, with everything ready, she could not escape. The police watched her. The house was under guard. Even her own nerves betrayed her, for I had seen her myself in a state of utter collapse.

But I brought myself up with a jerk, for on Sunday night she herself had been killed.

She had not expected to be killed. She had gone downstairs and eaten an apple! Whatever guilt she may have felt, at least she apparently felt secure. Had eaten an apple and then wandered out into the warm night air. For all her complaints of someone trying to enter the house at night before her mother's death, now quite calmly she started out. There were guards about, but no one saw or heard her.

What was she after, that Sunday night? The bird cage? Then what was in it? Did she keep, in a seed cup or under the sliding bottom, the keys to that hidden room of hers and to the Liberty Avenue house? That would explain a great deal, but not all. Perhaps the key to the chest had been there too, taken from her mother's neck after the killing! They had found it not far from her body.

But then who had taken the bird cage? Was it Holmes?

It was possible, I thought. Almost certainly on that Thursday he already knew about the gold and where it was. But so far as he was concerned, the killing of Mrs. Lancaster did not help him, but rather hindered his plans. There was the chance of quick discovery that the money was gone, and also that Miss Emily would break down and confess. Yet he had made no immediate move to get the trunk. It was six days before he made that final and fatal move of his.

I went back to Emily. Was it Holmes on that Saturday night after her mother's death, when someone had tried to enter Emily's room from the porch roof, and she had escaped to the Talbot house? But she had seemed to know or suspect who the intruder was, or rather the intruders, for she had said: "Hide me, George. Hide me somewhere. They're after me."

She had known then, or guessed, who it was. She knew she was in danger, for all her locked bedroom door. Yet only the next night she had walked that path toward the Talbots', and been shot.

My mind went back to Friday. It was on Friday night over the telephone that I had roused her from a heavy doped sleep with the word that there was someone on the roof; a man, apparently searching it with great care and some risk. Who was it, and what was he looking for? One thing was certain: he was capable of quick action, for in the interval between the ringing of the telephone bell and Margaret's appearance in the cedar room with her father's revolver, he had not only escaped. He had closed the trap door and replaced the ladder!

Perhaps I was oversuspicious as I looked back, but it did not ring entirely true, that story of Margaret's as she had told it to me on Saturday morning. Why had this unknown, escaping somehow through a darkened house, not only managed to do that, but also to replace the trap and ladder?

I looked out at the Lancaster house. It might have been possible to climb from one of the third floor windows to the roof, but I doubted it. Then again, Margaret had asked me not to speak about it. The more I thought over that the stranger it seemed; unless at that time Margaret suspected Emily of her mother's murder.

Was the man on the roof by any chance searching for the missing money? Or perhaps for the bloodstained garments of the killer for which the police had looked without result? They had to be somewhere, those clothes. There had been no chance for Emily, providing she was guilty, to have got rid of them.

But my mind kept going about in a circle, for after all Miss Emily herself had been killed only two nights later, and now even Holmes was gone.

I tried putting some of this down. I even tried repeating the chronology of that previous Thursday, for it was Mrs. Lancaster's murder, I knew, that had started the entire chain. Yet that day had varied little from any other day, up to the time of the death. It was entirely usual for Lydia Talbot to carry Mrs. Lancaster some delicacy for her tray, and Lydia had left at half past two. At three-thirty Mr. Lancaster and Mrs. Talbot had gone; he had returned but under oath had stated that he had gone directly out again. At three-forty-five Emily reported her mother asleep, and at four o'clock Jim Wellington had found her dead.

When in all that closely checked time had the murderer, with or without a key to the house, been able to enter, kill and depart without discovery. And whom had Mother suspected of being both capable and able to do such a thing?

I sat back and thought about that; about that day when Mother, having read in the paper that the gold was missing, had instantly sent for Mrs. Talbot to apologize to her! Apology comes hard to Mother, and this apology seemed to have been for something she had thought rather than said. So far as I knew she had said nothing.

What had she thought? That Mrs. Talbot, after being a good friend and a kindly neighbor for years, had somehow reentered that house after Mr. Lancaster went for his walk, and killed a woman who was not only helpless, but who was related to her by marriage? She could have done it. It came to me almost with a shock that she could have done it easily.

Nobody had checked on her movements after she left the house. Even Miss Lydia was out and did not return until around five o'clock. As for motive, why demand one of a woman who was as definitely eccentric as she was? Or there might be one; a part of that hidden story to which Mother had now and then referred, something out of the past of which I had never heard, some ancient enmity carried secretly for years.

I sat back in my chair and tried to face that possibility. It was not credible, of course; but it is never credible that people willfully commit savage and brutal crimes. And as I sat there I realized that there was more than one point to support my suspicion. The shooting of Emily with what was apparently George Talbot's automatic was only one of them.

I had remembered suddenly that there was a vine of poison ivy near the Talbot stable.

I sat then with my notes before me, staring incredulously out into the Lancasters' sunny garden. Eben was cutting the grass again, and save for the notes on my lap it might have been the same Thursday afternoon the week before, when the Lancasters' side door had opened, and Miss Emily had run out screaming and fallen flat on the newly-cut lawn.

As I looked I saw Jennie come out the side door and make a gesture to Eben. He stopped his mower at once, and something in the two attitudes told me that we had another death; that old Mr. Lancaster had drawn his last uneasy breath.

Chapter XXXV

The police in the meantime were subjecting Mrs. Mac-Mullen to a severe grilling. Herbert Dean was there also, and it is his account which I am using.

They had found her in bed in a small hot back bedroom on an upper floor. She looked ill, he said. She had deep circles under her eyes, and she had evidently been crying. So pitiful an object was she that they tried being gentle with her; but at that she grew defiant and they had finally to change their tactics.

It was after that that she admitted she had known Holmes well, but she maintained stoutly that she had never suspected the Merriam woman's identity, or that the stolen money might have been in the trunk.

"Why should I?" she demanded. "And if it comes to that, why would I go to that Hall girl this morning and tell her all I did, if I'd any idea of it? So far as I can see, all I had to do was to keep my mouth shut, and I was all right."

"But you knew him pretty well?"

"Oh, I knew him all right. Not so well as you may think, but one of my daughters brought him here once or twice. I don't know that I'd ever mentioned the Merriam woman to him at all; or her trunk either."

"How did you explain his bringing you that word about it, if you knew he was the Halls' driver?"

"I guess I might as well tell you," she said, looking around at that ring of determined faces. "He'd been bootlegging a bit. Not much, but now and then, and so he knew a good many people. Nice people, too. When he walked up the steps and said Miss Merriam wanted her trunk that night it didn't surprise me. I just thought she'd seen him somewhere and asked him to bring the message. But I told him he'd have to bring the key to her door. She had a special lock on it."

"And he brought the key?"

"He must have. He got in. I didn't go upstairs to see."

They got little further of any importance from her. She blamed a bootlegging gang for his death, and she insisted over and over that she had had no suspicion of what might lie in the trunk, although she admitted buying a certain number of boxes of dress weights for Miss Emily, who said her patient used them for potting flowers and weighting vases. Now and then too a heavy parcel arrived by express addressed to Miss Merriam, and was placed in the hall outside her door until she appeared.

"Once she said it was books, and I remember I said they'd be heavy reading, the way it took even to lift it. And another time she said she'd been having some old flat silver replated, and she showed me a spoon. But I wasn't suspicious. If I watched all the queer things my roomers do I'd go crazy."

"Yet you had read about the substitution of the dress weights for the gold, hadn't you?"

"How on earth was I to connect this Lucy Merriam with the Lancaster family? Everybody knew they didn't have a nurse."

"This paper now, with the photograph. You were interested enough in these murders to put up a chain on your front door, and on the kitchen door too. But you never saw that picture until this morning. Is that your statement?"

"See here," she said, raising herself in bed. "I'm not under arrest, am I? If I am, I'll get a lawyer. If I'm not, you'll take what I'm telling you I told you about that picture. Why should I have gone over to Crescent Place this morning, if I had anything to hide?"

And here I believe the Inspector smiled grimly.

"Well, you see, Mrs. MacMullen, the trunk was already

gone, wasn't it? And the money!"

It wa onto this scene that without the slightest warning a new figure projected itself. The bedroom door opened and a girl rushed into the room, a pretty girl in a uniform with a thin summer coat over it, and with a face the color of chalk.

She took in the picture instantly, and with a quick gesture she wrenched the door open again. But she was not quick enough, for Herbert Dean caught it and slammed it shut. But I gather that he was gentle with her when he spoke.

"I see you've heard, Peggy."

"Then it's true?"

"I'm sorry. It is true."

She stood there leaning against the door and looking at nobody.

"Dead!" she said. "He's dead. My husband's dead, mother; and I'm going to have a baby!"

They were all most uncomfortable. Peggy was hysterical and beyond questioning, and some instinct of delicacy got them out of the room. They were on the whole well impressed by the mother, and whether Peggy was or was not implicated in the theft of the trunk as unimportant just then.

"We were on a murder case," the Inspector said later, "and Holmes hadn't killed Mrs. Lancaster. He was a bootlegger and a thief, but he wasn't a killer. So we let her have a little time to herself."

They found an overworked servant somewhere, and she showed them Miss Merriam's room. It was still unlocked, and so far as evidence went it yielded nothing whatever. It was a front room on the second floor, and its strategic value lay in its outlook, according to the police.

"She could be pretty sure no one she knew was anywhere around before she started out. And that was important."

The public library was just across the street.

The room itself contained little of a personal character: a few simple toilet articles on the dresser, books on a table, a pathetic and half-eaten box of candy and some writing paper, pen and ink on a small desk in a corner, about completed the list. The desk blotter had been used, but nothing on it was legible, although Herbert Dean took it with him when they

282

left.

The only thing of any value they had extracted from Peggy was the location of Holmes's little place in the country. This, as they had expected, was out the North Road and some six miles beyond where the body had been found; and it was to this property that they went at once, Inspector Briggs, Mr. Sullivan, a plain-clothes man whose name I never heard and Herbert Dean, still carefully holding and protecting that desk blotter.

"Be careful, Smith!" the Inspector admonished the uniformed driver. "Mr. Dean back here has got the whole story of these crimes in his lap. Spill him and you lose your job!"

There was no difficulty whatever about finding the place, which they reached rather late in the afternoon. Reticent as Holmes had always been about it, there was no attempt to disguise his ownership of the property, for on the narrow dirt road leading in from the highway a mail box on a post was marked W. Holmes in plain black letters.

The car turned in there and the officers got out at the house.

It was a neat and not unattractive cottage of the bungalow type, built of wood and with a small detached garage, and surrounded by a dozen acres or so of land which had at one time apparently been a market garden. Now it lay uncared for and weed-grown in the August sun, and after a glance around the officers turned their attention to the bungalow.

It was locked; locked so securely that even Herbert Dean, who was according to the Inspector one of the best picklocks out of prison, was unable to effect a peaceable entry. They broke a window finally, and one after the other they crawled inside.

The place was untidy but comfortable. There was a living room of sorts, a bedroom, a kitchen and a dining room which had clearly been devoted to other purposes. The Inspector glanced around him and sniffed.

"Packed it here," he said. "Where's the cellar, Sullivan?"

"Right under the house, I imagine," said Sullivan cheerfully. "They mostly are."

Three of the men went down the cellar stairs finally, to find there what they had expected; a small still, or "cooker" as the Inspector called it, a vast array of bottles and so on. But Herbert Dean did not go with them. He was making a slow and painstaking inspection of the living room and the bedroom, which in the end yielded him nothing except a half-dozen books — entirely of the crime variety — a box of labels of an excellent English whisky, and a notebook containing the names of some of our best citizens.

He did better in the kitchen, however. Holmes had evidently done everything in his little country place but eat there, and the stove revealed itself as a dumping place for everything from broken glass to old newspapers. When the others emerged from the cellar they found him on the dirty kitchen floor, with a bed sheet before him and on it a miscellaneous assortment of old razor blades, defective corks, cigar ends and what looked like a book until it was opened, and then revealed itself into the type of receptacle sold in a good many stores and generally used for cigarettes.

"See you're happy, Dean!" the Inspector said, rather grimly.

Herbert grinned and held up the box.

"Here's the thing I told you about, anyhow," he said. "Made it himself purely as an experiment; but rather a neat job at that. It would be interesting to know just how long he watched those library trips of Emily Lancaster's before he began to suspect, wouldn't it?"

The men examined the box. It was an ordinary book of fair size, with the center of each page neatly cut out but leaving an inch or less of margin. These margins had then been carefully glued together, and the interior strongly reinforced with a lining of adhesive tape. The result, which I now have, is a substantial box which looks like a rather well-worn book.

"Simple, isn't it?" Herbert said. "She carried two or three books each time, but the duplicate of this one went back and forth pretty regularly. They'd be fastened together probably, with a strap or a piece of cord. Cord probably for I imagine it broke once, on the path to Euclid Street."

The Inspector was less humorous about the box than he had been about the blotter. He took it and examined it carefully.

"He made it?" he said, "How d'you know this isn't the box

Emily Lancaster used, herself?"

"Because Miss Louisa Hall saw him making it. As a matter of fact, he made it last Saturday night."

The Inspector looked annoyed.

"Look here, Dean," he said. "I'll admit you're a valuable man. Maybe I don't always see eye to eye with you on this case, but I'm glad to have you. Just the same, I'm damned if I'll have you holding out on me, and that's what you're doing."

"You'd have jailed Holmes in a minute if you'd got anything on him, Inspector. And I needed him. If he knew how that gold and currency had got out of the house, he might know where it went. I was watching him pretty closely myself."

"Oh yeah? And you lost him, didn't you?"

"I did. I had a man of my own on him; but he lost him Wednesday morning, at the cemetery."

"And because you lost him, he's going there himself!"

But Herbert shook his head.

"I'm guilty on one count, Inspector," he said, "But not on the other. None of us can allow for accident, and I think Holmes's death was an accident. It wasn't in the original program, anyhow. Maybe there was a fight. Maybe he'd been put off the truck and ran in front of it to stop it. But he died because a car went over his chest, and it's pretty hard to run down and kill an active man just because you want to do it!"

Chapter XXXVI

They were still arguing over that, I believe, the Inspector truculent and rather flushed, when Sullivan quietly came in from an examination of the garage and reported that Holmes's uniform was in it, and a small light truck.

"Haven't gone over it," he said, "but it looks like the one we're after."

It was, they discovered. There was the nail in the tire, and the unmistakable evidence that it had been driven through a freshly tarred road. Careful examination of seat and body revealed nothing else, however, although some fresh scratches in the rear looked as though it had recently carried something heavy and unwieldy.

There was no sign of the trunk.

It was almost six o'clock by that time but still broad daylight, and so they set out to cover the dozen acres or so as well as they could. For now of course it was at least possible that Holmes had reached his garage safely, and had been killed on his way back into town. In that case he might have emptied the trunk, buried or hidden its contents and been on his way back with it to dispose of it in any one of a dozen ways, Even to return it to the MacMullen house.

They divided, the Inspector going back into the cottage and the three men searching the ground outside. It was the plain-clothes man who found the hole, and called the others to look at it.

The spot was well chosen. A bush had been lifted and carefully wheeled in, about three hundred feet from the house; and beside it lay the top sod, cut from an area about two feet by two. This space had then been dug out to a depth of about thirty inches, and an empty box with a wooden lid placed inside it.

The work was recent; about twenty-four hours old. The bush showed no signs of wilting, and under the surface the pile of soil was still moist. In the Inspector's words:

"It was all ready, you see. All he had to do was to fill the box out of the trunk, replant his bush, replace his sod, water the lot, and then sit tight until the excitement died down. Only it didn't work that way."

For that hole in the earth told its own story to the men who stood around it. Holmes had been killed on his way out with the gold. He had never reached his little place in the country with it, and somewhere safely hidden away or perhaps traveling respectably tagged on a train going nobody knew where, was Miss Emily Lancaster's trunk with its valuable contents.

I have written in detail of this expedition and its result; for it was the search for that trunk and its ultimate discovery which revealed the last and most shocking of our murders. But there was another discovery made late that afternoon which helped to prove Mrs. MacMullen innocent of any connivance as to the trunk itself.

Herbert Dean, going through the pockets of Holmes's uniform, found a letter in it addressed to that lady. It was in a fair imitation of Miss Emily Lancaster's hand, and it read:

"Dear Mrs. MacMullen: I am sorry not to see you again, but we are leaving in a hurry. This is my authority to give my trunk to the bearer, who will also have the key to my room." Signed. "Lucy Merriam."

"All set" as the Inspector says. "Note ready in case the landlady refused without it. And of course he had a pretty good general idea of the lock on that door, or maybe he had made an impression of it. He had plenty of chances."

It was too late when at last they got back to the city to do more than teletype a general description of the trunk, and to send operatives to the various railroad stations. Mrs. Mac-Mullen, again closely questioned, could give no details by which it could be identified, and had not even noticed from what store it had been delivered. Peggy was in danger of losing her child and a woman from the neighborhood and a doctor were with her, so that she could not be questioned; Mr. Lancaster had died that afternoon and any information from Margaret as to where her sister might have gone for a trunk was not obtainable, for she was shut in her room and reported to be in collapse.

The four men ate some dinner and decided to call it a day. And that night I had a brief but rather comforting talk with Herbert Dean. Comforting in spite of the fact that he started it with a warning. Mother was over at the Lancasters', for although Lydia Talbot always presided over our funerary ceremonies, it was and is one of our traditions that in cases of grief the family must on no account be left alone with it; and I understood from Mary that all the available Crescent, including Jim Wellington, was also there. I had begged off with a headache myself, which was real enough, and I was sitting on the porch in the dark when I heard his light active footsteps on the street and recognized them.

At first I thought he mean to go on by, and I ran out along the walk and called to him. It was then that he read me my lecture, right there on the path.

"I've been criminally remiss with you, Lou," he said severely. "I've warned you not to wander around alone, but apparently that isn't enough. Among the numbers of things I don't know about this case is why you were attacked the other night; or why anybody wanted to get into this house at all. Nevertheless, you were attacked and you might have been killed. If it were not for the fact that you have a lot of hair — very lovely hair, Lou! — well, it doesn't stand thinking about. Anyhow, we've got to keep you safe."

He laughed a little, as he led me back to the porch. "I

seem to be increasingly interested in keeping you safe, Lou. Odd, isn't it? That you should walk into my life at the instant I was being blown out of the Wellington kitchen! Still, I dare say many a romance has started less romantically."

He did not pursue that, however, although I dare say I colored.

"I've had a wretched afternoon," I told him. "You've left me feeling that I can't trust anybody; not even Jim Wellington."

"Well, that's something gained," he said rather drily. "And you are quite right. Don't trust anybody around here for a while anyhow. Don't trust them until you can see the whites of their eyes, and then run like hell!"

"Herbert," I said, "you must tell me about Miss Emily. Somehow I can't bear it."

And then he became grave, almost tender.

"Who are we to judge her?" he asked. "She took it; we can take that for granted. What we don't yet know is why. She may simply have wanted it for herself. After all, she had given up her life to that old woman. She may have been in inner rebellion for years; then suddenly she saw her chance to escape. Almost fifty and liable to the emotional upsets of that age in women, Lou my dear. She might have been in an abnormal state of mind. Such things happen.

"Or there's another possible explanation. She may have felt that too many people knew about that gold, and so she had to protect it. That is simply another guess. There's a third one, but less likely; that she and another member of the family, say, Mr. Lancaster, developed the plan together to protect the money. I don't believe it, myself. And I don't think that this third person was Margaret, for I have an idea that Margaret all along has suspected Emily of just what she did; and maybe more than she did."

"You mean that Margaret thinks Emily killed their mother? Oh, *no!*" I wailed. "She never did. How could she think such a thing?"

He reached over in the darkness and took my hand.

289

"Listen, Lou," he said. "I agree with you, but try to get Margaret's point of view. You see, there are degrees even in crime. There's cold-blooded calculated murder; and there's the picture of Emily Lancaster, not allowed to marry, getting on in years and heavy and tired, and that old woman nagging her until she'll do anything, even kill, to escape her. Margaret has had her share of it, too, so she's afraid it was Emily. That's all. And in twenty years or so, if you stay where you are, you'll possibly understand that fear of Margaret's yourself."

And he added:

"The terrible domination of the old and helpless, Lou. Think of it!"

I did think, to my own shame. I realized that along with the rest of us I had watched Emily Lancaster for years without ever thinking about her at all; had taken it for granted that she asked no more of life than her three meals a day, her broken sleep at night, and the servitude from which her only escape was into the books she read so avidly.

But he was entirely convinced, for more reasons than he gave me that night, that Emily Lancaster had never murdered her mother. It was more to reassure me than anything else that he explained that afternoon as he saw it.

"Just take the question of time, for instance," he said. "The killing didn't take long, but remember that she was fully dressed at three-thirty, and differently but fully dressed again at four. And she was a slow-moving woman. Even if she had stripped off her clothing and entered that room entirely naked—and that's been considered—she would have had to go back and bathe and clean the tub. And the police examined every tub in the house, including the outlets. The soap, too. Then there's that story of Jim's, that when he went up she was talking to her canary. If that was acting, for whose benefit was it? She may have known he was in the house. She could hardly have known he was upstairs in the hall."

My mind was too confused to work properly, but I was trying to think as best I could.

"Still, if she knew Jim was coming that afternoon to get out the gold, wouldn't she be pretty desperate?"

"But did she know? It was Margaret who did the telephoning. Emily was out at the library at the time, getting some books. But wasn't she prepared even for discovery, if it came before she could get away? I think she was. I'm not so sure about the window screen, but that flower pot was overturned; and they're not easy to overturn. I've tried it. How about those stories of someone on the porch roof at night, before the murder? Weren't they pure camouflage for her theft? — if it is theft to take what will be yours some day anyhow, and what you may feel you have earned a dozen times."

"Still, Herbert," I objected, "there was no reason for her running out of the house last Saturday night, unless there really was someone there. Or she thought so."

"That's different," he said almost roughly, and released my hand. "There was someone there that night, and if I knew who it was I'd have this case settled and out of the way."

After that he told me some of the steps by which he and the police had reached certain conclusions. He held out much I have already told here, but as a résumé it is not without interest. He had recaptured my hand, and I felt that he was amused at my feeble effort to free it.

"I'm holding it out of sheer gratitude, Lou darling. Nothing sentimental about it, so let it alone. You see, you set me on the track of that money."

"*I* did?"

"Certainly you did. You told me about Holmes and his book. Do you remember? It was like an answer to prayer. You see, my dear, that money wasn't taken all at once. It wasn't taken even in three or four packages, or whatever they might be. What had been going on was evidently what has been going in some of our banks, a sort of slow seepage, or so it looked. That meant somebody who had pretty steady access to the chest, so the first thing the police went after was the servants, particularly the upstairs maid, Peggy. But it was obvious from the beginning that in the twenty or so afternoons and ten Sundays that they were out of the house, none of these women could have carried off the gold. Add an evening out each week for good measure, and you'll see that, all other things being equal — chances at the chest and so on — any one of them would have had to carry each time several pounds of gold coins. It simply couldn't be done, for there was plenty of evidence that these women carried out only small hand-bags. That is, unless some one of them had an outside accomplice.

"We considered that, but the two older women seemed to have no outside life at all, and Peggy's mother we found to be a widow named MacMullen who kept a highly respectable lodging house on Liberty Avenue. Yes, we knew about Mrs. MacMullen before she came to you. Then you came along with your story of Holmes and his book, and suddenly I saw a light."

"I wish I did," I said despondently.

"Well, you see, from the first it was clear that Holmes occupied a highly strategic position in that room and bath of his. Also that he had plenty of time to use it. And Holmes wasn't tearing leaves out of a book. He was cutting them, one or two at a time. In other words, Holmes was making an experiment with a book, some glue and a spool of adhesive tape."

"I see," I said slowly. "He was making a box out of a book."

"Precisely. His experiment proved that, given a fair-sized book, it could be made to hold a good bit of flat gold money or currency. And Holmes was no angel. He was on the track of something, and that something was a fortune to him. Here was Miss Emily, making her almost daily trips to the library, and carrying two or more books each time, probably tied together.

"He had access to the MacMullen house, too, through Peggy; he almost certainly knew that Miss Merriam was Emily and the papers had told him that the gold had not been found. Then *he* saw a great light, and I'm sadly afraid, Lou, that he followed it to his death."

He told me then about the cottage, and about the

conclusion he had come to as to how Holmes had met his end.

"There were one or two odd things about the way he was found," he added thoughtfully. "They're rather hard to explain. In the first place, he was neatly laid out on that road, and his white handkerchief was placed on his chest and anchored there with a stone; as if to insure that the body would be seen. Then again, the autopsy showed nothing that would indicate that he had been struck down and then deliberately run over. If it didn't rather strain my imagination, I'd say he'd been run over by accident, and that by his own truck!"

But he added, after a pause:

"We have to remember this, of course, little Lady Lou; and maybe it will make you more careful. Holmes, tragic and puzzling as he is, only enters the picture after that first murder. In a sense, he was only an interruption. He interfered with a carefully laid plan; much as did Margaret Lancaster the other morning."

"Margaret interfered?" I asked. "How did she interfere?"

"She sent away the bird cage," he said, rising and smiling down at me. "And the cage had Emily's keys in it. Do you see? Holmes didn't need those keys; not enough at least to kill her to get them. But somebody else did. When we know who that is—!"

Across at the Lancasters' the front door had opened, and a broad beam of light gleamed out on the trees and the walk. He got up quickly.

"Just one question, Lou," he said, "and we'll have to be quick. After Mrs. Lancaster's murder somebody burned what might have been a photograph, on very heavy board; one of the old types of mountings. Or it might have been something else, pasteboard anyhow with a beveled edge and gilded. Does that mean anything to you? I think, but I'm not sure, that it came out of the Lancaster house."

There were no voices on the porch across by that time, and I had to think quickly.

"They had quantities of old pictures," I said. "Some were

293

framed, but I haven't missed any. Of course I haven't been there much since. And there's the old photograph album, of course. Margaret gave it to Mother."

"Margaret gave it to her," he said slowly. "When? Since her mother's death?"

"Yes. It's upstairs now somewhere. I think it has never been unwrapped."

"Unwrapped? You mean it was tied up when it came? Lou, I've got to have that album, and I've got to have it soon. It'll be back here at twelve o'clock, and don't open the door until you've turned on the porch light and seen who it is. Is that a promise?"

I agreed, and to my stunned amazement he bent down and kissed me lightly on the lips.

"That's for being a good girl," he said, and a moment later he had disappeared down the street.

It was not until he had gone that I remembered that I had not asked about the poison ivy.

Chapter XXXVII

The neighbors were leaving the Lancaster house now. I could hear their low decorous voices and the subdued sound of their feet on the steps of the porch, and it was almost a shock to hear that even Mrs. Talbot had ceased to boom. At the street pavement they separated into two groups, the Talbots turning right, the others coming toward me; Jim, the Daltons and Mother. The men in their dark clothes, the women in black, as they approached their faces looked like four disembodied and slightly swaying white balloons; and this illusion was increased by the fact that they were not talking at all. As they came closer I saw that Jim was slightly ahead, and that with his hands thrust deep into his pockets he was apparently lost in thought.

At the foot of our walk he stopped and faced them, like a man who has made a decision of some sort.

"Look here," he said. "I suppose there's no use expecting an honest answer, but isn't there a chance that *he* is mixed up in this somehow?"

"Nobody has heard of him for years," Bryan Dalton said. "In any case, since you've brought the matter up, why the Lancasters? He was fond of Emily, even if he hated the old lady."

"He had plenty of reason to detest her, I gather! What's the use of all this secrecy anyhow?" Jim demanded. "I didn't know it myself until a day or two ago—I dug it out of the Talbots' Lizzie, if you want to know—and George Talbot doesn't know it yet. If that isn't like this Crescent, I don't know what is. I've kept quiet on George's account but I'm damned if I care to go on. That story's got to be told. If he was crazy then he's crazy now."

"He was just about as crazy as I am," Bryan Dalton said shortly.

"Would you know him if you saw him? Any of you?" Jim persisted.

They were all certain that they would, but Jim himself, it appeared, had never seen this unnamed individual at all; at least not since he was a small child. He was impatient and irritable, as I could tell by his voice.

"He may be right here among us," he insisted. "He may be your Joseph, Dalton! Or he may be this new butler of ours. He's a queer egg. If he's a butler than I'm a housemaid!"

"Joseph has been with us for years," Bryan Dalton said stiffly.

"And John Talbot's been missing for years too!" Jim persisted.

I sat up suddenly in my chair. So it was John Talbot they were talking about, the man of the crayon portrait in the stable loft, and of whom Lydia only that very morning had said that he was the gentlest soul alive. And at one time he had been considered a lunatic, but not by everybody!

Mother was speaking, in her clear high-bred voice.

"You are being absurd, Jim," she said. "For years all of us have tried to keep that unfortunate story from George. Do you want George to learn it? Or the police?"

"The police! My God, why shouldn't they know? It's their business to know. What sort of a conspiracy of silence is this, anyhow? If John Talbot liked Emily, how do you know she didn't let him into the house last Thursday? She might have thought he was sane, and then he got out of hand; and then later on he killed her too. Are you going to ignore a thing like that to conceal an old scandal or whatever it was?"

"Listen, Jim," Laura Dalton said. "If anyone of us really thought John Talbot capable of such a thing, we would tell it. We simply don't, that's all. That other was a crime of passion. She'd ruined his life and cut him off from his family."

"Someone," said Bryan Dalton, "might say to my wife that I do not regard that as an unmixed evil!"

But Jim was not listening.

"Nevertheless," he persisted, "he shot the woman he had eloped with, and was shut up with the criminal insane, wasn't he? Is he there now? Does anybody know?" And when he received no answer I saw him under the street light make a furious and hopeless gesture.

"There you are!" he said. "And I'm not to tell the police! Well, I'm saying here and now that I intend to tell the police, and you're all going to take it and like it. By God, I believe the whole lot of you would let me go to the chair, if it came to that, rather than admit that a man tried under another name in another state for murder was a Talbot of Crescent Place!"

He turned angrily and swung away toward his house, leaving them staring after him.

Mother went into the house without seeing me, and she asked no questions when I followed her into the library. She looked tired and all she said was that Margaret Lancaster was taking her stepfather's death very well, but that she looked rather dreadful.

"I wouldn't say anything about this, Louisa," she told me, "but she is uneasy. You see, she cannot find her father's revolver. He always kept it in an upper bureau drawer, but it is not there now. She has searched everywhere for it."

I was startled.

"When did she miss it?"

"Last night, I think. It's really odd, for only the nurse and the doctor went into that room. And Margaret herself, of course."

She was more disturbed than she cared to admit; and it was very late before at last I got her settled into bed, with the usual vases on her window sills and her hall door locked.

"You *will* lock your door carefully, Louisa?"

"I always do, Mother, where is the album you brought from the Lancasters' the other night? I'd like to look at it."

She looked surprised, but not at all startled.

"The album?" she said. "I did put it somewhere. Yes, I took it up to the third floor. Surely you don't want it tonight?"

"I just wanted to know where it is," I said evasively, and went out.

It was almost midnight before through the connecting bathroom I heard the click of her lamp as she switched it off. Even after that she turned restlessly for some time, and I was almost in despair when at last her deep and regular breathing told me that she slept. Then at last I was free, and the next half hour stands out in my memory as one of a general misery leading gradually to sheer terror.

As I may or may not have said, in both the Lancaster house and our own only one staircase leads to the third floor. This takes off from the rear hall on the second floor, and it was on this staircase that Mary and Annie had established their absurd barricade. The first thing I had to do therefore was to move the chairs, which seemed just then to have as many legs as a centipede and the viciousness of all inanimate things in the dark at night. Then, having at last aligned them in the second floor hall and climbed the staircase as silently as possible, on the top landing I stepped without warning into a pan of cold water, evidently also a part of the defense system, and then and there in the dark I almost sat down and wept.

Time was short, however, and with that complete loss of self-respect which comes of wet feet and bedraggled skirts, I at last reached the cedar room and having closed the door turned on the light. Like the same room at the Lancasters, it too had a trapdoor to the roof, and I looked at it nervously. It was closed and bolted, however, and with increasing courage I began my search.

It was not difficult. The Crescent not only wraps what it stores, but labels each parcel; and thus I found myself confronting packages of all sorts ranging from one marked "L's first party dress," to more recent ones tagged modestly as "woolen undergarments, medium weight." Of the album, wrapped or unwrapped, there was not a trace, and my wrist watch told me that it was already five minutes past twelve.

There was only one other place possible, and that was my former schoolroom over the old part of the house; Mother used it now and then as a sort of extra storeroom for odds and ends, and I went there with rather a crawling of the spine. Early impressions stay with us, I find, and although it was twenty years since it had happened, I could still remember the sheer horror of the night when, the governess out of the room and the dumb-waiter bell ringing, I had heard my supper tray coming up and had seen instead a dreadful black face making horrible grimaces at me from the shaft.

It had caused quite a stir in the neighborhood, for I had fainted flat on the floor; and even the discovery that it had only been "Georgie" Talbot on the top of the slide had not entirely removed the horror of that moment. Indeed, the first glance I took after I had switched on a light was toward the shaft. But the sliding door was closed, and thus reassured I set about my search.

The album was there, still wrapped as it had been, and lying on my scarred old schoolroom table. I picked it up and stood for a moment looking about the room. I was a child again, being told to be a little lady. I was an adolescent girl, curious about a thousand things which no one thought I ought to know. And I was a young woman, slipping up there to write my first and almost my last love letter, and crying my heart out because if I married I would leave a still grieving mother alone.

But mostly I was a child, left alone in a room where there was a horror; a sliding door which at any time might open again and show a grinning monster. Then, just as I had put out the light and was working my way in the dark toward the hall, I heard something fumbling at that door again.

I could not believe it. I could feel the very hair on my head fairly rising, but still I did not believe it. Nor could I move. There were weights in my feet, and my legs were like the legs of a sleeper with nightmare, who must escape and cannot move them. And still that dreadful fumbling went on.

So familiar was I with the door to the slide that I knew to the instant when there was space for fingers to catch the edge of it, and I could follow inch by inch its slow movement upward. Infinitely stealthy, all of it; as though time were nothing and only caution mattered. Then at last the power came back into my legs I ran as I have never run before, crashing into the pan at the top of the stairs and accompanied by it and in a deluge of water fell the entire length of them and brought up in a sitting position in the hall below; without breath left in me even to scream.

Chapter XXXVIII

The next sound I heard was Mary's voice, spoken through a crack in her door above: "The saint's preserve us! Who is it?"

"It's all right, Mary," I gasped. "I'm sorry, but it's me again! I fell over your pan."

"Are you hurt, miss?"

"No, I think not. Mary, there's someone in the dumb-waiter shaft. I've just heard them."

But with that I heard her give a low wail, followed instantly by the closing and bolting of her door. There was plainly no help from that direction, and I dare say with the instinct of the woman who saved the parrot and left her baby during a fire I picked up the album and flew down to the front porch and Herbert Dean.

Fortunately, Mother had not awakened.

The search which followed, while revealing no intruder in the house, clearly proved that I had been correct about the shaft, and Herbert Dean showed a capacity for sheer rage which surprised me.

"Damn them all!" he said. "I've told them this thing isn't over, but they take the guards off! I'll have that Inspector's hide for this, and the Commissioner's too." Which was followed by a bit of rather stronger language than I care to repeat.

The search revealed certain facts. One of these was that as our basement is shut off from the main floor by a strong and well-locked door, it had not been considered necessary to watch the windows with any great care. One of them in fact was wide open, and had been so in all probability since Mary had raised it earlier in the week.

Curiously enough, the use of the abandoned old dumb-waiter as a means of access to the house had never occurred to any of us. It went to the basement, since before Mr. Lancaster and my father had done over the two houses the kitchen had been there. But it was years since it had been used. Once Mother had found Annie dropping soiled linen down the shaft, and had sternly forbidden it as a slovenly habit. After that the shaft door into the laundry had been closed and nailed.

It was neither nailed nor closed that night when Herbert Dean reached it, with a revolver in his hand and me at his heels. It was standing wide open, like the window, and examination showed that the old wood had rotted around the nails and must have given way easily.

He looked exasperated as he examined it.

"Why the devil didn't you tell me this was here?" he demanded. "It's a port of entry for anybody who wants to get into this house. Whoever hit you the other night probably came in this way, for I'd had an eye on the kitchen door; and you trapped them at the foot of the back stairs. Didn't anyone remember it?"

"Do you imagine we deliberately concealed it?"

He laughed a little then, and getting up on a chair he examined the top of the slide itself with meticulous care.

"Does the Crescent housekeeping extend to things like this?" he inquired. "That is, is the top of this thing kept dusted? Or was it actually forgotten?"

"I imagine no one has seen it at all for five years, or dusted the top of it for fifteen."

"Somebody has. It's been cleaned lately. Carefully wiped. Very canny, this unknown of ours. Taking no chances. I suppose the ropes are all right? I'm going up on it anyhow; but not until I've taken you up myself and shut you into your room and heard you lock your door."

A program which he would have carried out with entire success had he not on emerging from the schoolroom in the dark bumped head-on into Annie, who had finally determined to fill the pan again and was on her way to replace it.

The resulting uproar was one to waken the dead, and although in the midst of it Herbert Dean managed to escape, to this day Annie insists that an enormous creature that night rushed at her in our upper hall, made an effort to strangle her, and only fled when she doused him with a pan of cold water. This last was true enough, for Herbert spent most of the remainder of that chilly August night on guard outside the house, drenched to the skin and furiously annoyed, and clutching a large and heavy old photograph album by which he seemed to set considerable store.

Not that it was really as simple as all that, for Mother was up by that time and on hearing Annie's story had at once called the telephone central and demanded the police. Herbert Dean's insistence on my silence was put to a heavy premium after they arrived, but I kept my own council and let Annie tell her story. The result was a thorough searching of the house, followed by the discovery of Herbert himself, with the album neatly tucked under his arm, hidden away in the limousine and obviously not courting discovery.

It was a cruising radio car which had come, and the men did not know him. So for the second time within a few days Herbert found himself under arrest. It took a half hour at the station house to get himself identified and released, and before that happened an officer who had seen him taken into the Lancaster house only a few nights before stopped and stared into the room where he was being detained.

"Where did you get *him* again?" he asked the sergeant.

"Over on Crescent Place. Hiding in a garage."

"And what's that he's got?"

"Old photograph album. Holding onto it like nobody's business, too."

The officer eyed Herbert with cold suspicion.

"He's crazy as a loon," he said. "Last time I saw him he was after an empty bird cage. Told somebody after he was grabbed that he was a dickey bird of some sort, and that he wanted the cage so he'd have a place to sit down in!"

We knew nothing of all this that night, and I did not see Herbert again until later that day. Mother was too disturbed to sleep again, however. The officers had discovered the open window in the basement and the chair we had left by the dumbwaiter shaft. One of them had even taken the trip to the schoolroom on it and had been stuck between two floors and only rescued by herculean efforts. But the whole result was that Mother's carefully built case against Holmes seemed to have collapsed, and that when I finally went to sleep at dawn she was still up and gazing thoughtfully out of her window.

That day the intensive search for the missing trunk went on. The store where it had been bought was located and a careful description and photographs obtained. Both were sent out to all precincts and detective squads, and to all state troopers, as well as to railways, hotels and even storage warehouses, with an enlargement of the special lock Emily Lancaster had ordered to supplement the regular one. By telephone, short-wave radio and teletype the search was taken up, and by afternoon the press had the photographs and ran them that night as "Mysterious Trunk Wanted by Police in Crescent Place Murders."

One paper offered a reward for its discovery, and within a day or two the others followed suit. But nothing happened, and when in the course of time it was discovered, as everyone knows who reads the papers, it was too late. As the Inspector says:

"What threw everybody off was those foreign labels. It was a smart trick, that. Pretty well plastered with them, it was; everything from steamer tags to hotels in Europe. It made the same difference that a beard and a pair of false eyebrows would make on you, Miss Hall!"

But all they learned that first day of the search, Friday

August the twenty-sixth, was the identity of the colored man who had helped to carry the trunk down to the waiting truck. He had not noticed the white helper, save that he had a short beard and was not young; and he had an alibi to bear out his statement that he had remained behind when the truck drove off. He added something to that, however. The white helper had gone along.

He had waited until Holmes was in the driving seat, and had then got onto the truck and curled up in the rear. He had supposed it was by prearrangement, but Holmes might not have realized that he was there.

"I dunno, boss," he said. "That heah white man, he jes' got in over the tail. Engine makin' a mighty lot o' noise jes' then, so mebbe the other fellah didn' know. This white man, las' I saw of him he was sittin' flat behin' the trunk."

But that Friday, beginning with two o'clock in the afternoon, stands out in all the history of the case as its one most significant day. Not only because it was that night that Lydia Talbot disappeared, but because at two o'clock that afternoon Margaret Lancaster got into a taxicab and, driving to the District Attorney's office, proceeded of her own free will to make a statement so surprising that even the stenographic notes were in places almost unintelligible.

No one of us saw her go, or had any idea of her intention. She left Miss Lydia in the house, got into the taxicab and was driven downtown alone; and I have often wondered since what must have been her thoughts as, bolt upright in that cab and as carefully dressed as usual, she went determinedly to expose at last what she had fought so hard to conceal.

She looked exhausted and old, Herbert Dean says, as she went in. She threw back her heavy black veil, took a seat across the wide desk from the District Attorney, and simply said:

"I have come to tell the real story of my mother's murder, and of my sister's death following it. I suppose you will want a stenographer."

The District Attorney could hardly believe what he heard.

He stared at her.

"You are—you want to make a signed statement?"

"I do. It cannot hurt anybody now."

They kept her waiting for a time. It was dangerous, for they knew she might weaken at any moment, and for all her quiet manner it was clear to everybody that she was close to actual physical collapse. But there would be points to check and questions to ask; and for this they needed the Inspector and Mr. Sullivan. The Commissioner had taken his ivy poisoning home to bed, but Herbert was already there.

Someone in that fifteen-minute interval asked her if she needed some spirits of ammonia, but she shook her head.

"I am quite all right," she said.

That was the only time she spoke until, with everything ready, she asked if she should start. The District Attorney said "Please," and she drew a long breath.

"As you all know," she said, "I am Margaret Lancaster. And I am here to say that to the best of my knowledge and belief, my sister while mentally deranged killed my mother; and that last Sunday night, out of fear that she would do further harm, my stepfather shot and killed my sister.

Chapter XXXIX

"I shall try to be as brief as possible, and I am telling what I know because you already suspect my stepfather. I have learned from the nurse that you have his pistol; that she gave it to you. But what you cannot know is the reason he had for killing my sister. While he could not tell me, I am convinced that he considered her unbalanced mentally at times, and dangerous.

"I had noticed nothing different in my sister Emily until last spring. At that time Mother began to worry about her personal fortune, and she finally decided to have some of it turned into gold, this gold to be kept in a chest under her bed. None of us approved, and Emily least of all, but Mother was determined.

"She arranged with her nephew, James Wellington, to make this exchange for her, and this he did under protest. I need not go into that. You know all that already.

"It was in April that I began to notice a change in Emily. She came in one day very white, and went into my mother's room. There they had an argument of some sort, and my mother was very angry after it. From that time on I felt that the relationship between them had changed. Emily was tearful at times, and once I found her in the storeroom with an old family photograph album. She was crying over it. Later I saw it in my mother's room. She kept it in the top drawer of the chest beside her bed.

"I am telling you this because the album caused me so much anxiety later, although I do not yet understand just why. I have wondered — but I must get on with this statement.

"Emily was my mother's nurse, and was in and out of her room at all hours. It was early in the summer that I began to wonder about the gold under Mother's bed. Emily had been the soul of honesty, but late one night I heard her coming out of Mother's room, and I opened the door. She heard me and she looked very much alarmed. There was a low light in the hall but I could see her plainly, and she was carrying something that looked like one of the canvas bags from the chest. When I knocked at her door she was some time in letting me in, and then she looked frightened.

"I did not know what to do. I went to Mother's room, but she had had her usual opiate and was sleeping soundly. The chest was closed and locked.

"After that I watched Emily as well as I could. I examined her room over and over while she was out, but I could find nothing. She hardly ever carried a purse, and the only places she went were to the library and to a woman on Liberty Avenue across from the library who she said was dying of a cancer. I even followed her once or twice, but she went nowhere else.

"If she had not been in such a state of terror I would have given up then. There was no gold or money in her room, and she evidently had no box in any bank. But she was so queer that at last I went to Bryan Dalton. He laughed at me at first, but he too saw the change in her and at last we agreed to keep a watch and see if she left the house at night.

"We established a sort of post office in our woodshed, and he would drop a note there. Usually it said: 'All quiet.' Sometimes he said she had come downstairs at night apparently for something to eat. But she never left the house. This will explain why Mr. Dalton has been involved in the case. He had nothing whatever to do with it.

"It was about the first of this month that my father became suspicious. Emily had professed to believe that someone was trying to get into the house at night, and that they were after the money under Mother's bed. On the night of August first Father was sleepless and anxious—he had never approved of the hoarding anyhow, considering it dangerous as well as unpatriotic. That night he heard a sound from Mother's room, and he went in.

"Emily was on her knees beside the bed, and she screamed when Father spoke to her. That wakened Mother, but Emily said she was after a sleeping tablet herself and that it had dropped under the bed.

"I knew nothing of this until my father told me later on, after Mother's death. When Emily had gone Father managed to examine the chest, but it was locked as usual and so he went back to bed. He asked Mother after that to have the chest opened and the money recounted, but that annoyed her and he had to let it go for the time. It was more than two weeks before he finally decided to have it done, with or without her consent. Then, on the morning of Thursday August the eighteenth, he told me exactly what he had seen and I foolishly told him what I knew.

"While Emily was out at the library I telephoned to Jim Wellington to come at four that afternoon, for what Father called an audit. Father had not told Mother, and it was to tell her that he came back after he had started for his walk that afternoon. He changed his mind, however, after he was in the house. She was asleep, and he decided to wait until Jim was there.

"I do not yet know how Emily learned about the audit, and the early afternoon was as you know it. Lydia Talbot brought Mother some things for her lunch, but was too late with them. Her sister-in-law, Mrs. John Talbot, left with Father at half past three. It was my afternoon out, but I had arranged with Father not to go and was in my room.

"At three-thirty—or a little later—I saw Bryan Dalton walking from his garage toward our woodshed. Our servants could not see him from the lower floor, but I saw him from my window. Instead of going inside and leaving a report, he took up a position where he could watch the house, and that puzzled me. I thought at first he was merely waiting for the result of the audit and I paid no attention; but at last he saw me and waved to me to come down.

"I had turned on my shower, but I began to dress, and then I heard Emily screaming and as soon as I could get into my dressing gown and slippers I ran out. What I thought was that Jim had come earlier than usual, that the theft had been discovered, and that Emily was having an attack of hysteria. But you know what I found."

Here I believe she stopped for the first time. Someone offered her a glass of water, but she refused it and after steadying her voice she went on.

"I need not go into all that. You know it as well as I do. For one thing, Bryan Dalton had thought as I did about Emily's screams and her fainting attack, and when he saw Louisa Hall bending over her he did not go to her. Instead he came up to our kitchen porch and waited there outside. It was locked, of course. The servants were upstairs in the hall by that time, and nobody saw him.

"But I kept one thing from you then, and I am telling it now because I understand that you have certain suspicions about Bryan Dalton. When I went into that room after Emily had rushed downstairs, I found the album I have spoken of open on the bed, and the two pages were covered with fingerprints in — in blood. Fresh blood.

"Emily was still screaming, and I had only a second or two. Mother's sewing scissors were on her bureau, and I cut them both out. I still had them in my hand when I called down the stairs to tell the servants; I hid them inside a radiator cover in the side hall. Later on, when I went back to get Father a glass of wine, I gave them to Bryan Dalton. They were stiff, but he put them inside his overalls; and as soon as he dared, at my request, he burned both the overalls and the pages of the album, out in No Man's Land. He was afraid there would be traces of blood on the overalls.

"My father believed as I did. We knew that every door into the house was locked, and neither one of us believed that Emily was normal. All the Talbots have a queer streak in them.

"You all know what followed. My father — he was really my

310

stepfather—was convinced that Emily had done it in a fit of insanity. What is more she had worn a glove of his, one of a pair Jim Wellington had left, and which Father had found lying about. He kept them in the housemaid's closet on the second floor, and used them when he blackened his boots. But after the—after she had finished in Mother's room she didn't even try to hide it. She threw it down into our lower hall, and when I came back into the house with her after she had pretended to faint outside, I picked it up almost under the nose of a policeman.

"I hid it behind the pillows of the library couch when I fixed it for her, and later I got it out of the house. But Father saw in that glove an attempt to place the crime on him. He never spoke to Emily again after I told him about it.

"I tried to shake this conviction of his, to save a dreadful scandal. But he was certain that she had done it, and I myself have never doubted it. She herself knew that he suspected her, especially after that first night when both of us found him in the cedar room. You see, the police had found no stained clothing, and he thought perhaps she had hidden what she wore on the roof. He had been up there, anyhow, and Emily knew as well as I did why.

"The next three days were too horrible to talk about. Doctor Armstrong was keeping Emily under opiates, but Father would not even go into her room. What he thought until Sunday night was that she was definitely dangerous; not to him, but to almost anybody. And on Sunday night things reached a climax.

"He was never able to tell me, but I believe he heard me call to Emily and knew that she was going downstairs. When she left the house he must have followed her, and when she went first to the Daltons' and got a spade—for that is what she did—it meant only one thing to him. That was that she had buried Mother's money and then killed her.

"That meant more than insanity. It meant that it was a crime to conceal a crime, and he must have gone mad himself. He went back into the house, got his automatic, followed her to the Talbots' and shot her. I know that, for I found his pistol on top of his dresser the next morning, and it had been fired.

"I am not guessing about this. The next night while George Talbot was asleep in our library — Monday night — I found his automatic on the floor, and I remembered something he had told me last spring at a picnic. That was that the barrels of two similar automatics can be exchanged, and that an innocent man could in this manner be charged with a crime he had never committed; since every barrel left its peculiar marks on a bullet.

"I make no defense. I knew there could be no case against George. He had no reason whatever for killing my sister. And my father was dying. He and I had been very close, just as my mother cared more for Emily than for me. I changed the barrels that night, wiped both the guns and put my father's back where it belonged. I am sorry now, but at least he died in peace."

That was the end of the official statement, and I shall eliminate the questions which followed it, with the exception of one, and that was asked by Herbert Dean.

"I would like to go back to that Thursday afternoon, Miss Lancaster. Just why had Bryan Dalton waited by the woodshed? We knew that he had, but he has refused to give a reason."

"He wanted to see me."

"Is that all?"

She hesitated, but he was relentless now. He walked forward and confronted her.

"Shall I tell you what Bryan Dalton saw, Miss Lancaster?"

"But he's wrong!" she said wildly. "I swear that he is wrong."

"Shall I tell you what Bryan Dalton saw that afternoon from somewhere near his garage, and what brought him over to watch your house? Or will you tell us?"

She said nothing, and he continued.

"What he thought he saw was an axe, moving slowly up the back wall of the Lancaster house. But that garage of his is some distance away, and anyhow the thing was incredible. He walked over and looked into the woodshed, and the axe was mixing; but he is not a quick thinker, and he was puzzled more than anything else.

"It was not until Emily ran out shrieking that he began to

understand. Even then he would not believe it. He went to the house, but the kitchen door was locked and the servants upstairs. After that I imagine he went to the ground underneath the window, and he thought he saw marks showing that the axe had lain there hidden in the planting for some time. All day and maybe part of the night. That's true, isn't it?"

"But he's wrong, I tell you," she said, more calmly. "I swear that he is wrong."

"What was he to think?" Herbert said, still sternly. "Here was your sister, in spotless white, still in the side garden. She had not killed her mother. And when you came with those fingerprints from the album to be destroyed—! Of course he thought it was your window."

"It was not. I swear that."

"No," he said quietly. "I know it was not. But you should be grateful to a very gallant gentleman, Miss Lancaster, who thinks to this moment that you had hidden that axe and later on fastened a cord to it; and that at or about three-thirty that afternoon you drew it up and through the window into your bedroom."

"And you don't think so?" she asked.

"I don't think so. He simply mistook the window. The axe went into the housemaid's closet next door."

Somewhat later they let her go. They were of two minds about her, that group in the handsome office which as Mother would have said represented a considerable outlay of taxpayers' money. They compromised on having her followed, but she went directly home.

There was a long argument after her departure.

"You can see how it was," the Inspector said when it was all over. "Here was Dean; I'd watched him work and I had a good bit of confidence in him. But the D. A. and the Commissioner when I called him up were hell-bent on holding her.

"What they figured was that the affair of Holmes and the money was out. You know what I mean. Emily had hidden the money, Holmes was carrying it off and somebody else had got wise and took it from him. But this Margaret Lancaster not only knew it was gone. She knew, according to them, where it had gone to. All this story Emily had made up about a woman with a cancer probably hadn't fooled her at all.

"You've got to remember this, too. Margaret's shower was running. She could have done the thing mother-naked—if you'll excuse me, Miss Hall—and then gone back and had a shower and been as clean as a baby. Only mistake she made, as they saw it, was that she sent away the bird cage, and that had the keys to the MacMullen house and the trunk in it. Then later on she followed Emily when she went to get them, and killed her with her father's gun.

"Unnatural? Sure, but the whole thing looked unnatural, didn't it? She'd changed the barrels of those guns, and it was what you might call an open question whether she did that to save him or to save herself.

"Then again, when they got Dalton back that afternoon after she had gone home Dean turned out to be right. He believed she did it, was sure it was her window that axe went into. He admitted he might be mistaken, but that's what he thought. She was about frantic when she gave him that stuff to burn. At first he thought that was natural enough, seeing that she was so sure Emily had done it. Later on he got to thinking—about Emily's white dress and Margaret taking a bath and so on, and he wasn't so sure."

Chapter XL

It was that evening that Lydia Talbot disappeared.

None of us at that time knew about Margaret Lancaster's visit to the District Attorney's office, and the afternoon was the usual afternoon on the Crescent when a normal death has taken place among us.

We called up our various florists and ordered flowers according to our tastes and means, we pressed or ordered pressed the black clothes we kept for such occasions, and from behind our immaculate window curtains we watched the cars of various old friends and city dignitaries drive up, leave cards with messages of sympathy on them, and drive away again.

Lydia Talbot had as usual taken over the duties of hostess, and stood gravely in the lower hall. To those of us who went in she gave the last details with a certain gusto, and she was talking to me while instructing the mortician, as to the moving of the parlor furniture so as to leave room for the casket.

"I understand that it was really quite peaceful at the end, Louisa. It's very sad, but of course after all he wasn't a young man. 'Over there, *over there!*' she startled me by adding. 'Put the piano there, I told you that before.'"

She darted into the parlor in her rather rusty black dress, and I do not think she even saw me when I left.

That was at five o'clock. Margaret must have been back at that time, but none of us saw her return and officially she was still prostrated in her bed, with the nurse in attendance.

315

Save for the discovery of the bird cage that afternoon, I can remember nothing of any consequence. Both our servants were jumpy, which was natural, and Annie's story of the man on the third floor now included a glittering knife in his hand, although how she could have seen it in the darkness seems rather unusual. Mother fortunately had been able finally to lay the whole disturbance to hysteria, and had not missed the album; and the trunk was still undiscovered, as was the identity of the white man who had helped to get it out of the MacMullen house.

Peggy was still there, very ill after losing her child; and a careful inventory of the roomers in the MacMullen house had resulted in nothing. All of them were women with one exception, and this was the pianist at a local theater, who had been on duty all evening of the night the trunk was taken.

The discovery of the bird cage was valueless. The gimlet-eyed man and Daniels' cart had gone with Daniels himself was back on the job that day. It was on my way back from the Lancasters' that I encountered him. He looked white and drawn, and I stopped.

"I'm glad you are back," I said. "You haven't been sick, I hope?"

"Yes, miss. I haven't been myself. I see they've had another death next door."

"Yes. But this at least was natural."

"Well, maybe, miss. Although there's such a thing as being killed by troubles. Still, as Shakespeare says: 'what's gone and what's past help should be past grief.' I meant to tell you, miss; I think there's a bird cage belonging to Miss Emily Lancaster over on Euclid Street. I've seen it hanging in her window many a time. But it isn't the same bird. It doesn't sing any."

I still wonder why he told me that. Was Daniels himself suspicious of the truth at that time? I think not. It sounded like and probably was purely a piece of information, passed on in case the cage was wanted again. Nevertheless I telephoned the fact to Inspector Briggs, Herbert Dean being somewhere unknown, and they got the cage that night. But it revealed nothing, nor had the family which had it any information.

One of their children had found it lying abandoned in No Man's Land some days before and had brought it home. The housewife had simply scrubbed it thoroughly, furnished it with a new bird, and thought no more of it.

If it had borne any fingerprints they were certainly gone.

It was Mother who brought the first news about Lydia Talbot. She had relieved her to go home for dinner at half past seven, and she had not come back when Mother returned, visibly annoyed, at a quarter to ten.

"Really," she said, "it is too annoying of Lydia. She said positively that she would come back as soon as she had eaten her dinner and steamed a crêpe veil for Margaret."

"I'll go over and find out, if you like," I offered. "She may be sick."

But Mother, who had insisted on Annie as an escort both to and from the Lancaster house, refused to let me go.

"The nurse is there," she said. "And it's too late for anyone to call now anyhow."

I was puzzled about Miss Lydia, but not alarmed. As I may have said, it is our custom in times of death to regard the body as a sort of neighborhood trust, and to separate the family from it with the same firm kindliness as that with which we separate the family from the world. Also we guard over and watch it during the daylight and evening hours, although in recent years we have ceased sitting up with it at night. Little by little this duty toward our dead has been passed to the spinsters of the Crescent, as being presumably free of domestic obligations, marital or otherwise; and for years Lydia Talbot had been the high priestess of our funeral rites.

She had enjoyed these brief hours of importance, and I was slightly uneasy after Mother had gone up to bed. I tried to get the Talbot house by telephone, but evidently someone had left a receiver off and I could not do it.

It must then have been nearly eleven when I went out onto our front porch to look across at the Talbots', and to wonder if I had the courage to go over and see if everything was all right. To my astonishment I found George on the walk, and at first I thought he held a revolver in his hand. It turned out to be a flashlight, however, for he switched it onto my face.

"What is it, George? What's wrong?"

"Nothing. At least I hope not. But I thought I'd take a look around. You see we can't locate Aunt Lydia. I went to the Lancasters' just now to get her, and she hasn't been there since dinner. I've been along the Crescent. She isn't at Jim's or the Daltons', and your house was dark, so I knew she wasn't there. I—well, I just thought I'd look around. The way things have been going here—!"

"When did she leave the house, George?"

"About a quarter to nine, and it's eleven now. She hadn't a hat or anything," he added. "I haven't told Mother, but—well, where could she go, like that? All she had was a small box with a veil in it. I believe she'd repaired it for Margaret Lancaster."

"You're sure of that?"

"I saw her out myself. I suppose it's all right. She's perfectly capable of taking care of herself, but where could she go? She wasn't even wearing a hat."

"We'd better get a policeman," I said. "And we can look around, anyhow."

I dare say I sounded worried, for he looked at me quickly.

"You don't really think it's serious, do you? Great heavens, Lou, who would want to hurt her? She isn't particularly pleasant or agreeable, but people don't—well, they don't kill because they don't *like* somebody."

It was not difficult to find an officer around the Crescent during all of this period, and so we picked one up near the gate and took him with us. He was frankly skeptical, although polite enough, when George explained to him.

"It was dark when she started," he said, "and I wanted to go with her, but she didn't want me, and said so. She's been rather more crabbed than usual this last day or so, and I didn't insist. But I waited until I couldn't see her any more. She had no hat on and she carried the flat box with the veil under her arm."

"She hadn't said she might go elsewhere?"

"No. Where else could she go?"

"Well," the officer said reasonably, "she might have gone to a movie. Lots of women go without hats these summer nights. She might have changed her mind later on. I wouldn't get excited yet. There's a movie house on Liberty Avenue, isn't there?"

There was, of course, and both George and I knew that Miss Lydia often went there. But it would have been difficult to explain to the policeman that on occasions of death in the Crescent we do not go to the movies, or that Miss Lydia was the high priestess of our funeral rites and therefore far removed from such diversions.

"She didn't go to the movies," George said stubbornly, and let it go at that.

The three of us turned and went slowly along the street. The officer had got out his flashlight, a powerful one, and was throwing it along the grass inside the curb, and then into the shrubbery on our left; but without result until we were almost exactly halfway to the Lancasters'. Then he swooped down suddenly and picking up an object from the bushes held it out.

"This the box?" he said.

"It looks like it. What on earth—"

George took the box and stared at it. It was slightly broken at a corner of the lid, but otherwise unharmed. Inside, when he opened it, lay Margaret Lancaster's black veil, and George's face was as pale as his chronic sunburn would permit when he looked at it.

"I can't go back and tell Mother," he was saying. "It would about finish her."

The officer himself looked grave. He wandered about over the grass, and at last he stooped and picked up something else. He brought it to us in the palm of his hand, and turned the flashlight on it.

"Don't know what it is," he said. "Maybe been there a long time. It was kind of trampled into the ground. Either of you ever see it before?"

We stared down at it, and then at each other. Lying there under the lamp was the butterfly head of Lydia Talbot's hatpin. I can still remember George's dazed expression.

"It's hers, all right," he said. "But listen, Lou. She went out without a hat!"

The general alarm was raised at midnight, and for once in many years the Talbot house was unlocked and unbolted, and blazing with lights. Inspector Briggs, Mr. Sullivan and two plain-clothes men had inspected it inch by inch, but they had found nothing. Lizzie and Mrs. Talbot, examining Miss Lydia's room, while the police looked on, were certain that nothing was missing except what she had worn that night; a rusty black silk dress, a black mohair petticoat, and undergarments, and her usual black shoes and stockings.

On a stand near the window sill stood the electric iron with which she had pressed Margaret Lancaster's veil.

Lizzie was as calm as usual; a tall thin figure of a woman, not unlike Miss Lydia herself. Mrs. Talbot, however, was profoundly shaken. She could hold nothing, not even the glass of wine George got her, and her voice was a mere echo of its usual boom.

"Her habits?" she said. "She had none, except going to the movies. As to being kidnapped for a ransom, who's to pay it? She hadn't a penny, and I haven't much more. Not since this depression set in."

"You don't think it might be a case of loss of memory?"

"She hadn't any memory to lose."

"Now," said the Inspector, "you have no reason to believe that she had any enemies, I suppose?"

"Neither enemies nor friends. She lived a life of her own, and she was as nearly negative as any human being I ever knew."

That was as far as they got with Mrs. Talbot. They tried to tell her that such disappearances were either compulsory or voluntary, and they asked her if she knew of any reason why Miss Lydia would have run away. Her only answer was that she had taken nothing to run away with, and that she had had a good home. Why leave it?

By two o'clock that morning the search was in full cry. Both the Common and No Man's Land had been searched without result, including all outbuildings facing on the latter, and the one or two policemen who had been on duty reported nothing suspicious. It was not until three A.M. that the first clue was picked up, and that proved to be the missing woman's bag, found on Euclid Street with its beaded strap broken, and looking as though it had either broken of itself or been jerked from her arm.

It contained only a clean handkerchief, a dollar or two in money, and an old hunting case watch with which everyone on the Crescent was familiar. It made a terrific noise, and all of us could remember Miss Lydia's bag on a table or a chair, ticking away like a grandfather's clock.

Scarcely any of us went to bed that night. We gathered in small groups in each other's houses; Margaret and her nurse in the Talbots', where Ms. Talbot sat like a woman stunned and Lizzie moved inscrutably about with coffee for everybody, and Jim Wellington and the Daltons with us.

Something possessed me then to tell about the dumbwaiter incident, and I remember Bryan Dalton examining the outlets, and at four in the morning insisting on nailing them all shut again. Laura Dalton had little to say. She seemed puzzled, but she looked happier than I had seen her look for a long time. She found an opportunity to tell me that she was sorry for what she had said the other day.

"I was hysterical," she said. "Of course it wasn't true. And he hasn't been out of the house tonight, Louisa. Besides, why on earth should anyone kill Lydia Talbot?"

For that was what it had come to. Not one of us but believed that Lydia Talbot was already dead, the third and possibly the fourth in our list of murders.

Chapter XLI

The police in the meantime were working hard. One motive after another was examined and rejected. She had neither money nor enemies, and the two remaining possibilities were either loss of memory or a killing without reason. Subjected to this new test even Margaret Lancaster's conviction, as shown in her statement, lost much of its value; and was before many hours had passed to be proved entirely mistaken as to her sister Emily's death at least.

In the meantime the Bureau of Missing Persons had sent out its usual messages by teletype, with a careful description of Miss Lydia. It was not only local. It extended to other cities, and to the state police of nearby states. Her name was placed upon the general alarm, and men were visiting the morgue, our hospitals and even our hotels and jails. Already too by daylight that next morning, Saturday, circulars were being printed, using an old snapshot of Miss Lydia which someone happened to have.

I have one of these before me now. It reads: "Missing since nine-thirty Friday night August the twenty-sixth, Miss Lydia Spencer Talbot. Born in the United States. Age fifty-two. Height five feet eight. Weight about one hundred and thirty pounds. Gray hair, parted and worn in hard knot. Flat curls on forehead. Complexion medium fair. Gray eyes. Denture with four teeth (molars) lower jaw. No identifying marks on body. Wore black silk dress, not new, black mohair underskirt, black shoes and hose. No rings or other jewelry. No laundry or other marks on clothing."

In addition to all this radio broadcasts had already been sent out, police boats on the river were on the lookout for a body, and the night police reporters assigned to the various station houses had abandoned their usual poker games for what promised to be another sensation. With one result that none of them had anticipated, which was the return of Helen Wellington.

It must have been ten o'clock in the morning when she telephoned to me from the same hotel downtown where I had found her before, and her voice was strained with excitement.

"Can you come down right away?" she asked. "I can't locate Jim or Herbert Dean, and I'm blithering all over the place. I suppose it's true?"

"Lydia Talbot has disappeared, yes."

"Good heavens! Lydia! Listen, Lou; I called Jim early last night, and he said Margaret Lancaster thinks her father killed Emily. Is that right?"

"Margaret thinks that? You don't mean it, Helen. You can't."

"No, I don't and can't," she said, with something of her old manner. "She may think that, but it isn't true. I *know*."

I was in her room by half past ten, and found her still in traveling clothes and pacing the floor. She was lighting one cigarette after another, and under her make-up she was very white. She hardly greeted me at all.

"Don't blame poor old Jim for this," she said. "I swore him to secrecy, but if he had any guts — but that's neither here nor there. We split on the thing anyhow, and now with old Lydia gone he'll never forgive me."

"Just what is it all about, Helen?"

She made a gesture.

"It's just that I'm a plain damned fool," she said. "Things looked black for Jim, and if they found *I'd* been out that night — !"

"What night?"

"Last Sunday night," she said. And finally she told her story. She and Jim had had a difference of some sort, and she had not gone to bed. She was nervous and angry. However that might be, at one o'clock or thereabouts—she was not sure of the time—she had gone out to the refrigerator for some soda, and from there to the rear porch. It was a hot night, and for some time she had sat there on a chair staring out over the tennis court and No Man's Land beyond it. Everything was quiet there, but suddenly she thought she saw a match lighted near the Daltons' garage to her left; a match or a flashlight.

It went out in a second or two, but it had interested her, and so she had left the porch and gone along the kitchen path which connects all the houses. She had just reached the end of their own shrubbery when she saw a woman coming from beside the Dalton garage. At first this woman was only a shadowy figure and she remained so until she emerged into the open. Then, by the walk and the heavy outline, Helen decided that it must be either one of our servants or— improbable as it seemed—Emily Lancaster.

Whoever it was, she was carrying something. And whatever it was she carried, it seemed to be long and awkward to manage.

Helen had followed her quietly. She was quite certain now that it was Emily, and her first horrified idea was that she was carrying an axe. But—and this was something not known before—as she rounded the curve of the walk near the Lancaster house itself she saw that the light was on on the kitchen porch, and that although it was Miss Emily, what she carried was a spade.

Helen was shocked almost into immobility at the sight. To her it meant only one thing; that after all Emily Lancaster had taken the money and buried it somewhere, and was now about to dig it up. So she kept on after her, making as little noise as she could, and now and then walking along the side of the path for that reason.

"You see how it was," she explained. "You know the sort of heels I wear, and when I heard the news the next morning I knew I'd left a trail about two inches deep every here and there."

Her suspicions were confirmed when Emily passed the rear of the Lancaster house without stopping, and started on the longish path toward the Talbots'. Here was to be the direct proof that Jim was innocent, and she was both excited and thrilled. Then something happened which scared her, as she said, into a fit.

There was someone behind them both! She slid into the shrubbery and hid there, with her heart going a million a minute. But after all it turned out to be old Mr. Lancaster, in his bare feet and a dressing gown, coming along at a half trot, and with his right hand in his dressing gown pocket. Helen had only a second or two to observe him clearly before he too left the light behind. It was long enough, however.

"If ever I've seen a man mad with fury it was the old gentleman that night," she said. "He'd always seemed a mild little man, but he was a raving lunatic just then; and Margaret's right about one thing. There isn't a doubt that he was out to shoot Emily. I suppose he'd been watching her ever since the murder, and that spade settled it. After all she wasn't his daughter, and he thought she had buried the gold and then killed her mother. Well, I must say it looked like it just then."

Helen herself was too scared to think of anything to do. Mr. Lancaster was coming on, and ahead somewhere in the dark was Emily. She stayed in the shrubbery until he had passed, but she was not far behind him when he came to the door of the old stable which was the Talbot garage.

For it seemed that Emily had not gone on into the waste land at all. She was inside the Talbot stable, with her spade on the floor beside her, and with a flashlight she seemed to be inspecting a corner behind a barrel. Then Helen, not far behind the old man, saw his hand come out of his pocket and saw that it held a gun.

"It was a close thing," she said. "I don't think Emily ever saw me at all. I had just time to knock the thing out of his hand, and it must have gone a mile. But Emily had heard something, and the poor old thing looked up and saw her stepfather. She looked startled, and neither of them said anything for a minute. Then she braced herself and managed to speak.

" 'I'm sorry I wakened you, father,' she said. 'Margaret told me tonight that my bird was dead and that George had put it here. I wanted to bury the little thing.'

"He never replied to that at all," Helen went on. "He looked queer, however, and I didn't stop to look for the gun. I took him by the arm and led him back to the house and got him inside. I don't believe he even recognized me. He seemed dazed."

But after she had got him back into the house — he had left the kitchen porch unlocked — and she helped him up the back stairs, he rallied somewhat. He said: "Thank you, Helen. I'm afraid I am not myself. I have been through a great deal."

He asked her not to waken Margaret, and if she would mind getting his pistol. But she did not leave him at once. She gave him time to get into bed, and then she went in to see if he was comfortable. She knew where Margaret kept the whiskey too, and although he protested she went downstairs and brought up the tantalus from the dining room.

"All the time," she said, "I was wondering what I would say if Emily came in. It would have looked pretty queer, my being there, and of course I couldn't tell her he'd tried to shoot her."

But, although she had been in the house all of twenty minutes, Emily did not come back, and at last she started out to find the pistol. The old man seemed better, although according to her he still looked pretty ghastly.

The lock was still off the kitchen door, and she left it so.

"Well, I didn't much care to go back," she said. "Not with guards around the place and likely to find me on my hands and knees looking for a gun. Not to mention Emily herself! But I went. I crawled about where I thought it had fallen, but I couldn't find it. I was pretty shaky by that time, not because I suspected any trouble but because I couldn't think up any likely story if I was discovered. I couldn't very well tell the police the old gentleman had tried to kill Emily, could I? And Jim in the mess up to his neck anyhow.

"There was no sign of Emily, and no light in the Talbot garage either. I thought probably she was still out there somewhere burying her fool bird. But it wasn't any fun, there in the dark. I could see a little against the lamps on the street, but I couldn't very well light a match, even if I'd had one. Finally I decided it had gone farther than I thought, so I tried the Talbots' drying yard; and I found it there, by stepping on

326

it!"

"You hadn't heard any shot?"

"Never a shot, or anything else. I suppose George had been out and gone back before I got there. Anyhow the Talbot house was dark. When I got back to the old gentleman he was asleep, so I put the gun on top of his bureau and beat it. That's the story. You can believe it or not."

She had been utterly incredulous when she heard of Emily's death. Mr. Lancaster could not have killed her. He was asleep and breathing stentorously when she left him. After that she began to worry. Explain as she might, that story of hers had nothing to support it but her bare word; and not only was Mr. Lancaster beyond interrogation, but it seemed dreadful to her to tell of a dying man that he had made that irrational attempt on Emily's life.

"I simply decided to keep my mouth shut," was the way she put it.

Just when she realized that Jim knew something she was not certain. He was queer all of Monday and Monday night. She would find him gazing at her, and then looking away quickly before she could catch his eye. He drank quite a little that day, too. She found herself watching him also; and it became a rather dreadful game according to her. For by Monday night each of them was suspecting the other of what she called "something."

It was not so irrational as it sounded, she said. If Jim knew that she had been out on Sunday night, then he too might have been out of the house. He might have slipped out after her and returned before she did.

"Of course it was crazy," she explained, "but I wasn't normal, any more than the rest of you along the Crescent. There's a queer streak in the Talbots, too, and his mother was a Talbot. I began to wonder if he had it. You know his uncle ran away with a woman years ago and then up and shot her one day. I knew that, because Jim has wondered lately if the old boy had come back and was trying to exterminate a lot of people he didn't like."

By Monday night she had worked herself into a modified sort of hysteria. That was when she had walked into our house and said what she had said. But after the attack on me Jim's nerves had given way entirely, and they had a rather dreadful scene after she left me on Thursday where each accused the other of all sorts of unnamed crimes.

When she had jerked open the door to leave the room she found their new butler in the hall outside, and knew that he had been listening. After that she simply threw some things in a bag and escaped.

The night before she had weakened and called Jim. She had had time to think.

"You have time to think in the country," she said, lighting a cigarette and forcing a grin. "There's nothing else to do. And if Jim suspected me it suddenly dawned on my weakened brain that he couldn't have done it himself! He'd heard of Margaret's statement from Bert Dean, and he was sorry as hell and quite decent. But what am I to do, Lou? If I tell, won't they come down on Jim again? And I can't locate Herbert Dean anyhow."

I did the only thing I could think of at the time. I took her firmly by the arm and into the elevator, and half an hour later she was telling her story to the Police Commissioner, who beyond a tendency to scratch now and then had apparently overcome the poison ivy.

Chapter XLII

That was on Saturday, August the twenty-seventh. The reign of terror had extended over nine days, and there was talk about evacuating the Crescent to save further killings. Two or three timorous families on Euclid Street behind us had already moved themselves, their children and their family pets to remote spots in the country. Even the Avenue in our neighborhood was largely deserted at night, the press was screaming about the homicidal maniac who was still at large, and one tabloid having exhausted all other resources, dug up from an unknown source the old story of John Talbot and his love affair, with its tragic ending. From that moment the search for Mr. Talbot was almost as intensive as that for Lydia herself.

Mr. Lancaster was buried that afternoon, police reserves having been called out to control the crowds around the gate and elsewhere, and a half dozen motorcycle men escorting the body to and keeping the cemetery clear. I had flatly refused to go there, much to Mother's indignation.

"I had never thought that a daughter of mine," she said, "would be found failing in respect to the dead."

"I am not going, mother."

"Is that any way to speak to me, Louisa? Really, sometimes I wonder if all this trouble hasn't done something very strange to you."

"I'm afraid it has, mother."

She whirled from where she was standing in front of her mirror, pinning on her hat with its long dull-beaded black pins.

"Just what do you mean by that?" she demanded.

"I suppose," I said carefully, "it has taught me my right to live while I can. To live my own life, not yours, mother. Not anyone's but mine. My own."

She stared at me with incredulous eyes.

"And that to me, from my own child! All I have left, after years of sacrifice for her!"

"Just what have you sacrificed, mother?" I said, as gently as I could. "Haven't I been the sacrifice? Isn't this whole Crescent a monument to the sacrifice of some one or other? And to what? To security? Then where is it? To how things look? They don't look so well just now, do they? If you believe in either one or the other you might look out the window!"

She made no answer to that. She gathered up her dull black bag, straightened the folds of her mourning veil, and went to the door. There she stopped and turned.

"I would like to know," she said bitterly, "if Doctor Armstrong has put these—these outrageous notions into your head."

"No," I told her. "It was someone else, and if he ever asks me to marry him I shall do so."

I doubt if she heard much of the funeral service that day. I know that when she returned she locked herself into her bedroom, and that she did not speak to me again for twenty-four hours. But as those twenty-four hours were filled with excitement I am afraid I felt this punishment less than I should.

There had been no sign whatever of Lydia Talbot through all of Saturday. Downtown in the District Attorney's office Helen was being examined on her story of Emily Lancaster's last night, with the usual group about her, and the only result the complete destruction of Margaret's theory. And, although

330

no one knew this at the time, Herbert Dean had spent at least a part of the day going from one hairdresser to another, carrying a photograph with him. The remainder of the time, or some portion of it, he spent in a lodging house on a narrow street behind the hospital; the address of which he had obtained, not without difficulty, from the blotter he had taken from Emily Lancaster's desk in the MacMullen house.

There, as I know now, he got permission from a reluctant landlady to examine a small furnished room, extremely tidy, but from which all traces of its recent occupant had been taken the night before. Except for the books. The room was almost filled with books.

"Must have been quite a reader."

"Yes, sir. He didn't do much else. I was sorry to lose him. He'd been here ten years."

"Is he sending for these books?"

"Well, now, that's funny for a man as fond of them as he was. They were like his children in a way, if you know what I mean. But he said I was to give them to the library. He wouldn't need them again."

The net result of all this being that a puzzled and irritated Commissioner of Police was that afternoon asked for another guard, this time to watch the house behind the library; was also requested to issue a general alarm for one Robert Daniels, street cleaner to the Department of Public Works; and was left to read and study a mass of aged and not too clean clippings from a city in an adjoining state.

"What's the big idea, Dean?" he demanded. "If you think this fellow Daniels is the killer, why don't you say so?"

"I haven't any idea that he is the killer," Dean replied soberly. "What I want to do is to save his life."

But on the Crescent we still remained in ignorance of all this. The only news I had was that Lizzie, from the Talbots', had not returned from Mr. Lancaster's funeral. That came to me at my lonely dinner, via Annie and the grapevine telegraph, and lost nothing in the telling.

Briefly, Lizzie had been acting in a strange manner all

331

week. She had eaten scarcely anything, and had been so hard to get along with that she and Mrs. Talbot had had a frightful fuss early that day. The whole house had heard it, and no one had been greatly surprised when Lizzie at once went to her room and packed her old-fashioned valise. They were surprised, however, to see her come out to the servants' car — it is our custom on such occasions to supply our domestics with transportation — and to drive quietly enough to the cemetery. The valise she placed in front, beside the driver.

It was not until the return journey that she spoke at all, and then it was only to the chauffeur. She reached through the window in front of her and touched him on the shoulder.

"I'll get out here," she said.

Some one of the women tried to say good-bye to her, but she paid no attention; and the last they saw of her she was standing with her valise at her feet and apparently waiting for an interurban car.

"Well, we understood well enough, miss," Annie said. "Her sister's got a farm out near Hollytree. But to go off like that, with all of us knowing her for years — well, I suppose she felt pretty bad, with one thing and another. I'm not one to hold a grudge against her."

It seemed natural enough to me, knowing Lizzie's dour manner. During all my early years she had terrified me. She had beaten George within an inch of his life when he had frightened me with the dumb-waiter, and had then taken the black and some of the skin off his nose with sapolio. And she had smacked me soundly once when she found me in the Talbot stable trying to smoke a seedpod from their Indian cigar tree. A hard dauntless woman, Lizzie, whose other name I have never even heard up to that time, and whose jet-black dyed hair was as familiar to me as the ancient cameo pin with which she pinned her high collar.

But I was less easy about her after George Talbot had been in to see me that evening. He had been following all sorts of police clues throughout the day, and he looked dirty and tired. Mother was still shut away in high dudgeon when he came into the library and put a copy of the tabloid into my hands.

"I suppose you've seen this dirty stuff, Lou?"

"Yes."

"And you knew the story before?"

"I really don't know any story, George. I overheard some talk a night or two ago, but—"

"And that's been the Great Secret!" he said disgustedly. "All these years I've known there was one. I've known damned well too that everybody else along here knew it, except you perhaps. And now this filthy paper brings it out and just about intimates that my father's back and at the old tricks. By God, for a plugged nickel I'd go down and beat up the lot of them!"

He quieted down after a time. He seemed indeed more annoyed that this Great Secret had turned out as it had than for any other reason.

"Look what it's done to us!" he said. "We lived locked up and bolted away! And why? He wasn't crazy. That was a trick to save his neck, and I'm darned glad he did. Glad he escaped from their lunatic asylum too. A man gets caught by a pretty face, runs away with it, takes another name, and then is found one day in a hotel room with a gun in his hand and the woman dead. She's wrecked him, and he finishes her. And for almost thirty years Mother expects him to come back and shoot her too! Why? She didn't mean anything to him. I doubt she ever did."

With which unfilial remark he got up.

"The only decently normal person left in the house was Lizzie," he said. "Now I suppose you know she's left. Driven off, I suppose, like Aunt Lydia."

"George! Do you think your Aunt Lydia simply went away?"

He made a despairing gesture.

"How do I know?" he said. "She'd wanted to go. Wanted it for years. I never blamed her much, although I didn't like her. But Lizzie is different. She didn't want to go. Why should she leave what's been her home for more than thirty years? There's something very queer there, Lou."

333

He got up.

"Well, I'll take that rotten sheet and get out," he said. "I've still got to take my sleuth for his walk before I go to bed!"

He took the paper and went away. I had read it, and its implication was plain enough. But both George and I were wrong that night. The tabloid contained only a part of what he called the Great Secret, and we were to have another tragedy before we learned the rest of it.

Chapter XLIII

If George Talbot was tired and dirty that night, he was nothing to Herbert when, at half past nine, he rang the doorbell. He had abandoned all pretension to being other than he was, and that Annie appreciated this was shown by the avidity with which she agreed to bring him the tray of any sort of food she had, which he asked for.

"I hope you don't mind, Lou," he said. "I haven't eaten today, and tonight I'm worried. That's feeble for the way I feel. Where's your mother?"

"She's in bed. I'm afraid she is sulking."

He ignored that and at once stated his intention of spending the night in the house, and on guard.

"On guard? Here?" I asked.

"Where else? In the first place, I want to be sure you're safe. That's vital. But in the second place, so long as our killer thinks there are dangerous prints in that album, and thinks that that album is here, there may be other attempts to get it."

He went on to explain, leaning back like the tired man he was, in his big chair. There were new lines on his face, and he looked fairly exhausted.

I cannot recall all that he said. It had something to do with the fact that a carefully premeditated killing like that of

Mrs. Lancaster, implied more than the sequence of events leading to it. It meant another sequence to follow it, and this sequence could only be planned in advance. If then any part of this following sequence was altered, even in the smallest degree, every other part of it was changed.

In this case the album had slipped, or it was the gloves perhaps. They were too clumsy; the wearer could not take something badly wanted out of the album. The gloves had to be abandoned and an attempt made to tear out the page. But the page was mounted on cloth, and time was at a premium. Then there was probably an alarm of some sort. That might have been when the desperate attempt was made to raise the screen.

Whatever it was, the original plan had slipped then and there and with it all the rest of the sequences which had been meant to follow.

Annie brought the tray about that time, and he ate like a famished man. I had asked no questions and I let him finish in silence. It was after he had pushed away the tray that he came over and put a hand on my shoulder.

"What a restful person you are, Lou," he said. "And when this is all over —"

Annie came back for the tray then, and whatever he had meant to say never was finished. He was absorbed in our crimes again, the lone wolf in spite of his disclaimer, still following an idea of his own against the open cynicism of Inspector Briggs. What he maintained, and what has since been accepted as a fact, was as follows:

On the day of Mrs. Lancaster's death an unknown person had gained access to the house. The method was still in doubt, although he himself was fairly sure of it. At some previous time this unknown had visited the housemaid's closet on the second floor, and after tying a long cord to a pipe there, had slipped it under the window screen, where it hung concealed beside or behind the tin drain pipe from the roof. If discovered, it would mean little or nothing. If not discovered, it offered a practical method of bringing the axe into the house.

That Thursday was chosen because it was the housemaid's

day out, and the closet would presumably be undisturbed that afternoon.

Having then got into the house and being concealed there and probably locked in, one of two courses was followed. Either the outer clothes were taken off or something put on over them which could later on be discarded and destroyed. The closet offered a wash bowl and running water, and it was close to the head of the back stairs. Escape had been made later on by those kitchen stairs and the kitchen porch; and the killer could walk away or even be seen, without any trace of blood to betray the grisly secret.

Both the police and he had agreed on this theory of his, provided the crime was not an inside one. The purpose of the glove thrown down into the hall had been to indicate an escape in that direction, but for some reason the second glove had been kept. The problem of disposing of it had been solved by placing it in the top of the drain pipe, and the heavy rain that night had washed it down to where I had found it.

"The Providence of God, Lou," he said gravely. "For that glove could only have come from the pipe, and the only access to the pipe was that closet window! There, in that closet, you see, was the story."

The Inspector and he had come to the parting of the ways, however, over Margaret Lancaster's story; and Helen Wellington's testimony that day as to Sunday night had resulted in a definite schism between them.

"That blows it wide open, Dean," the Inspector had said, banging a fist on his desk. "I don't care what you think or say. What about that closet anyhow? It's my opinion that it was Margaret who was in it. You've got to go a long way to get some outsider through a locked door into that house, but this woman was there all the time. Then what does she do? She gets that first glove out, by giving it to Lou Hall. She gives Dalton something to burn, and we've only her word as to what it was. And after Emily is shot she switches the barrels of those two guns and keeps it quiet until she misses her father's from his room.

"That scares her. Maybe that nurse told her we had it. So

337

she cooks up a story and brings it to us. The old man is dead, so she hangs that second killing on him. It's safe, and it's good. I'll say it was good! Only the Wellington woman turns up and knocks it over the fence and out of bounds."

Apparently he went even further. He considered it highly probable that Margaret had either employed Holmes to get the trunk, or had known it was to be taken and had found someone else to take it from him. "Easy enough these days," was what he said. "One grand would get fifty fellows to do that job—unless they knew what was in it!"

Herbert had pointed out the absurdity of that. If Margaret knew where the money was, why steal it? It was hers anyhow. All she had to do was to tell the police that she suspected where Emily had hidden it, and she had it.

"Not if she'd killed her sister," the Inspector said stubbornly. "Maybe Emily kept a diary in the trunk, or something to show that she was afraid of her. She may have told Margaret that. For she was afraid. She was scared stiff, and that's a fact. She had more than three days after her mother's death to tell the truth, but did she? She did not. Then on Saturday night someone tries to break into her room and she beats it! For where? She gets out of that house, and when the Talbots let her in she says that 'they' are after her. Who are 'they,' Dean. Her own people, that's what."

It was all rational enough, although Dean pointed out the device by which the axe had been taken into the house as destroying much of it. It was awkward and inept, he maintained. The axe was not used in the summer, and Margaret could have taken it in at night—any night—without discovery. The very fact that Bryan Dalton had seen it in that cautious ascent showed that the method was dangerous in the extreme.

But his case, he said, lay largely in the old albu,m and that, he added, was why he had come out that night.

"Not that I don't always want to come, light of my life," he said, with something of his usual cheerfulness. "But if I'm guessing right there have been two attempts to get the thing, and there is likely to be another. That lets Margaret

Lancaster out. She knows those fingerprints are burned. But there is someone who doesn't know it, and who thinks that the album is still here."

Then he grinned at me.

"I've been rechecking the alibis for that Thursday afternoon," he said. "About the only one we can check absolutely is your mother's, and there is an old axiom that the more perfect the alibi the more suspicious it is! And how do we know, my love, that you were sitting sewing at your window, as you say you were? Or that Helen was shopping and running up more bills? Or that Jim after all didn't need that legacy to pay them?"

"But you know better," I said sharply.

"Oh, yes, I know better. I even know who did it, or think I do. Someone, my dear, who had easy access to that house. Who knew its habits to the last minute. Who was ordinarily calm on that surface, but was capable of terrible rages. Maybe someone who was sane enough but not quite normal. But how am I to prove it?"

Suddenly I thought I saw a real light. I sat bolt upright in my chair.

"It was Lizzie!" I said. "Lizzie from the Talbots'! It must have been. She loathed Mrs. Lancaster, but she was always in and out of the house. And she's terrible when she's angry. I've seen her angry."

He was lighting his pipe.

"Well," he said thoughtfully, "let's consider Lizzie. I've done it already. She—"

"But she's gone, Herbert. She ran away this afternoon."

"Ran away? Where?" he asked sharply.

"I don't know. To her sister's, perhaps."

I told him what Annie had said, and he sent for her and questioned her quickly. He looked sober and anxious, and after making me promise not to leave my room that night and assuring me that there would be a guard outside, he merely put a hand on my shoulder for a second, caught up his hat and left.

A minute later I heard him driving out of the Crescent like a crazy man.

That was at half past ten on Saturday night, August the twenty-seventh. But it was not until almost midnight that the police located the driver of the interurban car Lizzie had taken, and discovered that she had left it some four miles beyond Hollytree at a stop which was nothing but a dirt road crossing the track. Within fifteen minutes of that time city police, the sheriff's car and two or three hastily notified state troopers were converging on the Hollytree district, their orders being to trace if possible a tall thin woman dressed in black and carrying an old-fashioned valise, who had left the car at that point; and also to find the farm belonging to her sister.

They found the farm; a small down-at-the-heel place, and finally roused the family. But Lizzie had not been there. From the moment she had stepped off the platform of that interurban car she had apparently disappeared into a void.

It was ten o'clock the next morning before they had any clue whatever. Then a man living on the outskirts of Hollytree telephoned in to Police Headquarters in the city.

"I've got a white dog out here. He's a wanderer, and he came home about an hour ago covered with blood. He isn't hurt. He looks as though he'd been swimming in bloody water, and I thought you'd like to see him before I wash him. It looks queer to me."

Chapter XLIV

Herbert and Sullivan went out at once, and the Inspector followed with the Police Commissioner, who was in golf clothes and rather irritated at losing his Sunday morning game. The dog was in an enclosure behind a small house, and a half dozen curious neighbors were staring at him over the fence. He wore a muzzle "so he couldn't lick the stuff off, sir."

There was no doubt among any of the men that "the stuff" was blood. There was a serious question, of course, as to whether it was human or not. The result was that Herbert Dean cut off some of the hair and went back to town with it to make the usual test, and that he missed the search which followed.

Judging from the newspapers the next day it was an exciting one. It was a Sunday morning, and that part of the local population which had not gone to church turned out with a will. Orders were to look, not necessarily for a lake or stream, but for some small and stagnant body of water where blood would lie. They were warned also that blood changes in sunlight, or even assumes the color of its background, and were to mark and report any suspicious body of water, however small, whether it bore any indication of what they were after or not.

In the meantime Dean had telephone that the microscope

showed that the specimen was undoubtedly human blood, and as soon as possible he rejoined them. He was too late, however.

On the outskirts of the town itself, and only a hundred feet or so from the main road, was an empty house which had a local reputation for being haunted. It had been for rent, furnished, for the past five years. Recently, however, it had been rented. A week or so before a man had called the owner over the telephone and taken it for the summer. He had sent two months' rent in advance and had ordered the key left in the house on a certain day.

Strange as all this was, the owner had formed a theory. Once or twice members of the local psychic society had held sittings there, and as those people often preferred to be anonymous, he had accepted the terms without question.

He had not been asked to make any repairs, and he had made none. No tenant had moved in, although on the Wednesday night previous the neighbors had reported that a car had stopped there and that something had been moved into the building. As the nearest house was five hundred yards away, the identity of this object was not known. But on that Sunday morning while the search was going on this owner, a man named Johnson, decided to walk over to see if his new tenant had arrived.

He was uneasy, for the drain pipe which carried the waste water out of the house had broken, and if used the water would collect in a low-lying bit of ground behind it.

He saw no signs of occupancy, and walked around the house to the rear. Here he saw a largish pool, covering an area about eight by eight feet and several inches deep in the center. But he saw more than that. He saw that this pool was covered with a thin film of what looked like blood.

He did not enter the house at all. He rushed back into town and got the police, and together they broke down the door.

If they had expected to find any sign of crime, they were mistaken. The house, was bare, clean and without signs of occupancy; but a damp spot on the bathroom wall over the tub looked as though it had been washed recently. This wall was papered, and the washing had loosened the paper, which was still moist.

"How long ago, Dean?" asked the Inspector.

"Six hours, maybe. It's hard to tell."

The first search revealed nothing else. The cellar floor had not been disturbed, nor could they find any indication outside that anything had been buried on the property. A second and more thorough examination, however, revealed something of vital importance.

In the cellar, piled behind a stack of cut wood, they found the drawers of a new wardrobe trunk of good quality, and not one of them doubted their significance. Whether all this related to the disappearance of Lydia Talbot or not, they were on the heels of a crime, and none of them but felt confident that a body had taken the place of those drawers in a trunk.

Here they found unexpected corroboration. A dairyman in the vicinity, driving with his cans to the station early that morning, had seen a trunk being taken out of the house by the Hollytree expressman, whom he knew well by sight.

"And right there," said the Inspector later, "we ran into the worst luck of all that unlucky business; for this fellow who does the local hauling had piled his whole family in his truck and gone for a week-end camping trip. And he never showed up until late Monday night!"

In spite of the hot trail, however, inquiry for the trunk brought no results that day. It had not been shipped from Hollytree or any station nearby, and at last they fell back on the city itself. Here they faced the usual baggage room congestion of the summer months, and they were in the position of men certain that a terrible crime had been committed and without a single clue as to where to find the body.

The frantic search included one for the camping party, but without result; and it was not until noon of a hot Monday that a trunk, waiting to be called for on the blistering platform of a way station a hundred miles from the city began to excite the interest and apprehension of the agent.

He sent for the police, and the trunk was opened, about six o'clock that night. It contained the body of a middle-aged woman, all but the head, and was at once identified by the clothing and so on as that of Lydia Talbot. The head had been removed to allow the body to be placed in the trunk, and the entire body had been wrapped in an old piece of carpet from the house at Hollytree.

I have gone as little as possible into detail. The trunk, as I have said earlier, had been disguised by a number of foreign labels, but was readily recognized as the one Miss Emily had bought and sent to the house on Liberty Avenue. There was no sign of the gold and currency it had once held, however, and an almost microscopic examination of the premises near Hollytree revealed no trace of it there.

This was the situation then on that Monday evening, the eleventh day after our first murder. Mrs. Talbot had collapsed; no sign had been found of Lizzie, although a nation-wide search had been instituted and a general alarm had gone out at once; George Talbot had been violently sick after viewing the body; and Laura Dalton had crept on Monday night to her husband's room, knocked at the door and been heard crying hysterically after he had admitted her.

The general demoralization on the Crescent was utter and complete. One by one our old servants began to give notice, the Daltons' Joseph being the first, and on Tuesday morning our colored laundresses one by one put down their irons, walked upstairs and handed in their resignations.

Helen Wellington came in on Monday to say that John, her new butler, had vanished without pay, and that the remainder were packing their trunks.

"I've told them how absurd they are," she said, "but it's no use. Lizzie's done her dirty work and she's got the money. Why on earth should she come back? Jim says she is crazy, but I wish I could be crazy for the best part of a hundred thousand dollars!"

A dozen Lizzies had been found by Monday night, and every hour new ones were turning up. She was a common enough type of middle-aged spinster, and the numbers of spinsters of that age who had dyed their hair black was an embarrassment to the police.

Such information as we had in our house during those two wild days was practically entirely from the newspapers. I did not hear at all from Herbert. But the new tragedy had at least brought Mother out of her retirement, and renewed our relationship on a cool but talkative basis.

She was entirely convinced that the killer all along had been Lizzie.

"She never liked Hester Talbot," she said, "but she was fond of Lydia and John. She never got over the fact that when Mrs. Lancaster's first husband died she kept all the money. He left a will leaving part of his property to them, but after he died she produced a new one cutting them off. Lizzie Cromwell always said she'd forged it! Of course that wasn't true, but I think they all believed it.

"Then when John got into trouble and shot this woman he'd run off with, Hester Talbot wouldn't pay a good lawyer for him, and neither would the Lancasters. It was just by luck that he was found insane, although he really wasn't — and sent somewhere. But there was no scandal here. He had assumed another name, and he was tried and convicted under it. It was a great trouble to all of us, and although Lydia got over it all I don't think Lizzie ever did. I always thought she was a little in love with John herself!"

But she added something which I now believe to be the truth.

"I have wondered lately about poor Emily and that money she took, Louisa. She never cared anything about money, and sometimes I think — Do you suppose she had met John Talbot somewhere — he'd escaped years ago, you know — and that she took it for him? It was all so unlike her, somehow. And she was always fond of him."

Curious, all that, when I remember that it must have been almost at that time on Monday night that an elderly man, with thick spectacles and one side of his face drooping from an old paralysis, walked into the seventeenth precinct station house and collapsed onto a bench.

Chapter XLV

He sat there for some time before anyone noticed him. Then the sergeant sent an officer over. The man had dropped asleep by that time, and the officer shook him.

"What's wrong, old timer?" he asked not ungently. "Snap out of it!"

The man blinked at him through his spectacles.

"I don't know," he said, in a rather cultivated but halting voice. "I can't seem to remember my name, or who I am." And he added, with an apologetic smile: "Memory is like a purse, officer. 'If it be over full all will drop out of it!' "

The officer eyed him, and then went back to the desk.

"Old boy's lost his memory, or so he says. Better put him somewhere for the night, eh?"

The sergeant agreed, and this story might have had a different ending but for that very decision. For it was when a jailer was taking him back to a cell that he noticed some stains on the man's white shirt. He stopped in the long stone-paved passage and looked at it.

"Ain't hurt anywhere, are you?"

"No, I don't think so."

The jailer was mildly curious. In the cell he got his prisoner to take off his coat, and was shocked to find that the turned-up cuffs of the shirt were also badly stained. The unknown eyed them himself through his spectacles.

"That's strange," he said haltingly. "Now how did I get that?"

"You're asking me!" said the policeman. "What you been doing? Killing a pig?"

The man shook his head, and then slowly drew something out of a trousers pocket and gravely handed it to the officer.

"This doesn't belong to me," he said in his halting voice. "I have no idea how I got it."

The policeman took it and held it up. Then he grinned.

"Looks like you been playing Santa Claus!" he said, and still grinning carried the object out to the sergeant at the desk.

It was a short grayish beard of the cheapest variety, and made to hook over the ears by small wires.

When the sergeant, curious himself by then, went back to the cell, it was to find the unknown quietly asleep on his hard bed. The two men inspected the stains on him, but he did not rouse. And he was still asleep when Mr. Sullivan got there an hour later. Sullivan examined him before he roused him. He was neatly dressed, but it was evidently two days or more since he had shaved. His clothing too was incredibly dusty, and his shoes worn and scratched as with long walking over rough ground.

Sullivan, with his usual memory for faces, had known him at once for Daniels. He himself was tired and rather sick, for he had come from examining the contents of that ghastly trunk, and his next step is excusable under the circumstances. He turned to the sergeant and pointed to the stains on the shirt.

"There's the Crescent Place killer," he said. "And he's shamming. I'll give you fifteen minutes to bring his memory back while I get in touch with Headquarters."

I do not know what followed. But I do know that when the Inspector and Herbert arrived they found Daniels stretched out on the floor of an upper room, and that there were some words between Sullivan and Herbert that, as the Inspector said later, fairly blistered the paint.

In the end they called an ambulance and took the unconscious man to the hospital on Liberty Avenue; and both Herbert and Sullivan sat with him the rest of the night. He was not hurt, it developed. He had collapsed from a combination of fright, hunger and thirst. But if they hoped that when he came to he would remember his identity, they were disappointed. He refused both food and drink, and could be induced only with difficulty to speak at all.

"Sullivan thought he was still shamming," Herbert has said since, "but I didn't believe it. It was either genuine amnesia or straight hysteria. I'd seen both in the war, from shock. I thought the poor devil had had a shock. That's all."

They tried to rouse him by questioning him.

"Listen, now. Your name is Daniels, isn't it? Robert Daniels."

"Daniels?" he said after an interval. "No. I'm sorry, but that's not it."

He did not reply at all when Herbert suggested that he was John Talbot, and shortly after that he lapsed into what Doctor Armstrong calls a definite catatonia. He would or could not reply to any questions at all, was stiff and rigid in his bed, and could not be roused for the nourishment he evidently needed. Some time in the night, however, after the two men had gone, he wakened in a condition of frenzied excitement. He was still confused, made terrible grimaces, and the policeman on guard in the room had some difficulty in keeping him in bed until he could be tied there. After that an interne gave him a hypodermic of some sort, and he became quieter.

Police swarmed in and out of his room all that day, Tuesday, but without result.

"You can get my point of view, Miss Hall," the Inspector said a day or two later. "We knew by that time he was Talbot; Dean had wired for his prints the night before, and they came in that day. And we knew his history; knew he'd killed a woman, been sent to a state institution as insane, and had escaped from it years before. You can see how it looked, and I'll admit the whole thing had me fooled, or Dean did, I've often wondered since what you told Dean to put him on the right track. He didn't get *that* out of a microscope!"

It was of no use to tell Inspector that I had told Herbert nothing, because I knew nothing. And Herbert Dean today says that the police still regard his entire success in the case as due to me!

Nevertheless, although they believed that they had the Crescent Place killer under guard in the hospital, the search for Lizzie Cromwell still went on. She had not visited her sister's house; and with one exception, from late Saturday afternoon when she had left the interurban car four miles beyond Hollytree she had seemingly dropped out of existence.

She had walked back that four miles along the track, carrying her bag; for a man had seen her and so reported. He had seen her clearly in the light of another car; a tall thin woman with a valise, who had stepped aside to let the car pass. "Like one of these flashlight pictures," he said. "But I got a good view of her. She wore black clothes with some sort of a big pin at her neck, and she had a kind of old-fashioned satchel in her hand."

That had been about ten o'clock at night, and was only a mile beyond the house where the pool and the drawers from the trunk had been discovered. Where and how she had spent that interval while she presumably waited for darkness nobody knew; possibly, according to the police, resting somewhere in that darkening countryside and waiting to meet the man Daniels.

"One thing was sure," said the Inspector. "This Daniels was in it up to the neck. We took that darky to the hospital and with that fake beard on Daniels he identified him as the man who helped carry down the trunk. Only thing in our minds was whether he'd done away with this Lizzie too, as well as the Talbot woman. You've got to remember that if he *was* Talbot — and all of us were sure of it — he'd been crazy once, and he might be again."

For Lizzie had not been located, although the general alarm sent out for her described her as meticulously as it had described Lydia Talbot. At Headquarters everyone but Herbert believed that our murder mysteries were solved, and that the story was written large for everyone to read. Indeed, the Commissioner himself gave a statement to the press some time that day; much against Herbert's advice.

In it he stated that the various crimes had been committed as part of a plot to secure the gold taken from the Lancaster house; and, although he rather hedged here, he intimidated guilty collusion between the street cleaner, Daniels, and one Elizabeth or Lizzie Cromwell, still missing but likely to be discovered before long. The gold had not yet been located, but here too the police expected results very soon.

Nevertheless, that statement of the Commissioner's, coupled with a further description of Lizzie, brought some result that night. Lizzie had been seen early on Sunday morning. A woman answering her description, but without a valise, had gone into a restaurant of the cheaper sort downtown and had eaten a small breakfast. For this she had rather apologetically tendered a bill of large denomination in payment, and had waited until the cashier sent out for change.

She had seemed very tired, but she had been neat in dress and quiet of manner; "very ladylike." And the cashier remembered a cameo brooch.

From the beginning the police had believed that this valise had held the missing head, and now to the search for Lizzie was added an intensive one for the satchel.

Late as it was, men were sent out again; not only to cover the check and baggage rooms of the railway stations and such express offices as they could reach, but outside the city line the county officials collected troopers and local constables to search beside all railway tracks and public roads leading into town. But as everyone who followed the case will remember, the bag was not recovered until much later. Then in dredging a new channel under one of our railroad bridges, it was brought up one day with a load of sand, with its gruesome contents still inside.

I knew very little myself that day of what was going on. The Crescent had sunk into a lethargy which amounted to fatalism. Our servants were packing to leave, and Aunt Caroline was demanding over the telephone that we close the house and stay with her downtown. At noon the police had asked Margaret Lancaster to identify the man in the hospital, the prints sent by mail not having yet arrived and Mrs. Talbot having refused to leave her bed. She came over first to us, a mere shadow of herself and looking incredibly old.

I remember thinking that Laura Dalton could never be jealous of her again; and as she had come without a hat, noticing with a shock that the hair I had always admired had been dyed hair, and that it was now gray at the roots.

I admitted her myself, Annie being upstairs packing a trunk.

"May I come in, Lou?" she said. "I have to go to the hospital, and I shall need that album I gave your mother. I don't know why Hester Talbot won't go. It's certainly her affair, not mine. If Uncle John is so changed that he could work here for months and none of us recognize him, how on earth am I to do it now?"

She wanted the album, she said, because there was an old photograph of John Talbot in it. She could take it with her, and it might help. Anyhow it was all she could think of.

I did not know what to do. Mother came in just then and said the album was in the old schoolroom. But of course it was not, and at the end of an hour of frantic searching Margaret went away without it.

That was the first of two visits that afternoon for the same purpose. The second was George Talbot, in a savage humor and looking as though he had not slept for days on end.

"Mother wants that album Margaret Lancaster gave your mother," he said. "I'm damned if I know why. And I'm to bring it as it is, tied up and everything! I give you my word, Lou, that house is like a madhouse. She won't open her door until she knows who is outside, and I've had Doctor

Armstrong there twice, but she won't let him in. As for getting her to see that poor old chap in the hospital—! After all he's my father. I've told them to give him the best there is."

"Then you don't believe—?"

"Believe? Don't be a fool, Lou. As far as I can make out he was living the life he liked. He had his books, and he had work to do." And he added: "I wish I'd known who he was, Lou. Imagine me passing him day after day, and giving him a nod when I felt like it. Well, where's the album?"

I had to tell him then that we could not find the album, and he looked rather dismayed.

"More hell!" he said as he got up. "Let me know when it turns up, will you? There's a picture of him in it, and she wants it. God knows why!"

I remember watching him as he cut across the Common to his house, and wondering whether I should have told him the truth; that the police had taken the album for some mysterious purpose of their own. But I am glad now that I did not.

Chapter XLVI

That night stands out in my mind as one of gradually accumulating horror.

It started with confusion, for at a dinner that evening served by a neat but sullen house-parlor maid Mother suddenly determined to go to Aunt Caroline's.

"You and Mary," she told Annie, "can stay for the night or go. As you are deserting me after all these years, I feel that I am quite right in abandoning you."

Annie then retired in tears, and then followed a period of hectic packing. When Mother travels, even if it be only the equivalent of thirty city blocks, she travels; and I spent a wild hour or two collecting the small pillows, the slumber robes and bed jackets and even the framed photograph of my father which always accompanied her.

Both maids were ready before we were, and I remember the bumping noise of their trunks as they were taken downstairs, and my own sense of loss as I paid them off and saw them go.

To all this was added the hottest night of the summer, with a heavy storm threatening and the incessant roll of distant thunder; and when at nine o'clock the doorbell rang, I was distinctly nervous as I went downstairs. I turned on the porch light before I opened the door, but it proved to be Herbert

Dean and I let him in.

"Getting out?" he said when I told him. "Well, that's sensible, darling. I'll be a lot easier in my mind."

"But if you've got the killer, as the papers say—"

"We're not entirely through yet," he said evasively. "The main thing just now is to keep you safe at least until—well, until somewhere around the end of September."

"What is to happen the end of September?" I asked him in an unguarded moment.

"Haven't I told you?" he asked, in surprise. "Our wedding, of course. Naturally I have been pretty busy; but it does seem odd that I should have told Helen and forgotten to tell you!"

"I hope Helen declined, for me!"

"Declined? Great Scott, no. She leaped at it. She says she will never be happy until you are out of Jim's way."

Incredible, all of that, in view of what happened later that night; and as I have said, this is not a love story. Nor is it. But in that fashion was I wooed and won that same evening, although Herbert today maintains that he proposed to me in an entirely conventional fashion, and that I lowered my eyes modestly and whispered a "yes."

That, as I happen to know, occurred the next day, and of all places in the world in the hospital on Liberty Avenue where a half-conscious John Talbot in another room was talking garrulously to a police dictograph, and a stenographer behind a screen was also taking notes.

The first step in the sequence of that night was when I told Herbert that two people had wanted the album. It had almost an electrical effect on him, and he made me recite the conversations as completely as I could remember them. He was almost boyishly excited when I had finished.

"We're close to the end, Lou!" he said triumphantly. "And thank heaven for a girl like you who doesn't talk. You're going to talk now, however." He looked at his watch. "See here," he said, "give me thirty minutes, will you? I'll be back by that time, and then I'll want you to do some telephoning. Can you hold Mother half an hour?"

I thought I could, and he left, driving off at his usual rocketlike speed. Fortunately the storm was close by that ime, and Mother is afraid of lightning. I found her upstairs, ready to go but apprehensive, and I managed to delay my own packing for another thirty minutes before I carried my overnight bag down the stairs.

The house was empty and queer that night. I could never remember it without at least one or the other of the maids in it, and the wind which preceded the rain made strange sounds as I waited in the lower hall for Herbert. I was shivering for some reason when I heard his car again and admitted him.

"All here," he said cautiously, and produced the album neatly tied up in paper. "Now I'll get out again, but first you're to do a little work on the telephone. And while you're doing it I'll unlock the kitchen door. Right? I want to get back into the house after you've gone."

I agreed, although I was puzzled. I was, it appeared, to call up George Talbot and Margaret Lancaster, and to tell them that the album had been found in the schoolroom after all. But I was also to say that we were leaving at once, and that I would give it to each of them the next day.

"Better not do it until the taxicab is at the door," he said, and after a quick and excited kiss he had gone again, driving away more sedately than usual.

I obeyed his orders to the letter. I took the album up to the schoolroom, not without some nervous qualms, and while Mother was gathering up her last possessions for the taxi, I was at the telephone. She caught something of what I said, however, and was rather peevish about it.

"Really, Louisa," she said, "why didn't you tell me? I shall take it to Margaret myself. The taxi can stop there."

It took some argument, including the approach of the storm, to get her into the cab without the album, but at last I managed it and we drove away. She was still offended as well as highly nervous, I remember; and she was continually opening bags on the way downtown to be certain that she had brought everything.

All in all it was a wild ride, for the rain was coming down in torrents by that time and Mother insisted because of the lightning on taking a roundabout route to avoid all trolley tracks. To add to the general discomfort the wiper on the windshield refused to work and for the last mile or two we went at a snail's pace.

And then, within four blocks of Aunt Caroline's, Mother remembered that she had taken my father's picture out of a suitcase and forgotten to put it back again!

She insisted on returning at once, and it was only with difficulty that I persuaded her to go while I took the taxi back for it. She agreed finally and gave me her key to the front door; I had never had a key of my own.

"It is on my bed," she said. "You would better take the taxi man in with you, just to be safe."

One look at the driver convinced me that I would do nothing of the sort, although here and now I apologize. He was to be a valuable ally that night. But I knew that Herbert was in the house, which Mother did not, and I may as well confess that I was rather pleased than otherwise to go back.

Nevertheless, the sight of the darkened building in the midst of that storm daunted me. The taxi man sat in his seat, stolid and immovable. Beyond reaching a hand back to open the door he took little or no cognizance of me. Rain poured from the roof of the cab and fell in sheets from the porch, and I had no sooner gained its shelter than following a terrific flash of lightning every light on the street went out.

I let myself into the hall and felt for the light switch there. To my horror the house lights were off also, and there was neither movement nor sound to tell me whether Herbert was inside or not.

I groped my way into the library and found a box of matches. With the bit of illumination my courage came back, and in the dining room I found a candle and lighted it. There was still no sign of Herbert, and at last I called him cautiously. There was no answer, and I was beginning to be alarmed. Then suddenly the wind blew open the kitchen door behind me, my candle went out, and I had not groped my way five feet before a man had caught me in his arms and held me with a grip like a vise.

"You devil!" he said.

It was George Talbot.

I believe he would have killed me then and there, but at that moment the light in the hall came on, and he released me and stood staring at me.

"Sorry Lou!" he said thickly. "I thought—look here, there's all hell loose in this house tonight. Beat it; I'm telling you! O God, there go the lights again!"

I had time to see that he held a golf club in his hand, however; and with that my shaken courage returned.

"Listen, George," I said. "I can't go. Herbert Dean's here somewhere, and we'll have to find him. If there is somebody here who is dangerous—I'd better bring in the taxi driver. He'll help us to look, anyhow."

And at that moment four shots in rapid succession were fired somewhere in the upper part of the house. I heard George groan in the darkness, and the next moment he had dashed out of the room and up the front stairs. Some sheer automatism took me into the front hall, and as I reached the foot of the stairs a flash of lightning showed the taxi driver in the doorway. Then everything was dark again, and out of that blackness something rushed at me from the rear of the house and knocked me flat on the floor.

Someone ran over me as I lay there, going with incredible silence and speed. Then there was a shocking scream, and by another lightning flash I saw that the taxi driver was struggling to hold a black and amorphous figure. Then there was another shot, the hall mirror fell in a crash of glass, and I fainted.

I never heard George Talbot come rushing down the stairs nor his frantic call over the telephone for the police. I never saw the inside of the library, where a grim-faced taxi driver had tied up a figure with a blackened face with the cords from the window curtains, and was now standing with a pistol pointed at it.

But the arrival of a police car finally roused me, and I was sitting dazedly in the hall when a few minutes later they carried down Herbert Dean, with a leg broken by a bullet and evidently in pain, but with a faint smile for me on a practically bloodless face.

It was midnight before I reached Aunt Caroline's again. I

357

had been left to recover in the hands of a strange policeman who seemed to know as little of what had happened as I did. But I did not go until the hospital had assured me that Herbert was in pain but not gravely hurt.

I must have presented a queer sight to Aunt Caroline's butler when at last, delivered like a warrant by the officer, he admitted me to the house and showed me up to my usual room. My hat was at a strange angle and my face dead white, save for a small cut where I had hit the edge of the hall table. I felt that I would never sleep again, but I fell into what was almost a stupor the moment I got into bed, and it was bright daylight on Wednesday morning before I wakened again.

Aunt Caroline had sent up the morning paper with my tray, and the first thing I saw was an enormous headline: "Crescent Place Murders Solved. Social Registerite Held Deranged."

Chapter XLVII

All of that was on Wednesday, August the thirty-first. Our murders were solved, and a grateful public having read the morning papers began once more to go about its business. Editorials congratulated the police, and certain old residents of the city shook their heads and sighed.

But the police were not entirely happy. Although they now knew the answer to that baffling problem — and a surprising enough answer it was — they still did not know the whole story. There was, as Herbert says, still the question of John Talbot. How much did he know? Was he an accomplice or an innocent victim? On the one hand, they faced the stubborn silence of their prisoner; on the other, the inability to rouse Talbot out of a complete and hopeless apathy.

Herbert believed that Talbot was entirely innocent. He had formed a sort of attachment for this elderly man who for months as Daniels the street cleaner had pursued his quiet vocation among us, mildly interested but largely detached from that long-lost life of his, and returning at night to his tidy room and his books. Until at last some violent current carried him out of his eddy and into something so dreadful that his mind refused to accept it and so shut down on it; as one may draw a curtain.

The arrest had been made on Tuesday night, but the problem of John Talbot still faced the police on Wednesday. His condition was unchanged, and so it was that later on that day an interesting experiment was performed on him in his hospital room close to Herbert's, and at Herbert's suggestion.

The results more than justified it, and very possibly have added a new arm to crime detection, but it was not done without protest. At eight o'clock that morning Herbert Dean had called Doctor Armstrong on the telephone and had asked him to come to the hospital. There they had a long talk, Herbert pale but insistent, the doctor objecting.

"Damn it all, man, it's still in the experimental stage. There's a technique too. I don't know it. If this is an actual catatonic stupor— But it may be hysteria."

"I don't care what it is. You can get the stuff and the technique too, can't you? Come, doctor, this isn't a time to hesitate. Use the long distance telephone. Use an airplane. Use anything you like, but do it."

Finally Doctor Armstrong agreed, and by ten o'clock that morning a dictograph had been installed in John Talbot's room, a screen ready for a police stenographer placed in a corner, and a lengthy long distance call to a great Western University had been charged, as Mother would say, against the taxpayers of the city. Shortly after that Doctor Armstrong came back, bringing with him a professor of neuropsychiatry from the local medical college and a package of a certain drug; and asking for a basin of ice, some towels, and a syringe for making intravaneous injection. The drug, a preparation, I believe, of sodium amytal, was dissolved in distilled water, and with Daniels still in his stupor it was injected into his arm.

I have largely Doctor Armstrong's description of what followed. The man on the bed relaxed almost at once, according to him. All rigidity disappeared, his breathing increased but was somewhat more shallow, his pupils on examination showed some dilation, and he himself was sunk in a deep sleep.

They allowed this sleep to last for an incredible time, according to the impatient men who by now crowded the room; the District Attorney, the Commissioner, Inspector Briggs, and Mr. Sullivan. Herbert, having fought to the last ditch for a wheeled chair and having been refused, at last bribed an orderly and got one; appearing in the doorway just as, the Inspector having pinched his lip into a permanent point and the Commissioner having called it a lot of tommyrot and threatened to leave, one of the two medical men took a cold towel from a basin beside him and placed it on the patient's face. He repeated this twice, and then John Talbot roused, not fully but to a certain level of consciousness; enough to answer all their questions, but not enough to allow the brain censors, whatever they may be, to close down and alter the facts.

For three hours he talked, that long lean figure on the bed which bore so little resemblance to that crayon enlargement I had seen long ago in the stable loft. He told what he knew and what he suspected. He answered every question they put to him. He told them things they had never dreamed of, and without any emotion, so far as they could see, he recited the tale of that Saturday night and early Sunday morning; when he had had to cut the head off a human body, and had been actively sick in the middle of it.

The statement is too long to give here. I quote one or two lines of it, merely to give the idea of the method.

"Why did you shoot that girl in the room of the hotel at—?"

"I didn't shoot her. I had been out, and I came back to find her dead, and the room full of people. It was my gun but I never did it."

Then followed a long statement of his love for this woman, his unhappiness at home, the long struggle before he decided to go away with her. The police listened patiently through this flow of talk, which included his escape from the state institution.

"I was lucky to save my neck, at that. None of my relatives would put up any money, and my wife hated me. I don't know that I blame her."

Later on they asked him why he had come back to the city, and particularly to the Crescent.

"I came back to see my son," he told them. "I've been watching him for a good many years. After the war I had a job with the iron works as a bookkeeper, but my eyes went bad, and I had to have them operated on. I drifted from one thing to another, and then I got this work for the city. I was uneasy when they put me on the Crescent, but nobody recognized me, except Emily Lancaster. She did, but I asked her to keep quiet."

There is a good bit here in the record about George, and the tragedy of seeing him day after day. "He looked like a fine fellow. Sometimes he spoke to me. I always wanted to sit down somewhere and have a real talk with him. 'To sow a thought and reap an act' — that's a father's part. But the way things were —"

They could not shake him on the Hollytree situation, although they went back to it again and again.

"What did you find when you got to the house near Hollytree?"

"It was done when I got there. All I could do was to get rid of the body. I put it in the trunk."

"What did you do with what you took out of the trunk? The money?"

"I buried it that night. I never wanted to see it again. I buried it under some willows by the creek. Then I hid the drawers out of the trunk in the cellar. After that I walked into the town and got the expressman to take it away."

"Where did you get the foreign labels for the trunk?"

"I'd traveled a great deal. I had some on some suitcases. All that I had to do was to soak them off."

"Did you want this money for yourself?"

"God, no. Why should I want money?"

"What became of the head?"

"I don't know. It was in the satchel."

On only one point was he vague at all. He had walked ever since, all of two days and a part of two nights, until he

362

had reached the police station. But he did not know where he had walked. The horror had closed down on him. He was not thinking. He was simply moving on and on, like a machine. He had noticed some things, for here the record speaks of "August, tarnished by the sun's hot breath."

It rang true, all of it. Even those cynical policemen knew that. Their attitude softened, although his revelations made them shudder. When it was all over Inspector Briggs put a hand on the thin shoulder and held it there a moment.

"Now you go to sleep," he said, "and quit worrying. We'll fix this up. And we'll send your boy over to see you when you wake up."

It was not until that long séance was over that an indignant surgeon trundled Herbert back to his bed, and growled fiercely that he was to get in and stay in. But that night I was allowed to see him, and it is from our talk then that I give Herbert's summary of the case as well as I can.

"From the beginning it seemed clear that the money Mrs. Lancaster had hoarded was involved somehow in her death. When Emily's part in taking it became known, then, we had two guesses. One was that she had taken it for herself, that her mother was secretly able to get about and so discovered her loss, and that Emily had killed her. Against this was Emily's total disregard for money and her actual devotion to Mrs. Lancaster. There were other elements too; her unspotted dress that day was only one of them.

"Nevertheless, Margaret believed from the first that she had done it, and that her stepfather had killed Emily. We knew that the old gentleman had not done so, however, after Helen's story. I never did believe it, for that matter.

"What seemed evident after the death of Holmes was that we had, outside of the murders, two definite plots to get hold of the money. The one was that of Holmes himself, possibly with Peggy to help him. The other was not so clear. I figured that more than one person was involved in it, since we were pretty certain that on the night Holmes was killed no one had left the Crescent. What occurred to me then was that somewhere near where the body was found this outsider—

363

whoever it was—had tried to get Holmes off the truck and had perhaps run over him by accident. There was the handkerchief on his body, for one thing, so that he would be seen by any passing car.

"That was not the act of a murderer; I thought then of an inexpert driver as an explanation, and as we know now, poor old Talbot hadn't driven a car for a good many years.

"What we now know took place is that Emily had recognized Daniels as the uncle she had been fond of. This would have been in the spring, at the time the coolness sprang up between her mother and herself. Probably Emily urged some sort of help for Talbot, and the mother refused.

"That makes it likely that Emily took the money for her uncle. Maybe not, but someone was to escape, either John Talbot or herself, and I think it was Talbot. That's the reason for the steamer folders in her room. However, one thing is certain. She never told him what she was doing. He learned that elsewhere, and he learned it after the old lady was killed. That was when, under a threat of being sent back to the asylum, he took Peggy's bag from her and tried to enter the MacMullen house; and the chain held him up! He says—and I believe it—that this threat was used all along to force his cooperation.

"But it was a fatal mistake that Emily made when she told her mother. The old lady could get about, as we know, when there was no one there to see her; and she took to watching this street cleaner, whenever she had a chance. He was changed, of course. She wasn't sure he was Talbot. Then one day she asked Emily to bring down the old album, and there was a picture of him in it. Day after day she compared him with it, and she saw that Emily was right.

"That settled it, for she had a weapon now. It involved a lot of people, and especially one person. She was not a pleasant old woman, and she had hated the Talbots for a good many years.

"However that may be, this knowledge of hers gave her a weapon against them. They are a proud lot, and at any time she could spring the glad tidings that John Talbot, a fugitive

364

from the law, was sweeping the street in front of their very house! And I'm afraid—I'm very much afraid, my darling—that she did just that, a day or two before she was killed.

"You see, she was killed for two reasons: to keep her quiet and to get that identifying photograph of Talbot out of the album. The money in a way was incidental, and even the second reason was not vital; it only became vital when those prints were left in the album itself.

"That killing, by the way, was as reckless and yet as cunning a piece of work as I have ever seen. There was in all that careful preparation only the one slip, and that was beyond control; that was the leaving of the album with the prints, as the result of some alarm. You see, time was vital, and she had found the old lady out of bed! That meant getting her back and covering her, to delay discovery as long as possible. She got back, but she was *on* the sheet! Little things, all of them; but not in the plan. Then one other thing went wrong also, for the screen would not lift. That careful method of showing an escape by the porch roof was out. No wonder she forgot the album!

"Perhaps the grass was put there then. Perhaps it was an accident. Perhaps poor old Emily, terrified of the discovery that the money was gone and trying to shout 'wolf' for the family to hear, put it there and overturned that pot herself. I don't know, and it doesn't matter now.

"What does matter is that the killer had to indicate an exit from the house while still remaining it in. Hence—and that was quick thinking—the glove thrown down into the hall. Then the slipping into the housemaid's closet, the door locked, and the careful stealthy removal of all signs of blood.

"But there were some bad minutes in that closet or later on. They came when the album was remembered, and they must have been pretty terrible. How could this killer know that Margaret Lancaster had destroyed those prints, or had had Bryan Dalton do it for her?

"The next step was the gold itself; for there it was, with all its potentialities. I don't suppose we'll ever know the truth about it. For instance, how would this unknown know about it? Was Emily seen going into the MacMullen house? Was it via Peggy and the grapevine telegraph? Did someone else besides Holmes get onto the book trick? One person at least had picked up a piece of gold after that unlucky spill in No Man's Land, and may have mentioned it. Or—and this is worth consideration—did Emily in her distress take a confidant.

"She may have. She may even have told where her keys were kept in the bird cage. I think myself that she did, or why did poor old Talbot have to climb that porch roof to try to get them? For that's what he did, game leg and all, on that Saturday night.

"The cage was gone, however. You'd seen to that!

"Then, to come to the night of Emily's death: it was late when she heard where the cage was, and having slept all day she was wakeful. But she was not the only person who had learned late that night that the cage was in the stable. When George Talbot came home he was told that Emily had been inquiring about it, and he told Mrs. Talbot and Lydia, in the presence of Lizzie Cromwell, just where it was.

"Nevertheless, probably no murder was intended that night, and it is a strange fact that had not one of those three women been in the laundry later that night, secretly washing those bloody undergarments which had been hidden away since Thursday, in all likelihood Emily Lancaster would still be alive. But one of them was there, and she heard a sound outside; perhaps when the gun fell.

"I have no doubt but that it was the intention to secure the keys that night anyhow, although the washing was more vital. But however it happened, one thing is sure. This woman found the automatic, shot Emily and got the keys from her. By the time George was aroused she was safely inside the house by the basement door.

"But the keys were valuable only if they could be used, and there was a period of uncertainty following that. Talbot says that although he had been relieved of his job to let a police operative take his place, no plan was made at that time. For one thing it was too dangerous. There were police and detectives all over the place, and although this killer of ours knew by that time that the money was in the trunk, she could think of no way to get at it. And I'd better say here that until Saturday night Talbot had believed what Margaret Lancaster had believed about the two murders: that Emily had killed her mother, and that the stepfather had shot Emily.

"It would be interesting to know if that theory originated with Margaret, or if someone else did not suggest it to her!

"Still acting more or less under duress, Talbot finally agreed to rent the house near Hollytree, and to take the trunk there if and when some plan could be arranged to get it. In the interval he hung around the MacMullen place. Those were Lydia's orders, and he had to obey them. If he didn't it meant back to the asylum for him. What hope had he of proving his case, even if it could be reopened? And to give up his job meant the bread line.

"That is why he was on the pavement the night Holmes took it away, and he rode right out into the country on the tail of the truck, with Holmes not suspecting he was there. The rest is about as I had imagined. He threw Holmes off the truck, after forcing him to stop it. But the poor little devil made a lunge toward it just as Talbot let in the clutch, and the thing went over him. Talbot went on. He had to go on. He had known from Holmes himself where his place in the country was, and after he took the trunk to the Hollytree house he simply took the trunk back there and left it. Simple, isn't it? But he was feeling pretty sick about Holmes himself. He went back to the place where he had left him, lying there with that handkerchief on his chest, but the body was gone.

"After that it was plain hell for him. He had been in Europe, as well as a lot of other places, and with that search for the trunk going on he disguised it with those labels from his own baggage. But he was terrified by that time. Here were three deaths already connected with that money, and he began to fear that he would be involved, and perhaps too to grow suspicious. He gave up his room and left his books, going to one far downtown, and waiting there for a message.

"Then at last it came, on Saturday. That was when he went out to the house at Hollytree late in the evening; and what he found was Lizzie Cromwell shot to death in an upstairs bathroom, and his sister Lydia trying to get the body into the tub."

Chapter XLVIII

So Lydia Talbot had been our killer!

She never made a statement, and she died of pneumonia shortly after her arrest. Perhaps Doctor Armstrong is the only one among us who feels any pity for her, and he quotes now and again that theory of murder being a reaction from extreme repression. But she had, he says, been a psychotic for many years, and he laid that terrible two weeks to a definite unbalance at the end.

"Like most of you, she lived an unnatural life," he said. "Maybe she started only by wanting to escape that, and the money would do that for her. But there was something else, too. She'd shot and killed that woman years ago, and her brother had suffered the punishment for it. That must have weighed on her for many years, and now came the old woman's threat to send him back to it, and she went plain crazy."

Here, however, he added something which explains a great deal that puzzled me for years.

"You can take one thing as a fact. Mrs. Talbot wasn't only locked away from her husband. She was locked away from Lydia. And Lizzie Cromwell was as much Lydia's keeper as anything else. For Hester Talbot not only knew that Lydia had killed that other woman in a fit of jealous rage—Yes, jealous, Lou! You find things like that now and then. The human mind is a queer thing—but that she had been abnormal for years."

Even now I have no details of that early crime of Lydia Talbot's, save that she had resented her brother's flight, had followed him and in some wild fury killed the girl in a hotel bedroom. What was outraged pride and what was actual jealousy no one now can ever know. But she had let him take the punishment and never spoken; and if Mrs. Talbot suspected the truth she had never whispered it.

In a way, harboring Lydia after that must have been her revenge on the husband who had deserted her—

I was married—by edict!—late in the September following, and if Mother was resentful she at least provided me with the usual dozens of this and that which the Crescent regards as essential to any bride. But Helen Wellington and I bought my trousseau, and I can still see Mother eyeing a chiffon nightgown, and then stiffly leaving the room.

We are very happy, Herbert and I, but now and then since I have found myself still wondering about different incidents of our crimes which I had failed to understand. Naturally too as a bride I was interested in Herbert's part in the final capture of Lydia Talbot. And the entire story, as I have gradually learned it from Herbert, is interesting as showing the manner in which he reached his own conclusion as to the criminal.

From the beginning it seemed probable that the murderer of Mrs. Lancaster either lived in the house or had been able to enter it without suspicion. He and the police were agreed on this. But ever since the hoarding had commenced the house had been kept locked, and it was Mr. Lancaster's custom to make the rounds two or three times a day, examining all doors and windows.

The cellar windows were also protected by iron bars, and the door to it was padlocked. All other windows and doors were found to be locked, and although by inside collusion this might have been arranged, careful investigation of the servants drew a complete blank. Two of them were quiet and respectable women who during the entire investigation were carefully watched without result. Peggy MacMullen, or Peggy Holmes, was young and pretty; but she had been on the back porch, carefully dressed and made up for her afternoon out, when the alarm was raised.

The family then came under consideration. Unnatural crimes are not new to the police, and the overturned flower pot, the bits of grass on the porch roof and the raised screen looked like something prearranged to show escape by the roof. But in the family the police included Jim Wellington. His presence in the house, his later admission that he had been in the room, his own production of clothing stained with the dead woman's blood, and the final argument that he stood to win by her will were certainly all suspicious.

Added to this was the fact that a substitution had been effected for the gold in the chest. There was not one of them, on the morning the chest was opened, who did not believe that whether Jim had killed his aunt or not he had certainly systematically robbed her; and there is not a doubt in the world that had they found that old glove of his which Margaret had smuggled to me on Thursday night, he would have been arrested and later on indicted for the murder.

But intensive search of his house and of the grapevine path, as well as all open ground in the neighborhood, produced no gloves. They had even — all this was news to me — examined the ashes of Daniel's fire in No Man's Land; but all they found were a few buttons from an old suit of overalls, and one of these went back to Headquarters, but was ignored there.

The search, however, included more than the gloves. Miss Emily's wild excitement over the missing key and chain from her mother's neck puzzled them; and in fact it is still not quite clear to Herbert, or to any of them, just why it was found where it was.

"You can see why Emily was worried about it," he says. "If she could find it and hide it it might mean a delay in the discovery that the chest had been looted. On the other hand, the taking of the key and chain may have been a clever move on Lydia's part to prevent the opening of the chest until she

371

had managed to get away with Emily's trunk. I imagine that's the real answer; but things got too hot for her. She buried it where it was found later on, and I've wondered since whether Lizzie Cromwell didn't see her do it. Something made Lizzie suspect her even before the night Emily was killed. That's certain."

Before I leave the keys and get back to the first murder, I should explain here that Herbert is confident that Emily had a second key to the chest, since she could not have used the one her mother wore around her neck.

"And I fancy that there is where Holmes first came into the case," he says. "He was handy with tools, and either she gave him a tracing of the key she wanted and had him make her one, or she asked him to get one from a locksmith. That would have been in the spring, but Holmes was shrewd. He knew through Peggy that the gold was in the house, and he knew of that room she had taken at the MacMullens'. When he learned that the money was missing, all he had to do was to figure how it had been taken out, so he made his book into a box and — well, it killed him."

The District Attorney that first night was unwilling to hold Jim. He had made a good witness. Also he was well and favorably known, and the police could not afford to make any mistake.

But also Mr. Sullivan, who had had more than one axe murder in his experience, had examined those clothes of Jim's, and he maintained that the stains on them were not the stains which would have come as the axe was lifted for one blow after another. They looked, according to the detective, to be exactly what Jim had said they were. If he had raised the axe there would have been drops on his coat and shirt. There were none there.

In the end they let him go, but he was under careful surveillance from that time on.

Up to that point Herbert and the police were in agreement. But now they split.

"They had made two divisions," he explains. "The people in the house and someone outside. I made three, for I included the visitors that day, Jim himself, Mrs. Talbot and

Lydia, and it was at the inquest on Saturday that I got a bit of light.

"Lydia Talbot had been admitted by the front door with her basket for Mrs. Lancaster, had later taken the basket to the rear of the house and gone out by the kitchen door. Natural enough, probably; but if you are up against a locked house where no one could get in but someone apparently had, you have to begin somewhere.

"And I didn't like her. She was a neurotic. It was in that flat voice of hers, was written all over her."

What he wondered that day was just what Lydia had done after she left Mrs. Lancaster's room and before she appeared down the back stairs to the kitchen porch to leave her basket and its contents.

"What she could have done, if conditions were right, was obvious enough. She could have slipped down the front stairs, unlocked the front door, gone back up to where she had left the basket and taken it down to the kitchen porch. She had two witnesses there to prove that she had left the house. Then, under cover of all that shrubbery, all she had to do was to circle the house, going by the empty laundry wing, and enter it again by the front door, locking it behind her."

It was only a possibility at first. He knew nothing of the Crescent, or of its interrelationships. There seemed no object in her killing her sister-in-law. They might have quarreled, of course. There was Emily on the stand saying she had left Lydia with her mother while she cleaned her bird's cage. But the presence of the axe was the rock on which he almost foundered.

"Grant a quarrel or anything you like, she had carried no axe in a ten-inch basket, although we know now that she carried some other things besides food! A ball of cord, for instance, and a knife or a pair of scissors. And that axe had to be taken into the house somehow."

By the Sunday morning after the first murder, however, he had veered to the idea that it was an inside job after all. He had got us all straightened out in his mind by that time, and he had had my story of the glove. He was still working on his own, and I have already told how I got him into the Lancaster house.

What he wanted was the second glove, or some proof that it had been destroyed. But he also wanted to examine the house itself. Already he had a fair idea — through Holmes and his experiment with the book — as to how the money had been carried out. He knew too that the Crescent was not as arrogantly at peace as the front it presented to the world, and he was turning over in his mind Mrs. Talbot and her locked house.

"Either she was crazy," he says, "or she was afraid of someone inside the place. She didn't lock only her windows and her outer doors. She had the inner doors locked too. And I'd watched her on the stand. She was scared almost to death. That voice of hers was — well, a shout of defiance. She knew something, or she suspected someone."

That Sunday morning, however, he was still suspicious of Margaret Lancaster. He had not missed the significance of her shower, and he had been practically certain that the man he had seen on the roof was her stepfather. He came pretty close to knowing what he was looking for, also.

Still, back in his mind was that idea that somebody could have entered the house, locked as it was, and hidden away until the moment came; that moment which to anyone who knew the family habits was the one time in the day when the thing could be done.

"There were a number of such places," he says. "Any room in the guest wing would have answered. But I happened to find something in the housemaid's closet on the second floor which made me fairly jump. The key was on the inside of the door! That was absurd on the face of it. Why lock such a place at all? And especially why lock one's self in it?"

He had spent all the rest of his time there. It had two smallish windows; one opening onto the roof of the kitchen porch, and a larger one which overlooked No Man's Land and a flower border beneath. He opened the first one, and found the opening to the drain pipe just below it. Then he examined the closet itself.

It was clean, with no bloodstains whatever. The walls and

loor were of white tile, and he switched on the light and
went over them carefully. Also he examined the sponge and
cleaning cloths, as well as Mr. Lancaster's boot-box, but
they suggested nothing. However, he slipped the sponge into
his pocket before he left, and analysis of it later on showed
faint traces of human blood.

Just before he left he looked up, and he saw tied to a water
pipe a short length of heavy cord. It had been cut, as if time
had been too short to untie its knots, and when he left the
Lancaster house that morning he was certain, not only that
Lydia Talbot had committed the crime, but that he knew
how she had brought the axe into the house.

Chapter XLIX

What I figured was that she had previously — the night before, perhaps — hidden the axe in that flower border. If it was found it might be mysterious, but nothing more. The rest was easy too. Here was Margaret in her room and Emily and Mrs. Talbot with the old lady. She had the run of the house for some time, and even if she were discovered in it nobody would have questioned it.

"But she wasn't discovered. What she did before she went down and out the kitchen door was to drop that string of hers down the outside wall, beside the drain pipe. Then after she was outside — in case anyone was looking — she could tie the end of it to the axe, and seem only to be looking at the flowers. That's what she did anyhow. Maybe she picked one or two as an excuse, for she had to pass the kitchen porch again to get around the other end of the house. Eben was at the end next to you. She did pass that porch again, for both the girls there saw here. They thought nothing of it, naturally."

When, that Sunday morning, I had found the second glove, he felt that he had everything against her save actual proof. He was confident that she had locked herself in that closet, knowing the housemaid was out that day; that she had there taken off her hat and dress; that she had with infinite caution drawn up the axe, assisted by the chatter and noise below; that at the last moment she had seen Mr. Lancaster's gloves in his shoe-box and had put them on; and that having committed her furious crime she had returned there, locked herself in and safely and systematically washed, cleaned the closet, redressed and finally escaped by way of the back stairs and the deserted porch after Bryan Dalton had gone.

Unfortunately, other things had happened, or began to happen. There was Emily's wild flight to the Talbots, and her cry that "they" were after her. There was the undoubted fact that someone had climbed a porch pillar and tried to enter Emily's room, and as Herbert says:

"Not by the wildest flight of my imagination could I see Lydia Talbot doing that — unless she had wings."

And then on that Sunday night there came the shooting of Emily, and following that the mix-up about two identical makes of automatics. His theory did not fit any of all that, nor did the death of Holmes. It was a Chinese puzzle, and he began all over again, this time on Margaret. By that time he was openly working with the police, and he had seen Annie's anonymous letter.

He could not fit either Margaret or Dalton into the picture, however. It is true that he began to suspect some outside assistance, and he knew before long that Bryan Dalton had stood by the woodshed that afternoon, and had burned his overalls that night and something else as well. But why should Margaret have used the closet when her own room offered a safer refuge? Or why should she have brought the axe in by that method when she could have carried it in at night, any night?

What deceived him too for a time was Lydia Talbot's own demeanor. She was moving much as usual around her narrow orbit; neither overacting nor underacting her part.

The reason for Emily being out that Sunday night also worried him. Every inch of No Man's Land had been gone over, but neither the police nor he had missed the possible significance of that spade. It had been his theory that Emily had secreted the money elsewhere, possibly in a rented room not far away. But no keys to such a room had been found, nor was there any trace in the house of the book which she had almost certainly used as a receptacle for it.

It was my own story of the lost bird cage which gave him his first clue to the whereabouts of the keys, and as we know the police themselves prevented his finding them in time. "If I'd got Talbot that night I'd have had the story," he adds.

Then came the attack on me, apparently purposeless, and shortly after that the MacMullen woman's story and the death of Holmes. Also Herbert had made that night examination of Mrs. Lancaster's room, and was convinced that she had been out of bed when at least the first blow was struck. In that case she might well have known that the money was gone and been killed to gain time until it could be placed somewhere in safety.

The discovery of Emily's hidden room did only one thing to help solve the murder. A photographic enlargement of the blotter found there enabled Herbert to read on it the address of the house behind the library, and to enable him to examine the family history for a possible connection with the man Daniels.

"The only real brain-storm I had was right there," he says. "There could be no logical connection between the two of them, on the facts. But she had written to him, and more than once. It was then that this story Jim had told about John Talbot popped into my mind. I got the details from Jim, but it was your Aunt Caroline, my darling, who remembered the date and the name under which he had been convicted. Which was *not* Daniels, by the way. After that I sent for old files of the newspapers where it had happened, and—"

"Aunt Caroline! Whatever made you go to her?"

"Because, O light of my life, your mother would not talk! Aunt Caroline, thank God, did not live on the Crescent."

It was then that, being fairly sure of his ground, he went to see Daniels, or Talbot rather. But in the interval Lydia had disappeared, and Talbot's room was empty. And Talbot was Lydia's brother. Herbert found himself back once more to Lydia as the killer; although there was a chance that

378

Talbot himself was guilty. If she could admit herself to the Lancaster house, she could have admitted him also.

Then came Lydia's disappearance. Herbert had never for a moment believed that Lydia had been killed. To him it was a plain case of escape, and escape with sufficient money to last her the rest of her life. But how had she escaped? He says:

"There was that old bead bag of hers, found over on Euclid Street; and there was that damned butterfly from her hatpin. Why a hatpin if she wore no hat? I didn't believe she left without a hat. She would be too conspicuous. I suspected that she had a flat hat of some sort in that box along with the veil, and maybe a transformation too. And on Saturday morning I asked Lizzie Cromwell to see if all of Mrs. Talbot's transformations were in the house. They were not. One was missing, and Lizzie knew as well as I did what that meant.

"She told Mrs. Talbot and wanted the police notified. But you know your Crescent! She absolutely refused, and so that afternoon Lizzie simply packed her valise, put George's automatic into it, and went after Lydia herself."

No one will ever know, I dare say, how Lizzie knew about that house at Hollytree. But know she did, poor creature; just as she knew from Amanda on the Monday morning before that someone had washed clothing in the laundry the night before.

And she found Lydia in the house when she got there. She knew her danger, and she followed Lydia's flight to that upper bathroom with George's automatic in her hand. When the bathroom door would not lock things must have looked quite simple to her. She walked in, and Lydia probably hit her at once with a chair.

However that may be, the one thing we do know is that in some such manner Lydia got the automatic from her and shot her dead. And that when her brother came back from burying the money that is what he found.

"What could he do," Herbert says, "except to give her a chance to escape? He helped her with the undressing, and to put her own clothing on the body. And it was he who took

379

the drawers out of the trunk. Right there, however, I got my clue.

"For you see, my dear, that trunk, once the drawers were out, was large enough to hold the body. There was no real necessity for — well, for amputating that head. The only real reason I could see for such an act was to conceal the identity of the dead woman. The trunk was certain to be found, but with Lydia Talbot apparently inside of it she was safe. I tried to tell Briggs that, but he wouldn't even listen.

"The rest is easy. While they were looking for a black-haired Lizzie, I was looking for Lydia Talbot, gray-headed and flat-voiced. But I couldn't find her, and so I sat down and tried to think what I would do if I were Lydia Talbot, waiting to make my escape when the time came and with leisure now to worry about any clues lying around.

"It seemed to me that the album was still the danger point, if as Lydia believed my fingerprints were smeared all over it. Suppose on her disappearance her prints had been found in her room at the Talbot house, and then some day — long after she had made her escape — someone opened that album? Can't you see it? And not only that, but let them be found and identified, and that desperate expedient of the body in the trunk would fail of its object. Let her once be identified as the killer, and she saw the body exhumed and a world-wide search made for her."

So he believed that she would, sooner or later, make her third attempt to get at the album. But not even Herbert until the last few hours suspected her of the audacious method she had used, both to get it and to hide herself from the police. For what she had done on that Sunday night was to slip back inside the Crescent itself, enter by a basement door to which she had hidden the key, confront her sister-in-law and tell her the truth.

She knew the Crescent. Best of all, she knew her sister-in-law: her horror of scandal, and the fact that she had already learned from Lizzie Cromwell that Lydia was guilty. She went to Mrs. Talbot, and demanded sanctuary!

From that night until the night of her capture she had been hidden in the Talbot house, in that bedroom of hers which had been locked after her departure. Not even George suspected, or the servants. What her thoughts were during those long hours no one can know. She must have seen again and again the horror on her brother's face when, looking up from that awful bathtub, she had said:

"I had to do it, John. She knew."

"Knew what, for God's sake?"

Some things, however, we do know about her; for Mrs. Talbot's statement to the police says that during all the time she was hidden in the house she was obsessed by only one thing.

"She neither ate nor slept," she said. "When I went with food at night she would be sitting by a window in the dark, and all she would talk about was the album.

"I wanted to get her away, but she refused until she had it. So that last day I sent George for it. It wasn't to be found, but later that night Lou Hall telephoned that it was there, and I told her.

"She slipped out soon after that, but George must have seen her and followed her. I had not told him she was in the house, but he may have suspected it. He may have suspected all the rest, too. I know he and Lizzie Cromwell had a talk on Saturday, before she left.

"That is all I know, except that my son has stayed at his club since that night, and he seems to feel that I am guilty of something, I hardly know what. I protected him from her for many years, and I consider that he is most ungrateful. Especially since she learned from him when he was a boy that trick of blackening her face."

For that, as it turned out, had been the secret of her uncanny ability to get about at night during the three attempts she made to get the album. With her black clothing and a pair of black gloves she would be almost invisible on any dark night. Certainly her face was blackened the night of her capture, and I can understand the taxi driver's statement later on:

"I got a look at her with a lightning flash when I caught her. And I was so scared that I pretty nearly let go!"

381

Now and then we go back to the Crescent. The Lancaster house is closed, and Margaret lives in Europe; somewhere in Southern Germany. We hear that she is about to be married. Jim and Helen are still there, however, getting along rather better than before, but every now and then the Daltons' Joseph gravely announces that "Mrs. Wellington has gone again, sir."

The Daltons are the best of friends, and probably rather more than that. Mother has Aunt Caroline staying with her, and Annie and Mary are back. They all seem to manage quite well together, and Mother is thinking of wearing a little mauve this year. But she has never quite forgiven me my marriage and she left the room abruptly one day when Doctor Armstrong, tapping cheerfully on his black bag, asked me if I wouldn't soon want him to bring a baby in it.

Although we have buried most of our tragedies, there is still one which survives. In the last house by the gate Mrs. Talbot sits alone; although George goes out dutifully to the Sunday midday dinner, fried chicken and ice cream in summer and roast beef and a fruit pie the rest of the year. He and his father share an apartment downtown, and as an act of pure justice Margaret has turned over to Mr. Talbot the money recovered from under the willow trees.

Otherwise the life goes on much as before. On any summer day Eben's lawn mower can be heard; children are still taboo on No Man's Land, Mr. Dalton still practices short golf shots there, and what Helen called its smug and deteriorating peace has again settled down on the Crescent.

Nothing has changed, and it is Herbert's contention that people really learn nothing after a certain age.

Perhaps that is true. It is certainly a fact that during our last visit there something went wrong with the gas stove, and that he experimented with it after his customary fashion. There was a tremendous report, and Herbert himself was hurled out onto the back porch, almost at my feet.

"Are you hurt?" I asked.

He broke off in the middle of a flow of really awful language to look up at me.

382

"Hurt?" he shouted. "I've damned near broken my leg."

Then he saw that I was laughing, and he grinned boyishly.

"Let's go home, Lou darling," he said. "Let's go where Monday doesn't have to be wash-day, and nobody ever saw a hatpin, and we can use our newspapers to start a fire and sit by it, and not to roll the doilies on. Let's go!"

And so we went.